WAR
BOYS

WAR
BOYS

M. A. Schaffner

>‹

WELCOME RAIN PUBLISHERS
New York

War Boys
Copyright © 2002 by M. A. Schaffner.
All rights reserved.

Library of Congress CIP data available from the publisher.

Direct any inquiries to
Welcome Rain Publishers LLC

ISBN 1-56649-244-0

Printed in the United States of America by
HAMILTON PRINTING COMPANY

First Edition: August 2002
1 3 5 7 9 10 8 6 4 2

For Captain L.J. Schaffner, MSC, USN

CONTENTS

WAR
BOYS

THE DINING ROOM WINDOW

As Charles first tried to pull his gritty eyelids open, a white sheet of light slapped them back shut. He rubbed his eyes till tears came then tried again. This time he succeeded. At the foot of the bed a window—three feet square, lined on either side with a panel of green corrugated fiberglass, and set in a concrete wall—opened on a view of vast, cloudless sky.

The window radiated heat and glare; he turned over in starchy, sweat-damp sheets and kicked away a wool blanket. From the look and feel of things he might have come to in a hospital or juvenile detention center; momentarily he forgot which. Then he remembered. Some hours before he had gone to sleep in the U.S. Naval Station, Subic Bay, Republic of the Philippines. By now his father had probably left for work.

He remembered some other things. Over the humid layer of his own sweat and morning breath an icy stratum of perfume reminded him that his mother, too, had gone out on a mission. That tinge in the tropical air of industrially processed roses told him that he had not dreamed when she'd come in to kiss him and call out a piercingly happy "good morning!"

Charles sat up and shook his head to clear away the fuzz. They'd gotten in at two in the morning after a long drive from Clark Air Force Base, and though he tried so hard his brow actually knitted with the effort, he couldn't quite tell his real memories from the ensuing dreams. In one or the other he had seen a pale yellow moon over distant hills reflected in rice paddies; crowds of ragged children in towns of compressed squalor, their hands waving packets of gum and cigarettes, and two naval officers in the front seat of a van suggesting the family not roll down their windows, their tropical white uniforms shining in the mugginess like a pearly gate between civilization and savagery. In one or the other little lizards crawled across the concrete ceiling of the Barkers' tiny new kitchen while a Filipino carrying their luggage assured his mother "Boutiki very good luck, ma'am, eat bugs." And in one or the other he sat in a dank hot terminal in Guam surrounded by young soldiers and sailors going to or from Vietnam, and when one boy in tiger stripes found out Charles's age he said, "Shit man, I was *born* older than that," and then a large lizard in the next chair folded up his copy of the *Washington Star* with a headline about the battle for the citadel of Hue and calmly observed that no more planes would come: the terminal itself had just taken off for Vietnam.

Charles wiped his face on his damp T-shirt and tried to orient himself. He knew where Commander Barker had gone. He didn't have to see his father leave to know that the old man had put on his service khakis, pressed sharp, with the new commander's oak leaves on the collar and the bright gold scrambled eggs on the shiny visor of his cover. He'd have worn brown shoes you could see up girls' dresses with and a breastplate of fifteen or twenty silk ribbons from all his campaigns and achievements since 1944, including the one he had the most pride in, the maroon Good Conduct Medal that only enlisted men could earn, and that told everyone he met he'd worked his way up, step by step, from E-1 to O-5. They'd see it and know that behind the open smile and easy, down-home manners of this slightly chunky, balding former Texas farm boy stood a man who knew more about the navy than any officer who'd gotten his stripes straight from

Annapolis or NROTC, including all the tricks and wiles of his sailors. They'd trade handshakes and salutes with him all morning, thought Charles, imagining his father as he stepped into the AO billet at the hospital. Officers and men alike would try to get on his good side from the get-go.

But Mrs. Barker would also have suited up for a first day on the job. Charles caught another whiff of her perfume and thought of how she would have prepared, her morning rituals as complex as those of a knight donning armor: the lotions, powders, and paints; stockings, girdle, garter, bra—a whole network of straps and buckles and buttons—then the narrow skirt ending a precise two inches above the knee, the white silk blouse, discreet pearl earrings from their tour in Japan, and, topping it all, a helmet of Lady Clairol Blonde. She'd have a full day ahead of her. She'd have to reconnoiter the PX and the commissary, ordering air conditioners and a week's supply of food. She would call on the CO's wife, then lunch at the O Club and make at least two dates for cocktails later in the week. Somewhere in her rounds she'd hook up with at least one other navy wife she'd known, or known a close friend of, in Arlington, Bethesda, Yokohama, Corpus, Mare Island, or any one of a dozen other places the Barkers had lived before, and she'd get the straight poop on maids, houseboys, yard boys, and cooks—how much to pay, hours, gifts, recommendations. She had a lot to take care of, but Charles knew his mother could do it. She'd done more than twenty years in the navy, too—nearly as long as his father—and the fact that she didn't have a commission or rating didn't mean she didn't have a rank and the accompanying responsibilities. And she'd volunteered, too, same as his father. She could've stayed in the next small town over from the old man's on that south Texas highway and married any of half a dozen boys destined to become feedlot owners, local bankers, undertakers, florists like her own father, or other varieties of leading citizens, but when Charles's father put on his white monkey suit with the third class's stripes and got down on his knees after six weeks of dating and said he had orders to sail, the wide expanses of prairie and pasture with their endless crops and herds of cattle seemed suddenly small. Or so she had told her son.

So Commander Barker had his job and Mrs. Barker had hers, and Charles, he guessed, had his own. "Look around some," his mother had said lightly, "make some friends." And Charles knew where his duty lay. Make friends. Get along. Someday, when he became an officer, all of his friends would wear stripes, too, and together they'd come back to the places they grew up in, already knowing the habits and the rules, the geography of place and the geometry of hierarchy and process. Charles's parents expected, whether they even knew it or not, that he'd step out of their quarters on SOQ Hill and run into some other boys his age and just naturally fall in with the good and secure and honorable future before him.

And he wanted to, he thought, despite leaving his friends in Arlington. The Barkers had lived there six years and Charles had gotten settled, even though most of the kids he knew came from civilian families and some had even begun to turn into hippies, sort of. As he once more noticed his mother's perfume, he thought of Sally with her long, straight peroxided hair, pink arms, white stockings, and a blue jumper over the white blouse that somehow first made him notice her breasts, and he remembered how his mother leaned close to peck him lightly (to avoid smearing her lipstick), her breasts right by his face in a cloud of womanly scent, and how she'd ask him to zip her up when she and his father dressed up to go to a change-of-command or retirement ceremony or dinner at the O Club, and then he saw Sally again and thought of her in two years when they got back if his father didn't extend the tour and then—damn, he thought— he realized he had an erection, and jumped up and ran to the bathroom right across the hall.

About fifteen minutes later Charles reemerged, having urinated, masturbated, and showered for the first time in this particular country. Back in his room he threw on a fresh T-shirt, shorts, and rubber sandals and wondered what to do. He imagined he'd find a base like any other: low, off-white buildings like the "temporaries" on the Mall in D.C., the insides pale yellow or green with shiny linoleum floors and walls lined with framed prints of warships and fighting marines among steam pipes and conduit, and offices of wired glass dividers, metal battleship-gray office furniture, clanking typewriters, and a smell of aftershave, perfume, and carbon paper.

He stepped out of his room for the second time, turned left, and got halfway down a short hallway before he stopped. Something did look different after all. He brushed his hand through his newly cropped hair and stared at the view before him. While he had whined to himself about the friends he left behind, who'd get halfway through high school before he returned, with their own little cliques and clubs that he'd never have time to break into, and while he'd tried to console himself with the thought of the friends he'd have all over the world, in one big white-hatted clique with everyone's role and status clear as the badges and stripes on the daily wear, another world had waited in ambush.

He took a few more steps to the end of the hall. He noticed, peripherally, an open space some fifteen feet long and ten wide, all concrete, with two windows like the one in his bedroom on the left and a stairwell on the right going down. The first half of the room had a layout of rattan furniture loosely parodying an American living room. The farther half, separated from the first by a low cabinet, which Charles knew his mother would soon fill with books, records, and local gewgaws, held a dining room table and six chairs. But just beyond this table, in the far wall, Charles saw a window twice the size of the others that opened on a scene unlike any he'd viewed before. At the top, the morning sun backlit a narrow band of clouds in a rich blue sky. Just below, a row of distant mountains the color and shape of sharks' teeth formed a jagged horizon and a backdrop for three more rows of hills, the first deep turquoise, the next bright green, and the closest a baked, grassy brown. These last ended in a steep drop into a valley that separated the mountains from the hill that the Barkers' duplex sat on. The valley, which occupied most of the lower half of the window, choked on jungle—an expanse of canopy, vines, and massive trunks so tossed and varied and contorted that Charles half expected the clouds rising out of its depths to open like a curtain on a tableau of dinosaurs or King Kong and all his cousins.

"Wow," said Charles. He stepped to the right, around the low cabinet and table, up to the window, then turned right into the kitchen and opened the refrigerator. One carton of reconstituted milk, one loaf of rather official-looking bread, and a snack pack of Kellogg's cereals. In the cabinet over the sink he found glasses and pale green plastic plates and bowls. In a drawer under the counter he found steel cutlery stamped USN. On the counter lay a copy of the *Manila Times*.

He opened the milk and the snack pack and made himself a bowl of Frosted Flakes. He found the appearance of Tony the Tiger vaguely reassuring. Out of curiosity he unwrapped the bread and took out a slice. It tasted okay despite the grainy texture resulting from countless little pellets of unmixed flour. He took the bowl, bread, and paper into the dining room and sat at the table facing the window. The Barkers' duplex shared the hill with perhaps twenty others, all squatting like a lonely string of bunkers defending the chain-link fences of their backyards. It occurred to him that he could easily spend the whole day staring at the jungle, so he forced himself to start eating and then, more deliberately, unfolded the paper and began to read.

Although the *Manila Times* seemed to rely primarily on English, it had enough Tagalog, odd names, and strange stories to assure Charles of its foreignness. Instead of Vietnam it had a feature about Sabah, or North Borneo, and the possibility of a war between the Philippines and Malaysia over it. Charles followed the article inside and saw a comparison of the two nations' armed forces beneath a photo of Filipino paratroopers patrolling a beach in Mindanao. He laughed. The navies were mostly composed of patrol boats—the ships that just happened to berth in any U.S. Navy base on any given Tuesday could take out both fleets in the time it had just taken him to make breakfast. And the soldiers in the picture wore tennis shoes instead of boots. How could two little noncommunist countries even think of fighting each other? He shook his head, confident that the United States would not let it happen.

Other articles struck him as interesting in the same weird, quasi-comical way: the jeepney driver who "ran amok" and machine-gunned three bystanders; a profile of a senator and his private army; a picture of handfuls of long, spaghetti-thin worms pulled from sacks of rice donated to the poor. But strangest of all, even in the inside of the paper he could find nothing about the war, the war he'd grown up with from the age of eight, the one that promised to meet him at twenty-one when he graduated from Annapolis or NROTC. With no daily victory with its hundreds or thousands of NVA or VC dead that the *Washington Star* never failed to deliver, Charles suspected that the *Manila Times* would probably also omit the weekly scorecard tallying the cost of inevitable triumph in another measure of several thousand of their, and a few hundred of our, lives. He would miss that.

Charles put down his spoon, drank the sweet milk remaining in the bowl, then looked out the window again, right to left and up and down. These didn't look like the woods in Virginia, which he remembered rolling away in well-groomed order from the road to Dulles Airport. Those woods seemed like U.S. Navy men, while this jungle resembled the scruffy Filipino paratroopers on a grand scale. As the sun rose higher and the mist grew thinner, he could see leaves in dozens of shapes and sizes carpeting or clumping, dark in shadow or bright in the sun, deep rich green to glowing bronze with streaks of silver. Where trees had fallen or a sudden escarpment broke the sloping side of the valley, he could see great trunks with rocket-fin roots and high branches hung with vines. Strange birds flitted unexpectedly past and tendrils of the dissipating ground fog reached haltingly after them. In some places gaps in the trees hinted at even stranger forms, and lattices of branches and vines stretched like the webs of giant spiders. *Anything could live in there*, Charles thought. Anything at all.

He forced himself to look nearer to the house and its neat square of lawn no bigger than the yard in Arlington. Even here a touch of the alien showed, in the plantings surrounding the suburban grass. He noticed first the short scrubby tree with blossoms of scarlet fire, the clump of sugarcane, and the banana tree centered against the fence that held back the jungle. Only then did he notice the monkeys.

"Oh wow."

About ten yards from the banana tree, at the same height as its top, stood the huge crown of a tree whose trunk had risen from the bottom of the steep hill some hundred feet below. All along the branches of this tree, peeping from the leaves or crashing from one limb to the next, danced the members of a large troop of apes—thirty or forty, Charles guessed. The leading three had already scaled the Barkers' fence and now stood ready to jump on the banana tree.

Charles ran into the kitchen and the door that led to the back stairs. As he stepped outside the sun struck his face again and he stopped, shaded his eyes from the glare, and tried to see. The cries of a dozen children competed with the buzz of a hovering rhinoceros beetle, fat and horned and about the size and color of an HO model tank. Without thinking, he struck at the beetle and blinked; when he opened his eyes he saw it scuttle off the landing and take flight again. Sweat collected in the small of his back. The sound of the children grew louder as they approached from neighboring yards, pointing and waving in excitement. Two more monkeys materialized on the fence; when the first child came within twenty feet, all five apes bared large canines and hooted, while the largest leapt down from the fence and flexed his biceps. The children screamed and fled a few yards. Charles walked halfway down the stairs before the monkeys saw him, too, at which two more ran into the yard and howled. He sat down on the steps.

Gradually more monkeys came into the yard, in groups of two and three. They looted bananas and fruits new to Charles, ran toward the children and their attending maids, ran back into the jungle, or, in the case of one gray and rough-looking beast, simply sat on the fence and observed. None of them looked like any monkey Charles had seen in the National Zoo. They stood three feet high and showed bright, varied expressions. Without bars or walls, they moved quickly and confidently, knotted with muscles and unexerted power. The scene resembled one at the zoo only in that a metal wall separated the two species. But here, as the old fellow on the fence made clear, the people stayed inside while the monkeys came and went at leisure.

After several minutes the crowd at the fence peaked and the monkeys settled in enough for one mother to take time out to nurse and several couples to drop their bananas for some quick and casual coitus. Charles watched the mother with her child. The kid sucked at her wrinkled breast while she picked bugs out of its hair and ate them. The two made themselves at home, as if they could tell the natives from the transients. Slowly and quietly he made his way down the steps and into the yard.

"You the new kid?" A boy stepped from behind a bush. About five-two, freckles, blue eyes; he had a medium build, a round face, and blond hair cut boot-camp short along the sides but left longish on top. Like a stillborn surfer cut, thought Charles, or, less kindly, something the Stooges might have thought up. To balance this he wore faded chinos, desert boots, and a Jim Morrison T-shirt.

"Yeah. Name's Charles."

"I'm Billy. Some folks call me Killer." They didn't shake.

"So how old are you?" Billy asked. Charles looked away, then told him, hoping he didn't sound uncertain. The Barkers had left Travis Air Force Base in California less than thirty-six hours earlier. When they crossed the International Date Line the day that they lost coincided with Charles's fourteenth birthday. He thought of it as somehow still hanging there, in the middle of the Pacific at thirty-five thousand feet, with the gray-green waves shushing below and the sky above fading abruptly into a spangled indigo void. He nodded toward the monkeys and the jungle. "This happen often?"

Only two monkeys remained. The others had just vanished. "Nope," said Billy. "Must have been special just for you."

"Pretty incredible," said Charles.

"Yeah. Fucking freaked me out, man. Why do you suppose those two are still hanging around?"

Charles ignored the profanity. Billy looked at least a year behind him. "Must be some sort of rear guard. They sent an advance guard of bulls to clear the way. These two are probably supposed to warn the rest if we try to follow." As he finished, one monkey grabbed the other's buttocks, mounted her, and, while she munched on a banana peel, pumped away for a few seconds and scratched himself.

"All right!" said Billy. "Looks like they're fooling around on the job. Go for it, man! Git some!"

Charles looked around but all the maids and little kids had gone, too. When Billy stopped laughing he asked Charles what Commander Barker did.

"He's the new administrative officer at the hospital. What does your father do?"

Billy spat. "Fuck if I know. I could give a shit, too. Do you really like to be called Charles? It's kind of pussy. How about Chuck?"

"No. Charles."

"Okay, that's cool. What the fuck, it's your name. Where you from, Charles?"

"Arlington, Virginia. That's right across the river from Washington, D.C. Where are you from?"

Billy shrugged. "California, I guess. Long Beach, San Diego, Treasure Island. Wherever. I been in Seattle, too, and Guam, and Jacksonville, they tell me, but I was too young to remember. I was born in Corpus Christi. That's right across the river from fucking nowhere."

"My parents are from Texas."

"BFD. I was two months old when we moved."

"BFD?"

Billy smirked. "You don't know? How about DILLIGAF?"

Charles looked back at the jungle. It bothered him that he didn't know these acronyms. It also bothered him that Billy didn't know what his father did.

"You really don't know what your father does?"

"He told me, but I don't give a shit. My old man's a prick. He made me get my hair cut just 'cause school's starting next week. Now I look like an asshole. One of these nights he's gonna wake up with his balls in his throat. Cocksucking, motherfucking son of a bitch!"

Charles frowned. The conversation was heading rapidly nowhere, but he could do this or go back to the *Manila Times*. Besides, didn't his mother want him to make friends?

"What's school like here, anyway?"

Billy hawked up a wad of phlegm and spat again. "It's like the rest of this place, man. It sucks dick. The principal's a prick. He can lick my balls, man, he's so fucking lame. He don't know jack shit. He's this weaselly little shit who runs around at lunchtime with a whistle making sure nobody leaves any trash around, and he whines alla time about kids smoking. When I get to be a senior, if I'm still in this shit hole, we're gonna do like they did at Sangley and pay some Joe ten bucks to waste his ass. Either than or I'll cut his legs off and ram them up his poopchute. What a dickhead!"

Charles couldn't resist. "You don't like him, huh?"

"No shit, Sherlock."

"I don't want to change the subject, but what do you do around here for fun?"

Billy looked ready to spit again but apparently decided the question didn't warrant the effort. "Fun? There's no fucking fun here. Shit. You can go to the Teen Club if you wanna hear Joe bands and watch the Aces and Kittens show off for each other. They got reefs so you can snorkel and shit. That's a lot of fun if you like being wet ninety-five percent of the time. They got free movies if you wanna see shit that can't make it stateside and like seeing the same flicks four times a week. Or you can let your parents take you to the O Club so you can watch the officers get drunk and barf on each other." He stopped as if reconsidering the logic, then pointed over the fence into the jungle. "And if you're really stone crazy, ninety-nine percent of this fucking *naval* base is pure raggedy-assed, bug- and snake-infested bush. And some motherfuckers like to go out in it for fun. Shit. So what do *you* like to do?"

Charles studied the trees. The last monkeys had left. "I like war games," he said. "You know, board games and miniatures . . ." Before he could continue a woman's voice called out "Billy!"

"Ah shit," said Billy. "Get back. If she sees you you'll have to come over for lunch and answer a buncha questions and I'll hafta sit around and listen to all that crap."

Charles stepped back to the cover of a bush.

"Oh Billy!" the voice cried again.

"Yeah, I'm comin' Mom!" Turning to Charles he said, "Listen—
BFD means 'big fucking deal' and DILLIGAF means "do I look
like I give a fuck.' Got it? If you don't know shit like that kids'll
think you're an asshole. Okay?"

"Sure. Thanks."

"All right. Put it there." He held out his hand. Charles went
to take it the normal way but Billy wrapped thumbs and pulled
them into a double-fisted soul shake.

"Billy!"

"Coming!" he yelled, then said to Charles, "Silly bitch. Check
ya later, man. Be cool." Charles watched him leave then went
back to do his dishes and put away the *Manila Times*. When his
mother returned he met her at the door. Hanging in the humid
air behind her, like a rich humus under her flowery perfume, he
smelled the rot baking out of the jungle. She seemed surprised
to find him at home.

"Why Charles," she said. "I would have thought you'd already
be out playing and making friends."

"I was, Mom. Really."

"Well, I don't see anyone here. I hope you haven't spent the
whole time in your room dreaming about those games and toy
soldiers. We'll only be here two years, you know. You don't want
to miss everything."

"Yes, ma'am."

"Come on—since you're home you can help me unload some
things. I found a beautiful lazy Susan at the PX that will look just
wonderful on our dining room table."

"Okay, Mom," said Charles, but when he imagined her new
whatsit sitting in the middle of the table in front of that view he
thought—suddenly, and without meaning to—*BFD*, and he had
to bite his cheek to keep from laughing.

II

THE EXPLORER SCOUTS

Subic Bay opens south-southwest into the South China Sea—
a slightly irregular, vaguely angular, capital U with a mouth
more than five miles wide. The heart of the base—the ship
repair facility with its huge floating dry docks, piers, stores, and
workshops—lay in the bottom of the U in front of the Philippine
town of Olongapo. The rest of the base spread along the left, or
southern, arm, holding more offices, shops, and stores for the
myriad ships that stopped en route to or from Vietnam some
seven hundred miles to the west. After a few miles, near the end
of the U's left arm, the thinning trace of the naval station linked
with the naval air station at Cubi Point. There aircraft carriers
docked, looking like ghost gray cities rising from viridian sea into
cobalt sky, while their white warplanes waited on the adjacent
airfield like a well-organized flock of nesting seabirds.

From this thick corridor of ships and buildings, slender fingers
reached inland into the hills, two-lane asphalt roads ending at
little pockets of construction: officers' housing, high school, PX,
golf course, riding stables and sawmill, enlisted housing, hospital. But none of these took up much space. The hills occupied
most of the base, and bore fifteen thousand acres of mostly uncut

and unvisited rain forest, the last of its kind on the island of Luzon, protected from the local citizens and all other enemies foreign and domestic by the U.S. Navy.

In these first few days Charles didn't think much about the jungle except as a potentially annoying backdrop to his planned activities for the next two years. He resigned himself to having left home, for apart from a handful of friends he'd only left a society that he never quite felt comfortable with. He thought that now that he'd escaped the cliques of his high school in Arlington—those tight clubs of civilian children who'd lived there all their lives—and returned to his real home, the Navy, he might have a better chance of finding a girl. Or, if not that, maybe he could teach some of the boys here his modified Featherstone rules for war games with tin soldiers and, using his replicas of the Austrian and Prussian armies of the Seven Years' War, gain a local reputation for military genius that might serve him well years later, when he and his opponents met again in the commissioned ranks of the Navy. But either way he didn't see getting far away from air-conditioning. Too many weird things waited for him outside: not just the monkeys in the backyard, but the swarm of flying ants he found coating the front door on his second day (so thick he could only get rid of them with a whole can of bug spray and a broom), the mole crickets in the utility room, the copulating lizards on the living room ceiling, and the squadrons of flies rising like gunships from the imitation suburban lawns. It made everything seem not quite right, as when his father drove him and his mother to the Naval Hospital the day before. On the way they passed the camp of a marine battalion landing team (a different creature altogether from a civilian "BLT"). The sign at the gate showed the Marine Corps emblem of an eagle sitting on a globe and anchor. But an enormous fan-rooted jungle tree rose up behind it, so on the whole the emblem looked no bigger than a pimple on the base of a ten-story leafy erection.

Charles supposed his mother objected to the jungle as much as he did, but Commander Barker seemed to enjoy it: he laughed as he told his wife and son that monkeys came out of the jungle at the hospital, too. One monkey, he'd heard, found that the ambulatory patients often had lunch outside. The monkey quickly learned to grab away their crutches and canes, and then take their food. This continued for weeks, Commander Barker chuckled, till the staff finally called the master-at-arms and had him shot.

Commander Barker took his family all over the base those first few days. But on a Thursday night marking the end of their fourth day, he turned right from the road to Cubi at a sign that read FICPACFAPFAPL and dropped Charles off in front of a two-story concrete office building, telling him to call when the meeting ended. Commander Barker had his own ideas about how his son would spend two years in Subic, and they had something to do with scouting.

"I *know* you didn't get any off her, Jim."

Charles sat in the briefing room that a sailor at the front desk directed him to. A boy in the row before him sat sideways and looked to his right, scornfully disbelieving of the boy directly in front of Charles. The boy's brown eyes shifted a little and he ran his hand nervously through close-cropped, tightly curled brown hair before rubbing an acne-pocked cheek and Roman nose. Even as he leaned back in the metal chair and assumed a casual air his athletic frame tensed as if expecting an ambush. Charles found him unsettling. The second boy kept his eyes on the podium and smiled.

"Fine, Joe," he said. "I ain't asking you to believe me."

Charles thought Jim looked friendly. His straight, dirty blond hair hung too long, brushing the tops of his ears and forming Beach Boy bangs on his forehead, and his purple-tinted granny glasses made him look a bit hippie-ish. But his green eyes and pouty lips, half closed over braces, didn't look like they belonged to the sort of boy who would give him any trouble.

"I mean," said Joe, "I *know* you're bullshitting me."

On Joe's left a tall lanky boy with thick black hair, olive skin, and chocolate eyes laughed and twisted in his chair as if it formed more of a mooring pin than something he sat on. In a lilting accent Charles couldn't place, he said, "Jim's a cat, man.

He had half the women on this base, baby. You better watch you mama . . ."

"You better watch your ass, Luiz." Joe seemed angry. Charles sat back in his chair. The two boys at the podium looked up from some papers. One sat tall and square, bigger than any of the three in front of Charles. The other appeared shorter than Charles, lean and mean with a blond crew cut; he stepped in front of Joe.

"Cool it, Barone."

Joe smiled the way guys did when they looked around a gym and realized that they had just managed to choose all the hard-core jocks for their own team. He stood up, a head taller than the other boy, stared into the latter's ice-blue eyes, and said, "Say what, shorty?"

"Oooh . . ." said Jim and Luiz, smiling, the low sound joined by the half-a-dozen other boys in the rows behind Charles. The small boy let the sound die out into an expectant beat of silence, then replied. "I don't mind being short. It puts my fist just that much closer to your balls."

"All *right*, Finch," said Jim.

A little flustered, Joe said, "Yeah? Your lips, too, shrimp."

"You wanna see which gets there first?"

Charles saw Joe's hands clenching and unclenching as Finch leaned forward, hands on his hips.

"Girls, girls, girls," said the big boy at the podium. "Are you going to quit the grab-ass or do I have to come over and play sheriff?"

Jim and Luiz chuckled, Finch leaned back and folded his arms, and Joe sat down, saying, "Yeah, yeah, yeah." A voice at the back said, "Way to go Edgefield," and Finch stepped back to lean against the wall behind the podium, just under the blue-and-gold drapery of the banner of Explorer Post 360, Subic Bay.

Edgefield took the podium like a skipper at the conn. His gray eyes played over the small group before fixing on Charles.

"There's no old business worth a wet fart, so for our first order of new business I'd like to welcome Charles Barker, son of Commander Barker, the new AO up at the hospital. Howdy. Is that Charles or Chuck or Charlie or what?"

"Ah, Charles."

"Okay, Ahcharles it is."

"Is that like 'Ah-choo,' man?" asked Joe.

"Hey Charles," said Jim.

"Good to meet you, cat," slurred Luiz. Other boys murmured greetings; Finch stepped up between Joe and Jim and took Charles's hand in a quick, firm grip. "Welcome aboard, Barker," he said.

"All right," said Edgefield. "Now that we're all asshole buddies with Ahcharles here, let's talk some serious bullshit. I want to see us do some real scouting this year, guys. I'm sick of all this tourist crap. I been to Baguio, I been on sixteen goddamn destroyers and carriers, I seen the Joe-fucking-schoolhouse, and I've stood post on sixty-fucking-five wives' club bake sales, right?"

"I hear ya, man," said Jim, brushing back his bangs.

"Damn fucking straight," said Joe.

"Yeah, Jesus Christ for sure," said Luiz.

"You guys get to go on carriers?" said Charles. The room groaned.

Then Luiz said, "Hey, what's wrong with Baguio anyway? They got mountains, and it's real cool . . ."

"And there's that Flip whore you ended up with last time," added Joe.

"Did that shampoo ever do it for you?" Jim asked.

"Shi-it, man . . ."

"Okay, okay, that's enough," said Finch.

"Fuck Baguio, man," said Edgefield. "I'm talking *scouting*, you pussies. I'm talking hiking, swimming, camping. We're supposed to *do* that kind of shit, man. We're the Explorer-fucking-Scouts, not a home for wayward pussy-dependent jerk-offs. I mean, Jesus, you fuckheads, some day I'd *like* to be a motherfucking Eagle Scout. If I'd been back in the World in a real post I'd have merit badges up the ass, instead of what I got from dicking around in this hellhole, which is jack shit."

"You be lucky have your dick in any hole," laughed Luiz.

"Yeah, right," said Edgefield. "I'll remember that the next time I hear you screaming in the boys' room. But no shit, fellas, listen up. I still haven't been able to line up a counselor for an overnighter, but that doesn't mean we can't get out during the day for a few hours."

"What are you thinking about?" asked Joe, nervously fingering a fresh pimple on his jaw.

"Not much. A little hike from Kalayaan to Binictican."

"Oh blow me, man," said Joe. "That's all hills and cliffs and shit."

"Yeah," Jim added, "that's bad country. Isn't that where that little twerp got himself offed a few years back?"

"No, man," said Luiz, "that was out back of Cubi some place."

"Killed?" asked Charles.

"Yeah, killed," said Joe. "Some poor little asshole just like yourself got lost and eaten up by wild boar."

"No, no," said Finch. "It got dark and he kept moving. He fell off a cliff."

"Then the pigs got him . . ." said a voice in the back.

"I never heard anything about any pigs . . ." someone replied.

"It don't matter," said Edgefield. "We're just going to walk from the officers' housing area to the golf course. It's no big deal. It's just a start. It's only about six and a half klicks."

"Four miles as the crow flies," said Joe. "More like ten on the ground. Where you going to start?"

"Finch?" said Edgefield. Finch unfolded a detailed contour map of the base. Charles leaned forward and noted a red, rubber-stamped CONFIDENTIAL over the key. He traced a route. "There's a series of firebreaks leading up to the Kalayaan beacon. We can take compass bearings there, get an idea of the ground, then head out."

"That's fucked," said Joe. "Once you get all the way up to the aviation beacon you got to find a way down into the jungle. *Then* you got to clear four or five ridges before you hit the greens and the last one's a *real* motherfucker. You can count my ass out."

Charles heard boys whispering behind him. No one sounded enthusiastic.

"I'd go," said Luiz. "When do we do it?"

Joe turned away and sneered. His eyes met Charles's. "Hey, Ahcharles," he teased, "you going too?"

Edgefield broke in. "He doesn't have to go anywhere. Nobody has to go anywhere yet. Before we do anything I want to take a little dry run up to the beacon. Soon. Like maybe next Saturday afternoon. After that, after we figure out what we're doing, maybe we can all of us get together for the real thing."

"Well, I'd love to join you boys, but I'm going to be in on something else next Saturday," said Jim, his braces flashing in the fluorescent light.

"Short time or long time?" asked Joe. "Maybe I'll go with you."

"Sorry, only room for one."

"Well, I'll go to the beacon," said Luiz.

"Okay," said Finch. "You, me, and Edgefield will check it out."

"Shit," said Joe. "How about you, Barker? You don't look like you got anywhere else to be on a Saturday. And who knows, maybe your mommy will find you before the pigs do."

Charles glanced at Joe, then away, wondering if he gave off some kind of scent that bullies could key in on, like dogs with fear. He forced himself to brighten and say—jokingly, he thought—"Oh goodie. Can I?"

"Jesus," said Joe.

"Stow it, Barone," said Finch.

"Stow it yourself, you little dickhead."

"That's enough," said Edgefield. "If that's a joke, Barker, you're gonna have to try harder 'cause I ain't laughing. But if you're serious, it's not a bad way to get your feet wet."

"Yeah, your pants, too," said Joe. Jim and Luiz laughed, then Jim said, "I make a motion we adjourn."

"In a hurry to be somewhere?" asked Edgefield.

"Always, man, always."

"I second it," said Joe.

"Fine," said Edgefield, "go get the fuck out of here."

With that the meeting officially ended. As Charles went down the hall to find a phone Finch came up beside him. "You sure you want to go?" he asked.

Charles looked at him. Finch had fine features and a bearing that projected a level of confidence out of all proportion with his size. His white short-sleeved shirt and khaki dress slacks would have looked nerdy stateside but here seemed a kind of dependent's uniform, a uniform Finch wore with invisible shoulderboards. Charles didn't want to go anywhere near the jungle, but he'd said something in front of the other boys and now felt that he'd either have to follow through or hear about it for the next two years. Besides, he had nearly a week and a half till next Saturday, a healthy amount of time in which to work on an excuse.

"Yeah, sure," he told Finch.

"Well, you'll need some stuff, then."

"Stuff?"

"Yeah—you can't just walk out into the jungle in your street clothes. Listen, I'm getting a ride back with Edgefield. He's got our stores. We can fix you up tonight."

"Yeah, okay, but I told my dad I'd call him after the meeting."

"We'll get you home, shipmate. Don't worry about your old man."

Charles nodded and followed him outside. They stepped first into a viscous wall of humidity, and then into a screen of little green caterpillars dangling from filaments that glittered faintly in the dark. Charles recoiled but Finch casually brushed them aside and led the way to a hulking old Buick. Finch took shotgun and Charles got in the back. Edgefield winked at them, revved the V-8, and slowly tooled down the road for about a mile until he reached the intersection near the commissary where the road split. To the left, the main base blinked and hummed. Ahead, the road ran straight across a mile or so of flat, cleared land, then shot up into the hills where it wound its way another couple of miles to the Kalayaan housing area. As he passed the commissary, Edgefield cocked his head to the throaty growl of his car and said, "Shit man, listen to this bitch drink gas. She's just lapping it up." He made some slurping sounds that really did sound a lot like his car and stomped the accelerator, saying, "Let's see how fast she goes in second!"

The engine now roared like an old, sick lion and the car lunged forward, pushing Charles back into the seat. He closed his eyes, then opened them and looked at his hands. He had never ridden in a car driven really fast. When he glanced over Edgefield's shoulder the speedometer read eighty. Right after that they hit the hills.

It seemed to Charles that time slowed even more with fear than with boredom. An hour in church might seem to him like four, but he couldn't count the ones he'd spent in the shot ward getting inoculated for the trip overseas. That had seemed like a two-year tour itself, although now he remembered only a single moment, when a Navy doctor wielding an especially long hypo said, "This one's for cholera."

The Buick sailed, up into the night, outracing its headlights along the twisting unlit road, while Edgefield and Finch sat as silent as pilots on a sortie over Haiphong. At every turn shadowy trees loomed in newly bizarre shapes, while the brights brought out a constant train of ghosts. After a while the stars froze in the gap in the canopy above them and time slowed so much that it seemed they didn't move at all; the motion came from the earth as it slowly turned beneath their wheels.

Charles had a lot of time to think then. Mainly he thought about fear, the little fears like shots and bugs (when just a little boy in Yokohama he'd seen centipedes under the couch near where he played, first two legs, then three, then four, and he began screaming, because four or six seemed about the maximum number of legs any of God's creatures should have and anything more spoke of an ingenuity more diabolical than natural), or not having the answer in math class, or trying to speak to a girl one liked, or worrying about one's parents walking in during a bout of masturbation. He saw these as little fears because he had so many of them they seemed no more than tiny parts of the one big fear, a fear he couldn't name or describe, but that he thought might find him anywhere, especially in a place like the jungle.

He hung on tight to the armrest to keep the centrifugal force from throwing him across the seat each time they cornered. When the car and his body sailed over the crests his stomach had all it could do to keep up. He went rigid, fixing his eyes on the slowly undulating double yellow line, shaking with the surging automobile, then suddenly realizing, with little room for embarrassment amid his fear and surprise, that he had an erection. At any moment, he thought, they might sail right off the road and fly into the trees on the inevitable turn that Edgefield couldn't handle and then they would crash, and the next day a rescue team would find Charles just as Charles found himself now. His mother, his father, and the whole U.S. Navy would watch as workmen pulled his lifeless body from the wreckage of the Buick and laid him out: pale blue shorts, white T-shirt, tennis shoes, and big ol' boner. He laughed. Edgefield and Finched turned around and they laughed, too. They thought he enjoyed this.

When they arrived at Edgefield's it felt like landing at Clark again after the nineteen-hour flight from Travis. Charles got out on shaky legs and followed the other two boys to a house just like his own: two stories, prefab concrete slabs, roof sloped to the rear, living quarters above, utility room, maid's quarters, and carport below. In the screened-in area between the carport and the maid's quarters Charles could see the shadows of metal racks piled with gear. Edgefield opened the door and motioned them inside.

"Most of our parents know somebody somewhere who's getting rid of something for some reason," he explained as he switched on the light. "So we get a lot of shit. Some pretty neat shit, too. I keep telling my old man we need some sixteens, or even some surplus fourteens, so we can really take care of ourselves out there, but no dice. Look around though."

Charles gaped, then shut his mouth and walked slowly down the aisle between the two rows of shelving. The scouts had a bit of everything: green fatigue pants and shirts and lightweight jungle jackets; web belts and packs and boots—even a few pairs of the new nylon-sided jungle boots. They had personal med kits with battle dressings, water purification tabs, and snakebite kits, even a big medical bag with atropine injectors, just in case they ran into some nerve gas. They had ponchos and camouflage poncho liners, pup tents, hammocks, and mosquito nets. In one

corner Charles saw entrenching tools, issue machetes, and bay-
onets. Edgefield pulled two items off a shelf and held them out
for special notice: a field compass and a drab pack of marker
dye. He explained the dye: "It's for pilots who get shot down
over the sea. So people can find them. Dyes a piece of ocean
orange, man, big as a fucking football field. I swear to God one
of these days before I leave I'm gonna toss this fucker into the
pool by the O Club—maybe dye the *admiral's* ass orange!"

The three of them laughed and then Finch and Edgefield
helped Charles pick out boots, jungle fatigues, web belt, knapsack, and canteens.

"Take at least two," Finch said of the canteens. "You'll get
thirsty. Besides, they're not all alike. The new ones are plastic.
They won't ever rust, but all you can do is drink from them.
The old metal ones sit in a cup with a fold-out handle you can
cook in."

Edgefield brought out some sodas and a church key and
popped the top on a can of pretzels. Everything here came in
cans. You couldn't ship a bag of chips across the Pacific. Not with
a war on.

They looked over the equipment for a minute or two more
before Edgefield raised the big question. "You're not scared, are
you? You know, of snakes and shit?"

Charles shook his head and took a quick swig of Pepsi. Finch
added, "You know what they say: there are a hundred different
kinds of snakes in the P.I. Ninety-six are poisonous and one will
choke you to death."

"What about the other three?" asked Charles.

"No one's ever seen *them*," laughed Edgefield.

Although Charles got home early his mother and father both
wanted to know where he had gone after the meeting and why
he hadn't called. Once his father heard that Charles had ridden
home with Captain Edgefield's and Lieutenant Commander
Finch's sons he nodded and said, "That's fine, boy. Just give a
ring next time. Your mother worries."

Indeed. Mrs. Barker held her after-dinner Scotch and soda
absently to one side and stared at her son as he held a knapsack

stuffed with fatigues in one hand, combat boots in the other, and a pair of canteens on a web belt draped around his neck.

"Charles, honey," she asked, "what is all of that for?"

"Uh, some of the guys were talking about taking a little hike next Saturday."

"Where to, sweetheart?"

"Just a little ways into the jungle." That's it, he thought. That should do it. Sorry guys, parents won't let me. Honor and ass saved at the same time.

"Oh, no. No, no, no. That can't be safe." She smoothed the front of her skirt.

Right Mom, thought Charles. *It can't be. Plus, all of the boys here seem to be lunatics.*

"Now dear," said Commander Barker, putting his arm around his wife's shoulders, "those boys know what they're doing. Hell, Edgefield's son is a shoe-in for Annapolis." He gently turned her away and, looking over his shoulder, gave Charles a conspiratorial wink.

"Thanks, Dad," said Charles. *Thanks a lot.*

III

NAVAL STATION YOUTH
ACTIVITIES

The twenty or so concrete duplexes that made up Senior Officers' Quarters sat on a hill so distinctly higher than and separate from the rest of the base that Charles had to ask Billy if it had a name of its own. Billy squinted a platter of freckles and said, "Sure. SOQ Hill."

They'd met up a few minutes earlier, at eighteen hundred, in front of their homes. They now walked the half mile down the hill toward a crossroads. If at that point they kept going straight they'd end up in more housing, of lower-ranking officers and civilians. If they turned right they would eventually reach the main Naval Station several miles away. They planned to turn left, which after about a hundred yards would bring them to the Teen Club.

"You're not really going," said Billy after a minute or so.

Charles looked up into the narrow band of sky that followed the road between the canopy of high trees on either side. He then looked down into the depths of the jungle to his left, bizarre shadows and weird varieties of shapes of shades of green, all subtly shifting as they walked past.

"Sure, why not?" he replied. In truth, he still hoped his mother would nag his father into telling him he couldn't. Then Charles could complain to his peers about his parents and still not have to climb that hill in the jungle.

"Why *not?*" said Billy, turning and tugging that same sweaty Jim Morrison T-shirt from his pudgy thirteen-year-old torso. "Because it's fucking stupid, man. It's not even like crazy brave, you know? It's just fucking crazy."

Charles picked up his pace, knowing Billy would have to sweat harder to stay even and hoping maybe that would shut him up. An entire week lay between tomorrow and the date of the hike, and he didn't want to spend the whole time afraid. After only five days it seemed a bit early for the tour in Subic to end in disaster. In another ten minutes they'd reach the Teen Club, which had a live band for its Friday-night dance and, as far as Charles knew, other boys who would make better friends than Billy, and girls who might fulfill the fantasies that up till now he'd had to fake his way through on his own.

The lighting changed abruptly, as if a blue lamp shade had dropped over the sun. Shadows swelled from the depths of the forest, the tunneled mouth at the end of the road down the hill began to close, yet everything near—tree trunks, curbs, the lines in the sidewalk—took on a glowing outline. The effect intensified for several minutes, the world burning like a slowly puffed cigarette end under a growing layer of ash. Then somewhere behind the two boys the sun sank into the South China Sea and the cigarette became a blown-out match head, the orange rapidly fading to black. Twilight ended in a deep wilderness night, punctuated at great distances by the Navy's streetlights, their glare softened by the translucent wings of billions of newly wakened insects.

"Shit, man—look out!" Charles felt Billy jerk him back, but he couldn't see anything to fear. Bad joke, he thought, and turned around to set his foulmouthed friend straight, but Billy pointed down and, wide-eyed, said, "Motherfucking *cobra*, man!"

Charles turned back around. A slender shadow perhaps eighteen inches long slithered across the walk in front of him with an easy mobility that came closer to scaring Charles than its hoodless form. "You're joking," he said to Billy, who shook more now that he could see his fear hadn't caught on.

"Yeah? Well it was, too! Man, I wouldn't go out in the jungle if I was as fucking hopeless as you are."

"Well, you're not going out there anyway, are you?"

"Ah, fuck you," said Billy, but so defensively that Charles let it ride. When they got to the Teen Club itself he felt a touch of disappointment. A cinder-block building—one story tall, a few classrooms wide, with a small parking lot in back—it had all the visual appeal of a rural radio station or VFW hall. Kids stood in little knots roughly segregated by high school grade and laughed or chatted with sidelong looks at the other groups. Nearer the door some of the kids turned their attention briefly to Charles and Billy but gave no sign of having any opinion of them. Charles became suddenly conscious of who walked beside him on this first critical visit, but the awareness came too late. Besides, he needed a guide.

"Pretty fucking lame, huh?" said Billy. Charles nodded and pushed ahead into a fog of bass notes that began several yards before the front double doors: just inside, a bored girl took a dollar from Charles and stamped his hand while a layered noise surrounded him with strained electric guitar riffs and a cacophony of adolescent voices. Billy and Charles stood briefly in a kind of lobby, perhaps ten feet square, with a glassed-in office in front of them and double doors on either side through which passed a light but unending stream of boys and girls on a series of apparently vital errands. In marked contrast, a boy sat on a gray vinyl couch in the right rear of the room quietly reading from a large book. Billy tugged Charles in the boy's direction and called out, "Hey jerkwad!"

The boy looked up with a weary, cynical expression. Smaller and thinner than Billy, his thinness came to an extreme in his face, which grew outward like a hatchet blade under lank black hair spotted with dandruff, and came to a point at a beak bearing glasses with heavy black frames. He wore clunky dress shoes, khaki pants, and a long-sleeved white shirt under a dark jacket.

He conceded to the Tropics only to the extent of omitting a tie. Despite the adult costume he looked about ten, except for his eyes and mouth. He had serious eyes, like Finch, and a sardonic twist to his lips that made him seem a lot older than the rest of him. Like seventeen, maybe. When he saw Charles he closed the book, marking his place with his finger, and rose, soberly offering his right hand in greeting. "Name's Ford," he shouted over the background noise.

"Barker. Charles Barker."

Just then a pair of tall boys brushed them aside. Perhaps juniors or seniors, the boys wore white denim vests with large ace of spades logos on the back and towed a pair of girls with pageboy hairdos and powder-blue windbreakers. The four passed through quickly, laughing and opening the nearest double doors to unleash another concussive sound wave from the dance floor. When Charles recovered his balance he asked, "Who were they?"

"Fucking Aces," spat Billy with jealous disdain. "Buncha assholes. The two chicks were Kittens. Cockteasin' whores."

Ford shook his head. "That last term is an oxymoron, Billy. To be precise, some of them are cockteasers and others are whores."

"Moron yourself, dickweed," said Billy.

Ford ignored him and addressed Charles. "Both Aces and Kittens are old groups, perhaps even predating the Teen Club. For all I know they trace their ancestry back to prep school frats of the officers in Dewey's fleet. I like to think that earlier members were tortured to death by the Japanese."

Charles bent down to hear Ford's shouted history and asked, "So why are they here? Are they official?"

"Sure," Ford replied. "They tend to keep all the kids on this base from noticing how stupid the adults are. You see, they provide us with our own, even more inane, social hierarchy. All the real 'popular' kids belong: jocks, princesses. They toil not, neither do they study, but lo they getteth good grades and many rumors of sex."

"Ford, just what the fuck are you talking about?" Billy yelled. "They're just a buncha dickheads and I wouldn't join if you paid me."

"Trust me, that won't be a problem."

"Ah, fuck you. C'mon Charles, let's see what kind of ass is on the dance floor."

Charles nodded to Ford. "You'll have to excuse us. We're going to get some ass." Ford smiled wanly in response. As Charles turned away he got a glimpse of the spine of the book in Ford's hand. *Nausea*. Sartre. So perhaps Ford planned to become a doctor someday. Commander Barker wouldn't mind Charles having a friend like that. It might even get him off the hook for hikes in the jungle and whatever other gruesome initiation rites the old man intended for him.

The preview in the lobby didn't prepare Charles for the decibel level in the dance hall, which took up half the Teen Club but still looked no bigger than a standard classroom, though it had to hold all the noise of a Filipino rock combo banging out top-forty hits over cheesy amps. Some twenty kids sat or stood along the walls, most of them wearing what Charles began to see as the regulation navy dependent's uniform: girls in jumpers and blouses or shifts with skirts no more than two inches above the knees, boys in dress slacks and short-sleeved shirts, often plain and buttoned down, the more daring in loud batik patterns acquired in Olongapo. A few boys went so far as to have their shirttails hanging loose outside their trousers, but none that Charles could see had hair that more than touched his ears. Several couples jerked uncertainly on the dance floor, and from time to time a boy would cross from one side of the room to the other and ask a girl to dance. For the most part they agreed.

After a brief pause in the music Charles heard a cheap electric organ spring into the opening chords of "Light My Fire." Billy stood transfixed; everything negative he'd said about Filipinos and the Teen Club fell away as he swayed to the theme of his favorite group. Charles, too, found himself taken as the portentous lyrics—expertly mimicked by the local vocalist—gave way to a long instrumental passage in which the plaintive organ and melancholy lead guitar played snippets of melody off each other and twined the Doors' original motifs with their own, only vaguely familiar, variations, while the drums and bass settled into a trance-inducing, transcendental pattern, saved from monotony, Charles thought, by the mere power of seeming so very right for this moment. As he looked around the half-lit room filled with children fixated on their own boredom, with no desire to leave for the outside world of parents, but content to stay here in this room, in this music, forever and ever and ever, it seemed to Charles very nice that the Navy had done this for them—given them all their own place, with refreshments and music and full light or half light as they wished, here in the middle of a U.S. Naval Station, deep in the jungle in a strange country thousands of miles across the bottomless Pacific from a country they all wanted to go home to, though many of them had spent most of their lives in places that only reflected it dimly, surrounded by warships and warplanes in linoleum-floored havens like this.

Mom and Dad are at the O Club right now, thought Charles, imagining them all dressed up and attended by uniformed stewards. He hadn't seen the O Club in Subic yet, but knew that when he did he would find no surprises.

The song finally ended. Charles didn't know whether to ask Billy to show him the rest of the club or to stay and maybe get up the nerve to ask a girl to dance. He weighed the danger of continuing to appear with Billy against the potential disaster of rejection from the first girl he approached. He escaped the dilemma when a boy in a Nehru jacket and beads, with blond hair that actually half covered his ears, approached the stage and whispered in the ear of the lead guitarist. The Filipino smiled, lit a cigarette, and spoke a few words to the group. Then he picked up his guitar and hit the opening chords of "Purple Haze."

A few laughs and shouts indicated the general disapproval of the crowd as the quasi-hippie clapped his hands and unfolded into a kind of slow-motion, swimming dance. When he grabbed the mike an Ace stepped onto the dance floor and yelled, "Get a haircut, pussy!" and another boy called, "Hey bacla—blow job, two pesos!"

Others shook their heads, but the boy in the Nehru jacket jumped into the lyrics with such fervor that, inspired, the band members one by one crushed their cigarettes on the stage with the toes of their mod boots and gave their full attention to taking off from Hendrix and the Experience's buzzing, stomping drama into dark reverberations of their own. When in an ecstatic gesture the blond singer excused himself and kissed the sky, his passion and intensity even began to move his fellow dependents. Billy shouted an explanation into Charles's ear: "Lucky fucker's short. He's going back stateside—to the World, man—in about two weeks. He's so fucking short he can sit on the edge of a dime and dangle his legs. Plus, do whatever the fuck he wants." He gave one more disgusted look at the stage before pulling on Charles to go: "C'mon man. Nobody's dancing. There's nothin' but a buncha scags around anyway."

They went out another door into a snack bar little bigger than the lobby, with half a dozen booths and ten or twelve stools at the bar. To their right, Jim, Luiz, and Edgefield shared one of the booths with a slender and beautiful Asian girl. Farther on the right in the corner, Joe and two other boys wearing Ace vests stood around a fourth, apparently a pledge. Charles and Billy watched as the boy held out his hand for Joe's cigarette. As the boy sucked in his cheeks and squinched his tearing eyes, the other Aces liberally peppered a hamburger for him and a pair of nearby Kittens giggled.

Edgefield waved Billy and Charles over. The Explorers ignored Joe and his companions. They didn't seem to see Billy, either, but they all said hello to Charles. The Asian girl snuggled up to Jim, who sat back with a teasing and yet relaxed expression, looking with his braces a bit like an earless Bugs Bunny on tranquilizers. Edgefield, sitting across from the girl, told her, "Lee Ann, this is Ahcharles, our new bro. Says he wants to try the jungle with us."

Lee Ann looked up at Charles from the shelter of Jim's arm and tenderly said, "You are so brave."

At that, Charles started to get hard right there in front of them, but Luiz, sitting next to Edgefield, took care of that by explaining, "No, he just more afraid of looking scared," and laughing as if he'd made a joke, though Charles thought they could all see the truth in it. He felt a hand on his shoulder and turned his head into the cloud of cigarette smoke Joe blew in his face.

"Yo, tenderfoot," said Joe, "you still planning on certain death?"

"Ah, Christ," said Jim, "leave him alone."

"Why? You ain't goin', are you?"

"Well I would," smiled Jim, "just because it sounds so god-damn heroic. But me and Lee Ann were kinda planning on some other kind of action . . . ouch!"

She pinched him and they all laughed, but then Joe blew more smoke in Charles's face and demanded, "What are you laughing at, new kid? You think you got balls? You ain't seen balls till you feel mine bouncing off your chin."

"Yuck, man," said Luiz.

"Hey, there's ladies present," said Edgefield.

"Yeah," replied Joe, "that sweet chick in the booth and these two little scags here. Well, Ah-choo, it's been real nice seeing you again." He wet his finger, quickly ran it across Charles's lips, and turned to walk back to his friends. Charles winced and rubbed his mouth on his sleeve as the others looked on without expression.

"Jesus," Charles said, "why is that guy such a prick?"

"Just trying to be a hard-ass," said Edgefield. "He don't mean nothing by it, much."

"Yeah," added Luiz, "he never really get in trouble, so it just pisses him off more."

"What do you mean?" Charles asked.

Billy explained, as if a gun had suddenly pointed away from his head and he could now speak: "His old man's some big fart in Base Security. Every time Joe screws up somebody steps in and it gets taken care of."

"Think about that," said Jim, polishing his purple lenses with a paper napkin. "If I go out in town and tie one on or get it on with some Joe whore—not that I ever would, Lee Ann honey— I'm really risking something. But him, he could do anything short of murdering a round-eye and nothing happens. But we all know why nothing happens and it really frosts his ass."

"Yeah," said Luiz, "like how would you want everybody to know your daddy always, *always* takin' care of you?"

"That's got to be humiliating," said Jim. "I mean, that's got to be even more humiliating than actually getting busted and thrown in some Joe prison and butt-fucked to death."

"Well, not really," said Edgefield.

"Still."

"C'mon," Billy said to Charles, "I got more things to show you."

"Well, don't try to show him your dick," said Luiz, "or you be looking all night."

"Lick it," said Billy, and walked away. Charles followed as the other boys laughed and Lee Ann said, "I get so tired of all you guys talking about your little old dicks all the time."

Billy led Charles out the back door, where the noise of the band made only a distant thumping and six rough-looking boys sat at a picnic table next to the crowded parking lot. With their hair generally long and slicked back, and two or three of them in jeans, they looked like greasers back home. Perhaps to reinforce that impression, they met Billy and Charles with hostile stares. A yellow-blond pimply boy, large enough for a junior, stood up and came toward the two. A heart tattoo showed under the rolled-up short sleeve of his right arm. He said, "Man, you should knock before you come out that fucking door. You coulda been somebody's parent."

"Or the fucking manager," said another.

"It's cool," said Billy, "he's with me. Got my bottle?"

"Got my money?"

Billy gave him two dollars. He gave Billy a bottle in a brown bag.

"Hey man," Billy protested, "this shit is half empty!"

The boy smiled. "Excise tax, punk. You want a full bottle you can go out in town and get it yourself."

Billy turned and walked into the parking lot as one of the boys commented, "Asshole." When Charles caught up with him Billy pulled out the half-filled pint of Tanduay rum and flashed it in the streetlight as if he had found some rare and precious booty. Charles nodded appreciatively but shook his head when Billy suggested they spike a can of Coke. Billy seemed disappointed, but then brightened as with sudden inspiration. Motioning Charles back toward the club, he led him past the boys smoking and drinking at the picnic table and pointed to a gray metal box on the exterior wall of the Teen Club. A switch handle jutted out, a smaller version of the one Dr. Frankenstein pulls at a Very Important Moment in the film.

"See that?" asked Billy. "That's the power switch for the whole damn club. One of these days I'm gonna pull it and shoot everybody who runs out the door. Neat, huh?"

"Yeah. Look, I'm getting a little tired. Maybe I should leave." Charles felt sticky and worn. The walk down the hill had heated him up, and with all the kids in the Teen Club its AC couldn't cool him down again. Now he found himself standing out in the muggy night immersed in mosquitoes and the mingling smells of cigarettes, booze, soda pop, and something worse: just around the corner he could hear someone vomiting while other kids laughed and cheered him on.

"Sure you don't want some of this?"

"Maybe later—tomorrow night—I don't know."

"Fine. All the more for me."

Charles went back through the rear door and found the snack bar packed. The band had taken a break and everyone had come in to fill up on burgers and fries. Finding a door on his right, he opened it and stepped into another room about half the size of the dance floor. It had two Ping-Pong tables and four for pool, at one of which Ford and Finch played eight-ball. Charles pushed his way past the kids at the other tables, happy to see Finch.

"Where's Billy?" asked Ford as he advanced on the table with his cue.

"Out back. He just got overcharged for some rum."

Ford nodded and took careful aim. He sank the cue ball.

"Drat. I need new glasses."

"You've needed new glasses for the past year," said Finch. "Why don't you try chalking your cue?"

"Ah, of course. A simple oversight. May I have the shot over?"

"No way."

"I'm surprised you wouldn't have done something about those glasses earlier," said Charles. "I mean, given your medical interests." He pointed to Ford's book, which lay on a chair by the wall.

"Alas," said Ford, "that this generation would be so ignorant."

Finch explained. "*Nausea* is a novel by some pinko Frog philosopher, not a medical book. Ford keeps trying to get me to read it but I tell him I'm still working on Mahan's *The Influence of Seapower on History*."

"Warmonger," said Ford.

"Damn straight. You wanna break again?"

"I don't know. I'm trying to decide whether this string of defeats is good for my soul or yet another source of enrichment for some future shrink."

Finch shook his head and turned to Charles. "Ford says Billy said you're into war games."

"That's right."

"What kind?"

Finch and Ford played another entire game of eight-ball while Charles explained the structure and rules for Avalon Hill board games with hexagonal mapboards on which players could re-create entire battles like Gettysburg and Waterloo, and how someone could make up his own battles with armies of toy soldiers using either groups of several figures glued to stands as in the Morchauser rules, or single figures grouped together for purposes of fire and melee as in Featherstone's. He went on to expound his special passion for the Seven Years' War and the campaigns of Frederick the Great, known, he told them, as one of the Great Captains of history. He didn't add that Frederick had a reputation as a sensitive boy who spoke French, played the flute, and suffered from an oppressive father who kept canes in every room of the Prussian palace so he could beat his son wherever he happened upon him. That would have made things too complicated.

"Let's do it," Finch said to Ford. "We'll get you and me and Billy to fight it out at Charles's place some time. Who knows, Ford—with no strength or physical coordination required, you might just have a snowball's chance in Subic of winning. So tell me, Charles, we use a table or floor or what?"

"The dining room table, I would think," said Charles.

"Fine." Gesturing to the table with his cue he added, "Eight ball in the corner pocket."

"Great," said Ford. "Let's do play with toy soldiers. I'm sick of getting my butt kicked in these grown-up games."

"Shut up and take it like a man," said Finch.

"But I'm not a man yet," protested Ford, pushing his voice into an even higher falsetto than normal. "I'm too young to die!"

They laughed, the three of them, then Finch said, "Speaking of which, one of us should check on Billy."

"I'll go," said Charles. "I was ready to go home anyway. I'll take him with me."

"Good man," said Finch. "If you run into any trouble with the hoods out back let me know."

"Me too," said Ford, "so I can crawl under a table."

"Right," said Charles, and left, wondering only briefly what the diminutive Finch could do about the big guys in back besides bowl them over with his style of command, which, when he thought about it, didn't seem too implausible.

But out back trouble had already found Billy. Charles found him in the dirt to the left of the rear door accusing the blonde with the tattoo, anger and agony twisting his voice into a rising whine. "You fucker! You asshole! I said you could have a swig and you drank the whole damn thing. You took my money and you took the bottle . . . you—you—*asshole!*"

"Better watch who you call asshole . . ."

Two steps out the door and Charles found himself between Billy and the blonde. He thought about turning around and getting Finch but the greaser staggered forward a step, pushed into him, and cut off his retreat. Charles took another step back, got his balance, and turned to face the kid. He'd had beatings from bullies before; he'd prefer that to leaving Billy and later having to explain why to Finch. He formed his hands into uncertain fists and said, "Look, why don't you just leave him be?"

The blonde looked from Billy to Charles. Charles saw eyes as red and bleary as Billy's. The greaser blinked, said "huh?" then stumbled over to the corner of the building and puked.

"Motherfucker," whimpered Billy. "*Fuck you!* Fuck *all* of you!"

Charles stepped over and took his hand. "Come on, Killer," he said quietly. "Let's go home."

>< >< ><

When school started three days later Charles found that only one of his teachers seemed to understand the kind of combustible mixture they had to work with. The rest had other, more personal needs, which they expected employment in the DoD overseas school system to meet. The second-period history teacher, for example, with his barong tagalog shirt, Filipina wife, and four children in a house off base, had gone native, and when he mentioned America he might just as well have spoken of some historical entity now equally distant from him, like Tombstone in the 1880s or the settlement at Jamestown. And the young third-period math teacher in a pale shift, who nervously fingered her faux pearl necklace and spent the hour glancing from window to clock, had no more on her mind—the kids said, and Charles believed—than which young officer she would meet in the O Club each night, and the intricacies of sneaking guests into her room in the BOQ.

But Mr. Las Casas seemed different. No taller than most of the boys, balding with short black hair and a thin mustache, and probably already past thirty, he moved with a special intensity, like a shark in a tank. He talked to his class directly while his hands waved with a life of their own, as if straining to leap from his wrists to his students' necks and shake some learning into them. He said he wanted to teach them. He wanted to teach them English. In a thick Brooklyn accent he said, "I know what you're thinking. I heard the same thing when I applied for this job. 'Why do you want to *teach* English?' they asked me—'you can't even *speak* it!'" The class laughed but his own smile rapidly switched back to a pinched-lip fervor. When a student asked why they would have to read Shakespeare, Mr. Las Casas said, "Gee, I don't know. I don't know what could possibly interest you in *Romeo and Juliet:* street fights between teen gangs, illicit underage sex, and clueless adults handing out useless advice and otherwise gumming things up. I guess none of that sounds familiar to you so you tell me."

Apart from Las Casas, George Dewey High School seemed to offer only an unconvincing parody of the school Charles had attended in Arlington. On the first morning the bus even broke down: attended by Jim and Luiz, the Filipino driver got out, opened the hood, and made improbable adjustments with sisal twine and a large flat rock, the two scouts meanwhile offering gratuitous advice, smoking cigarettes, and translating his Tagalog curses for the edification of the less traveled passengers. Later, when the first morning's classes ended, Charles discovered that the school had no cafeteria. Students either ate in one of the dozen classrooms in the low building perched in a clearing on the hillside, on benches in the covered walkways leading to the administrative building next to the parking lot, or in the large grassy courtyard the walkways and buildings enclosed. Edgefield, Joe, and some of the other juniors and seniors could get in their souped-up cars and speed down the half mile of road to where it T'd with the road from Kalayaan to the main base, then hang a left and pick up a burger and fries at the snack bar next to the PX. But no one invited Charles for a ride, the benches seemed to belong to particular groups, and he didn't want to spend all day in a classroom, so he took his brown bag to the courtyard and there found Billy and Ford. They had apparently enjoyed their morning. Among other items of note, Luiz had loosed a rhinoceros beetle in Miss Auckland's speech class, another boy had jammed the library door shut by breaking off a pencil in the lock, and other boys had driven the bald science teacher to send them to the principal's office for refusing to stop combing their hair in front of him. The morning's crowning touch came in the break between second and third periods when yet another group of boys had surreptitiously deposited a shopping bag's worth of Tanduay and San Miguel empties, used condoms, and lipstick-smeared tissues in front of the guidance counselor's office. This all led to a speech from the principal, Mr. Schutt, which they heard over a loudspeaker as they sat down to eat. Charles didn't get all of it—he found himself distracted by the approach of several inch-long jungle ants as well as a fellow freshman's sudden panic over another imaginary cobra—but he did catch some of the key phrases: ". . . it has been noticed that certain illegally procured alcoholic beverage containers have been wantonly abandoned on school premises . . . U.S. naval regulations forbid the possession of . . . Naval Investigative Service personnel have been requested to review for fingerprints . . . in the future it is hoped that all dependent personnel will comport themselves . . ."

"Jesus I hate that fucker," said Billy.

"Tell us something we don't know," said Ford as he released a piece of waxed paper onto the lazy noontime breeze.

"I mean it, man."

"You always mean it," Ford said. "So what?"

"So," said Billy, leaning a little closer and dropping his voice, "if you just help me like I wanted you to over the summer we can take this place out."

Ford winced. "Quiet, Billy. You're really gonna get us in trouble."

"What are you guys talking about?" Charles asked.

Ford looked around, put his finger to his lips, and said, "Sodium chips. I found jars of them packed in wax in the lab storeroom. They're really old—I don't think anyone else knows they're there."

"Fuckers blow up when they touch water," Billy added excitedly. "That's what you told me, Ford. Jesus—think of it! There's probably enough there to take out every head on the base! Just think of what we can do to this school!"

"*Shhh!*" said Ford.

"Are you serious?" Charles asked.

"Shit yeah," said Billy.

"But we must exercise caution," Ford added. "If you act the wiener and tell everybody, Billy, we could get in serious trouble."

"You want in on it?" Billy asked Charles. Ford looked at him, too.

"I don't know guys. I don't want to get caught—I just got here. Something like that would look pretty bad on my record when I apply for Annapolis."

Billy sneered. "Ah fuck, man. You don't wanna be a pussy officer."

"You saying our dads are pussies?"

"He's right, Billy," said Ford. "I don't wish to interfere with my chances of attending a decent university just to blow up this lousy place."

"Shit, you guys are both pussies. Just get me the shit and I'll show you what balls are." Billy punctuated his remark by quickly downing the rest of his soda, belching, then karate-chopping the tin can a few times so he could bend it in two and tear it apart. He left the pieces at his side and got up. "I'll see you fuckers later," he said, and strode off like John Wayne keying on a sunset.

"Well, *I'm* impressed," said Ford after a respectful pause. "I admire a man who can rip up a tin can on the tenth try."

Charles shook his head. "That young man has a serious adjustment problem. How can you even think of giving explosives to someone like that?"

"That is a profound and thought-provoking question," Ford replied, "but look at it another way: there are a lot crazier people with a lot bigger bombs around here."

"You think so?"

"Trust me."

The next day Luiz wanted Charles's trust, too. "Cat, you gonna love wrestling! You not so skinny. Look at your arms: I bet you could take one twenty easy. Come on out with us, man. We get to travel, man—go to Manila and Clark. Check out some embassy and air force chicks, you know—maybe stick it in something different, you know?" Here he laughed and gave Charles his first-ever conspiratorial wink on that particular subject. "Come on, cat. Jim's comin' out, too. We'll take care of you."

So Wednesday after class Charles found himself in the multi-purpose room in the administrative building, stripped to gym shorts and his old Kenmore Junior High T-shirt, lined up with a couple of dozen other boys trying out for the wrestling team. After they weighed in, Charles found, with some surprise, four other boys competing for 120. All five of them stood in a loose circle and looked each other over. Charles scanned the rest of the room. He saw most of the Explorers, including Joe and Edgefield in the upper weight classes and Finch in one of the levels below Charles. Just outside the 120 group stood Jim and Luiz, appraising them.

"You fucked up, dude," said Jim.

Luiz replied, "How I know they all show up? You say get me somebody for one twenty, right?"

Jim shook his head. The coach, a squat man with fingers like bricks, said, "All right, boys, listen up . . ." and soon had them doing push-ups, jumping jacks, sprints across the room, and a variety of other fatiguing exercises that seemed, to Charles, to have little to do with wrestling. When they finally got to some basic holds and positions Charles made the pleasant discovery that the other boys in his group had no more energy than he did, and that in any case wrestling had as much to do with balance and leverage as with strength, which meant that the art of reversals and pins might not end up so very different from that of moving toy soldiers across a dining room table in a flanking maneuver. Still, after an hour of skirmishing he felt that although he could pin two of his opponents, the other two would have to lose on points, if at all.

After the coach dismissed the boys for the evening Luiz and Jim asked Charles to stay for a little while.

"Listen," said Jim, "you gotta take one twenty."

"Yeah," said Luiz, "so guys don't think Explorers take pussies. Besides, I promised you a trip to Manila."

"In addition to which," said Jim, "I don't know you well enough to want to see you get your ass kicked. Here, let me show you some shit. Luiz?"

Luiz dropped to all fours and Jim knelt beside him in the standard opening position. "Okay Charles, pay attention. Say you're lucky enough to be on top, right, and you got the guy like this. But he's a real bad mother and you don't know if you can take him. Check it out. Normally dudes'll have their heads resting on the other guy's back anyway. What you got to do is get your chin right in his spine and dig it in . . ."

"Ah, shit, man!"

"Sorry, Luiz. See, Charles? Or if you've got him in this hold . . ." Jim went on, with Luiz gamely assisting, to demonstrate pressure points and ways to conceal quick jabs or tickles from referees and onlookers, and even how to slip a hand under the opponent's cup for a quick testicle-squeeze.

"I don't think I could do that," said Charles.

"Well, think about it anyway. There's always the possibility that you'll get caught, or end up with some real hard-core stud who'll try to stomp the shit out of you for that kind of action, but I figure that if they're in the same weight class and I get in the first blow, I don't have too much to worry about. I'm not saying you should cheat or anything like that, I just thought I'd let you know what works for me sometimes—you know, my personal style and technique."

"What about you, Luiz?"

"Well, sometimes I lose."

"Yeah?"

"Other times, cat, when maybe nobody looks, I just give a little kiss, you know, on the neck, and like they go totally stupid for maybe three seconds."

"Long enough for a reverse," Jim winked.

"Yeah. Well thanks, guys."

"Anything for a friend," said Jim.

Thursday night Charles went for a walk after dinner and at twilight reached the wooden park bench at the crossroads at the bottom of SOQ Hill. Ford sat there with another book but sunset came over them before Charles could make out the title. After nodding hello, Ford said, "I guess we won't be seeing Billy at the Teen Club for a while."

"What do you mean?"

"Well, the little wiener tested out a sodium chip in his kitchen sink, like totally freaking out the maid, and that worthy denounced him to the authorities, i.e., his father."

"Wow. Did his dad find out where the stuff came from?"

"Negative. Billy refused to confess the names of his co-conspirators. That's why he's grounded for a month."

"Geez. How's he taking it?"

"As one might expect. He wanted to kill the maid. You know Billy. He said, and I quote: 'I'm going to kill that fucking bitch Joe cunt.' Unquote."

"Sounds like Billy."

"And I said, oh, right. Start an international incident because now you can't blow up the toilets at school and have to stay away from the Teen Club, which you think is so lame anyway. You can imagine what he said to that."

"Yeah. But I guess he's not *too* much of a wiener."

"Enlighten me."

"He didn't talk. You could really be in trouble, too."

"No, I believe *wiener* remains the correct term. He didn't talk because he hates his father. And he tries to catch me in the boys' room and toss those cursed incendiaries over my shoulder while I'm attempting to micturate. I wish I knew how many he had left: I'm starting to get a complex."

They watched a few Navy sedans drive past from the rear gate while the lights came on at the O Club and swimming pool across from the Teen Club. Behind the O Club SOQ Hill took on a sharp edge against a sky that first turned royal blue, then indigo. When the sun left the hill entirely, the sky became one swath of black with only a string of four widely spaced streetlights to show Charles the way back home. Charles realized then that he hadn't walked up that hill alone before, still less alone in the dark. And he remembered that on the day after tomorrow the other Explorers expected him to join Finch, Edgefield, and Luiz for a march through the bush to the Kalayaan beacon.

"What are you thinking?" asked Ford.

Charles hesitated, looked around. "Nothing. You?"

Ford wiped his glasses with a frayed linen handkerchief and put them back on. "Epoxy in all the locks at school. Smoke bombs in the main base theater. And there's some stuff in the lab that would make a great stink bomb. You know, Billy isn't really a wiener. It's just that he thinks small. And that bothers me. It bothers me almost as much as this place does."

"Why are you guys so bothered by this place?"

Ford shook his head. "O Clubs, enlisted clubs—Teen Club. Uniform regs—dress codes. Tours of duty—you know, sometimes I feel like *I'm* in the Navy, but my dad's a civilian, Charles. *He* took a job here, but I never signed up to be low man on the totem pole, and my mother never volunteered to leave her house and gardening club so she could come over here and be snubbed by officers' wives. I mean, I guess she did volunteer, sort of, but who knew, Charles? I mean, there are men being killed in Vietnam every day in the name of democracy and freedom from communist dictatorship, and here we are, like peasants in this funny little kingdom where all the lords wear white suits and gold braid. Don't you think that's strange, Charles? Doesn't it kind of get to you?"

"I don't know; I kinda like it here."

Ford smiled ironically. "Yeah, your dad is a commander. But you're no vapor head, Charles. You'll learn. Give yourself time. Anyway, I'm going home and finish another chapter of Camus." He got up, gave a little mock salute, and walked off, away from SOQ Hill.

Charles almost called out after him, but he knew he could hardly ask Ford to walk him home. Charles, after all, had a date with the jungle on Saturday.

He sat a few minutes longer, feeling the humidity thicken and swatting at some of the mosquitoes that insinuated themselves against his neck and arm. A bus ought to come by, he thought, but he didn't know when and, if he caught it here—just to go up the hill in the dark—anyone on it would think him scared. And yet he did feel scared. But then he felt scared and on his feet and walking up the hill.

The road led under an archway of trees that almost met above him but let just enough moonlight through to cast serpentine shadows in the black areas between the four patches of light. Each of the lights stood like a milestone to Charles, a little piece of the Navy to guide him through the hundred yards of barbaric wilderness separating each from the next. Or perhaps, he thought, he shouldn't overdramatize: as he walked—in the middle of the road to avoid the branches reaching right up to the sidewalks—the very act of moving gave him some sense of control over his destiny, and as he reached a point halfway up the hill without having let terror take him over and lead him to run away to only God knew where, he felt almost as if he had accomplished something great and wonderful. But as he reached the edge of the third streetlight's circle a small figure with a gun stepped out from the jungle on his right.

Charles froze and would have shrieked, but all the noise he could manage came out as a sort of half-drowned snort. He hadn't quite reached the light. Maybe, he thought, the armed man hadn't seen him. He might still have time to run. But the little man had seen Charles and now turned his way. Charles had no choice; he stepped into the light.

"Hey Joe," said the little black man, laughing. "I scare you?" He wore gray fatigues and an American helmet liner. A riot gun hung from his shoulder on a sling of twine. He stood about four and a half feet tall.

"N-no," said Charles, quickly smiling at the obvious lie.

"You go home now?"

"Yes. Yes, I think I will."

The little black man touched his helmet, grinned, and vanished.

Another light lay ahead, on the other side of another stretch of blackness. But by the time he decided that he really had seen the armed dwarf Negro, Charles had gone well beyond it, to the top of the hill and the door to his family's quarters.

✦ IV ✦

THE BEACON MARCH

Just after the road to the main base left the Kalayaan officers' housing area, a gap appeared in the security fence on its left. Beyond the gap the ground rose sharply and a bulldozed firebreak waist-high with elephant grass led ten yards up the slope before turning right and disappearing among the high, vine-knit trees of the jungle.

When his father made the U-turn and pulled over, Charles could see his three companions already waiting: Edgefield and Finch as short and long versions of the same unarmed warrior, in pale gray-green fatigues the color of the tall, dusty, sun-bleached grass around them; Luiz in an open, untucked fatigue shirt with jeans and tennis shoes. When Charles got out, Commander Barker smiled and waved at the boys. Edgefield, gray eyes wide, took off his fatigue cap with its faded USMC insignia and scratched at fine sandy hair barely longer than a crew cut. As the car pulled away he stared at Charles.

"You *told* your old man?"

That stunned Charles. *Great*, he thought, *just great—I don't even want to be here.*

"*My* dad knows," said Finch, looking up at Edgefield. Charles wondered how Finch managed to get a uniform that small.

"You're shittin' me," said Edgefield.

"My dad don't give a fuck," laughed Luiz.

"Really," Finch continued. "I didn't figure it was a secret."

"Shit, my mom'd have a cow if she knew I was doing this without some squid chaperone. She thinks there are still Huks around here."

Luiz said, "But there are. Some, anyway. And bandits and smugglers. Mainly smugglers. Hell, man, it's *easy* to get on base."

"Huks?" said Charles. "Communist guerrillas?"

"Yeah," replied Luiz. "Something like that."

"Christ," said Edgefield, "let's get humpin' before my mom or one of her wives' club buddies drives by." The other boys nodded, adjusted web belts sagging with two or three canteens each, and set off quickly up the firebreak. The tall boys—Luiz and Edgefield—loped easily, but Charles and Finch occasionally stumbled over the innumerable small gullies and incompletely rotted stumps that broke up the track. Charles found the canopy narrowed to a thin vent and the jungle closed to within six feet on either side before he had time to think about what that meant to him. As he struggled up the hill he focused on Finch's dull black combat boots treading through the grass in front of him and only peripherally noticed the tall columns on either side with their thick skeins of dead brown or vibrant green vines, and the febrile burst of ferns and saplings at their roots. Luiz stopped and, when Charles caught up, pointed back to the road now hidden by the forest. "You know that fence, cat? Navy put it up two years ago, keep out smugglers. Had to hire three new guards, you know? Three more Negritos come out of the jungle, get uniforms, shotguns—somebody's family, right? But they worry they lose the job if the fence not needed."

"Hey, come on, dammit!" yelled Edgefield from somewhere up ahead.

"Okay, be cool! Come on, cat." Luiz strode off and Charles followed, his ponderous boots taking two steps for each of the Guamanian's. At the roadside, in the sun, he felt baking hot; here in the close shade the air felt nearly as hot and a great deal heavier. Sweat formed a thickening film all over him and began to trickle down his ribs. Hoping to get Luiz to slow or stop again, he asked, "So what happened?"

"So they kill some people, man. Every week they drag another Joe to the fence and tell the MAAs, 'See man, another Filipino try and smuggle on the base.' Finally Security say, 'Okay, okay, we keep the fence,' and they don't kill nobody no more. Not too much, anyway."

The trail turned and leveled off for a few yards; here they found Edgefield and Finch waiting for them. Charles wanted to stop. "What are *Negritos?*" he asked Luiz.

Finch answered: "They're pygmies, Charles. Little Negros—Negritos. They're the people who were here from the beginning, before the Malay came."

"They live in the jungle, cat. They're real good at it."

Edgefield lit a cigarette and added, "Navy hires 'em for perimeter security and to walk the neighborhoods. You might have seen them; they come out at night like geckos. I think they hate Joes or something. They don't have any problem killing them or bringing them in. And you can't bribe 'em. They don't even know what the fuck money *is*, man." He tossed the barely smoked cigarette to the ground and crushed it out with the heel of his boot. "Okay," he said. "Let's move on."

They slogged on for what seemed to Charles like another half hour. The other boys gradually slowed their pace, so he just managed to keep up by maintaining his own at no small cost. He'd worn down quick. Nothing fit right: his issue machete pulled on his shoulder and his canteens bumped awkwardly on his hips. His jungle jacket turned black with sweat under his arms and on the sleeve rolls where he wiped his forehead; his cap turned black, too, not only on the band but halfway down the visor. They got to a straight stretch perhaps two hundred yards long and, looking up, Charles could see the others strung out at wide distances in front of him. Edgefield, in the lead, looked back, saw them all sagging, and motioned for a halt.

"No," said Finch, "not till we get to the top of this rise."

Luiz turned to Charles and as he closed up said, "Yeah, you don't never want to stop at the bottom of a hill, cat—you never get up again."

"Why do you call me 'cat'?"

"You got a cat smile," grinned Luiz.

"Okay, okay, let's move," said Edgefield.

They reached the top of the rise and saw that the path took a short dip before turning slightly to the left and rising steeply to the last peak. Edgefield raised his hand and they fell out. Charles staggered to the side, leaned against a tree, and began to slide down into the mess of living and dead leaves at its base.

"You don't wanna do that," said Edgefield. "Snakes."

Charles shuffled back to the middle of the trail and sat by the others, accepting a drink from Luiz's canteen because he felt too tired to pull one of his own from its heavy canvas pouch. Here near the top of the hill they could see a bit more sky through the canopy and, in front of them, where a tree had fallen not long ago, the sea appeared through a vertical slash in the green. At this distance, through the midday haze, it looked like dirty blue-gray glass; at the horizon the sky seemed a paler shade of the same, but as it rose over them it turned into a brighter medium blue flecked with shining white clouds.

"What do they pay them?" Charles asked no one in particular.

"Huh?" asked Edgefield.

"The Negritos. If they don't know what money is, what does the Navy pay them?"

Finch said, "Their king has rights to the dump. If he wants anything there, he's got it. You know, scrap metal and stuff."

"Well," said Edgefield, jumping to his feet, "that just about did me right. Let's move out."

Finch and Luiz got right up but Charles slipped. To his surprise, both of them reached down to help him. Then their eyes met and they smiled.

"Nah," said Luiz, "cat gotta help himself."

"Don't fall behind," Finch said, and they turned to catch Edgefield.

Charles flushed but quickly caught up and they all reached the top together.

The beacon stood on a rocky summit some twenty yards in diameter and cleared of all vegetation but a few saplings and clumps of weeds. The summit rose just a few feet above a canopy that, even this close, looked as dense and solid as a shag carpet. The boys blinked at the sunlight flashing down from the vast sky and scanned the panorama of sea to the west and unfolding green in all other directions. The land made a roiling flow of rough-textured waves, pools, and eddies variously shining and shadowed. The only hint of the naval station's existence came from a few gray darts leaving white wakes on the distant bay, some faint incrustations of metal and concrete on the shoreline, and the beacon behind them, a ten-foot cube of concrete with a gray metal door and a short steel tower holding a light and three antennae.

They tried the door, just for grins, but a heavy padlock kept them from mischief. Charles sat down against the side of the beacon while Finch and Edgefield took compass bearings and Luiz scouted. The hike left Charles tired but happy. He'd made it, and now, with a relatively cool breeze wafting in from the sea and a great picture of the jungle rolling in forested breakers down to the smooth water, he almost forgot what had frightened him.

"Read in on that big hill there, man," Luiz suggested; "the one on the right of that ridge. Yeah, yeah—you got it." Edgefield peered through the sight of the field compass and recited numbers to Finch, who wrote them down with a black U.S. government ballpoint in a little green book. Luiz looked back at Charles and explained, "The golf course is right over that ridge in a valley. I worked there this summer."

"How can you tell anything from anything else down there?" Charles asked.

Edgefield looked back and shook his head in pity; he folded up the compass and said, "Let's hang out here a while. It's still early. Maybe we can figure out how to get down this hill on the Binictican side."

"Yeah, we should," said Finch. "We wouldn't want to get the whole post up here and have to turn back."

Charles sat up at hearing them talk about going down through the canopy into the forest itself. Luiz saw him and laughed. "You want to go home, cat?"

"If we can find a way down somewhere along here," said Edgefield, pacing the western side of the hilltop, "it should be okay pretty much till we get to the ridge overlooking the golf course."

"It's not as smooth as it seems looking down on the treetops," said Finch.

"Yeah, I know, but I checked out the contour map and there's nothing too severe. I mean, we can hack it no sweat if we can just get down this fucking hill in the right direction."

"Yeah," said Luiz, "we can hack it."

Charles stood and joined them at the edge of the hill, keeping silent as the others discussed the possibilities. If they tried to back down the trail and circle around to the western side they could get hung up on some unforeseen terrain feature or too turned around for the compass readings to help. Or they might simply take too much time and end up caught by nightfall. Finch insisted on the most direct way down; if they couldn't find one that seemed safe, then they should give up the idea of the hike. Luiz nodded and slowly retraced Edgefield's search on the western edge. After about a minute he said, "Here," and pointed to a spot that to Charles looked as dense and forbidding as the others. They all walked up to take a closer look.

Charles still saw nothing promising. Between two trees a stretch of rocky slope trailed off into shadowed undergrowth at an average angle of about forty-five degrees. Edgefield whistled thoughtfully and Finch cocked his head like a bewildered puppy.

Edgefield said, "Looks pretty hairy, Luiz."

"No, no," insisted Luiz, "look"—he pointed out the litter of vines and saplings and explained that they could make it by creeping down and using these for support. He offered to go first and clear away some of the branches hanging in the way. Once at the bottom they could look around for a little while and then climb back up on the same route.

"I don't know," said Finch, "you can't even see the bottom."

"Maybe one or two of us should stay up here," offered Charles.

They all looked at Edgefield, and stood around as he got on his hands and knees and peered down for what seemed a very long time. They all looked: Charles wondered what the others saw. The accidental trail appeared to him like a gap in the wall of a bombed building; an occasional sea breeze caused the tree-tops to sway ever so slightly and allowed pinholes of sunlight to play across the inner chambers of the woods, where the trunks rose like columns in a ruin, vines hung like conduit and wire, and the ground heaved and dropped like collapsed flooring. Everything about it spoke of danger to Charles, and he could think of any number of creatures perfectly at home there that might make the danger worse: spiders, snakes, scorpions, wild boar, and, for all he knew, rabid monkeys and dinosaurs. And yet he also felt an attraction. If he didn't go down there he would only know what it looked like—he might just as well have seen it on TV.

"I'll lead us down," Edgefield said.

"I can go first," said Luiz.

"Uh-uh. If somebody behind me falls you can catch them. I don't want Ahcharles riding my ass down this cliff."

"Okay. Let's go, cat. You come after me."

Finch said, "I think I'll just wait till you guys make it down and then jump. I'm bound to land on one of you."

"You can land on this," said Edgefield, giving him the finger. He slid forward and down on his behind, then grabbed a handful of vines and, still half sitting, began to lower himself. In a few moments he disappeared into the shadows. Luiz followed. Charles froze. Finch whispered, "It's okay. I'm right here. You saw how they both went? Start by heading for that vine. Right there. See that stump? Put your foot there. Yeah, you got it. No sweat. Outstanding. Try to keep an eye on Luiz. I'm right behind you."

Charles descended slowly, wrestling with a thousand little problems of balance and gravity. The jungle came up around him on all sides and he soon lost track of direction and height. Everything around him formed a confusing mix of arboreal motifs: branches, trunks, leaves, and vines crossed and recrossed in such profusion and variety that he could hardly tell where one plant ended and another began—they all seemed to belong to one living creature, like incredibly ragged fur on the back of some unimaginably huge beast.

He saw Luiz in the half light in front of him, sitting down and holding on to a thin branch with his right hand while raising his left in a signal to halt. Charles couldn't see Edgefield, but from the sound guessed he had made it another ten or fifteen feet farther before becoming tangled in a close web of vines.

"Hold up," Edgefield called, over the sound of his bolo slashing at vegetation. "I'm hung up here."

"Don't take too long," Finch called back, "I think this vine's giving way."

"Yeah, yeah." More furious slashing, then, "Ah, *fuck*!" followed by a sound like several sheets tearing as Edgefield fell, grabbing whatever he could.

Luiz leapt after him. "I'm comin', man!"

Charles felt Finch push past him, shouting, "Move, move, move—c'mon goddammit!" Charles tried to hurry after him, scrambling, sliding, pulling up saplings and vines, as he half fell to the large rock where the vines had snagged Edgefield. He'd cut these through, but Charles noticed a few smears of blood and that the rock formed the edge of a small cliff that dropped about six feet to another steep slope. This seemed to level off another twenty feet beyond, where Charles could just make out Luiz and Finch kneeling next to Edgefield like shadows in dusk.

He hurried down the rock, skinning his hands and banging his knee, then ran to the others, barking his forehead against a low branch along the way.

Edgefield sat against a tree, wincing in pain and disgust as Luiz split his trouser seam with a K-bar and Finch parted the fabric. The dark cut below the knee didn't look too wide but it had already bled a lot. Finch poured water over the wound from his canteen, then iodine from a bottle he took from the med kit on his belt. Luiz brought out a bulky battle dressing and wrapped the wound.

"You okay?" asked Charles.

"Just embarrassed," Edgefield said. "I must have clipped myself trying to cut my way out of there. I don't know *what* the fuck we do now."

"Nothing broken?" asked Finch.

"Don't think so."

"You lucky, man," said Luiz.

"Oh, yeah. I feel real fucking lucky right now."

"We gotta get you out of here," said Finch.

"I don't think I can make it back up that hill," Edgefield said. He fumbled in the breast pocket of his jungle jacket for his cigarettes, avoiding the others' eyes. Luiz began to rummage through the undergrowth, picking up branches and trying them out as walking sticks. Finch let out a quiet whistle and looked around. Charles looked around, too. They didn't have a lot of options. If they couldn't go back the way they came, then they'd have to circle the base of the hill to get back to the road. But they'd already talked about that up at the beacon—the distance around the hill might not come to much less than that straight to Binictican, and they might not find the terrain any easier, either. Someone could try to climb back up the hill and go for help. But that too could take a long time.

Mosquitoes buzzed nimbly in the thick air and large flies began to circle Edgefield's dressing. Somewhere a bird began a hectoring racket, ratcheting a series of staccato melodies up and down like an ornate sound test. Finch looked into the shadows through the compass sight. Luiz found a stick that seemed to meet his specifications. Edgefield blew a pair of smoke rings at the flies around his knee, then said, "Fuck it. Maybe we should just go on the way we planned. We've got compass bearings, we know roughly where we're going. I'm not that bad off. I can hack it. I just can't take point, that's all."

"Maybe I should go back for help," said Finch.

"I'm not waiting here for a buncha Negritos and grunts to rescue me, that's for sure."

"But I'm really not sure about the way," Finch said.

"Me, neither," said Luiz.

Charles's nerves made him impatient. Someone had to take responsibility. In the books he read, books like *Naval Battles and Heroes*, moments like these brought out the best in the least likely men. "I'll lead," he said.

Edgefield, helped to his feet by Luiz, leaned on the stick and looked suddenly weary. "No offense, Barker, but I wouldn't trust you with shit. Finch, take the compass and get us the fuck out of here. You follow him, Barker, and make sure he doesn't get too far ahead of Luiz and me."

Finch looked at each of them, checked the compass one more time, then nodded and walked off into the woods. Charles, trembling and blinking furiously, quickly followed.

For a time they had easy going. The thick canopy kept the underbrush sparse, and most of the time they kept their bolos sheathed. Even limping, Edgefield managed the same speed as the others, and though they sometimes stretched their line till six or ten feet separated each of them, they all stayed in sight of each other. The air grew warmer and heavier, but the ground rose and fell gently and didn't take too much work to cross. At length they came to a steeper rise where a storm had taken down a few trees and the undergrowth thickened into a wall. Finch decided to take five and check the compass bearings. Edgefield looked faint and they had to sit him down and bind on another battle dressing. Even hanging loose his trouser leg had become soaked with blood.

Charles checked his watch. Already past fifteen hundred. They could probably make it out before sunset if the way forward stayed like the way behind. But the mess ahead of them made that seem unlikely, and that worried him. He guessed he'd done okay so far, but he had daylight and his friends with him. If night found him still here he didn't know what he'd do. It made a lot of sense that that kid a few years back had just lost it and run off a cliff. Out here in the jungle with the strange trees and God only knew what sort of beasts, panic seemed a reasonable option.

They got Edgefield back on his feet and worked to the right of the blockade. After a few score yards they came upon a clearing of an acre or so filled with pale grass that reached above their heads. They found a well-beaten trail and followed it, hoping that it would lead them around the barrier of fallen trees. In a few minutes it crossed another trail and they took that to the left. Then the trail forked. They took a left there, too, but it then veered right and took them to a spot where the ground fell off, first on their right and then in front of them. Luiz said, "I don't like this. There's pigs here."

"Wild boar?" asked Charles.

"Whatever—what you think make this trail?"

"This isn't working," said Finch. "We gotta go back."

Edgefield slumped and Luiz had to catch him. They stumbled back the way they came, getting turned around twice but still ending roughly where they'd started. Finch checked the compass again and looked at Edgefield. "You okay?"

"Yeah. Just decide where you want to go, okay?"

"We can carry you if we need to," said Finch.

No, we can't, thought Charles. *Not even if we have to.* His fatigues weighed him down with several hours worth of sweat. He felt like he'd jumped in a pool of hot spit. He looked at his watch. Nearly sixteen hundred.

Finch seemed to have found an invisible marker in the jungle. He rolled down his sleeves as he stared at a tapestry of greens and browns growing up, down, and across from each other. Then he muttered, "Follow me," put his forearms up in front of his face, and simply walked into the mess blind. Charles followed, then Edgefield with Luiz.

They spent a good ten minutes pushing through grasses, ferns, and shrubs, trying to keep a reasonably straight line ahead. But then they came to an especially tight knot: it had everything they'd encountered before, but grew even denser, tied together with a lacework of dead vines at the upended buttress roots of a fallen tree so large the top of its prone trunk lay above their heads and its crown hid in the brush a hundred yards—or maybe miles—farther than they could see. At the sight of it Edgefield and Charles collapsed while Luiz looked around and panted like a fox listening for hounds. Finch checked the compass again, but without enthusiasm. He seemed not to know what else to do.

"Somebody tell me this wasn't my idea," said Edgefield, reaching for another cigarette.

"Those things'll kill you," Charles said, hoping for a laugh.

"Fuck you," said Edgefield without malice. "We're hopelessly lost, penned in by the worst terrain this side of Satan's asshole, with dwindling supplies of water and no food. The only comfort I have are my Lucky Strikes and the fond hope that if they do find my bones they at least won't mix 'em up with yours 'cause you're such a puny little fuck." Then he, Luiz, and Finch did start chuckling, and in a way that invited Charles to join. He did, wondering whether Edgefield thought it really as bad as all that and, if so, whether Commander Barker could get whatever remained of his son buried in Arlington National Cemetery.

"Poor cat," said Luiz, laughing and shaking his head. "He think he gonna die."

"It *is* pretty hairy," said Finch.

"Maybe," said Luiz. He looked around some more. Edgefield worked on his Lucky, blowing more smoke rings at his knees. Luiz watched him, then followed one of the rings as it rose and twisted into an ever-thinning curl. "Oh yeah," he said. "Easy."

"What's that?" asked Finch.

Luiz pointed to the trunk that rose five feet over Edgefield's and Charles's heads and said, "There's our road. Finch, you go up there first with Charles and I'll boost Edgefield. Don't you see—it's like a road, man."

The others exchanged glances, first doubtfully, but then broke into grins. Finch crawled up and helped Charles, then both dragged Edgefield as Luiz pushed from underneath. When they all got up they found themselves on a small highway more than a hundred feet long and a man's height off the jungle floor. It carried them over and through the worst of the worst and, when they slid off the branches of the crown at the far end, they discovered that they'd reached a patch of woods a fire had raced through no more than a year or two earlier. Almost nothing grew under the high canopy but the great tree trunks themselves, and the scouts moved easily over a floor of carbonized leaves and sporadic traces of fire retardant.

"Fucking A," said Finch to Luiz. "You did it."

Luiz shrugged and kept walking. They traversed the open jungle swiftly, sometimes in file, sometimes abreast, and sometimes as a rough constellation in a universe of leaves. Charles looked up and knew he had never seen so many or so many different kinds of leaves: some like oak, but huge and bulbous; some like clusters of knives. Others fanned out palmlike from squat miniature trees that sprang from the woody flesh of the full-sized trees. Luiz showed Charles a wild rubber tree and hacked it with his bolo so Charles could see the latex ooze. Once Finch had to turn back and help Charles untangle himself from a thin green vine, bright and shiny as a strand of plastic, the sort of toy plant one could buy with an aquarium and tropical fish at Woolworth's. It carried trios of short thorns in pale bulbs and when Charles absently waved to brush it aside it curled into him and the thorns in the little bulbs clenched together like a baby's fist.

After a few hundred yards they came down a soft slope to where the fire had quenched itself in a tumbling stream. Here the bush grew thick again and Luiz warned the others to watch for cobras. Finch called a halt by some rocks on the bank. Charles looked at his watch then looked away. "What's our bearing?" he asked.

Finch smiled and shook his head. "Doesn't matter," he said. "I'm pretty sure we're just about there."

Luiz nodded. "Yeah, that's right. Over the stream—this ridge. It must be just on the other side."

Edgefield, stretched out against a rock, raised his head and clapped slowly. One, two, three. "Good job. My dad'll kick my butt if I'm late for dinner." The others forced a few chuckles and let him smoke another cigarette. This time Luiz bummed one, too. When they finished they waded the stream, letting the icy water soak their boots and wet their trouser legs halfway to their knees. They found the last ridge tough going; it rose almost as sharply as the beacon hill but had no firebreaks. The scouts scrambled from one level spot to the next by pulling on whatever plants or stones came to hand, taking turns tugging or pushing on Edgefield. Halfway up they rested against the buttress roots of one of the larger trees, the four of them crowded together in the angle of two rocket-fin supports. About fifty feet from the crest the ridge plateaued and Finch, Luiz, and Charles raced laughing for the imaginary finish line at the golf course with Edgefield hobbling along behind as best he could. Charles came in third, nearly running into Finch and Luiz as they staggered to an abrupt stop.

"Goddamn," said Luiz. "How we gonna get down?"

Charles dropped to his knees. Edgefield folded up next to him. All four looked west, the lowering sun making them shade their eyes. The golf course spread out beneath them, a pattern of emerald splotches on a background of pale, scruffy native grasses. The scouts could see neatly trimmed Americans in pristine leisure wear attended by starched caddies, golfing while crews of sweaty laborers hacked infinitesimal fragments off the encroaching jungle. The people on the golf course looked like toy figures near enough to touch, like a little diorama set in a model train layout in a neighbor's basement back in the World. But to touch these toys the boys would first have to drop about eighty feet down the sheer escarpment in front of them.

"Ah, fuck," said Edgefield. "What a lovely view."

Charles nodded and wrapped his arms around his knees to keep them from trembling. He felt like someone had taken his stomach out and thrown it off the cliff.

Finch and Luiz walked off. After a few moments of silence, Edgefield said, "Cigarette? It won't kill you before nightfall."

Charles grinned feebly. He would have taken it, too, but he didn't want to unclasp his hands. In a little while Finch returned and led them to a spot about forty yards to the left. Luiz had already gone a few yards down, one hand on a vine and the other stretched up toward his friends. "Look," he said, "I got another road here."

"Jesus Christ," said Charles. From a straight drop on either side the wall here descended at an angle of about sixty degrees. It looked only remotely possible. They'd die if they fell.

"I know it looks pretty hairy," said Finch. "Maybe Luiz and me could use it to go and get help."

"No dice," said Edgefield, staring at the bottom. "I'm not hanging out here all night with this tenderfoot. If you guys wanna kill yourselves, fine. We'll all kill ourselves."

"It's no problem, man," called Luiz. "This a long vine I got here. It goes all the way down, almost. I'll show you."

"Okay," said Finch, "you go first. Be ready to catch bodies. I'll help you, Edgefield. Charles, you can bring up the rear."

"Fucking A," said Edgefield. "Let's do it."

Luiz set off, half rappelling and half scrambling. He faced out from the precipice most of the time, only turning around to point out vines and roots for Finch and Edgefield to use. Those two followed carefully, slipping badly at first, but Edgefield waved Finch off and struggled on with his hands and one good leg. Charles watched them descend and noted how the main vine shuddered and swayed. The three got lower and lower and he knew he either had to follow or stay behind and wait for someone to get him in the dark. The dark scared him, but not as much as not finishing the march with Edgefield, Finch, and Luiz. If he fell, at least they'd carry him the rest of the way.

"Hey, Charles!" called Edgefield. "You coming or should I call your old lady?"

"Fuck you," said Charles, "I'm already there."

"Don't worry, cat," yelled Luiz from the bottom. "You land on your feet!"

For the next several minutes Charles saw nothing but the cliff face and the minutely interesting details of each vine and root. The large vine they all used ended about fifteen feet from where the hill itself changed to a medium slope. He found a foothold, let go, and scrambled nearly half the rest of the way before falling at Luiz's feet. He stood up before the others could help him. His palms burned and bled and the knee that he'd banged at the beacon throbbed sharply, but he felt good, real good. The four boys stood in a circle and laughed at each other, all smudged with dirt, scratched and bloody, clothes and hair tousled and adorned with pieces of leaves and stray twigs.

"Fucking A!" said Edgefield. "We *made* it! *Explorer* fucking-*Scouts!* Post Three Sixty, Subic Bay, R.P. Fucking A."

"We look like Huks," said Luiz. "I betcha first guy sees us calls Security."

"Let's straighten up," said Finch.

They brushed each other off, hurriedly combed their hair, straightened their jackets and belts, and tucked their trousers into their boots. They couldn't do much about Edgefield's torn trouser leg, now black with dried blood, so they unfolded another battle dressing and tied it over. This done, they marched down the last slope, stepped through a few yards of high grass and brush, and strode onto the green. Half as a joke Finch began to whistle "American Patrol" and Luiz took up the tune. Charles could only manage a wheezy off harmony, and Edgefield, gritting his teeth, only smiled. They held themselves as straight and tall as they could, but now that they had finally made it none of them found it easy to put one foot in front of the other. Charles felt a weight on his shoulder. Edgefield's hand. He straightened up more and helped him along.

They marched past a party of officers in neat, civilian golfing togs trying to get in a last hole before dark. They ignored the stares and the turned heads. They ignored the people at the putting green and the Filipino caddies and lawn boys and workers in white sweat turbans clearing brush with sickles. They marched in a beeline for the clubhouse, not caring which lieutenant's shot they blocked or which commander's wife got grossed out by Edgefield's bloody and clumsily wrapped leg. When an ensign asked where they'd come from, Finch said, "Kalayaan," and they didn't even slow to watch his jaw drop. They parted the doors to the clubhouse and marched right into the dark and paneled and well-upholstered interior and took a polished table near a sideboy covered with a crisp white cloth and a glittering row of clean glasses.

Finch had a few dollars so he went to the bar to get some sodas. Charles had a few nickels so he went to the phone to call home.

Mrs. Barker answered on the second ring. Charles asked if he and his friends could get a ride.

"But where are you?" she asked anxiously.

"We're at the Binictican golf course," he replied. "In the clubhouse."

After a moment of silence she said, sounding confused, "Binictican? How did you get *there?*"

"We walked."

A longer silence followed.

"But Charles," she said at last, "why didn't you call me earlier? I would have given you boys a ride."

V

THE WALLED CITY

On a Saturday morning three weeks into the school year, Charles stood in front of the PX with fifteen other boys waiting for a bus. Across the parking lot he could see a field half a mile wide, of high grass dotted with scrub trees and, beyond that, jungle-covered hills. The rain forest trees stood improbably tall and twisted, as if someone had taken a photograph of normal stateside trees—say, oak, maple, or beech—and run a blowtorch over it, then draped huge nets of living and dead vines onto the curled mess. Two weeks earlier Charles had walked in that. Now he waited for a ride to a wrestling tournament at the American School in Manila.

"Hey cat!" Charles turned around. Luiz, his tall, half-Guamanian friend, stood with his hands on his hips and grinned at the jungle. Briefly, Charles imagined Luiz with a wire up his butt and a switch that flipped every time he saw a girl or a patch of jungle. "You wish you was back out there, cat?"

"Actually I thought I might stay inside and crank up the AC for the next two years."

"You crazy, cat."

A gray Navy bus pulled into the parking lot. The coach clapped his hands and the boys picked up their kit bags to a chorus of good-byes and good lucks from Navy fathers waving from behind the shields of open car doors. Some of the boys waved back, some even smiled, but most took on the grim, tired faces of soldiers going off to the front, in wars that had fronts—a look their fathers only half regretted. When the column of boys dispersed into the semi-isolation of bus seats, more of the boys waved, and a few even shouted, "See ya, Dad!" through windows they quickly shut again to lock in the air-conditioning. The bus grunted and they left, applauded by the muffled crunch of doors shutting in their family sedans.

God, it's hot, thought Charles. Inside the bus the AC kept him from getting hotter but hadn't yet begun to cool him down, and the bright sun in the wide sky baked the vinyl seat like a searchlight through a magnifying glass. The bus drove away from the bay, back toward Kalayaan and the jungled hills, toward the rear gate of the Naval Station. Looking behind, the boys could see concrete buildings and Quonset huts, well-washed streets, freshly painted warships on the glittering bay, and, just to their rear, fathers driving home to officers' quarters in Kalayaan, their cars escorting the bus like tin cans and cruisers convoying a carrier. After a few minutes the group reached Kalayaan; the escorts turned away one by one as if their charges had just returned home to port instead of leaving for unfamiliar waters.

Charles looked hard at the houses with their well-kept gardens, the O Club, the swimming pool, the Teen Club. *Everything looks different when you leave it*, he thought. The buildings ended and the bus rolled through a small stretch of jungle before reaching the rear gate. There, three marines showed the official face of America to the world beyond the perimeter: white hats, khaki shirts pressed hard as plywood, blue pants with red stripes, and shoes like polished obsidian. The guardhouse and its turnpike sat in the middle of the two-lane asphalt road as it curved downhill into the bush, so one could see only sky just above the road and trees rising high on either side, with a purple shadow straight ahead where, after a few twists and turns, the road climbed into the Zambales Mountains. They might have found a road to nowhere. To the left, two Filipino cops in Navy uniforms sat in a jeep behind two more marines, these in fatigues and carrying loaded M-14s. After a few words with the bus driver, one of the picture-book marines waved the team through.

Jim, sitting sideways in the seat in front of Charles, turned his sleepy rabbit face back and said, "Don't worry about the tournament, man."

"We'll do okay?"

"No, we're gonna get stomped. Tell you why. We got Wagner High from Clark Air Force Base. They ain't so bad, but they're a lot bigger school so they got more competition for the weight classes. Then we got the American School. Buncha corporate and embassy kids who think their shit don't stink. But they're big, too, and Daddy buys professional coaches and trainers. Then we got Faith Academy. Missionary kids. Fucking religious fanatics: they never get laid and hell's waiting for them if they beat off, so they have all that hormonal energy penned up. Freak me out—every time I get on the mat with one I'm afraid I'm gonna get raped or forcibly born again. That ain't a lot of fun."

"So tell me again why we're doing this."

"Hell, it's a chance to get out, isn't it? Besides, they all got sisters, and I hear those Baptist chicks fuck like lizards on a tin roof once you get 'em going. So relax. Some things are worth an ass-kicking."

Charles nodded as if he thought either of them had a chance with the kids from Faith, either on the mat or between the sheets. He looked wryly back at the hours after class spent in monotonous workouts in the multipurpose room and in running laps around the skeletal campus of George Dewey High School. Now he realized that he could expect in return only the questionable excitement of traveling through a shabby country he hadn't seen before and the possible joke value of explaining a GDHS letter jacket when he got back to his friends in the World.

As they began to hit the bumps and ruts that announced their arrival on the Filipino section of the highway, Charles thought of other places the Navy might have sent his father. Jim, for example, whose father worked in NAVSUP, had come over from Alameda just a year ago and, when not telling stories about his adventures with the bands and bar girls of Olongapo, could go into raptures about the runaway female flower children floating stoned around Haight Ashbury, just begging for an encounter with a savvy dependent with tales of faraway places, cruel parents trying to force him into a Navy career, dispensary condoms, and commissary cigarettes. And Finch had learned to surf before his father shipped out from NAS Coronado: Finch looked like a diminutive seminarian, but he could make more than Charles's hair stand on end when he described his breast-level view of beach girls bouncing over the sand to the sounds of Jan and Dean and the Ventures. And although Joe had come from Corpus, and Edgefield from Norfolk—neither great metropolises—at least those places formed a part of the World, with the perimeter fence a formality, and the natives strange only in that they didn't wear uniforms.

But the more Charles looked outside the bus the less he regretted practice. He had only seen the country outside the base that one evening a month ago when his family had landed at Clark after a nineteen-hour flight from Travis, and then had to drive three hours through the black steamy night to Subic. And everything about that drive seemed unreal. Now in daylight the bus full of boys coasted and crunched gears, turned right and left in near circles or hairpins, and rose then descended the switchback through the low mountains.

A few miles outside the base the jungle fell off into forlorn clumps of future firewood or wooded strips hugging the banks of rough, convoluted streams in deep valleys on first one side of the road and then the other, while opposite them rose steep grassy slopes burned off once a year in the dry season. Philippine houses appeared: shambling creations of wicker and bamboo on stilts or, in one case, thin branches framing walls of flattened cardboard boxes and a roof artfully crafted from tin cans. Philippine buses suddenly popped around corners—hacking monstrosities in gaudy colors with half their passengers hanging precariously from their sides with baggage and chickens. Honks and squealing brakes announced scooters and jeepneys—the latter decorated like Christmas trees, their drivers and riders smiling and waving at the Navy bus, shouting "oi!" and "hey Joe!" like clichés of friendly natives while the boys opened the windows and gamely hollered back "hey, Flip!" and "how much blow job?" When the road finally leveled, farmers knee-deep in muck stared from rice paddies while tending ponderously graceful carabao.

Along the road where the houses occasionally thickened into hamlets, strands of wire departed from roadside lines and led to one or two well-built homes of indeterminate age, some even with outside walls and courtyards, or to shantylike sari-sari stores with familiar blazing advertisements for Coca-Cola and Marlboro—signs at first so incongruous that Charles thought someone must have stolen them for decoration. But as more sari-sari stores appeared with similar signs for other American brands, and as he saw a Kentucky Fried Chicken only slightly more smudged than one at home, he got used to it. After a while as a sort of game he counted the similar signs for Philippine products, but even in a series of otherwise incomprehensible Tagalog words, Charles would find that one NEWPORT or 7UP that reestablished American superiority. At first this seemed right to him, like when the home team gets ahead, but after about an hour he felt a little more like he would had the home team run the score to sixty-to-nothing on the other school's field.

The ride got rougher. The Navy bus never got much above thirty because the road, forced to carry a full range of traffic from lumber trucks to horse-drawn calesas, had crumbled under successive wet and dry seasons and now had little more than sporadic, archaeological fragments of asphalt to distinguish it from the dirt shoulders. And they couldn't seem to travel more than a few miles without encountering a jam caused by anything from a broken-down jeepney to a carabao laboriously crossing the road to an encouraging chorus of car horns and shouting drivers. Yet the boys managed to maintain some sense of forward progress until the bus reached the first real town. There it slowed like a cow in quicksand, stuck in a bottomless morass of pedestrians, cyclists, scooters, jeepneys, trucks, calesas, and cars, all of them unrestrained by lights, signs, cops, or anything other than their own mass. On the road, the boys had just begun to settle down and pass the time quietly, reading paperbacks, peeking into the *Playboys* smuggled past the coach, or stretching out on the seats and dozing. But now they went to the windows as if ordered to repel boarders, and stared out, fascinated by the street life but uneasy with the number of people for whom those scenes comprised just part of an ordinary day. The bus bobbed past a market, coming within inches of stalls laden with mangoes, papayas, chickens plucked and unplucked, pigs live or hanging in butchered fragments, and an array of countless other household needs set out without packaging or advertisement.

"Jesus, look at that," Edgefield said, pointing, but not too obviously, to a huge, finned sedan that, from the .30-caliber machine gun mounted on the top, seemed to belong to a local politician.

"Hey, look—balut." Luiz touched Charles's shoulder from the seat behind and pointed to a small pyramid of eggs on a vendor's table only a few feet away. "Duck eggs, you know? They bury them in the ground and let them ferment. Real delicacy."

"Oh, man! Who cut the cheese?" cried Joe.

Finch took a camera from his kit bag and tried to take photographs through the windows without attracting attention. Jim winked past Charles to Luiz and nodded toward a group of uniformed schoolgirls escorted through the crowd by a pair of veiled nuns. As the bus jerked through traffic, Joe and Edgefield went up front and tried to give the driver directions as other boys shouted encouragement, yelled at other vehicles, screamed warnings of imminent collisions, and cheered with each jolt forward. The coach let them go for about a minute while he did his own window staring, but when a near-impact with a calesa brought the boys to a crescendo of neighing horse imitations, he jumped into the aisle and commanded, "Sit down and shut up!"

This worked for another minute or two until the coach himself became so involved with the world beyond the windshield that he too started advising the driver and hardly noticed when Joe and Edgefield joined him. After that the inside of the bus returned to cacophony until, with a lurch, a lunge, and a burst of dust, the bus freed itself, reached the other side of the square, and from there returned to the uneven but reasonably constant progress of the road.

After passing through two more towns of packed streets, market stalls, wooden shacks, and decayed villas behind stucco walls, they came to a stretch of dust-burdened roadway that led a level mile to a great house of dark wood. Covered with garish signs, it sat about thirty yards off to the left of the road. Several buses and a small flotilla of hired cars lay strewn in a field in front of it, parked by straggling trees wherever their drivers happened upon the least inconvenient spots.

"All right," said Jim. "Halfway house!" He and others jumped into the aisle, but the coach got up and blocked them from the front. Coach Simon didn't stand any taller than five-eight but he had the overall proportions of a cinder block and a smile to match. He didn't bother to tell anyone to sit down this time; he simply stared with an expression that resembled an Olmec copy of a bust of Caesar. Once the boys took their seats and the bus came to a halt, he said, "You ladies got half an hour and if you ain't back by then you can walk back to Subic for all I care."

He stepped aside, uncorking the aisle, and the team poured out carrying Charles along up wide rickety front steps, across a sagging veranda, and into a dim interior of baking air brushed by a few ceiling fans into a semblance of stale breath. Dizzy from the sudden change from the bus's air-conditioning, Charles sensed that he had entered a kind of dream where the Woolworth's at Seven Corners at home in Virginia had merged with the Horn Palace saloon near his grandfather's farm in Texas, with both of the original clienteles largely supplanted by Malays. At a bar in back drivers washed their lumpia and fried rice down with San Miguels or sodas; a few feet to the right the smell of the cooking first blended with and then surrendered to the thick ammoniacal fog that, together with a jittery line of American boys, identified the toilet.

Charles went to the end of that line. It curled by some shelves of souvenirs. He looked these over to take his mind off the recent discovery that he had to go pretty bad. An assortment of wood carvings made up most of the display: fruit bowls, hugely oversized salad forks, three-foot-high Igorot tribesmen, baroquely carved spears with rusty blades, and several platoons of Christs. They had small Christs and big Christs: Christs small enough to hang from the rearview mirror and Christs large enough to take a seat at the table for Christmas dinner. A few of the Christs prayed, but most hung from crosses, some in beatific swoons but the plurality in obvious agony, their emaciated rib cages straining for breath and their stigmata gaping like the smiles of gargoyles.

Charles noticed among the Christs a row of eight-inch-tall Moro warriors standing behind shields that reached to their feet like those of Roman soldiers. He thought about buying some of these; although much larger than all the others in his collection, he hadn't seen any other authentic Philippine toy soldiers and he felt enough of a connoisseur to want to pick up a few samples. As he left the bathroom, Luiz saw him and walked over. "You like these, cat?" Charles shrugged; not everyone understood the serious side of his interest in historical miniatures. "Well," said Luiz, "just don't buy one for your mom, okay?" He lifted one of the shields and a carefully carved penis the size of the figure's leg sprang up like a Nazi salute. Charles blinked and tried to clear the image before he took his turn in the toilet.

When Charles emerged and could breathe again without making his eyes water, he noticed one other kind of statuette that took up half a shelf of its own. Delicately executed, it portrayed a half-naked Filipina—very pretty, very pregnant—clutching an American sailor's cap to swollen breasts and gazing wistfully as a tear swelled in the corner of her right eye. The two-line legend carved in the base read, first in Tagalog and then in English, DAHIL SA IYO; BECAUSE OF YOU."

Charles tried to sleep the rest of the trip but the rough road and occasional loud traffic jams kept waking him up. When those didn't, the other boys did, either with another twenty choruses of "A Hundred Bottles of Beer" or "Roll Me Over," by projecting crumpled pieces of paper and rubber bands, or by other general grab-assing. No one much bothered old hands like Finch, Joe, or Edgefield—or Skunk, the boy at plus-180 distinguished by his shaved head and absence of vocabulary—but Charles had no such immunity and, worse, sat between Jim and Luiz. They didn't dislike him, but they did like to wait till he nodded off to play a kind of badminton by slapping an inflated condom back and forth over his head. Whoever woke Charles up by bopping him in the face or dropping it in his lap had to pay the other ten centavos, but Charles calculated that the same coin must have changed hands nearly a dozen times with neither of them trying very hard to hang on to it. By the time he finally gave up on a nap he heard Finch up front say, "Hey, we're almost there!"

Despite the air conditioner's brave and increasingly audible efforts, they had all become hot, smelly, slimed with sweat, and gritted with dust long before the bus turned its rump on the low western sun and nosed into the outskirts of Manila. Altogether they hadn't traveled more than fifty miles, yet it had still taken them most of the day.

Quezon City, the official capital, spread darkly to the left in closely packed low brown eruptions. They entered what seemed like a sea or, more, a vast stagnant pool of wood and metal tenements. Shacks stood in jumbled phalanxes, colored in places by faded advertisements in Tagalog and English that pushed their wares with the vestigial faked enthusiasm of overaged prostitutes. The streets showed even greater deterioration than the road through the country: rather than leading from one place to another, they seemed simply to exist where the buildings and vendors' stalls stopped and let them lie. Traffic lights existed too, but only as ornaments over the principal points of congestion; none of them actually worked. The side streets had so many potholes that it seemed no one had ever really paved them, but instead had laid down a network of ridges to suggest the former presence of a higher order of civilization.

The chaos and decay continued with no hint of an end until the bus crested a low rise and its passengers could see, less than a mile away, a kind of island in the marsh, a sort of Emerald City unexpectedly plunked down on the banks of the Styx, consisting of half a dozen tall glass towers on the right and large houses sweeping to the left. Even in twilight the contrast glared. Mud, rubbish, and ruin ended at a brick wall, and on the other side of the wall sat a suburban cutout of sprawling ranch homes, broad lawns, swimming pools, and more brick walls in lieu of picket fences.

"Makati," said Jim. "That's where we're headed."

"What are those lights?" asked Charles, pointing out the tiny green and amber flickerings along the top of the perimeter wall.

"Those aren't lights, dude. That's the sun setting on the broken glass."

"It's to keep the Joes out," Luiz explained.

At the gate to where the bankers and embassy people kept their big houses with guest rooms for the boys from Subic, four private guards in tiger-striped camouflage, black ball caps, and mirrored sunglasses halted the bus and checked the driver's and coach's identification cards. The boys kept quiet as the guards casually wielded their pistolized carbines and looked them over, but soon the guards waved them through and the faint sense of danger vanished.

On the streets of Makati Charles felt more disoriented than at any time since he'd left the States—not because things looked so strange, but because they looked so impossibly normal. It seemed as if they'd taken a bus across ten thousand miles of the poor, dark half of the world, passed through a looking glass, and arrived in northern Virginia on a summer night. Empty, well-lit streets led smoothly past cul-de-sacs where boys dribbled basketballs and girls skipped rope. Lights came on to show neat living rooms behind French windows. Station wagons parked in the broad driveways before two-car garages. Only the Filipina maids pushing strollers and Filipino chauffeurs bringing businessmen home gave the game away.

Coach Simon had the bus stop while he checked a list of names and addresses and examined a map. When they drove on again, he directed the driver to first one house and then another, dropping the boys off one by one. Charles went seventh, stepping out in the dark on the doorstep of a family named

Steiner. A maid let him in: as he stood and looked around a downstairs larger than any on base, except perhaps the admiral's, she giggled and went into a kind of pantomime that suggested that the family had gone out. Another maid stepped from the kitchen and led him down a hallway to a bedroom that smelled like a Holiday Inn and displayed the same pastel furnishings and superstarched linens. Charles liked that, and that the few family pictures on the wall—mother, father, teenage son and daughter—also contributed to the generic atmosphere. He preferred generic to out-and-out strange, of which he thought he'd seen enough that day.

As he set down his bag the second maid returned and led him to a large, eat-in kitchen. Two men in white stewards' uniforms smiled and pointed to a little table with a place setting and a dinner of steak, corn on the cob, and a glass of milk. They chatted in Tagalog and the maid said, "You eat now, okay?"

"Where is everyone?" Charles asked.

A Filipino in a black suit materialized at the kitchen door. He carried a peaked hat in his gloved hands. "Please have your dinner now," he said. "Your bus was late. The family is waiting for you down the town."

Charles nodded and sat. He forced himself to eat only half his dinner but then had to convince the staff that he enjoyed it and had no complaints. In truth he worried about his weight. To make sure he came in where the coach wanted him, at 120, he had eaten virtually nothing the last several days except as little of his dinner as he could get away with.

The driver led Charles outside to a black sedan with another Filipino in the front passenger seat who stared at Charles but didn't smile or nod. Charles got in the back and quickly noticed the absence of handles inside the rear doors. A glass partition sealed him off from the front seat.

He felt a protest rise to his lips but before he could speak the car sped away and raced down empty streets. After three or four screeching turns Charles felt for the Boy Scout pocketknife in his pants, but the Filipino in the passenger seat turned and smiled at him and very shortly they pulled up in front of a sixteen-story office building. Forgetting about the door handles, Charles tried to let himself out and felt a bit stupid when the driver calmly opened the door, handed him a green ticket, and said, "Please go to the eleventh floor. This will get you in. Good night!"

Charles walked up to the glass doors and a reflection of the Steiners' car turning back into the night. A Filipino security guard directed him into the lobby. A sign identified the building as belonging to a bank of some kind, but Charles didn't see any-place where one could get money. A Filipino elevator operator took him to eleven. There a large poster greeted him with news of an upcoming concert by the Philippine National Symphony. Brahms. A Filipino usher escorted him to a pair of wooden dou-ble doors. These he opened onto an auditorium of well-dressed Americans: mothers in matching skirts and jackets, fathers in business suits, and children in only slightly less formal versions of the same. Charles became acutely aware of his plaid, short-sleeved shirt and khaki slacks and what a whole day sweating on a bus made them smell like. He took a seat in the back and tried to make himself small.

On the stage the curtain rose to reveal the garden of an Eng-lish country house, complete with a meticulously painted back-drop, rows of real plants in large containers, lacy white iron chairs, and the effect of breeze-blown trees conveyed by fans and clever lighting. It all seemed very professional, but then the first actors walked onstage. They appeared no older than Charles. He glanced down at his ticket. The Freshman Class of the American High School, it read, in an English murder mystery called *Shall We Join the Ladies*.

Charles sat through three acts of Reginalds and Fotheringays whose elaborately attempted accents dredged up endless rounds of applause and hearty laughter from parents who, Charles thought, must have felt a desperate need to show support, because they couldn't possibly have felt that deprived of enter-tainment. About halfway through he stopped caring who killed whom and only stayed awake from fear of snoring in a strange crowd and in hopes that in this play perhaps everyone would die in the end.

They didn't. As the curtain fell a lady two seats over turned to him and asked, "Are you Charles?" in a voice that sounded quite sure of everything, including that. She looked something like his mother's age, but thinner, with deeper, rustier makeup, hair that fell straight to her shoulders, a dark skirt ending about five inches above the knees, and a kind of scaly reflecting turtleneck that Charles had only seen in pictures of models. But at that she didn't seem too different from the other ladies in the crowd. When Charles nodded she introduced herself as Mrs. Steiner and said that her son Robbie had acted the lead in the play they'd just seen. Charles nodded again but didn't know what to say. Robbie looked pretty big for 120.

Mrs. Steiner led Charles through the departing crowd to a spacious room down the hall. The room had a bar in one corner and a floor-to-ceiling glass wall that gave a view of all downtown Manila and a good part of the bay. Through the wall Charles saw a heavy sprinkling of lights over Makati and a few other stretches, but the rest of the city looked more like the sky on an overcast night. No one noticed. Charles saw only one other person looking out the glass, a tall man in a pin-striped suit. Mrs. Steiner pointed him out as her husband, a banker, whose office occupied a suite a few floors beneath them.

Mr. Steiner seemed distracted when his wife introduced Charles. He looked down at the boy in wrinkled, scruffy sportswear and said, "Good evening, how are you?" as if meeting an adult. Mrs. Steiner saw a friend across the way and left, saying that certainly Mr. Steiner could entertain Charles until Robbie showed up. Mr. Steiner nodded slowly and looked out the glass again. He seemed to find something very interesting out there. Charles tried to find it, too, but could only see a few lights and a lot of dark. Still, just to make conversation, he said, "Wow, you can really see a lot from here."

Mr. Steiner slowly replied, "Yes, Charles. You can see almost everything from here."

Charles nodded solemnly. He had never spoken with a banker before. Although only a civilian, Mr. Steiner surprised Charles with the dignity with which he wore a simple, undecorated suit, as well as the way he held his drink without ever raising it to his lips. After a minute or so Charles asked, "Why is so much of the city so thinly lighted?"

Mr. Steiner gave him a deeply puzzled look and seemed to ponder another, much trickier question. At length he replied, "The lights are thin, Charles, because they simply haven't many." He gestured out the window with his glass—a broad, sweeping gesture meant to cover a very large part of the city. "You see, it's the same old story," he said, "of the haves and the have-nots. We, of course, are the haves."

Charles looked at him and for a moment their eyes met. Mr. Steiner seemed to invest this statement with a special profundity, though to Charles it seemed not only obvious but, for a number of reasons, obviously right. *After all*, he thought, *who beat the Japs?*

Just then Robbie came up. He stood about an inch taller than Charles and apparently worked out. He had straight fine features, chestnut hair about an inch and a half over regulation (which he didn't have to worry about, Charles realized with a shock), and a strong jaw. *Damn*, thought Charles.

"Hey Dad," said Robbie, and Mr. Steiner smiled and turned from the window.

Charles felt groggy when the Steiners got him up for breakfast and tried to make him eat. He hadn't slept well, having spent most of the night in and out of troubling dreams. At one point Arlington County materialized in the middle of Quezon City and to get to school at George Dewey High School Charles had to take a bus driven by lizards from Binictican to the beacon through the jungle. Breakfast felt awkward, with Charles's concerns about weight compounded by the sight of Robbie wolfing down steak and eggs under the fondly approving gaze of his parents. Charles didn't begin to feel comfortable until he found himself in the locker room inside the vast American School sports complex lacing up his wrestling shoes and listening to Finch and Joe taunt each other about their upcoming opponents.

"I *hope* I get a preacher's boy," said Joe, "because he's gonna have to be born again just to get his head out of his ass."

"I want an Air Force brat," said Finch. "They don't know how to handle an opponent who's closer than ten thousand feet below them."

"Not by much," cracked Edgefield, ducking just in time to avoid Finch's towel.

"How do we usually do?" Charles asked Edgefield. "Jim says we usually get stomped."

"*He* may get stomped," said Finch, "by us for talking that way."

"Yeah," said Edgefield, "I personally plan on kicking some ass out there."

"Yeah, but just out of curiosity, how *do* we usually do?"

"It doesn't matter," said Finch, "we can win if we want to and work for it."

"That's the spirit!" said Coach Simon, overhearing.

"Oh blow me," muttered Joe.

Simon gathered the team around and said, "Boys, I've coached a lot of years and wrestled some myself, and I know for a fact that every man on this team can do just as well as anyone else in your weight class. As long as you put your hearts into it and don't get suddenly chickenshit on me, you're going to go out there and stomp the stuffing out of those pansies from Clark, Faith, and the American School!" He clenched his fingers into mighty blocks and thundered, "Let's go, men!" and the whole team jumped up and shouted, "Damn straight!" and "Fucking A!"

But out on the mat in the cavernous arena with thousands of friends, family, band members, cheerleaders, servants, and employees from everywhere but Subic, Jim's prediction proved the more prescient one. Jim himself actually won his first match against a boy from Clark whose protests about fouls went unheeded, but then got disqualified in the second match the moment he goosed the son of the American trade representative. Both Finch and Joe split their matches fair and square, as did Luiz under only slightly questionable circumstances. Edgefield lost twice narrowly, Skunk ran out of breath in the third round of his first match, and no one else really had a hope. Except perhaps for Charles. His opponent from Faith looked no bigger than he, yet Charles saw beneath his wiry red hair a weird glint in his eyes, and after initially scoring a point on a breakaway Charles just didn't want to get anywhere near him. And Robbie showed no particular skill, but he had considerable strength, and each time Charles got close to focusing on the moves that might turn things around he caught a glimpse of Mr. and Mrs. Steiner on the sidelines looking tense and worried and whatever killer instinct he had simply evaporated. He would never know whether he could have beaten Robbie or not.

When the last drops of sweat fell to the mat Subic came in a solid fourth in a field of four. Charles didn't know quite how bad he'd looked until Mrs. Steiner came up to him after the match and said, "The important thing is that you tried."

Mr. Steiner walked off with Robbie, talking intently. Jim, standing next to Charles, winked at Mrs. Steiner and said, "Yup, after that butt-stomping you got, Chuck, Dad's probably taking the young man out to get laid."

On the bus ride back Charles could hear a few muttered "almosts" and "should haves," and the word *pussies* seemed to escape a few lips, including Coach Simon's. But most of the boys kept quiet and to themselves. The final word belonged to Skunk, who hadn't uttered an articulate phrase the whole of the trip till they hit the switchback and the rear gate to the base suddenly emerged from the jungle.

"Christ," he said, "I feel like a Joe."

VI

THE BATTLE OF THE VC VILLAGE

"This isn't going to be like your last little jaunt," Commander Barker told his son. "I appreciate what it's like to be a young man and to want to go and do things on your own, but we can't have you out in the jungle without any supervision." He spoke calmly and firmly, making reasoning gestures with his right hand while his left steered the blue-and-white Chevy from the road to Cubi onto the narrow black strip leading to the pistol range. *Who's arguing?* thought Charles.

His father continued. "Now, I understand Captain Edgefield's found someone to go along on this overnighter. It wasn't easy, I'm sure. A young sailor on this base has a lot more interesting things to do than to chaperone a bunch of kids out in the wilderness. So I want you to mind him, hear? And no foolishness. Your mother'll give me hell if you boys pull another stunt like that little stroll to Binictican. Understand?"

Charles nodded and looked out the window at the jungle crowding the crumbling road. The creepers, the branches, the many-shaped leaves and the shadows between them, all seemed to him less inviting than threatening. It felt strange for his father to lecture him. Had Commander Barker actually asked his son whether he wanted to spend the night in the jungle, Charles could easily have acquitted himself of the charge of wildness. *But maybe he doesn't want to know*, thought Charles; *maybe he'd rather worry about me getting wild than wimping out.*

"Did you hear me, son?"

"Yes, sir."

After winding through a little valley, the road broke out of the jungle into a few dozen acres of grassy fields. Charles felt the crunch of gravel under the tires and saw ahead the Quonset hut offices, stalls, and targets of the range. These looked empty, but in the dusty lot Charles could see half a dozen cars, a gray pickup, and about a dozen boys and men, the boys in green fatigues and the men in khaki service dress. As his father drove the car into the lot Charles recognized the individual features of his fellow Explorer Scouts and their fathers. They parked; Commander Barker walked over to say hello to Captain Edgefield at the pickup while Charles retrieved his web belt and knapsack from the back seat of the Chevy.

Unloading the truck, the two Edgefields looked like only slightly different versions of the same military man—both nearly six feet tall and well muscled, the one in khaki a little grayer and taller, the one in green more deeply tanned. By the time Charles reached the truck the Edgefields had finished off-loading the son's knapsack and three large cardboard cartons.

"Will this do it for you?" Captain Edgefield asked.

"Sure, Dad. We're coming back tomorrow after breakfast and there's twelve of us."

"Hey," said Charles, "what's in the boxes?"

"Mortar rounds," said Edgefield. "We got a four-deuce in the front seat. Wanna help me get it out?"

"Sure!" said Charles, and took a step toward the front of the truck. Then he saw his father and Captain Edgefield chuckling while Edgefield shook his head in pity. *Ah, shoot*, he thought. What did he know? Perhaps the scouts actually did get to fire medium field artillery. They already wore uniforms and went on patrol.

"Those are C-rats, man," explained Edgefield.

"War food?"

Edgefield shook his head again and turned to look over the other scouts in the lot. Luiz stood a few yards away, hatless in a loose fatigue shirt and jeans, in the same Keds he wore on the beacon march; he motioned with his bolo toward the jungle two hundred yards beyond the range while Lieutenant Commander Finch and Jim's father, a lieutenant, nodded agreement. Next to them Finch, Joe, and Jim buckled on web belts heavy with extra canteens and began to help each other strap on their knapsacks.

"Hey, I wouldn't do that yet," said Edgefield, pointing to the cartons.

"Shit," said Joe, "why don't you have the last guy who shows up carry them?"

"Because I'm not going to trust my dinner to some jack-off who can't tell time."

Captain Edgefield looked at his watch. "I don't see all your men here yet, son. You losing your grip?"

"Right. I don't see your squid here yet, either. Looks like the whole Navy's going to hell."

"Son, I really do wish you wouldn't refer to enlisted personnel as 'squids' around me. You know I disapprove, and you really ought to consider how it would impact your father's career if your behavior compelled him to kick your ass in front of all these witnesses."

"Well, it wouldn't look any worse than if I kicked yours, sir."

"Kids," said Captain Edgefield to Commander Barker. "You can't live with them, and you can't run 'em over and leave 'em in the road."

Commander Barker laughed. He had already told Charles that he thought Captain Edgefield acted pretty decent for an academy man; he didn't put on airs.

After a few minutes some of the Explorers whom Charles hadn't scouted with yet began to show. First, three Negroes drove up in a Ford: Chief Petty Officer Sanders and his sons Tom and Ed. Charles knew Ed from his English class. Dark and stocky, Ed acted friendly enough, but a couple of times he'd referred to Cassius Clay as "my brother" and only last week he suggested that Charles might get to know "what's happening" by putting down Carlyle's *Frederick the Great* and picking up the *Autobiography of Malcolm X*. Tom, two years older, about four inches taller, and noticeably lighter skinned than his brother, looked uncomfortable and scarecrowish in his fatigues. Charles had first seen Tom on a Sunday afternoon in the Teen Club, sitting in a corner booth by the snack bar reading Dale Carnegie. While the two boys unloaded their gear, CPO Sanders exchanged a casual salute with Lieutenant Commander Finch and began to talk about the weather.

The last of the eleven scouts arrived when the Wong brothers drove in with MacReady. The same age as the Sanders boys, the Wongs also made an odd match for brothers. Carl, the younger, stood tall, lean, and mean like Luiz, but his brother George looked squat as a PX Buddha statuette, only with a crew cut and thick glasses. While they got their gear out of the trunk MacReady slowly began to lace up his boots. When the three joined the others around the back of the Edgefields' truck, Carl mentioned that they would have arrived earlier had MacReady not overslept.

"That cinches it, Not-Ready," said Edgefield. "You get the Ham and Lima Beans."

MacReady squinted, took off his fatigue cap, and scratched at his oily hair. "Again?"

Several pickups pulled into the lot at once from which a dozen sailors in dungarees dismounted and began to walk toward the Quonset hut. A marine instructor had already gone to the firing line. Charles saw him slap a seven-round box into the handle of a .45 and pull back on the slide. Back in the parking lot one sailor separated from the others. Tall, gangly, and looking a bit like Olive Oyl, only with wire-rimmed glasses and a shaved head, he strapped on a web belt hung with a single canteen and an issue machete in a canvas sheath. Apart from those items he wore the same dungarees, white hat, and black shoes that he would to chip paint or have a beer in the base bowling alley.

"Jesus," said Joe, "it's a good thing that bird's not going to the range. If they let *him* fire a forty-five the *recoil* would blow his skinny ass back stateside."

Edgefield looked incredulous. "You're kidding, Dad. *This* is our squid?"

Captain Edgefield seemed to wonder himself. "Petty Officer Fitzroy?"

The sailor looked at the boys in fatigues as if unsure. "Yes, sir?"

The captain sighed. "Get an extra blanket and poncho from the truck, son. This is your squid."

Fitzroy took a toothpick from his shirt pocket and began to chew thoughtfully. He nodded at the officers and raised his eyebrows at the boys. "Y'all the ones goin' campin'?"

"That's it," said Captain Edgefield, "and I want to thank you for agreeing to help out. You wouldn't know if your chief's on duty today, would you?"

"I 'spect he is, sir."

"Good, I want to give him a call. Son, you and your boys squared away here?"

"Yeah, Dad. We got it."

"They're all yours then, Petty Officer."

"Don't worry, Captain," said Jim with a wink. "We'll take care of him."

"Okay, men, let's fall in for the rations," said Finch.

The boys lined up. "I want the Turkey Loaf," said Luiz. Edgefield looked meaningfully at MacReady and said, "Mmm, mmm—I got your shit right here, buddy." Commander Barker caught Charles's eye, gave a quick nod and a smile, and walked back to the car. Captain Edgefield closed his door and started up the truck. In a few minutes nothing remained of the adults but a slowly dispersing cloud of dust. The scouts packed their C-rations and donned their knapsacks. Finch, dressed as if for inspection in pressed fatigues, trousers bloused over springs, and stiff brim pulled sharply down to his eyebrows, formed them into a file, taking care to have the more experienced boys spread among the less so they didn't split into two groups, one of which might get lost. Edgefield told Fitzroy to stay close to him. "You're gonna get those shoes pretty messed up out there, you know?"

"That's all right," said the sailor. "Not really mine, are they?"

"I've got the rear," said Joe.

"Good," said Finch, hands on his hips. The shortest of them all, he somehow made an upward stare seem commanding.

They marched behind the range and a few hundred yards to the left where the fields ended in weeds and shrubs; these increased gradually in size until abruptly meeting the trees. The file strung itself out on a thin path, two or three yards between each of its members. As Charles entered the shadows a sudden fusillade erupted back at the range and he flinched from the angry cracks as he might from a swarm of bees.

"That's right," said Joe. "Better get down; we might catch some strays."

Charles tugged on the straps of his knapsack and plodded forward. In a short while they came out of the band of jungle into a field of high grass and he pulled on the visor of his cap to shade his eyes. He looked down and noticed that he no longer had a path under his boots, but only flattened grass from the heels of the boys in front of him. The sun stung the back of his neck and pushed on his knapsack. Another hundred yards and he began to feel his pack and sweaty clothing pulling him down. When they came to the next wall of jungle the boys bunched up and Charles sat down where the Wongs and MacReady had already fallen out.

"Goddammit, get up," said Edgefield. "Nobody said 'take five.'"

"Thought you boys knew where you were going," said Fitzroy.

Edgefield ignored him. "Luiz, where's our trail?"

"Well, I know where this trail is. This VC village is up a stream, and the trail is on the stream. But I forget where the trail to the trail is."

"Shit," said Joe. "I think the stream's just ahead through these trees. The path we took last year's probably just grown over."

"Sure," said Luiz, "that's it."

Edgefield looked from one to the other, shook his head, and nodded to Finch. They formed up again and pushed slowly into the woods, by turns stepping and stumbling over roots and tangling and untangling themselves in brush and vines. They stayed level for a while but then came to a gentle downward slope that took them to the banks of a shin-deep stream about twenty feet wide. Here they rested while Edgefield and Luiz tried to find a trail, first on the near side, then on the far. After a number of minutes of thrashing in the brush on the other side, Edgefield and Luiz began to recross, Edgefield quietly cursing to himself, Luiz looking thoughtfully at the water. In midstream Luiz stopped.

"What is it, man?" Edgefield asked.

"I think maybe this stream is like a road, you know? The village is on the stream, the stream goes to the village. We don't get lost, we just get wet feet."

Edgefield thought for a moment, then said, "What the fuck: I'm standing here in the middle of a stream wondering if anyone else should get their feet wet. Finch! Joe! Line 'em up behind me. We're going up the stream."

"Oooh, I bet that water's cold," said MacReady.

"Remember Ed," said Tom, "we'll have to dry our feet very carefully when we get to camp so we don't get jungle rot."

"Yassuh, boss," Ed replied. Tom winced, turned, and gingerly stepped into the water.

Luiz led the way, trying to go from rock to rock, keeping in mind that most of the boys had shorter legs than he. For all his care, though, the rocks didn't always accommodate them and most of the others lacked his grace and balance. From his position toward the rear of the column, a man or two ahead of Joe, Charles could see the file move jerkily up the rippling roadway, the scouts dressed like disarmed infantry but taking long steps or short leaps with the awkward tentativeness of trainee tightrope walkers. Occasionally one slipped and fell with a dramatic splash and everyone would stop, some to help their comrade up, most to laugh. They made slow progress but no one seemed to mind. For Charles the pace allowed him to get used to the weight he carried, and in the stretches where they had no stepping-stones and had to wade, the water chilled him to his knees and lifted the veil of humidity from the entire jungle. The sun fell on them in a delicate lacework filtered through the canopy, and the high trees formed a lofty chamber over the water. To Charles it felt like walking down the nave of an oddly natural church, where the water burbling among the rocks made a kind of murmured prayer and the occasional cries of unknown beasts and birds resounded like the calls of priests and respondents.

After his second fall and the resulting chorus of laughter and jeers from the boys, Fitzroy sat on a rock, took off his shoes and socks, and rolled his bell-bottoms up to his knees. This didn't make him look any less ridiculous, but he did appear more comfortable; he poked his feet in the gravel of the streambed and announced that it felt just like looking for crawdads back home. While the file waited for him, Carl Wong and MacReady did a little dance on a large flat rock, stomping their feet and laughing at the tiny jets of water that squirted from the drainage holes in their nylon-sided jungle boots.

Jim knelt in the water and lit a cigarette, the act doing nothing to counter the effect of his baby face and granny glasses. "Just like a cold shower, this is. I'm going to have to take three or four of these if I have to spend a night without female companionship." At the rear of the column Joe lit up too and looked carefully around, his Roman nose and dark eyes evoking a watchful raptor. But Charles noticed that Finch, a few yards upstream, also silently scanned their surroundings. "What are you guys looking for?" Charles asked Joe.

"I don't know. Snakes, I guess." He saw Charles's look of fear mixed with skepticism and added, "No, Barker, I ain't shitting you. I mean, it's no big deal, just remember where you are."

"Right. Thanks."

"Don't thank me. Ah, shit; you're okay, Barker. For an asshole, that is."

Charles wondered whether to thank Joe again but Edgefield spared him the decision by waving them forward. And as they resumed the march Joe's warning had its effect: Charles checked the nearest vines for eyes and stared at branches fallen in the water to make sure that their undulations resulted only from an illusion of shadow and stream.

In another hour they came to a ford. On their right a trail twisted up a fifteen-foot embankment from the stream. Halfway to its top, next to the trail, they saw the mouth of a small cave half blocked by sandbags. Atop the bank stood a ragged palisade of half-decayed bamboo with one four-foot-wide gap to admit the path and several narrower ones where pales had dropped or someone had knocked them aside. Scattered glintings marked where spent cartridges lay among the litter of the jungle. As the boys scrambled out of the stream and up the trail into the VC village, Jim stopped and picked up one of the little brass cylinders.

"Thought so," he said, "this sucker's still live."

He showed Charles the brightly colored plug at the business end of the blank cartridge and let him feel the slight heft of the powder-filled shell. Then he pocketed it, saying, "We'll save this for a little later when things get too quiet around the campfire." *Great*, thought Charles. Now when it got dark he could worry about exploding campfires as well as snakes. He looked up into the vine-heavy canopy and shuddered.

Inside the village the post found five bamboo huts with thatched roofs, a sandbag emplacement, and a fire pit framed by four posts, bamboo crosspieces, and a largely rotted roof of woven grass. The stream curved around half of the circular palisade; the jungle came right up to the other half and in some places pushed through with a vigorous sapling or outburst of foliage. The windowless huts had their backs to the palisade and their doorways facing the fire pit. The scouts followed Edgefield to the center of the enclosure and fell out almost before he could give the command. They dropped their packs, unbuckled their web belts, then sat in the dirt and drank from their canteens. After a brief rest, Finch and Joe took MacReady and the Wongs out to rustle up firewood while the rest looked around the compound to see if the marines had left anything interesting behind in their war games—perhaps a mortar or a light machine gun. Charles stayed by the fire pit and took one of the rations from his pack. He found the act of examining his lunch curiously dramatic, like an initiation into some widespread yet nonetheless alien cult. The brown box contained several olive-green cans, each labeled, not with bright pictures of food or happy faces like ordinary fare, but with stark black letters referring to their contents in the same stilted language used for articles of equipment or ordnance: COOKIES, ICED, CHOCOLATE, for example, or BREAD, WHITE, ENRICHED. A dark olive cellophane utility pack came with each box and offered green moisture-resistant matches, chewing gum, a pack of four brand-name cigarettes, and a tight wad of white paper.

"Cool," said Charles, "you even get napkins."

Jim corrected him. "That's toilet paper, man. You can use it as a napkin if you'd like; just remember that the leaves out here are kinda chancy. By the way, you got some Salems for a pack of Pall Malls?"

Charles gave Jim his Winstons so he'd have an easier trade. Jim thanked him and pointed out one of the flat, shallow cans of strawberry jam. He said, "The jam sucks but if you slip one of the cans into the fire without anyone seeing a few minutes later it'll explode. Anyone near gets covered with sticky, boiling goo. Kinda like Boy Scout napalm."

"Jesus," said Charles.

"I'd thought of doing you, you know," Jim chuckled, "just so's you'd learn, but you gave me your Winstons and that was a righteous thing to do. I think I'll fuck over Fitzroy instead."

When the firewood party returned the boys got enough of a blaze going to heat their Pork, Sliced, and Beef, Chunked. Finch showed Charles how to open the cans with the tiny, flat, fold-out opener that came with every carton and that the boys called a John Wayne, as in, "Hey, toss me that there John Wayne so I can get at these crackers." Luiz showed his own idea of a noon-time meal in the Tropics by standing away from the fire but in its smoke, eating from a can of pineapple he'd cooled in the stream. He said the smoke kept away the mosquitoes.

After lunch the scouts further investigated the camp or split up to explore beyond the wall. The Wongs stowed their gear in one of the huts and discovered the tunnel leading to the cave in the stream bank. MacReady and Ed Sanders chased a frog up the stream while Tom followed, warning them about centipedes and scorpions. Luiz, intrigued by what Fitzroy had said earlier, took off his sneakers, waded in the ford, and soon came up with a large black crayfish. Fitzroy himself, as if vaguely aware of some responsibility for the post, strolled around the compound for a while and looked on thoughtfully while the scouts, engaged in their various pursuits, ignored him. When he tired of supervising he spread his poncho in the dust by the fire, lay down, and took a nap.

Charles approached Edgefield and Joe as they sat in the shade of one of the huts, smoking and chatting.

"The jungle's crap, man. I mean, this sucks," Joe said.

"Why the hell are you here, then?" Edgefield asked.

"I don't know. My old man, I guess. Thinks it'll help me get in Annapolis, or at least NROTC. Be an officer."

"Well, shit," said Edgefield, "just about every guy here wants that. Hell, the way the war's going, pretty soon they'll run out of us white boys and even the Sanderses and Wongs will pick up their gold stripes. Fuck, even MacReady—and if he's really lucky the VC'll blow him away and make him a hero before he gets court-martialed for fucking fish or something."

"Yeah, right," said Joe. "Goddamn war will probably go on for-fucking-ever. Guess I'd rather be an officer over a buncha squids at sea then get drafted as some sorry-assed grunt. Especially if it means humpin' through this kinda shit. I just wish I could get some points for the Aces instead of the goddamn Explorers."

"Right, I can see it now," said Edgefield, "brownie points for dry-humping your sorority sisters and puking on your shoes."

"Sounds good to me. Jesus, it's got to be better than the rest of what this place has to offer. I mean, back in the World camping don't mean this kind of savage wilderness shit, and varsity letters don't mean playing soccer in some half goddamn swampland . . ."

"Yeah, I remember that snake you almost tripped over last year in the game at Clark."

"Yeah, fucking *cobra*, man."

Charles left and walked over to the Wongs' hut. The Sanders brothers had returned from their trip along the stream and set up their bedding next door. Now both pairs of brothers stood outside their huts talking. Tom rubbed his pimply chin and asked George whether he thought they ought to drag some sandbags over to block the doorways against wild boar. George took off his glasses and squinted at them as if expecting an answer to appear in the lenses. The younger brothers laughed.

"Shit," said Ed, pumping his fist in a rough semblance of a Black Power salute, "if anything comes in here we can jump it with our bolos and waste its ass."

"Sure," said Carl, leaning against the doorway. "Besides, if something drops on you from that ceiling you want to be able to run away without breaking your neck."

"Gee, maybe we should build a fire in here," said Tom.

"Right," said Ed, "in a bamboo fucking hut."

"Hmmm," said George, "an interesting dilemma. I wonder if the Boy Scout Manual . . . Oh, hello Charles. Where were you planning to spend the night?"

Charles didn't want to think about spending the night. Despite this, he had. He'd noticed all the coffee in the utility packs and figured that between the caffeine and the terror he had of everything that crept and crawled and came out at night, maybe he could last ten or twelve hours wide awake with his back to the fire. Not that he'd admit it.

"I don't know," he replied. "Maybe I'll stay outside."

"Interesting," said Tom.

"Hard-core," said Carl, folding his arms and nodding in approval.

Charles shrugged modestly and left. He went through the gate and soon came across Jim sitting on the bank having another smoke. He'd found his Salems. Charles squatted beside him and kept a nervous gaze on the nearest underbrush.

"What's a guy like you doing in the jungle?" he asked. "Wouldn't you rather be with your girlfriend?"

Jim looked at him and smiled. "That is a good question, Charles my boy. Sure I'd rather be screwing Lee Ann right now. Like any fifteen-year-old male, my hormones rage day and night. And unlike many—including, no doubt, punk freshmen like yourself—whacking off has long since ceased to amuse me. But you got to understand women, Charles. You can't ever let 'em know how important that thang they sit on is. Every once in a while it pays just to say, 'no, dear, not this weekend—I think I'll just go out and commune with nature instead.' Makes 'em think."

"You're serious."

"Sure. And it is kinda sweet and peaceful out here, even with the snakes and the bugs. Of course, God only knows how I'll feel around twenty-two hundred hours. I suggest you sleep with your pants on." He inhaled deeply, tipped back his head, and blew several smoke rings.

"But why are you an Explorer, Jim? You doing it for your record?"

Jim pondered that. "Yeah, I guess so. I guess I want my daddy's white suit when I grow up. Shit, what else? Except for that last tour in Alameda I've lived—where? Yokohama, Rota, Guam, even Gitmo when I was too young to remember. *Not* going in the Navy would be like trying to start a business on another planet. Don't know the lingo, son; don't know the customs."

"Yeah. Me too, I guess."

"Besides, man, what would happen to us right now if we didn't do the natural thing? We'd get sucked in some other way, maybe drafted in as grunts, and then what?"

"I don't know. Maybe we'd be right back here, playing games."

"Maybe. But let me tell you. You got three kinds of grunts here. You got your base marines—you know, the garrison company. Oh yeah, they're a buncha bad motherfuckers, always going around saying shit like 'Haruh! Har!' and John Wayne–ing it. They can afford to be tough because they're here. Sabe?" Charles nodded; Jim continued: "Then you got the grunts going over to 'Nam. Giddy fucks, scared shitless all of them, because boot camp's just far enough behind for them to suddenly realize they're only eighteen and they're probably gonna die before they even begin to get enough pussy. And then you got the grunts coming back—the lucky fuckers who made it. Only they don't act too lucky, man, they're a buncha real quiet motherfuckers. Which ones you think we'd end up as? Tell me, man, because I'd really like to know."

Charles thought about what he knew of the history of the Marine Corps, about Belleau Wood, Chapultepec, Derna, Peking, Guadalcanal, even Khe Sanh. He remembered how the books described the battles. The men seemed to know what to do and the danger never seemed to bother them. He tried to imagine bullets cracking over this mock VC village and landing among the scouts, and then he wondered what he ever thought could change in the next four years to make him unafraid of that, or even of sleeping outdoors.

He stayed by Jim the rest of the afternoon, catching up with Luiz as the Guamanian explored the other side of the creek, then joining up with Finch for a four-man patrol of the outside of the palisade through the jungle. The patrol posed some serious difficulties. Thick undergrowth oozed up among fallen trees and the debris of previous generations of the bamboo paling that forgotten classes of marines had battered and smashed down. The four scouts pushed, tugged, hacked, and generally struggled to break through the several blockages, and when they finally reached the water upstream of the ford they washed their hands and faces and laughed at the leaves caught in each other's clothes and hair. Back inside the camp they found that Edgefield had stoked the fire for dinner. The sun dropped below the lip of the surrounding forest and cast the village into glowing shadow.

Joe looked around with an expression of intense boredom. He turned to the post president. "Okay, Edge: we walked in, grab-assed all afternoon, and now we got dinner on. What do we do after? Turn in as soon as it gets dark?"

Edgefield shrugged. George Wong said, "Why don't we get a whole lot of wood and have a bonfire? You know—sit around, tell stories, have cocoa."

"We'd have to be careful not to burn down the huts," observed Tom.

"Remind me never to put you guys on the entertainment committee," said Edgefield. "Anybody else got any ideas?"

"We could like maybe hunt boar," suggested Carl.

"I'm down with that," said Ed.

"You not going to find any boar," said Luiz. "They find you first."

"I got it," said Jim. "Let's have a war."

"A war? What the fuck you talking about?" asked Joe. "You trying to get hard-core on me, buddy?"

"What did you have in mind?" asked Finch, turning abruptly toward Jim.

Jim shrugged. "Beats me. The grunts use this place for training, right? We could divide into teams maybe. One holds the fort, the other tries to take it. Personally I'd prefer to go home and get laid, but if we're going to be spending the night here I think we owe it to ourselves to get a little crazy."

"I like this man's thinking," said Edgefield.

"Now wait a minute . . ." said Fitzroy.

"Don't worry," Finch told him, a fire kindling in his eyes, "we can take care of ourselves. If anything happens we'll tell our dads you tried to stop us, okay? That'll cover you with your CO."

"Y'all really do not know what you are doing, but if you want to do it anyway that's fine by me."

"You're a credit to the Navy, Petty Officer," said Finch, hands clasped behind his back like Napoleon before his marshals. "Okay, guys, this is how we could do it. We got flashlights, right? Whoever gets caught in a beam is shot, blown away. And sticks—sticks are like knives: whoever gets jabbed dies hideously, only nothing sharp, okay?"

Everyone agreed. Then they sat around the fire waiting for night. The post had three flashlights among them and decided that the defenders would get two because the attackers had more places to hide. Selecting the teams presented a problem. The darker it got, the more boys opted for the defense. Only after a fair amount of teasing and cajoling could Finch assemble an attack group. Jim joined because he had come up with the idea, then Luiz because he actually liked the jungle, day or night. The younger brothers, Ed Sanders and Carl Wong, joined primarily to shame their older brothers. Charles stepped up last, uncertain why.

Fitzroy agreed to umpire. "Let's just try not to get anyone really killed."

"Sure, Fitz," said Jim. "No more'n a few, anyway."

Twilight deepened into the brief afterglow of early evening and quickly faded to black. Finch led his squad out of the gate, over the stream, and into a patch of jungle he and Luiz had each explored earlier. About fifty yards from the village he motioned them down: they huddled around him as he whispered his plan. "Okay, listen up. I thought it over while we were choosing up sides. This'll be easy. Charles and Luiz, you come with me. Jim, you keep Ed and Carl on this side of the creek."

"What's the story, Finch? How come I get stuck with the little bros?"

"Somebody's gotta keep 'em in line. It's like this: the trail we blazed around the perimeter this afternoon, I don't think they're gonna look for us there. Even if they did they probably couldn't see. There's only five of them; they can't cover the whole works."

"Chief, there's only six of us. How're we supposed to surround them?"

"We're not going to surround them, we're going to hit them from two sides. I want you guys to wait exactly five minutes from when I leave. That'll give my team time to get across the creek. Then I want you to move up to the bushes across from the fort and make noise—you know, yell, shake leaves, throw rocks, whatever. Just stay under cover since they'll probably have both lights trained on you. We're going around to their rear and hit them from there. Charles, you'll recognize the basic maneuver from Frederick the Great's attack at Torgau."

"He almost lost that one," observed Charles.

"'Almost' means he won, then, doesn't it?" asked Carl.

"Sounds okay to me, man," said Jim. "Especially the part where you do all the work."

"What happens if they come out after us with the flashlights?" asked Ed.

"Then you probably die," said Finch. "But look at it this way: if they weren't already scared of the jungle they'd be the ones out here instead of us, right?"

"Right," said Jim. "What time you got?"

Charles looked on while Finch and Jim synchronized their watches, less because they had to than because it seemed the right thing to do. That done, they shook hands and Finch set off, followed by Charles, then Luiz. They had to halt under cover at the stream because the defenders had become anxious. Joe shouted out, "Come on you pussies!" and played his flashlight all the way to where Finch had planned to cross. Luiz led them another twenty yards up, all three taking care not to make more noise than they could help. They'd just crossed when they heard Jim yell, "Charge!" followed by the crash of stones and branches against the bamboo pales. Over their shoulders they could see the twin beams of the defenders lancing across the water into the trees, but whoever fired them gave no sign of leaving the shelter of the fort. They entered the jungle.

By careful steps Finch led Charles and Luiz from behind one tree to the next, silently pointing out stumps, low branches, and other obstructions, carefully brushing aside tendrils and leaves. They reached the palisade about ten yards in from the bank and inched around toward the rear of the fort, the point directly opposite the gate. In several places the light from the fire made knife blades that pierced the gaps between bamboo poles, but they passed these slowly without attracting attention from those inside.

Within ten minutes they reached their objective. Finch pressed against a crack and looked in. Only MacReady patrolled the perimeter here: Tom and George stood by the fire with Fitzroy while Joe and Edgefield fired their flashlights from the opposite wall, hidden from Finch's direct observation by the intervening huts.

Luiz widened a gap behind the nearest hut and slipped through, followed by Finch. As Charles covered with the flashlight the two snagged MacReady and dragged him to cover between the rear of the hut and the palisade. Charles stepped through and joined them.

"Say one word," Finch told Not-Ready, "and I really will cut your throat."

MacReady nodded and, when Luiz took his hand from his mouth, added, "Far out. Can I join your team?"

"No," said Finch, "but you can tell me where Joe and Edge are."

"Sure."

While Luiz and Charles huddled under cover with their prisoner, Finch crept into the village to reconnoiter. He returned a few minutes later with the news that Edgefield had figured out their plan and, covered by Joe, had advanced to the stream to attack Jim and the little brothers. They had to move now. While Charles held a stick on MacReady, Finch and Luiz pried a hole in the back of the hut and went through it to the doorway. They could see the older brothers still at the fire with Fitzroy. Finch brought MacReady and Charles into the hut and whispered a new plan. While they waited inside and counted to fifty he slipped out the hole in the back with the flashlight.

At fifty Luiz and Charles left MacReady and walked quietly toward the campfire. Fitzroy and the older brothers would probably not have seen them on the other side of the blaze even had they kept up their guard instead of watching Joe's and Edgefield's flashes. A few yards from the fire Luiz and Charles broke into a run. Luiz caught Tom before he could turn more than halfway around. George did get all the way around, arms outstretched as if he meant to catch Charles. Instead, Charles poked him in the solar plexus with his stick. "Ooof," George said, and dropped to his knees.

"Sorry," said Charles.

Joe heard everything and immediately faced the fire. "Goddammit, Edgefield!" he yelled, "Get back here! We've been flanked!" He ran forward and fired his flashlight at Luiz and Charles, but by the time he realized that it had no effect on targets standing in the full light of the fire on the other side, Finch popped up on his right, shot him, then grabbed his flashlight and tossed it to Luiz. As Edgefield stormed through the gate they caught him in a crossfire.

"Ah, fuck *me*," said Edgefield. "I wanna rematch."

"Fuck that shit," said Joe. "It was a silly goddamn idea to begin with."

A moment later Jim appeared at the gate with Ed and Carl. "Damn," he said, "in the absence of women what *can* you do but fuck your friends? Hey Joe—was it as good for you as it was for us?"

Joe turned to Finch. "You little shit. You think you're some big bad-ass because of these little Boy Scout games?"

Charles tensed, wondering if they would fight. He himself felt elated—his team had won, zero casualties to five. And he'd done his part. He helped George get up, brushed him off, and apologized again.

"It's okay," said George. "Hey guys! Let's make some cocoa and tell ghost stories!"

Edgefield stepped between Joe and Finch. "That sounds like a good idea to me. Doesn't it sound like a good idea to you guys?"

"Why are you always stepping in for this little shit?" asked Joe.

"Why do you think he's stepping in for *me?*" asked Finch.

"Both of you shut the fuck up and have some cocoa," said Edgefield.

A few minutes later one could forget that they had almost had a real fight. Around the campfire, their faces bottom-lit by its glow or highlighted by the smoldering tips of cigarettes, the boys sat on ponchos, rocks, or sandbags and told stories while Fitzroy dozed. At first they had to listen to Jim and Luiz talk about Olongapo, how b-girls smoked cigarettes with their vaginas or had intercourse with carabao on stage, but Tom and George steered them away with a few standard tales of lunatics escaped from asylums, which there in the midst of the jungle seemed oddly comical. When Tom and George had exhausted their stock, Edgefield began to talk of the White Lady. As he explained it, the White Lady used to live on a mountain next to the road from Kalayaan to the main base. But one year the Navy dynamited and bulldozed the mountain in order to put up some buildings that got cut out of the budget anyway, leaving only a huge flat field of cracked clay. The Navy thought they'd removed all the civilians, but they'd missed her, or perhaps she snuck back through Security to try to save her house by staying in it. In any event, they blew her up. Yet in a few weeks she began to show up all over the base—whole, not in pieces—a white, spectral figure who concentrated exclusively on haunting Americans. They would see her in their cars' headlights on dark nights in the rainy season, or drifting among the shadows of the orchids in carports in the hot dry weeks before Easter. And at least one boy swore she'd jumped out of a tree at him one night as he walked home from the Teen Club.

"But that was you, MacReady," said Joe, "and you were drunk off your ass."

They all laughed, except MacReady, who replied, "Hey, I *saw* her, man: I almost had a heart attack!"

"She ever kill anyone?" Charles asked.

"We don't really know," replied Edgefield. "But I tell you—and this is no shit—there's a lot of stuff that happens around here that never gets explained."

This seemed to satisfy everyone. After a few moments of silence, Tom stood and announced his intention of retiring. With that, most of the scouts got up, brushed themselves, and wandered off to the huts. Fitzroy stayed, still asleep. Luiz and Jim brought their ponchos and blankets out by the fire and Charles asked to join them.

"No problem, cat," said Luiz, "plenty room out here."

"Just watch your ass," winked Jim.

Edgefield and Finch walked the perimeter and gave assignments for the watch. Charles didn't hear his but decided that it didn't matter since he planned to stay up all night anyway. He removed his metal canteen cup with the folding handle from its canvas pouch, filled it, and pulled a packet of ration coffee from his jungle jacket. He put his cup over the coals as he'd seen Jim and Luiz do, and began to wait. Luiz curled up on his poncho while Jim smoked in silence. Charles sat warily, expecting any moment to have to fend off a snake or brush a huge hairy spider from his head. But now, in addition to his fear, he began to feel a certain irritation with himself—every itch made him imagine he had something hideous, like a centipede or scorpion, on his ankle, his back, his neck, and he finally became tired of swatting at imaginary perils and grew weary of his own fear. Still, the mosquitoes humming in his ears sounded and felt real enough. He rolled down the sleeves of his jacket and rubbed more of the oily repellent on his hands and face. Then his head fell forward on his chest.

"Shit! Oh my God! Help!"

Charles jumped to his feet, knocking over his half-evaporated cup of water and sending a hissing cloud of steam up from the fire. In front of the Wongs' hut he saw all four brothers, MacReady, and Joe gesturing excitedly, their unsheathed bolos shining back pieces of fire, their flashlight beams waving crazily on the wall by the left of the doorway like searchlights in an air raid. "Get it!" someone shrieked, and suddenly Charles could make out a big gecko, perhaps fifteen inches long, purple with green splotches, holding on under the thatched eaves and reflecting back the flashlights with huge, disturbingly placid eyes. "I got it!" someone else yelled—George, Charles thought—and the bolos flashed again, this time waving frantically toward the fat, stationary lizard. Three or four blades struck near it before it turned to scuttle off, but as soon as it turned one blade caught its thigh and in its hurry to leave its suckered toes released their grip and it fell to the ground. "Stop!" Charles shouted, but too late. The boys moved in, striking clumsily at arm's length, torn between their fear and their desire to kill it, but still dropping blows all around the frantic animal until it couldn't help but to run into one of the heavy, sharp blades.

"Cut that shit out!" screamed Luiz, springing from his poncho. He ran for the group and began pushing boys out of the way. In their own panic they ignored him, batting away at the lizard until Luiz had to individually push or pull each one of them off what now, in the dim glow of the firelight, showed only as a group of bloody pieces, the largest of which still watched them with the same calm eyes.

"Goddammit!" Luiz yelled. "Goddammit! You dumb sons of bitches!"

"What are you so pissed about?" asked Ed. "We thought it was poisonous."

Jim stepped up. "Congratulations," he said, then spat. "It's just a harmless fucking gecko. It *eats* shit like spiders and scorpions. It's a friendly."

"It's bad luck, man," said Luiz. "It's major fucking bad luck. It's a protector, understand?"

"Geez," said Tom, "it's just a lizard, Luiz. We're sorry if we like broke some taboo or something."

"Christ," said Luiz, and went back to the fire, brushing his sleeve across his eyes and shaking his head.

The boys stood and stared at each other. From a few huts away came the light rumble of Edgefield's snoring. Finch walked up. "What's going on?" he asked. No one spoke.

"Well," said Jim, "if you Explorer-fucking-Scouts are through slaughtering harmless forest creatures I think I'll return to my wet dream."

The crowd broke up. Charles told Finch what happened, then he and Carl Wong carried the lizard fragments away behind the hut on the flats of their bolos. They buried the pieces and then covered the bloodstains in front of the hut with dirt scraped up by their boots. Then Charles returned to the fire and retrieved his cup. He didn't bother to refill it. He knew he wouldn't get any sleep.

He lay down rigidly, afraid to move to either side. He didn't want to roll over on anything's stinger or fang, or—for that matter—something creepy but soft and harmless like the gecko. He watched the stars and smelled the smoke; he listened to Fitzroy snoring. *Lucky Fitzroy.* After the passage of hours he heard a soft, barely audible crunch. Something big and near. Without rising, his vision somehow shifted. He saw an enormous gecko slowly poke its head through the gate of the VC village and regard him with a cold, unforgiving eye. *But it wasn't me*, he tried to say, as it reached in and touched his shoulder with a suction-pad toe.

"Wake up, cat."

"Luiz. What time is it?"

"0-Dark-thirty, cat. Your time. You got the last watch. Remember?"

"You okay?"

"Me? Sure. There's one pissed gecko ghost out there, though."

"I think I saw him."

"Yeah? Well, don't worry. I don't think he pissed at you."

Charles stood up and immediately felt cold, colder than he had since early that spring back home in Virginia. He picked up his blanket and noticed that he'd moved around quite a bit as he slept, apparently without crushing anything, or getting stung, or getting bit by anything worse than a few mosquitoes. He draped his blanket over his shoulders and squatted by the embers of the fire. Luiz handed him a canteen cup half filled with hot coffee, then curled in his blanket and went to sleep.

Charles took the coffee and walked around a little, trying not to make any noise that would wake Fitzroy or the other scouts. The huts looked spooky in the dark and the bamboo in the palisade leaned like a chorus line of angry drunks, while God only knew what kind of creatures made the occasional howls and shrieks he heard in the jungle. Yet the stars shone, the fire glowed, and around him slept the peaceful forms of boys he suddenly thought of as friends—some better, some worse, yet still friends. He still felt afraid, afraid of a lot. But on the lengthy list of all the things that scared him, the jungle itself had dropped a long way down.

VII

CIVILIZE 'EM WITH A KRAG

C harles looked down at this hands, felt the little boat bobbing on the small but constant waves, and thought about getting sick. The sun forced his gaze down: his hands, glistening with salt water, still bore traces of acrylic paint—Prussian blue, grass green—from the toy soldiers he had started to paint that morning. He remembered the cooling hum of the air conditioner, the spotlight of his desk lamp in an otherwise darkened room. Had he ignored the concrete walls and the smell of lumpia coming from the kitchen where his mother's new maid busied herself making hors d'oeuvres for a party of officers' wives that afternoon, he could have imagined himself home in Virginia. Then the doorbell rang. A few moments later his mother came into his room.

"There's a boy here who says he knows you," she said doubtfully, her ruby nails playing with the cultured pearl necklace she'd bought ten years earlier in Yokohama. For the party that afternoon she had already put on the high-collared, sleeveless silk dress she purchased in Hong Kong on the same tour of duty. She seemed to like it, either because of the embroidered dragons or because it still fit. Charles liked it because the pale blue color reminded him of the coats of the Bayreuth dragoons.

He put his brush in the water jar and went downstairs. Mrs. Barker followed, curious. When Charles opened the door he saw Luiz standing in the carport, an improbably tall, lanky Guamanian in a white T-shirt and tiger-striped camo swim trunks. "Hey, cat."

"You remember Luiz, Mom; you gave us a ride back from Binictican."

Mrs. Barker arched one carefully painted eyebrow.

"We were all pretty dirty," Luiz theorized. "Gee, nice dress."

"Why, um, thank you. You do look familiar. Charles, why don't you invite your friend in?"

Once in Charles's room, Luiz said, "Hey, your mom's not bad looking."

"Geez, Luiz—that's my *mom*."

"Ah, don't worry, cat. Not my type. But your dad, he's not doing bad for himself."

"That's all I need to be thinking about."

"Damn, it's cold in here," said Luiz. He picked up one of the toy soldiers on Charles's desk and nodded appreciatively. Then he put it down and flicked off the air conditioner. Before Charles could object, Luiz threw open the curtains and raised the venetian blinds.

Charles staggered back like Nosferatu, only half in jest. Luiz said, "Come on, cat. This is great. You can see mountains and sea and all kinds of shit. We live down the hill—can't see nothing. Why you make it so cold and dark?"

"I like it cold and dark. It'd be getting cold and dark if I was home."

"Yeah? So? You crazy, cat. Let's go to the beach."

Charles blinked. "All that sand and sun?"

"Okay, we get some buddies and go diving. Once you see the reef, cat, you forget all about home. Come on. Rains'll be coming soon."

Charles thought for a moment. On his desk several fusiliers of the Erbprinz von Hessen-Kassel regiment stood next to an open copy of *Military Uniforms* by Preben Kannik. Outside his room he could hear his mother giving instructions to the maid. How could he concentrate on the lacework of his soldiers' lapels and cuffs once all the other wives showed up and began to chatter about their next shopping trip to Taipei?

Charles turned his hands over and examined the bloodless and wrinkled palms. A swell lifted the boat several feet, hesitated, then quickly set it down. He forced himself to look up. The cloudless sky took up nine-tenths of all that he could see with a flaring white, barely tinged with blue on the horizon. On two sides it met dry hills tawny with dead grass and here and there olive with patches of surviving jungle. On another side it gleamed with ships, aerials, warehouse roofs, dockyard cranes and machinery. On the last side, somewhere beyond the green of Grande Island, it faded into haze above the endless sea. The boat idled in the middle of the bay, a few miles from land.

Ten yards from the boat Luiz's snorkel peeked above the shining green and his body writhed beneath it like a giant salamander. Farther out, Joe surfaced and blew his snorkel clear with an upward spray of diamonds. Charles held on to the aluminum thwart, his T-shirt drying sticky on his back, and watched Edgefield empty a sock into the bottom of the boat by the outboard. Three seashells dropped out, each about four inches long, oval and bulbous, a bit like eggs flattened on the long side, but colored a glossy grayish green, and covered with fine umber lines in patterns evocative of alien calligraphy. They thudded in the hull; after a few moments of stillness, each slowly oozed out a fat snail head and a greasy foot.

"Arabian cowries," explained Edgefield. He nudged one with his flipper. "Harmless little fuckers and kinda cute, but you gotta watch out when you bring up a conch." He pronounced it *conk*. "They got that slit up the side and if you hold 'em too long they'll poke out a little tube and shoot you with a poison bone harpoon about so long. Hurts like a mother. Some of 'em kill."

Charles kept quiet and watched the Arabians waddle in their slime along the keel. The whole way out his companions regaled him with warnings about sharks, barracudas, sea snakes, moray eels, turkey fish, stone fish, fire coral, and giant clams, to the extent that Charles felt a profound and genuine surprise when, having reached the reef, they jumped in screaming in apparent delight as soon as Edgefield dropped anchor.

"You want to go back in?" asked Edgefield.

Charles nodded. He hadn't left the water because of any monsters, but because of the cold and the seawater he kept sucking out of his snorkel. Unless he wanted to spend the rest of the afternoon on the boat cultivating seasickness, he had to go back in.

"We'll follow Joe," Edgefield said. "He always leaves a little something."

Charles strapped on his mask and jumped in behind Edgefield. He cleared his snorkel, leveled out, and followed in the older boy's wake. The reef lay fifteen feet below them, a bright multicolored swath of fanned and feathered outgrowths covering each other with fantastic shadows. Charles could name no more than half the colors and very few of the shades that glowed and glittered in chaos around him. Fronds and spines mingled with waving gloves of glassy lace. Sea slugs crept along like frozen blue, neon-highlighted lava lamps. Fish parading satin sheens, particolored iridescences, and streaked contrasts coasted on hidden currents. Among all of this, secreted in pits and crevasses, mollusks hid, armored in lurid shells.

They had no trouble picking up Joe's trail. For all its seeming irregularities and wild variety, the reef had its own patterns. They established themselves intuitively and Charles could quickly sense where Barone had disturbed them. After a few yards Joe's crowbar had left a path like a bullet through a china shop. Charles stayed near the surface, sun warming his back, while Edgefield skimmed just over the top of upended, displaced, or shattered coral, occasionally pulling a jewel from the debris. They came upon Joe by the edge of the reef on the western side, where the filigreed garden ended and fell in a precipice to the bottom of the bay.

Charles stopped and treaded water, letting Edgefield go ahead where he and Joe dove in bright light over a huge, open pirate's treasure. Just behind them—only twenty or thirty yards from Charles—the sea turned deep indigo and swallowed the sun. It looked something like an approaching thunderstorm and something more like the end of the earth. Charles felt a fear like his fear of heights and turned to go back to the boat.

Directly below him he saw a perfect egg in the rubble of Joe's route. He sucked hard through his snorkel, getting a strong taste of rubber and seawater with his air, then swam down. The water grew increasingly thick and pinched hard on his nose and eardrums. He nabbed the egg, jumped to the surface, and blew out a spray of sparkling sunlight.

Luiz had already reached the boat. Edgefield and Joe joined them a few minutes later. As they dumped out their socks, Luiz said, "Joe, you chase shells like the goddamn Army go after Charlie."

"What the fuck do you mean?"

"What's that shit, Edge, you know, make a whole forest turn black and drop its leaves so nobody hide there?"

"A defoliant."

"That's it, Joe, you defoliant the fucking reef with that paint chipper."

"Lick my balls—you're just jealous."

"Oh yeah?"

Their treasure oozed in rough piles by their feet: Arabians, tigers, and eyes, poking up antennae and slithering tentatively like prisoners from a slave raid on a Martian city. Luiz grinned at Joe and pulled a final prize from his sock. "You got one of these?"

"Map cowrie?" said Edgefield. "That's sweet."

"Shit," said Joe. For a moment he seemed angry, but then he shook the water from his dark hair, rubbed his broad, worm-eaten-with-acne jaw, and grinned in resignation. When he saw Charles with his one egg cowrie he chuckled and tossed him a tiger and an Arabian. "You need a better excuse than one egg," he said. "We don't want your mom thinking you were cattin' around in town instead of out here."

"Thanks," said Charles, surprised and pleased. They told him how to clean shells. You left them in the shade in your backyard for several days until the jungle ants picked them clean. The shells would never lose their color after that. Charles listened, watched the cowries crawl, then looked at the waves lapping dully over the hidden reef. Edgefield started the motor to take them back to the Cubi landing. A Phantom streaked low over the bay. Three of the boys looked up. Charles slipped the egg cowrie over the side; it disappeared like a sinking moon.

He saw the same white that evening in the sky, and again in the morning when a few puffs of cloud drifted in from the ocean. "Rains'll be coming," Luiz had said. The white showed even stronger later that Sunday morning when Commander and Mrs. Barker and their son went to the Naval Station Chapel for mass and squinted in the brightness of the altar cloth and vestments in the blaze of high windows. Even the churchgoers hurt Charles's eyes with the white of starched tropical uniforms and ladies' gloves. Heaven itself, it seemed to him, could hardly look whiter though it rested on clouds. God had to love the U.S. Navy, with all this white and the ships in the bay gray like the pearls in heaven's gate. Charles saw another patch of white before him in the next pew: the neck of a girl he'd seen in the Teen Club. A few vertebrae mounded gently under the bottom edge of her deep red hairdo and led to the hollow between her shoulder blades where her green dress V'd down, leading his eyes farther to where it grabbed her hips. He could smell her perfume and a little taste of sweat like the sea and right there, despite all the white and God and the Navy, he could feel himself starting to get a boner. He looked up and began to sing with the others:

> *Eternal Father strong to save*
> *Whose arm hath bound the restless wave*
> *Oh hear us when we call to Thee*
> *For those in peril on the sea . . .*

After church the Barkers went to the big O Club on the main base. Here again they found high windows, bright sunlight, and a view of water and warships. They ate their late breakfast off white plates on white tablecloths served by Filipino stewards in stiff white tunics. A recording played over loudspeakers, a Filipino crooning a ballad in a mellow voice like an only slightly Oriental cross between Tony Bennett and Johnny Mathis. Mrs. Barker looked up from her Eggs Benedict and said that the singer sounded almost as good as Jim Nabors. Commander Barker sawed at a piece of bacon and nodded, his mouth full. Charles listened more carefully to the slow, simple melody and the singer's unashamed schmaltziness, hoping it would take his mind off the girl in the green dress, and wondering if he'd have to listen to that catchy but not particularly cool tune playing over and over and over in his head for the next week or more just so, right now, he could keep himself from getting another erection around his parents. At least, he thought, he would not have to remember the words—the singer sang in Tagalog. Mrs. Barker called a steward over and asked the name of the song.

"It's called 'Dahil Sa Iyo,' ma'am."

"It's very pretty."

"Yes, ma'am. It's very popular."

"What does that mean, 'Dahil Sa Iyo'?"

"It means 'because of you,'" Charles said.

Commander and Mrs. Barker looked at their son. "How'd you know that?" Commander Barker asked. Charles thought about the wooden statuette in the shop on the road to Manila, the one with the naked pregnant Filipina holding a sailor hat. "I don't know," he said, trying to psyche down his erection. "I just heard it somewhere."

"How romantic," said his mother.

"Yes, ma'am," said the steward. "I take your plate now?"

After breakfast the Barkers dropped Charles at their quarters and went off to a reception at the base hospital. Charles quickly changed from his church clothes to T-shirt and shorts, then disappeared into the bathroom with one of his mother's *Cosmopolitans*. A few minutes later after washing up, he emerged from the bathroom and went to work.

First he checked to make sure he had sodas in the refrigerator and cans of pretzels in the pantry. Next, he went to his room, opened his closet, and brought out several shoe boxes and a shopping bag that held a variety of cardboard and plastic objects. He brought the boxes and bag into the dining room, put them on the big table, and started to unpack. Tiny trees and houses from the bag became half a dozen forests and two villages on the table. Strips of brown construction paper became a simple network of roads connecting the villages with each other and the edges of the table. Strips of blue became a stream bisecting the table and forking about a third of the way from one side. He had no good hills but improvised with the volume of Kannik and two other books covered with scraps of green cloth. He looked out the window at the jungle and the Zambales Mountains. Someday, probably after he got back to the States, he would make decent hills of papier-mâché.

He folded the bag, tossed it under the table, and opened one of the shoe boxes. Peeling away layers of tissue paper, he brought forth an army—row after row of eighteenth-century grenadiers, musketeers, fusiliers, cuirassiers, dragoons, hussars, and artillery—all flat tin figures about an inch and a half high, some painted by the company that made them in Germany, the rest by himself. Charles lined them up on opposite sides of the table under their flags, the Prussians with Maltese crosses on contrasting backgrounds and the Austrians with the double-headed imperial eagle on one side and the Virgin Mary in a circle of flames on the other. He aligned them in groups of five as infantry battalions or regiments of cavalry so the other players could see what they had; they'd have to figure out their actual tactical deployment themselves. With the armies on parade Charles brought out the last items: a tape measure to determine moves and ranges, a pair of dice to decide the outcome of volleys and charges, and a few handwritten pages with the rules he'd modified from Donald Featherstone's *Tackle Model Soldiers This Way*. Ten minutes later Billy walked over from next door.

"Shit," he said, scratching his belly under a plain yellow T-shirt, "you got a serious problem. Hey, I know. Why don't I go home and get the Doors? We could listen to Morrison while we fight."

"No way. I got some Wagner overtures for these guys."

"I don't believe this."

Finch and Ford showed up about five minutes later, getting off the boxy yellow Blaylocks bus at the stop across Finback Drive. Ford wore a white short-sleeved buttondown oxford with black shorts and dress shoes that matched his clunky eyeglass frames. He bent down to tabletop level and carefully studied the ranks of toy soldiers. "Interesting," he said, "that this kind of embryonic psychosis should be so rare on this base."

"What in the fuck are you bleeding about now?" Billy asked.

"I just meant that since you all seem to want to grow up to be mass murderers in uniform someday, I'm surprised more of you aren't practicing like Charles."

Finch stood straight with his arms crossed, surveying the field. "This is outstanding, Charles; you can tell the different regiments and everything."

"If you're so down on war," Billy asked Ford, "why did you even bother to come over?"

Ford pushed his glasses back and stood up. "Strictly as an experiment. And, of course, because I'm only thirteen and still like toys."

They flipped for sides. Charles lucked out twice, getting both the Prussians and Finch as partner. Billy had a complaint about the uniforms.

"Okay, I think I got this. You guys are blue and we're white, right?"

"Well, mostly," said Charles.

"Mostly. Like some of the cavalry on both sides are green."

Finch looked over at Billy. Finch had a profile that reminded Charles of a bust of Alexander the Great, only a lot younger and with a crew cut. "Those are our Kleist hussars and your Archduke Joseph dragoons."

Ford let out a low sigh. "You catch on too quick, you know that?"

The battle did not last nearly so long as the ones Charles had played against himself with intricate maneuvers and counterstrokes. Charles and Finch looked over the terrain and agreed right off on a classic Frederick-style attack en echelon to the right, with Charles taking the lead brigades and Finch the refused left, while Billy and Ford led their soldiers up like two separate armies side by side—the same mistake, both Finch and Charles recognized, that the Franco-Bavarian army had made at Blenheim a few years before Frederick's birth. Charles's cuirassiers and dragoons swamped Billy's left-flank horse, then flanked his fusiliers when they turned to meet the lead battalions of Prussian grenadiers. Ford tried to move to his ally's aid, but got held up by a forest and the stream and, by the time he finally faced around to meet Charles, Finch charged to within a move of his right and rear. Two turns later the majority of Billy's and Ford's men lay flat on their sides on the tabletop.

It didn't surprise Charles to defeat Billy, because he knew the rules and Billy knew nothing about eighteenth-century tactics. But Finch's success, even against the pacifist Ford, seemed almost eerie in the ease with which he did it, as if he could not help but choose the right tactics.

Billy complained again. "It's because our guys had white coats. Who the hell would put soldiers in white coats? You musta been able to see 'em a mile away and anytime anybody got hit all the dudes around could see all the blood and get freaked out, man!"

"Come on Billy," said Ford, "we got beat because it's Charles's game and even if it wasn't you messed up."

"That's the spirit, Ford," said Finch. "Old Killer here's like your one best buddy and you just dump all over him."

"Yeah," said Billy, "that's the kind of shit that makes you so popular, you little prick."

"Yes, well, I'd just like to know how you think you're going to get away with egging the Blaylock buses this Halloween and not get caught like you did last year. You can't even get a bunch of toy soldiers halfway across a dining room table without getting them slaughtered."

"Oh man, that's bullshit," Billy protested. "That's a whole different thing. I only got caught last year 'cause of some dumb-ass MAA . . ."

"And the same MAA will probably get you this year," said Ford.

"You definitely need to reconsider your tactics," observed Finch.

"What's this about egging buses?" Charles asked.

He put some Cokes and ginger ales on the table and tossed Finch the church key while he worked an opener around the top of a can of pretzels. Outside, far off in the sky above the jungled hills, he could see one white cloud.

>< >< ><

The sky grew darker for days after the battle as overhead the clouds thickened into an immense Navy-gray blanket. From the shelter of the carport under the second story of the Barkers' duplex, Charles could see a broad stretch of the western horizon blacken with an approaching storm. Far off to the right, barren hillsides purpled in the false twilight; to the left, the trees around a spur of SOQ Hill changed to wind-tousled silhouettes while he watched. Ahead, the first flash of lightning cracked vivid white-orange across a score or so miles of sea, and beyond the jungle one could almost see the whitecaps burst under the steady push of the black wall.

Long seconds after the first flash, the first boom shook the ground under Charles's feet and the rain, previously gentle, bucketed down. Trees and shrubs contorted, branches thrashing or reaching for the ground as if to brace themselves. A car driving along Finback switched on its headlights and immediately braked at the sight of the rough flood forming in the street. Another flash shot vertically down to the mountains; Charles turned his head away and blinked; a moment later the boom rocked him on his feet. In the light of the next flash Charles saw Billy, hunched over like a soldier under fire, running across the sodden turf from next door.

"Jesus!" said Billy when he made the shelter of the carport. "Betcha the goddamn bus is late, too!"

They backed away from the edge of the carport. Raindrops pulverized themselves against the waterlogged earth and rose as a mist that the wind carried. Charles got as wet as Billy: they stayed under the carport not to keep dry, but to keep the rain from beating them to death. Billy shouted something. Charles couldn't make it out, so Billy stepped closer and shouted again. "Why aren't you out camping?"

"Oh right," shouted Charles, back in Billy's ear.

"Grunts do it in 'Nam alla time!"

"They don't have a choice!"

"Pussy!"

"You never come out at all, you little cunt!"

Charles startled himself, but the word fit. Billy bristled.

"Cunt yourself, pussy! I'm as bad as any of you mothers!"

"Not till you prove it out there, you little cocksucker!" Charles pointed across Finback to the jungle blurring behind a watery curtain.

"Look, the bus!" Billy shouted. One block down the Blaylocks bus unleashed a racing dependent and waddled back into the stream. Charles and Billy splashed down the driveway to intercept it, waving their arms and shouting to get the driver's attention.

Inside, the bus steamed and misted with wet bodies and the spray that came through windows that would not quite close. The driver used a rag to wipe the fog from the windshield and leaned forward to take his bearings during the one of every three seconds in which the wipers cleared the view. Billy and Charles sprawled over seats across from each other near the front and let the water drip off them onto the clammy vinyl seats and the slimy metal floor. They looked at each other and laughed, partly with the giddiness of survivors, and partly with mischievous irony. The Philippine bus system that worked the base had saved them from the storm, and they planned to repay it by getting off at the base commissary and buying enough eggs to turn it into tempura five days from now, on Thursday night, Halloween.

Billy couldn't tell Charles how, when, or why the tradition started, but neither wondered much. Perhaps the Blaylocks bus, with its crude lettering, clumsy construction, and frequent malfunctions, carrying a largely Filipino cast of maids, houseboys, and gardeners on a faithful half-hour run through all the American housing areas, reminded the boys too much of where they now lived. Or maybe they just realized they could get away with it.

The rain eased and the sky lightened. Charles looked back over the seats behind him, lightly occupied on this Saturday afternoon. He tried to imagine what it would feel like to ride this bus at the end of a workday when it teemed with Filipino workers leaving the wharves, warehouses, and ship repair facility. Billy had described his one experience with loathing: "Smelly Joes with bad BO and fresh grease in their hair chattering like a buncha goddamn monkeys! I just about puked, man." What Charles saw now seemed strange but not revolting. A few maids wore white dresses like nurses. A handful of men wore barongs or white dress shirts with dark slacks. They talked, not chattered, in a series of clearly articulated and musical, almost percussive twangs. They had skin the color of stained wood, from pine to oak to mahogany, and glossy black hair that the men combed straight back in trim pompadours. Charles thought about the British in India and the French in Algeria. Here America had its own.

When Charles's history teacher—the one who'd married a Filipina and lived off base with her and their children—learned of Charles's love for military history, he suggested some books on the Philippine Insurrection. Charles responded eagerly: having read everything the base library had to offer on Queen Victoria's little wars, he looked forward to reading about the American equivalent.

And so Charles learned that in 1898 the Filipinos had their own revolutionary army, the Katipunaan, and had nearly won their country back from the Spanish when Admiral Dewey steamed into Manila Bay and sank the Spanish fleet. When the Spanish garrison commander in Manila surrendered, he gave the Americans everything he controlled—rather, the ground he and his soldiers had just finished standing on—and responsibility for explaining to the Katipunaan that America now owned their country. The Katipunaan demurred, and the effort to convince them eventually employed the entire regular Army of the United States as well as most of the Navy and Marine Corps. It took several years, but with the assistance of modern rifles, Gatling guns, artillery, village burning, and the occasional torture and execution of prisoners, America prevailed.

Charles and Billy left the bus at the commissary and first bought a couple of sodas for cover. Then they each bought two dozen eggs. They might have picked more but Billy warned Charles not to do anything that would make them look conspicuous. At the checkout the clerk smiled; Charles wondered if she planned to ride the bus Thursday night.

Outside the commissary they ran into Joe and Luiz. Joe said they'd just made it: he'd read a memo his father had left out on their coffee table and saw that the next day the admiral would issue an order to prevent juveniles from buying eggs without adult supervision. Joe and Luiz had just come down to finish stocking their arsenal with another two dozen each.

On the ride back Charles kept his commissary bag rolled up tight and tucked closely to his side. At first he'd only worried about sneaking the eggs past his mother and hiding them from the maid. Now he wondered if any of the Filipinos on the bus knew what he had and, if so, what they would think. He also wondered for the first time what Filipinos thought about the names Americans called them. They had to know. *Joes,* for example, which came from all those kids running behind jeeps after the war and screaming for gum and cigarettes, yelling "Hey, Joe!" Could they resent that? What about *Flips,* a handy, only slightly disdainful, contraction? They must have heard worse. Around Clark, for example, for reasons now obscure, Americans called Filipinos *Beaks.* And around the turn of the century, while fearfully patrolling the sticky vined forests of Mindanao, inventing the .45 to knock down Moro warriors before they could close with bolos, interrogating guerrillas by pumping gallons of water into their bellies and kneeling on them, and plotting the kidnapping of Aguinaldo—the local version of George Washington—Americans called Filipinos *Goo-Goos.* But sometimes, even then, we called them their right name. A popular soldier's song, sung to the tune of "Tramp, Tramp, Tramp" went "Damn, damn, damn the Filipinos . . ." and concluded with the words "underneath the starry flag, civilize 'em with a Krag, and return us to our own beloved homes . . ." *Krag* meaning a Krag-Jorgensen magazine-fed, bolt-action rifle we killed insurgents with when they stayed too far away to pump up with a water hose. It occurred to Charles that he had no idea what the Spanish had called the Filipinos.

>< >< ><

Five nights later, on Halloween, Charles and Billy ranged the full length of Finback Drive, from the dead end on SOQ Hill all the way down to its intersection with the road from the rear gate. Near the Kalayaan O Club they met up with Luiz and the Wongs and caught the twenty-one hundred bus in a perfect ambush, several salvos hitting it front, flank, and rear, with the last egg breaking beautifully in a long smear across the windshield. That and some horseplay around the club exhausted the supply of eggs Charles and Billy had on them, so they walked back up SOQ Hill to their cache. They found their remaining eggs where they'd left them, under a bush in the front yard of a marine major. Two cartons. As they made the retrieval the twenty-one thirty bus drove by, passing before they could get into position. Not that it much mattered: by this time—its second run—the bus had received so many hits that it looked like a flock of vultures had spent the whole of the previous week using it for target practice. Still, they thought they might have one last grand go at it. They snuck back to Billy's house, through the yard, and hopped the fence to the ten-foot-wide strip cleared between the houses and the jungle. There they crouched, looked around for the Negrito perimeter guard, then moved quickly and quietly past half a dozen duplexes toward the end of Finback. Here the road dropped beneath a hill with a little playground and ended in a T lined with five more duplexes. The playground, Charles and Billy decided, would make a great firebase. When the bus hit the T it had to back up and change gears repeatedly in order to turn around, the whole time remaining less than ten yards from the hill that rose steeply to a few feet over its top. Yet when Charles and Billy got to the playground they saw half a dozen nine- and ten-year-olds already in the position. Charles pulled Billy down to the ground and whispered, "Okay, listen to me."

"Fuck that," Billy whispered back. "Let's just go up and waste them."

"Right. They got three times as many arms and probably four times as many eggs and at this distance even they can't miss."

Billy looked thoughtful, then suspicious. "What? You wanna just go away?"

"Nah. You help me pull this off and last year's bust is truly history. Plus, I might talk to the other guys about letting you into the post."

"I don't give a rat's ass about being a pussy Explorer Scout."

"Sure. Now listen up."

Charles carefully raised the bottom of the chain-link fence so Billy could squeeze through. The streetlight at the end of Finback lit the younger boys well but faded at the perimeter of the playground; a jungle gym and a pair of seesaws partially blocked the children's view of the back, had they decided to look back. After Billy set up, Charles circled around the outside of the fence, silently counting to a hundred. At a hundred he added another twenty, just to make sure, then lobbed one egg high into the streetlight's glow where Billy could see it. As it crashed down, Billy jumped up behind the younger boys and let fly, yelling, "Gotcha, ya little motherfuckers!"

The children yelled and leapt up in confusion, two running down the hill toward Finback, two cowering, and two turning to face Billy, eggs in hand. At that moment Charles rose, threw from enfilade behind the fence, and shouted, "Run for your lives, ya little fucks!" The two cowering boys bolted; the two with eggs threw wildly and ran off after their friends. Charles and Billy raced for the abandoned position, yelling and continuing to throw to complete the rout. They found three cartons, one half empty, one stepped on and entirely smashed, and one with ten more grade A extra large. At twenty-two hundred they bombarded the bus mercilessly on its fourth run of the evening. They still had half a dozen eggs left.

"Man, that was great," said Billy. "The way we got those kids and creamed the bus. Fucking great, just like a buncha hard-core grunts, man."

"Nah, that's not right," said Charles. "Grunts get ambushed, man—we were like Charlie. No, Charlies are in 'Nam. We were like the Katipunaan."

Billy frowned, ready to object. But below them a jeep suddenly pulled up, with four MAAs in whites, billy clubs and flashlights at the ready. Charles said it again—"Katipunaan!" and both boys quickly buffeted the sailors with the remaining eggs before hopping the fence and escaping to Billy's house on the path between the base and the jungle.

VIII

HEARTS DON'T MEAN SHIT

The seasons passed normally after Halloween, but not in a way familiar to Charles. No chill fall followed summer, and the jungle did not turn into a wholesale display of yellow, orange, and red. The wind did not roll carpets of oak and maple leaves into little streetside whirlwinds or bring the smell of wood smoke, apple pie, and cinnamon-spiced cider. The wind came instead off the ocean with a gift of several showers a day and the occasional three-day deluge. In between, periods of gray drizzle would haunt the jungle in the view outside the Barkers' dining room window, sometimes broken by an hour or two of bright sunshine and the heavy odor of rotting leaves.

Fall led Charles to think about girls and fantasize more than ordinarily about sex. During summer break back home, when he spent most of his time indoors painting toy soldiers and studying the campaigns of Frederick the Great, girls seemed an abstraction: confusing, diaphanous specters who invaded his dreams with new and troubling urges. With dawn they generally went away. But now, well into the school year, he thought about them all the time. He couldn't help it. They sat in all his classes, surrounded him in the schoolyard, and filled the Teen Club as objects of curiosity and unsettling desire. High school girls now—not the burgeoning children of last year, but young women, *chicks*, with the faces of angels and the curves of succubi, skirts clinging to rounded buttocks, stockings outlining supple legs, blouses revealing the promise of breasts, and hinting mysterious ecstasies in a hundred ways with scents, hairstyles, the color of lips and fingernails, the flash of a meaningful or torturing smile. He had only a tenuous idea of what sex actually involved, half of it coming from the health department pamphlets his father gave him in lieu of the mutually dreaded man-to-man talk about birds and bees, and half from the overheard boasts of boys who may or may not have known their subject. The pamphlet's line drawings could just as easily have illustrated a disease, and the tone of the overheard boys might just as well have described a military triumph over another species. So he spent his days immersed in sex like a new diver among the unfamiliar flora of a reef.

Charles mulled it over in a booth in the Teen Club the Friday night after Nixon's election. All the way down SOQ Hill Billy had complained bitterly about "chicks not putting out" when both he and Charles knew that the condition probably reflected an individual judgment rather than a universal prejudice. And now, sitting across from Luiz, with Carl Wong and Ed Sanders on the wall side eagerly listening to the Guamanian's stories over the sound of Santana playing on the jukebox off Ed's dime, Charles had to hear that judgment proved, at least as it applied to Olongapo. If one believed Luiz, the whole town existed for no other purpose than to collect the dollars and semen of American military personnel. The mayor herself, widow of the assassinated former mayor, oversaw the inspection of bar girls in an effort to keep the VD rate to reasonable levels, this despite the existence of clubs where nubile Filipinas demonstrated their willingness to accept anything into their vaginas by practicing with cigarettes ("Imagine," said Luiz, "smoke rings"), beer bottles, and, on special occasions, carabao. Carl shook his head and slurped the remnants of a soda through a straw in a manner hinting disbelief, but Charles could confirm at least part of it. Commander Barker had left a copy of a confidential report from the Naval Hospital lying out on the family's rattan Public Works end table one recent evening. After a brief account of the latest brawl between sailors and marines at the Navy recreational facility on Grande Island, the report noted that the 15 percent casualty rate suffered by the latest marine battalion landing team to enjoy a three-day liberty in Olongapo closely matched what it might have expected from a moderate firefight in Vietnam.

"You might not want to believe Luiz," added Charles, "but I'm pretty sure the Navy wouldn't lie about something like that."

"Damn," Ed remarked to Luiz, "why do you even bother with shit like that? Aren't you afraid your dick's gonna rot off or something?"

"It ain't that bad," replied Luiz, blowing his own smoke rings from a Kool. "I wash my rubbers out myself. And you just gotta watch out for a few basic rules, you know? Like never argue with a Joe pimp—some chief did that last week and *boom!* Shot him right in the head. Bleed to death in a jeepney before he get back to the main gate."

"Oh, man," said Carl, looking up from his straw.

"But more than that, cats," Luiz continued, "don't never act like a chick is a whore unless you know it, and never—like never, ever—insult any Joe's family, especially his sister or mother. That get you a Filipino haircut for sure." He drew his finger across his throat.

Lee Ann appeared, put her hand on Luiz's shoulder, then drew a cigarette from the pack in his shirt pocket with a gesture so seductively graceful that it held Charles in a state of awe. He recovered just in time to catch a drop of drool before it rappelled off his lower lip.

"Any of you boys seen Jim?" Lee Ann asked.

Carl, Charles, and Ed quickly shook their heads. Luiz reached up to light her Kool with a Zippo and said, "Hey sweet, he be here any minute; why don't we have a dance and give him something to worry about?"

"What, is the band starting?"

"Right now. I go tell them."

As if they overheard, the Filipino combo in the adjoining room kicked off their first set with a jumping cover of "Dancing in the Streets." Lee Ann led Luiz out on the floor, swatting his hand from her ass en route, and the three other scouts left their booth to wander into the dark inside the hall. There they separately attempted to look casual and only mildly curious while scanning the room for girls who might not say no.

Faces appeared in the dim light as if to challenge Charles. A girl from his math class with whom he'd once exchanged a few words about the weather; a girl from history who'd watched him the whole time he gave a report on the Philippine Insurrection and even asked a question afterward. It hardly mattered what they looked like—he saw a broad band of possibility between too-ugly-to-appear-with and too-gorgeous-to-even-consider. Still, his tension rose and he strongly considered going in to see whether Billy and Ford had a game going in the poolroom. But then he saw MacReady. Goofy-ass Not-Ready, his thick, oily orange hair curling up like waves slamming into rocks, his spacy blue eyes like headlights in his peeling scarlet face, boogying like crazy in beachcombers and flipflops with a girl who looked a lot better than one would expect. If even MacReady could do it, Charles knew he could never excuse himself. He spied the girl from math class—light brown hair, pink culottes, pale flesh of indeterminate contour—and moved to her like a tentative moray in a reef full of competing hazards. From the corner of his eye he saw Carl and Ed watching him.

The song ended just as Charles reached her, bringing a quiet that loomed like the cliff over the golf course, but at least he didn't have to shout.

"Okay," she said.

A minute passed while the band adjusted their equipment. Joe appeared at the entrance from the lobby wearing his white Ace vest and scoping the crowd with the same look someone would use to pick out gate crashers at a private party. Charles hoped he didn't see him. Two Kittens ran up to Joe and giggled some information they seemed to find important. Traci and Cissy—Charles knew their names from school—one blond, one brunette, medium height, pretty much the same down to the girdles and underwiring: everybody treated them like little Venuses but, Charles thought, one could just as easily get a stiffy for a Barbie doll.

The band hit up the opening of "Land of a Thousand Dances." Charles reached out to the math class girl, Beth—just narrowly brushing her hand—and led the way onto the dance floor. He had hardly ever felt so awkward, but at least he managed to sway as convincingly as most of the dozen or so other boys out there and no one seemed to notice him more than anyone else. With all his self-consciousness he didn't really notice Beth at all till the song had nearly come to an end: she swayed noticeably slower than the music and stared vacantly off to the side, either bored or doing a credible job of looking that way. When the song ended Charles asked if she wanted to dance again. She smiled and said, "Well, maybe later. I see one of my girlfriends," and ran off on her own gigglingly vital errand.

Flushed, Charles couldn't bear to try again. He headed back to the snack bar only to run into Joe and Jim.

"Tough luck," said Joe, "looks like you're gonna be dating your palm for a number of years yet."

"Assuming you haven't done this before," said Jim, "that was very good. Most dudes make the mistake of going right after another chick when they get turned down. Then they wonder why she says no. This *is* your first time, right?"

"Is it that obvious?"

"Is now," laughed Joe.

Over the next few weeks the weather gave signs of becoming hot and dry, which made it seem all the stranger to Charles that George Dewey High School would put on a Christmas pageant and that carols would play over the PA systems at the PX and commissary. Still, moments came when one could almost believe in the holidays, moments in the dark of the big movie theater on the main station when the AC cranked all the way up recalled memories of winter, or even at the GDHS pageant when Finch soloed on the trumpet in "White Christmas." Sometimes Charles's desire for a girlfriend became very strong then—not just for imagined sex, but for someone with whom to exchange gifts, to go places, or even to talk to about something other than sports, war, or other kinds of scoring. Charles didn't realize what a sucker he looked like until one day after English when he ran into Cissy and she batted her eyes at him, asked about the jungle, then suggested they meet after school in the library, hinting that she'd give him a ride home, which in itself hinted at even more. He should have realized his chances with a sophomore Kitten bordered on considerably less than nothing, but he went to the library anyway. After ninety minutes he checked out a book on the Boer War, walked half a mile to the main road, and caught the Blaylocks bus home.

His mother met him at the door. She had dressed for dinner at the O Club and had a manhattan in hand. Probably a bourbon and ginger waited upstairs for Commander Barker when he got home. Mrs. Barker looked worried but not angry.

"Where were you, honey?" she asked.

"School," said Charles. "I stayed after to check this out." He held up the book.

"Oh thank God. With this place I never know. Try to call next time, okay sweetheart?"

"Sure Mom." He went up to his room. Funny, he thought, that she should worry about him coming home late from school and not think twice about his going to the Teen Club. But how could she know about the drinking in back, the Aces and Kittens, or the way her son looked at girls on the dance floor after getting an earful of the adventures of Jim and Luiz?

"Tell me about town again," Charles asked Luiz. A light rain that may have ended fifteen minutes before dripped through the leaves over their heads and gradually changed their fatigues from pale green to black.

Luiz threw a smoldering butt into the stream lapping at his boots and made a soft kissing sound to accompany it when it hit the water. A few hours earlier their buddies or fathers had dropped them off at the riding rink several miles from the main road, where a few acres of fenced pasture sat surrounded by hills and jungle. After Fitzroy and MacReady showed up the post marched farther up the stable road to the base sawmill, then half a mile up a firebreak to a stream, then another mile till the stream bumped into a waterfall where a twenty-foot escarpment stood in their way. Edgefield had then ordered a ten-minute halt, at some point of which the hidden sky began to wring out a desultory rain.

Luiz took off his cap, leaned back against a rock, and let the drops fall gently on his face. He spoke as if reciting a pleasant, half-forgotten dream.

"Short time, twenty pesos. Five bucks. Long time, maybe twenty dollar. Blow jobs, maybe sometime only a buck. One time I'm sitting in a club and some Joe comes up, he say, 'Blow job, two dollar?' and I say, 'Okay, but no bacla boy, okay?' So I like unzip and move in to the table, right, and I'm waiting and waiting you know, checking out the bar girls who walk by, hoping she not be too ugly . . ."

"You're such a romantic," interjected Jim from a neighboring rock.

". . . and finally this asshole come back and slam a little bag of pot on the table and he say, 'Here, Joe—blow your mind!' and I say, 'Shi-it!'"

Charles sighed. Christmas approached with no likely girl in sight and all around him new kids appeared and others left as their fathers rotated in from or back to the States or other bases overseas. Even had he met someone, she might leave within weeks according to some secret schedule maintained by a nameless sailor in BUPERS back in the World. No time to lose and here he sat wet-assed in the jungle and why? He looked around at the boys in the post, soaking in the dripping wilderness: his gang, his crowd. *You have to hang with someone,* he thought.

And, not having a girl at the moment, he didn't see many alternatives. Billy and Ford didn't like to get defeated too frequently in toy soldier games, so sometimes the three of them would visit the Naval Station's bowling alleys and play ninepin, or they'd try the miniature golf course, best late in the day when the sun wouldn't make them blind yet before the mosquitoes massed for their dusk assaults. They could also see free movies, but the same one played every night for a week. Or the pool, where they might see Luiz talking up a senior in a bikini and, if they could focus on his patter rather than their own inexpressible aches, perhaps learn something.

None of that this weekend. Charles sat up, almost as an experiment, tugging at his rain-heavy pack with its useless change of underwear and socks and four clunky boxes of canned rations. His left foot slipped off the bank into the creek as he tried to balance himself, but his full boot couldn't get any wetter, only cooler. "A lot of squids take drugs?" he asked.

"A lot," said Jim. "Personally I prefer San Miguel . . ."

"Tanduay and Coke," said Luiz.

". . . I can go all night on that shit. But there's lots of reds around, and pot, and acid, and—this being your fucking Orient—opium. I guess you can get anything you want in Olongapo."

"Yeah, lotsa dudes be gettin' high," said Luiz, "but not enough."

"I hear you, bro," said Jim. "Some of those fuckers are downright dangerous when they get to drinking, which is another thing to look out for. You don't want to hang out if there're grunts and squids in the same bar. Usually it's the grunts on their way to 'Nam who're the worst. Those bastards don't care how many squids are around when they start something—they'd just as soon get busted up in Olongapo as in fucking Hue."

"The base marines, though," said Luiz, "they real careful. They like case a place before kicking up the shit. They got lookouts and a guard by the rear door and everything. They'll like womp up on six or seven squids then clear out thirty seconds before the shore patrol shows up. Never get caught, man."

"They say it didn't used to be like that," said Jim. "I mean, squids and grunts would fight, you know, but not this rib-busting ganglike shit. They had esprit, Old Navy style, you know? Guys from a ship would hang out in their own clubs, hook up with whores long time. Old chiefs would get their young swabbies bred careful by some old mama-san who knew how to do it right and hadn't had a case of clap in years. And them and the old gunny sergeants would make sure shit stopped before anybody got more than a few teeth knocked out. Real righteous people who loved their ships like their old ladies. Better, I guess. I swear to Christ, they'd even get together and sing in the goddamn bars, like 'Bell Bottom Trousers' or 'San Francisco, Here I Come' or even that shit about the monkeys in Zamboango. Old Navy, man, not like this crazy shit they got going now where nobody gives a fuck."

"That's what the whores say, anyway," said Luiz.

The bush fluttered and rustled twenty feet away across the stream and Edgefield appeared, back from a solo scout ahead. He looked over the rest of the post scattered on the bank and grinned broadly. "Ah, yes. Look at all the hard-assed mother-fuckers. I'm gonna miss ya, girls."

"What's that mean?" asked Charles.

"Aintcha heard?" said Joe behind him. "Edge's old man's waitin' on his orders. Probably move his ass out before graduation."

"Do they do that?" Charles asked. Everybody laughed except Tom and George. George said, "Well, Charles, you can't always expect the Navy to respect the school year in wartime."

Tom's voice nearly broke. "Marsha's father's supposed to get his soon, too."

"Oh man," said his little brother Ed, "that bitch was *never* gonna put out for you." The rest of the boys laughed even louder at that, but Tom jumped up, both fists clenched. "You little *animal!*" he yelled.

"Whoa, whoa, whoa," said Edgefield. "None of that black on black shit while I'm still here. Tom, sit down and relax. Ed, shut the fuck up. Finch, you come with me. I think I found a path that'll get all our young ladies up around this waterfall."

"Why him?" asked Joe. "Why you always picking him? Why the fuck should I have to be the one to stay here and baby-sit?"

Edgefield's gray eyes turned hard and fixed on Joe. Then they quickly tracked over the faces of the rest of the post as if to make sure everyone would stay shut up. The scouts all wondered what would happen. Not in the next moment, but weeks or months from now after Edgefield had gone. He could pretty much name his successor—Finch or Joe. Edgefield nodded. "Okay, Joe. Come on. Jim and Luiz, you guys keep Tom and Ed from going Zulu on each other."

"That's racist, man," said Ed.

"Oh shut up," said Tom.

Jim rose, walked over, and sat down between them. "Please don't hurt me bloods, okay?" Luiz laughed and joined him.

Edgefield, Joe, and Finch crossed the stream and disappeared. After a few minutes even the sound of their clambering up the escarpment faded. Fitzroy, still the nominal adult, still—after several trips—wearing his sailor's dungarees instead of fatigues, stood, stretched his Ichabod Crane figure, and yawned. "What you boys gonna do when that big fellow leaves?"

"Jeepers, I thought you were asleep," said MacReady.

"I was, but then somebody said the word *home* and I woke up."

Luiz said to Jim, "That Finch, he like a regular fucking John Paul Jones."

Jim nodded and wiped his glasses with the inside of his fatigue cap. "Yup. Like fifth-generation nav. He told me once there've been Finches jockeying U.S. warships in every scrap the Navy's been in since the Civil War, and he wasn't sure but that they didn't cover both sides of that one, too."

"Yeah, like when he make admiral maybe he can get *my* ass in Annapolis."

"But he is a *little* fuck," Jim continued, "and I get tired of all this rulebook shit sometimes. Joe's okay."

Charles felt he should say something. He liked Finch. Finch seemed a lot bigger than he looked. He couldn't tell about Joe.

"I don't know," said Luiz. "Joe more Ace than Explorer. And in town, you know, you and me and Edgefield, we'll hang out, watch each other's ass. Joe out with that Bandit group, fucking biker crowd. Don't see him much."

"Why are you guys talking like it's just those two?" asked George. He stood up a little uncertainly, brushed his broad behind, and adjusted his web belt over his belly. "Some of us others might want to run. I mean, some of us are good scouts, too, and get good grades."

Fitzroy let out a single contemptuous laugh and gestured at the overhanging trees. "Son, just look at where you're at. Just look at where all of you are at. I'll be shipping out in a little while myself, and my service'll be done with. But yours is all before you, and most of it's gonna involve places where grades won't mean shit."

"Oh, man," said Jim, perhaps thinking of Lee Ann, "why am I even out here?"

"Hey, cat, the jungle's cool."

"And you heard Fitzroy," said Carl, checking his bolo. "Might as well get some practice."

The next weekend the scouts did not camp out, and most of them ended up at the Teen Club. Charles walked down SOQ Hill with Billy as usual, but then they separated. While Billy walked outside to the back of the club to buy rum, Charles wandered through the club trying to look at girls without seeming too obvious. He'd brought along a copy of *Don Quixote*—a book Las Casas, his English teacher, had recommended—to help: if worse came to worse he could imitate Ford and simply sit in a corner and read. But he knew two or three girls besides Beth whom he talked to between classes, although usually about classes. They seemed attractive enough, but he knew he could get only so far with conversations about quadratic equations or the Ashanti War. And it remained unclear at what point in any conversation it suddenly became appropriate to hold hands or simply lunge. As he looked around the club at the girls there—white girls, Asian girls, black girls, girls mixed in combinations perhaps peculiar to the Navy, girls with full breasts, firm buttocks, or both—he realized that his thoughts about sex, all his fantasies and hopeful enactments, all somehow skipped that critical point between verbal introductions and frantic humping.

In the dance room he saw Tom in a dark corner talking to Marsha while the band set up. They looked funny together: Tom around five-ten, skinny and gangly, a light-skinned Negro with freckles and short-short hair with a slight reddish tinge. His eyes bugged a little, as if he wore invisible glasses. Marsha must have stood about five inches shorter though she weighed just as much. Stocky but not fat, her huge breasts jutted out like the engines on a B-52, while her long, straight blond hair framed a large-boned face. A real Valkyrie. Charles wondered how Tom ever thought they could make a couple. Tom seemed to plead with her now, though Charles couldn't hear what they said. Marsha's eyes glistened and she reached for Tom's hand. Tom turned away and put his hands on his face. When he turned back she had already begun to walk away crying. Charles didn't want Tom to see that he had seen, so he left in a hurry and went straight back to the poolroom where he knew he'd find Finch and maybe Ford. But Ford had not yet arrived.

"His family's sponsoring some new civilians," Finch explained. "He might be by later to show one of their kids around if they got any kids old enough to get in. Wanna shoot some pool?"

"Yeah, okay. Ford's probably just as happy home, reading."

"Could be."

Finch had time to beat Charles twice before Tom entered, staggering slightly, and almost weeping at the sound of "Hey Jude" playing over the PA system. He leaned on the pool table and sang softly to himself, "Remember to let her into your heart . . ." His brother Ed looked over from the next table and shook his head. Ed had let his hair grow out to the limits of the regs as a kind of embryonic Afro. Tom sighed, "That Marsha. We were talking about what was gonna happen once her dad got his orders, you know, and she said she'd write. She'd *write!* Can you believe it? 'We've been going steady *five months*,' I tell her. 'Doesn't that mean anything to you?' I ask her."

"Good Lord," said Finch, "what do you want her to say? You're sixteen years old for God's sake. You wanna get married?"

Carl Wong, who had the stripes to Ed's solids, laughed while his brother George tried to comfort Tom.

"Come on, fellow. Many more opportunities will present themselves."

Ed got angry. "You *know* what the problem is, man. Open your motherfucking eyes. You *black!* Ain't no way that white cow gonna hook up with you!"

"You are just so stupid," Tom said bitterly.

Joe walked in the door from the snack bar, saw the Sanders and the Wong brothers, and said, "Hey, what's this, the back of the bus?"

"You *see!*" Ed exclaimed.

Finch took a shot and without looking up from the table said, "Only one color in the Navy, Barone, or one at a time. White in the summer and black in the winter; khaki when orders permit."

"So how come the only color I see on officers is white?" asked Ed.

Finch looked up from the table. "Well, that'll change when you get in, won't it?"

The PA system cut off and they could hear the band tuning up. Joe grinned, saluted Ed, and went out the way he came. Charles wanted to leave but he had to remain while Finch finished beating him. The group playing tonight called themselves the In Crowd; Jim had told Charles about them. They played the Mod Club in town and couldn't really remember where they'd picked up the name. Jim couldn't believe they'd never heard of the song by the Mamas and the Papas so he taught it to them and they liked it enough to use as a kind of theme. Some nights they let Jim sing lead on it, amused at the sight of the skinny, rabbit-faced dependent in a white short-sleeved shirt with hair just an inch short of looking mod fronting for them in their dark, Teddy-boy outfits. Charles wanted to see if they'd do it tonight.

Still, Charles tried to give Finch a run for his money. He found it more difficult than usual, with Tom whining about Marsha and swearing to swim out to Corregidor and get eaten by sharks if she didn't promise to love him through eternity. Tom only shut up when Ford came in with the new girl.

They all shut up, suddenly occupied with the effort of assessing a dozen questions of desirability and accessibility. Like the others, Charles tried to look her over without seeming to, or without seeming to as much as the other boys. Like them, he failed.

Only Ford didn't stare. Instead he scrunched up in awkwardness at the thought of appearing in public with a girl, particularly one nearly half a foot taller, a discrepancy in height he accentuated by practically folding in on himself.

"Good evening, gentlemen," he murmured, "this is Joan."

Joan stood just a little shorter than Charles, slender, unmuscled, Hershey-brown hair side-parted and falling lankly down to an inch above her collarbone, her collarbone very white just above the round neck of her sleeveless pale blue shift. She had a fine, thin face, nose just a little long, brown eyes wide set and a little large. She didn't strike Charles as especially pretty, and not really sexy, but intelligent looking, attractive in a way that wouldn't draw competition from some jock he couldn't handle. If, of course, it ever came to that.

"Hello," she said quietly without focusing on any one of them.

Finch stepped forward, shook her hand, and introduced her around with the propriety of the host at an officer's retirement party. He suggested to Ford that they get a booth in the snack bar and have some sodas before introducing Joan to more people.

"Why thank you," she said, and Charles noticed that she had a soft, well-mannered southern accent. George Wong moved in to claim the pool table and shoved a cue in Tom's hand, so Joan went to the snack bar with Finch, Ford, and Charles.

As they took their seats she noticed Charles's book.

"Oh, you're reading Cervantes," she said. She seemed relieved, rather than enthusiastic, to discover a topic. Charles looked down at the fat volume. Years ago he'd read the Classic Comix version, a considerably easier task. It'd taken him more than a week to get halfway through the real book, what with its fine print, archaic language, and loose binding that shed pages one by one as he turned them. But the effort now seemed worth it.

"Yes," he said, "I'm rather enjoying the escapades of the man of La Mancha and his faithful squire. It's amazing how well the satire holds up after so many years."

Ford looked at him blankly. Finch smiled. Joan said, "Yes," and they kept the conversation going for another three or four minutes before the band cranked up again with "Satisfaction." Joan looked distressed, although she also looked like her manners kept her from saying so. Charles wanted to keep talking about *Don Quixote* but he knew he couldn't do it over the band. Even more, he wanted to ask Joan to dance, but she really looked like she wanted to get away. Had the music not filled in, his silence would have embarrassed him half to death.

Across the table from Charles, Joan looked down at her soda and sipped tentatively. Ford fidgeted at Charles's side, while Finch, Charles noticed, looked first at Joan and then at him. Their eyes met and for a moment Finch seemed to study Charles. Charles looked back to Joan: when she suddenly looked up, his mouth opened but no words came out. Instead he heard Finch.

"Charles, I don't care what you told me earlier. You can't possibly finish that chapter in here. Joan looks like she's had a long day. Why don't you walk her home? I know Ford wants to play a few rounds of pool before calling it a night, don't you buddy?"

"Well, I'm not sure . . ." Ford looked around the booth as if someone had just woken him.

"C'mon, don't be modest, champ."

"If you're sure you wouldn't mind," said Joan, already getting up.

"No, no," said Charles. He looked at Finch, ready to thank him, but Finch put a finger to his lips and jerked his head as if to say *just shut up and go*. Charles nodded and led Joan out, carefully parting the crowd of teens and steering her out the door just in time to pass Luiz who, seeing them, gave Charles a thumbs-up and a leering wink.

They walked slowly up the hill to the crossroads and stopped. Left led to where the civilians lived with the junior officers. Right led up SOQ Hill. Joan kept her arms wrapped around her, a little like she might if cold, and fixed her gaze forward and down. Charles kept his hands in his pockets with the book tucked under his right arm. He wondered what to say. He couldn't remember where they'd gotten to with *Don Quixote*. He looked at the park bench by the intersection and wondered whether to ask her to sit, but he could feel the mosquitoes brushing his arms and knew they'd get eaten up if they stopped long. She looked around, first at the few buildings not hidden by trees, and then at the sky over the jungle.

"It's strange here at night," she said, gesturing at the dark banks of foliage.

"The rain forest is all right," said Charles, almost meaning it. "Some of us go camping out there."

She looked shocked. "Isn't it dangerous?"

"Maybe," he said. "But not usually. Here, I'll walk you the rest of the way home."

"Oh, no. No, really. I can find my way. Thank you."

After a brief but tense silence Charles said, "Okay, you'll be fine. Just be careful not to step on any cobras."

Their eyes met. She looked scared. Then Charles smiled and they both began to laugh.

"That's terrible," she said.

"But it's true. C'mon."

"Okay. It's up this way, I think."

They only talked a little after that and it only took them a few minutes to get to her family's quarters. Charles found that they'd received orders from Charleston to Subic halfway through Joan's sophomore year, making her a year older than him. Her father worked with Mr. Wong in Finance on the main naval station. Charles talked about what Commander Barker did at the hospital but managed to avoid mentioning his own age and grade. Maybe going into the jungle would make up for it. They shook hands good night and Charles walked away.

Clouds passed overhead in patches, too high and thin to bring rain, but lit up by the moon and stars like something in a dream. Charles felt suspended halfway up to them, or at least far above the shadows of the trees on the sidewalks of the Kalayaan housing area. He didn't feel like going home or back to the Teen Club: early still, his parents would wonder if something bad had happened; his friends would ask him if something good had. On the way back to the intersection he saw the walkway on the left that led through a small patch of jungle to the BOQ where most of the teachers stayed.

He dashed through the glare of the streetlight to avoid the bugs swarming and the bats that made rapid elliptical dives and glowed with backlit wings. He guided himself along the dark walk with his hand on a steel railing and came out into a dim parking lot in front of a concrete structure that looked like the bastard offspring of a barracks and a motel. He found Las Casas' apartment by sound—the steady thumpathumpa of country bass from a stereo system bought new in Taipei the month before. He knocked.

"Ah, Charles!" exclaimed Las Casas as he opened his door and looked his visitor up and down. "And how are you enjoying the escapades of the man of La Mancha and his faithful squire?" He had asked the same question each time they met for the last two weeks. "Why are you here? You didn't find the Teen Club boring, did you? It's literature you should find boring at your age, you know."

"I wasn't bored," said Charles. "I just had to walk a girl home."

"I remember the first time I read Cervantes. What an experience! I got to feel I knew them, you know? Every day it was *hmmm, I wonder what he and Sancho are up to.* What do you mean you walked a girl home? Have you met someone interesting?"

Someone interesting, thought Charles. He looked at Las Casas, his balding, mustachioed English teacher standing there in his skivvies and T-shirt, and wondered what he did with his weekends.

"Yeah, kinda," Charles said, but realized he didn't want to say much more. Suddenly he didn't feel any better about his understanding and mature teacher interrogating him about Joan than he would about his parents or friends. So he said, "I was talking to Jim and Luiz again. They said they might show me around town if I could manage to sneak out."

Las Casas pulled him in, sat him down, and fetched a Pepsi. Johnny Cash boomed through the room growling about shooting a man in Reno just to watch him die. "Town? Olongapo?" Las Casas asked rhetorically. "Ah, Charles, let me tell you. The pleasures of Sin City are overrated. Believe me. All up and down the western Pacific, sailors and marines are telling salacious stories about their doings in Olongapo, real and imagined—I know, I've heard those stories. And I've been in those bars, too. But what do you think it means, Charles? What do you think of when people tell endless stories of endless booze and drugs and sex and more sex? What do you think it means?"

Charles scrinched up his face. "I don't know. They're getting high and getting laid and having fun?"

"*No!* No, no, no, Charles! Capital *N*, my boy. Nullo, nada, nihil, nope, nothing! Believe me. You know, I go out there, I get my beer, and I—well, you know, whatever—and whatever it is I do end up doing, it seems I always end up in some grungy goddamn bar and it's two in the morning and all I see around me— all the uniforms and all the mini skirts—are all just children and poor people, children and poor people. And I guess the poor people know what they're after . . ."

"Money?"

"That was easy. Money, yes; maybe power of some sort . . ."

"Power?"

"Well, forget them. But the children—the children! I don't know, Charles, but I sit there with my beer and look at all those little children in their uniforms, so tough, and I wonder what they get for their money. Short time, long time, blow jobs under the barroom table—I tell you, Charles, those kids'll come a thousand times but when they get over to 'Nam they're still gonna die virgins."

Charles stared hard, pondering Las Casas' words like a particularly difficult passage of Shakespeare thrown before the class.

"You don't understand, do you Charles?"

"I'm trying, sir, I really am."

"Well, listen. Forget about Jim and Luiz. They're very nice boys and I'm sure they know exactly what they're doing—in fact I've seen them out there and, yes, I'm pretty sure they do—but forget them. You've just met a very nice girl and walked her home and I think that's lovely. Don't let anybody ruin it by asking you if she put out."

"Hey!"

"I mean it, Charles . . ."

"Why are you so sure she didn't?"

Las Casas sat on a stool next to the dry bar he picked up on the same trip to Taipai and looked at his charge, first with a kindly and superior expression, but then with a sort of fatigue. "Of course," he said. "I'm sorry. I won't judge you again. Just promise me one thing."

"What, Mr. Las Casas?"

"Don't let this place get to you. Don't do anything here you wouldn't do back home. Don't feel anything here you wouldn't feel back home. You're not a sailor or marine, Charles. The war will end before it gets to you."

Charles took a swig from his soda and listened to the music. Convicts screamed joyfully whenever Cash sang another line about killing or hate. Just the other side of the South China Sea the war went on, just like it had for the last twenty-five or thirty years. Las Casas could kid himself all he wanted.

"Sure," said Charles. "Look, I gotta go. I just wanted you to know I was enjoying the book."

"Sure. Sure. Take it easy, okay?"

Charles didn't hear the door close behind him until he had already disappeared into the dark on the other side of the streetlight.

He saw Joan in school the next week and although she quickly discovered his grade, she didn't pick up too many sophomore friends right away and seemed happy to meet Charles for lunch and talk about books. Ford and Billy cleared out whenever she came near; Charles never asked them to, but he realized he would have done the same for them, and that made him feel closer to those two even as he spent more time with Joan. After a week he found the courage to ask her out to a movie and she said yes. He told Billy and Ford, of course, although when Billy hooted and said, "Right on!" he wished he hadn't. Ford said, "Good luck, I guess," and that made Charles feel even more dishonest, because he hadn't told them that she said yes the same way she might have said yes to a cousin or a girlfriend. Perhaps worse, he suspected he felt more comfortable with it that way.

When they went to the Kalayaan theater to see an odd and confusing foreign film, he didn't even try to hold her hand, although hardly anyone other than the sailor-projectionist had bothered to show up.

The next night he sat in the back of the conference room at FIC-PACFAPFAPL for Post 360's monthly meeting, watching the other boys come in and begin grab-assing. Luiz, obviously thinking of Joan, winked and Charles smiled in return, feeling every bit the liar he'd become. He might have brooded on that, but he heard the Wongs tell the Sanderses that they'd heard that Captain Edgefield had finally received his orders home. Edgefield himself seemed to confirm it when he came in, just by the new buoyancy in his step. Rumor also had it that Annapolis had already given him the nod.

Edgefield jumped to the podium. "All right, all right, all right," he sang. "Listen up, fuckers! We got some new business tonight, lots of new business, so let's get under way!"

"What's up, man?" asked Jim, trying to sound nonchalant.

"Besides you leaving, you lucky fucker," said Joe, a certain nervous hilarity in his voice.

"You jealous?" Luiz asked him.

"No shit, fuckwad. My old man fucking re-upped, son-of-a-bitch asshole that he is. I could kill the motherfucker."

"Oh yeah?" said Jim. "Then who would keep your ass outa Joe jails?"

"Fuck you, asswipe!" Joe seemed genuinely angry.

"Girls, girls, girls," said Edgefield, holding up his hands. "Let's not spoil my final moments with my bunkies by being rude. My heart's already torn in little pieces at the thought of leaving you."

"Suck my dick," said Joe.

"Whip it out and I'll go looking for a magnifying glass."

"New business, new business," said Finch.

"Oh fuck off, shrimp," said Joe.

"Okay, okay, okay," said Edgefield. "That's enough. Now, as some of you know, and as some of you will find out if you quit jacking off long enough to listen, my old man, God bless his ugly soul, has got his orders. San Diego. That's right, ladies: I'm short.

That means a couple of things. First, my last new member to welcome is Killer Billy over there. Yeah, the one holding hands with Ahcharles, whom some of you may know as our new Casanova, but Billy knows better, don'tcha? Yep, stand up and take a bow, Killer. Right—welcome aboard dickhead. Yeah, I'm real proud not to serve with you. Next, I'm gonna be missing out on this year's Death March. That's right, boys, the rumors are true. Come Easter the post is lined up to accompany about six troops of Boy Scouts on a fifty-miler from San Fernando right down the fucking Bataan peninsula. It's gonna be hot, dirty, and smell real unusual, but you know, I am actually gonna miss it. Just think, girls, five days off base! Talk about in-country: there's gonna be maybe one counselor for every twenty guys and half of them are going to be squids looking for the first chance to drop out and get loaded. There's no fucking way they can watch all of you! We went out two years ago and had the scouting experience of a lifetime, man. Six guys got the clap. Seriously. Anyway, I'm going to miss it and that does piss me off, though not much. Third—I am at third, right?

"I think that's C," said Jim.

"Listen up," said Finch.

"Third, whoever follows me in this job has got to do some serious humping to get a new counselor. We got Fitzroy to give his word of honor—I hear you laugh—to hold your dicks for the Death March, but don't count on him after that. The next president is going to have to find somebody permanento, right? Anyway, speaking of the next president, that brings us to the main topic for tonight. Who the fuck wants the job?"

A murmur ran through the group and all the boys shifted in their seats. They looked at each other, surprised to hear Edgefield just throw it out, but wondering if they could have done it any other way. Tom stood up.

"Ah, sit down, man," said Ed.

"Listen," said Tom, "I know no one can really replace Edgefield and you have other fine young men to choose from. I just want to tell you that I'm as ready as anyone to do what needs to be done. I mean, I work hard, I do the best I can, and I know that you guys will make your decision without regard to race, creed, color, or religion."

He looked around the room, nervous but hopeful. No one said anything.

"Uh, thank you."

"I second that," said George.

Ed turned to his brother. "Ah, man, if you'd just run as a black man, tall and proud, even I might have voted for you, even though you're my dickhead older brother. But who the hell you think gonna buy that Good Negro shit here?"

"Look," said Joe, standing suddenly, "we all know it's between me and Finch. Now I ain't saying I can kick his ass—though I can—and I sure as shit ain't gonna *beg* you pussies for anything . . ."

"Geez, Joe," said Jim, "you sure know how to go for *my* vote . . ."

"Blow me. Anyway, like I said, I'm the guy. So why don't we just vote and get it over with?"

"Is that, like, reverse psychology or something?" asked Luiz.

"What the fuck, man," said Joe. "'Reverse psychology'? Somebody teach you to read?"

They all looked at Finch. He stood and looked back. "I don't know whether I want this or not. There's a lot of responsibility in this job, whether you think so or not. I'll stay vice president if you want, and that's the truth. But if you do make me president, I'll take care of it. That's all." He sat down quickly while Joe and Tom still stood.

"Well, well, well," said Edgefield. "Looks like we got us an election here. Anybody got a deck of cards?"

Carl pulled a beat-up pack of Bicycles from his back pocket and held it up.

"Okay," said Edgefield, "pass it around and everybody take one. When you all got your pick, bring it up to me and I'll count them. If you want Joe, take a club—he's a real club kind of guy. If you want Finch, take a diamond. Fucker's little, but he's hard."

"What about me?" asked Tom.

"'That's easy," said Edgefield. "Spades."

"You see?" Ed told his brother. "You see? White man don't care for that Good Negro shit." ·

"But nobody take no hearts," said Edgefield. "Hearts don't mean shit."

They passed the deck around and everyone took a card. When the pack returned to Carl the scouts went up one by one to Edgefield and turned in their pick. Edgefield counted them and then announced that Finch had won.

"What was the score?" asked Joe.

"You don't want to know," said Edgefield. "But you came in second. How about vice president?"

"Oh sure. Why the fuck not?"

"That's it, then," said Edgefield. He looked around the room for a moment, then nodded to Finch. "They're all yours," he said.

"All rise!" Finch shouted, standing and saluting. Surprised, Charles nearly knocked over his chair as he got up. Beside him Jim whispered, "Salute with three fingers, man, not the whole hand. You're an Explorer Scout, not a squid."

Charles quickly corrected his salute as Edgefield walked past to the door.

That night Charles rode home with Edgefield and Finch one last time, listened to their tales of Death Marches in the past, and realized that he really didn't care to go. He could do overnighters in the jungle now, but he couldn't see any point in five whole days marching down dusty Philippine highways in the middle of the dry season. People died doing things like that, or at least got extremely uncomfortable. Besides, he'd just met Joan and she didn't know anyone else yet. She could meet anybody while he spent a whole week out in the boondocks working up a ripe smell. He couldn't think of worse timing for something like this. At least he knew how he could get out of it.

At dinner the next evening he sat at the side of the table facing the Zambales Mountains, the sky brutally clear in the late-afternoon sun, the hills in the foreground a tawny yellow. His mother sat across from him studying her rice; Commander Barker sat at Charles's right at the head of the table.

"So Charles, dear," asked Mrs. Barker, weighing a forkful, "how did your scout meeting go last night?"

"Oh great, Mom. Just great. The boys are talking about taking a hike."

"A hike?" she asked. "It's awfully hot this time of year. You're not thinking of the golf course again, are you?"

"Oh, we won't go for another few weeks. It'll probably be even hotter then. But no, we're not going to the golf course."

Commander Barker looked up from his copy of *Stars and Stripes*. "What are you boys talking about doing?" he asked.

"San Fernando to Bataan, dad. The Death March. You know, like in the war."

"Oh no," said Mrs. Barker. "Death March? You can't be serious. Honey," she turned to Commander Barker, "we can't let Charles do something foolish, can we? Who would send boys on something called the Death March?"

"Ah Mom," said Charles, trying to fill his voice with conviction.

Commander Barker looked at his son, searched his eyes, then turned to his wife. "I don't know, baby. Let me find out more from Captain Edgefield. Then we'll talk about it."

"I don't see what there is to talk about." She stared at her husband with an expression Charles had previously seen only in nature films that showed female raptors guarding their young.

"Okay, he won't go, then," said the commander, and returned to the headline story about a VC rocket attack on Saigon.

That seemed to settle it, but the next day at school Charles realized he had made a mistake. In the hall after second period he ran into Jim, who said, "Man, it'll be tough, but after five days Lee Ann's gonna wanna fuck my brains out." Then Charles ran into Joan.

"I've heard about this hike the Explorers are going on," she said. "You must be awfully excited. I mean, you'll get to see the real Philippines. There's nothing like that for girls here. Promise me you'll tell me all about it when you get back."

"Well, I don't know. I'm not sure my parents will let me go."

"Oh, Charles—you've got to make them let you. You won't have another chance like this. I mean it. I want you to come over as soon as you get back and tell me about it."

"To your house."

"My parents will be gone to Baguio for a few days, but I'm sure it will be okay. Can't you talk to your parents?"

That evening, while Charles relaxed on his bed, read, and tried to think of a new angle, his father came into his room. Commander Barker still wore his khakis from the office, but he'd taken off his hat and when he sat down at the foot of the bed the lamplight brought out the creases on his high forehead and glinted off his scalp where the thinning hair had started to gray, so he didn't look nearly as full of orders as when his son saw him at work. Charles folded up his book but at first his father didn't look at him. Instead he reached over to the desk and picked up a tin horseman.

"Which one is this?" he asked.

"A dragoon," Charles answered. "Regiment number twenty-four, Markgraf Friedrich von Bayreuth. Frederick the Great composed a march for them after their charge at the battle of Hohenfriedburg." He hoped that somehow enough militaristic detail would take his father's mind off the fact that his son still liked to play with toy soldiers.

"You don't say," said Commander Barker, his face crossed between a smirk and a sigh. At one time Mrs. Barker had talked about painting, and had even taken classes during their tour in Yokohama.

Charles still didn't know why his father had come in.

"Look, son: how bad do you want to go on that hike?"

Charles studied him, wondering about angles he knew he'd never see. "I don't know, dad. Maybe Mom's right. It could be hairy."

"But what do you *want*, son?" He put down the toy soldier and looked his son straight in the eyes, a move that always made it a little more difficult for Charles to lie.

"The guys'll be expecting me, Dad. I don't want to let them down."

Commander Barker smiled and patted Charles on the leg. "Then don't worry. I'll take care of your mother."

"Really?"

"Yeah. And one other thing. Those jungle boots of yours. They're two sizes too big. That's okay for those short little walks in the woods you've been taking, but you'll tear hell out of your feet if you wear them on a fifty-miler. I want you to take my old combat boots."

Charles felt a flush wash over him like hot surf. "But you wore those in Korea."

"Yeah, and there were a few nights when I'd have given anything to know that someday I'd be loaning them to my son."

⇥ IX ⇤

THE DEATH MARCH

Scouts and chaperones sprawled in the dust under the concrete bridge, propped against knapsacks, bundled tents, cases of C-rations, and the wheels of their four support vehicles. Some managed to sleep in the airless shade, others still gasped or stared back the way they had come: a view of several miles of white-hot sky over a dirty gray strip of road shimmering with ground haze from the heat. More boys staggered in every few minutes, groups of three or four, sometimes as many as a dozen, with or without scout leaders or adults. As each fragment straggled into the shade, Lieutenant Fleming greeted them, directing the more or less fit to a spot where they could rest and wait for the next move, walking the others to the side of a pickup where a Navy corpsman and an Air Force medic had set up an impromptu aid station. The medical staff, no older than nineteen or twenty themselves, worked casually but briskly, painting blisters, issuing salt tablets, patting their charges on the head or shoulder and sending them off to collapse with their fellows, barely taking time to knock the ashes from their cigarettes. Fleming himself would watch for a few moments, as if to assure himself that the boys would not actually die, and then walk slowly back to his post to wait for the next arrivals. Heavy, thirtyish, short legged—a naval supply officer lately accustomed to long hours in air-conditioned offices—he had not expected his first day on a Boy Scout hike to lead to what looked more than a little like a pending health disaster.

He squinted from behind his aviator shades at four children now about three hundred yards from the bridge and obviously having problems staying on their feet. He should send someone out, he thought, but he didn't have anyone on hand who could go and actually help, except for the medics. He took off his ball cap and wiped his bald crown with a dirty handkerchief. Every boy who came in looked overwhelmed, pushed beyond his limits, and surprised to find himself there. They answered his questions about their troop and the location of their friends as best they could, but in most cases Fleming might as well have asked about the movements of distant stars. Near as he could figure, half of his approximately 150 boys and twenty counselors had yet to come in and he had no way of knowing whether or not they ever would.

Charles watched Fleming from about fifteen yards away where he sat against the wheel of a deuce-and-a-half. He almost felt sorry for the man, but saved his sorrow for himself. His head ached horribly and his stomach felt like it had made plans to jump ship in no more than three minutes. His father's boots clung to his feet like medieval instruments of torture. He suspected that he had about thirty blisters but he had refused the corpsman's offer to take a look. He didn't really want to know.

"This bites," said Joe, and those around him nodded and groaned agreement. Finch looked up and around, then shut his eyes. They had all made it. Post 360 had come in together. No one helped anyone, but somehow Finch had kept the stronger, better-conditioned boys from leaving the others.

"How many miles was that?" Charles asked.

"Sixteen," said Jim. "Sixteen damn miles. They started it out too damn fast, too. We did four miles the first hour. Betcha we lose a few."

More nodding. Tech Sergeant Sipko, who led a troop of air force scouts out of Clark, came by looking crisp and amused. He'd driven one of the trucks; now he wanted to talk to 360's counselor.

"He's over here," said Tom, pointing to a recumbent form in blue denim with an unfolded sailor's cap over his face. "Want me to wake him?"

Sipko shook his head, squatted down, and lit a cigarette. "Hell, it'd be a shame," he replied. "I'll wait." Sipko carried a bit more weight than Fleming, a crew cut the color of smoke, and a complexion darkened more by a permanent flush than by the sun. That morning he had given them all a pep talk after the long bus ride from Subic and the first evening of camping outside Tarlac. They had stood in the searing Easter sun, the first streams of sweat trickling into their eyes, and listened enthusiastically, unburdened by any more than the most abstract concept of what the miles ahead might mean, while Sipko explained:

"They call it the Death March, boys, because this is the route the American and Filipino POWs took after the fall of Corregidor. There was thousands of prisoners but the Nips weren't ready for them. They wanted everybody moved fifty miles in two days but they didn't have the vehicles. So they force-marched them. Guys who'd fought all the way down the Bataan peninsula and holed up in forts for weeks—guys who'd been on half rations, then quarter rations, and only surrendered when they had nothing left to fight with—no ammunition, no food, no strength."

He looked around significantly. The boys ate it up.

"If anybody fell down, the Japs bayoneted him on the spot. If somebody fell out to help his buddy, they shot him down. Joe farmers risked their lives just to get a few mouthfuls of water to the guys, and a lot of them got killed for it. Thousands died those two days, mostly helpless prisoners who'd fought a brave fight and honorably surrendered. No doubt about it, that was a shitty thing for the Japs to do. Made a whole generation of Americans wonder how anybody could ever question why we nuked the slant-eyed little fucks.

"So what do you think, boys? Can you do it? Can you show the world how Americans can do a fifty-miler when they're not all beat to shit beforehand?"

The boys had roared approval and nearly jogged the first miles. Now they lay under the bridge half dead.

"Hey, Sipko," said Jim, "where was the Air Force on Corregidor?"

"They lost all their planes at Clark," said Charles. "Never even got off the ground."

Sipko looked around to find all the eyes of 360 fixed on him, some over contemptuous grins and some over lips tight with pain and resentment. He stood and stubbed out his smoke. "Just let Fitzroy know I was looking for him," he said before he left.

Charles leaned back and closed his eyes. They could not have picked a worse time of year for the hike. On the naval station at Subic, with an ocean breeze outside and air-conditioning inside, one didn't have to think too much about the height of the dry season. But here, miles inland, far in-country, they lacked those comforts; they even lacked the trees of the jungle to shade them. And beyond the physical distress brought on by heat and the direct, brassy assault of the sun, they faced the strange mental aspects of dragging their tired selves over dusty country roads during the days preceding Easter in the Philippines.

At home, in Arlington, Easter to Charles meant chocolate bunnies and colored eggs waiting in cool wet lawns for children returning from mass. The passion of suffering Jesus sounded a thin, incongruous note in the sonata of a pretty spring day full of candy. Yet in the Philippines, Charles learned, children did not have chocolate bunnies or colored eggs, only a lot of suffering Jesus. Some of their fathers and older brothers, although reasonably normal sinners 364 days a year, atoned for their own and their community's faults on the 365th as flagelantes. One of the few remaining traces of the period of Spanish colonization, the practice of flagelantism involved whipping oneself with a glass-tipped cat-o'-nine-tails for a number of hours and then washing the blood off in public, preferably in the salt water of the sea. Easter also brought out the penitentes: men who dressed like

Jesus in purple robes, wore crowns of thorns—real thorns—carried heavy wood crosses, and had friends and neighbors who dressed up as little theater versions of Roman soldiers and accompanied them on long marches through the countryside. Competitions occurred, and Luiz told Charles that every year the holiest penitente received the honor of an actual crucifixion in the main square of San Fernando, though modified for contemporary tastes with the use of stainless-steel nails through the palms and rope supports to keep the winner from suffocating during his twelve hours on the cross. They only occasionally died, usually from heatstroke. For women, each barrio had its contingent of passionaras, church ladies who dressed in black and wailed essentially nonstop from Good Friday through Easter Sunday, as well as intermittently the week before, as if to warm up.

Charles might not have believed any of this, but some weeks earlier he had seen a brochure his mother picked up for a DoD-sponsored tour to one of the southern islands. It promised a cultural spectacle rivaling the one in San Fernando, and Charles could tell from its tone and illustrations that had the natives failed to actually nail someone up, a number of Americans would have had every right to ask for their money back.

Further confirmation of the practices came on the bus ride up from Subic the day before, when the Scouts actually passed three groups of penitentes. Some of the boys laughed and waved—some of the Roman soldiers waved back—but Charles felt sorry for the Filipinos. Christ only had one hill to ascend. If He had a real heart, thought Charles, on Easter He would bring chocolate bunnies to all the penitentes.

So Charles felt the day before: now he had an even greater respect for men who carried crosses in the dry-season sun. That morning in Pampanga it seemed clear that a march made by starving men in two days wouldn't give too many problems to well-fed youths who had more than twice the time. That kind of self-assurance, combined with Sipko's pep talk, resulted in that four-mile first hour, despite the best efforts of the few counselors who knew what would happen. After the first break, when the whole column dribbled into the main square of a barrio for a rationed cup of water, energy and enthusiasm quickly dissipated. A dozen or so boys disappeared into nearby sari-sari stores for sodas or beers, and one of the counselors—Marine Corporal Dawes—joined them. Fitzroy attempted to round up the post, but Joe and Jim dodged him by slipping into an alley a few blocks away from the square and he gave up trying. When Fitzroy found the others Finch had already got them on their feet, ready to lead the loose, weak-willed column south to try to climb the wall of the sun.

Charles managed to stay up front that first hour without much trouble, but by the second he had begun to wear down quickly. He kept looking to the boys he expected the least from— MacReady, George Wong, and Tom Sanders—waiting for them to collapse so he could point out the need for another break, but none of them flagged or even looked half as badly off as Charles already felt. When they took a second break by the side of the highway, Charles's feet burned, his calves tightened, and he knew he'd have trouble getting back up, much less moving forward. Then Jim came by. He looked more than usually pale and his bangs lay sweat-plastered to his forehead like a line of commas, but he'd managed to stay on his feet and smile.

"You look all kinds of fucked up," he said to Charles.

"Fuck you."

"Yeah, promises—like you could get it up for me now. Look, why don't you hold back a few minutes when the column gets up. You can join me and Luiz in the rear."

"What good is that?"

"It's a laugh and a half, man. We get to mosey along at our own speed with Dawes, taking it easy, till word comes to close up the column. Then we push all the little Boy Scouts up and slack off again. Next best thing to riding in the truck with that bullshit artist Sipko."

So Charles tried that for the rest of the day, and although it didn't make him feel better, he didn't die like he knew he would had he remained at the front, and he did enjoy the occasional amusement of running up on straggling Boy Scouts and threatening to plant one of his father's boots up their butt.

The worst came after lunch, at which most of the boys either ate too much or too little of the canned combat rations, adding nausea or light-headedness to their other problems. Lieutenant Fleming, struggling to interpret his Philippine road map, kept passing the word that the evening's bivouac lay "just over the next rise." A "rise" in this country took more than a mile to roll up to its full height, from which the next one looked very far away indeed. The first such message encouraged the boys to push on, but the second simply pushed them farther along the path from disappointment to despair. After the third they just stopped believing that they'd ever reach the bivouac, and scouts and counselors alike began to drop out along the side of the road. The rear guard broke up when Dawes fell out with a group of younger Boy Scouts. Charles, with a grunt of effort, forced himself to keep up with Jim and Luiz. Looking ahead he saw that nothing remained of the column but scattered groups dragging themselves slowly along, watched by increasing numbers from the sidelines. The support trucks had disappeared over the horizon, ostensibly to set up the mythical camp, so anyone who couldn't make it on foot couldn't make it at all. Post 360 might have spent the night in several different roadside ditches, but Finch had pulled the group in front off the road and left Joe in charge with orders to pick up any of their stragglers who came by. Then he walked back a mile till he met up with Jim, Luiz, and Charles. When the four of them hooked up with Joe they found one of Sipko's colleagues from Clark berating him for not moving. Joe wouldn't take any of it.

"Who the fuck are you anyway?" he asked the Air Force man.

"Airman First Class Roberts, sonny," came the reply.

"I didn't know the Air Farce *had* any *first-class* turds," said Joe.

"Goddammit, you little shit," said Roberts.

"It's all right," said Finch, "I told them to wait."

Roberts turned around and looked at Finch, who looked frail and puny next to him. "Well, who the hell are you?" Roberts demanded.

"He's our post president," said Joe. "Now fuck off."

Roberts reached out for Joe but Carl Wong and Ed Sanders closed up on him with their elder brothers uncertainly behind.

Finch and his group formed on Roberts's right. A few yards away MacReady stood up next to the prone Fitzroy who, untypically awake, lifted his hat, peered out, and drawled, "I reckon you ought to do what the boys say, Airman. They be like to get totally out of control when y'all try to boss 'em." Roberts left.

A few hours later they all lay under the bridge listening to Fitzroy's snores and watching Lieutenant Fleming contemplate the possible trajectory of his career after managing to lose a few troops of scouts to heatstroke and, possibly, Huks. Yet by nightfall Fleming had managed to account for everyone. Most made it in by sixteen hundred; at seventeen hundred he sent Fitzroy and the corpsman out in one of the pickups for Dawes and a dozen others. Two of the boys had to go back to Clark for treatment but the rest only needed some first aid, fluids, and sleep. Dawes, a small wiry figure with pale eyes and a taste for Pall Malls and spitting, just grinned when Fleming asked him why he hadn't come in. "Hell, Lieutenant, I knew you wouldn't trust me alone out there so I just waited for my ride."

Fleming got camp set up within a fifty-meter radius of the bridge, with most of the tents set up more or less in a regular order. The Explorers spread their blankets in the dust and slept under the stars where a cool evening breeze could wash over them. They set up regular watches like they did in the jungle and Charles volunteered for 0-dark-thirty to dawn so he could see the sun rise over the plains.

At the beginning of his watch Charles walked over to the supply truck with his blanket draped around him like a cape and found Jim and Luiz playing poker by the light of a small fire. As about the oldest and biggest boys there, they and Joe had convinced Fleming to let them guard the truck against nameless Filipino marauders while the enlisted men caught up with their sleep. As a result they'd cornered the market on all the C-ration coffee and cigarettes that the counselors had removed from the utility packs before issuing meals to the boys. After they grabbed a few dozen four-packs each, Joe took his smokes and went looking for action in the next barrio up the road while Jim and Luiz stayed behind to play five-card draw for a pack a point.

"Lucky that boy's daddy is in Security or he could really get himself into some serious shit," said Jim.

"What do you think he scoring?" asked Luiz. "Pussy or reds?"

"I don't know, but I wouldn't try any serious shit out here. There's a limit to what your daddy can do for you this far in-country."

Charles stepped a little closer to the fire. None of the day's heat remained. "You guys mind if I watch your game?"

"No problem," said Jim. "You wanna cigarette? The Salems and Newports are mine, but you can have anything else you want. We got lots of Pall Malls and I don't want to waste them on Dawes."

"I don't smoke."

"Go ahead," said Luiz, "light up. You don't have to inhale. It'll help keep the mosquitoes away."

"Yeah?" Charles squatted down and picked up a four-pack of Winstons from Luiz's pile. He undid the cellophane, opened the box, pulled out the piece of foil, and tossed the excess packaging into the fire like he'd seen guys do on overnighters in the jungle. So far, so good. Luiz popped his Zippo and Charles leaned over to light up. He coughed on the first gentle puff.

"You really never smoked before, huh?" asked Jim.

"Don't," said Luiz, "it's a filthy habit." A Camel dangled from his lips. "You get that lit okay?"

Jim and Luiz played for what seemed like ages, picking up cards and laying them down with unconscious ease, seemingly unconcerned with whether the piles of smokes beside them grew or shrank, and keeping up throughout a quiet patter composed in part of more tales of town, partly of gossip about the other scouts, and partly of speculations on the erotic potential of their female classmates. Charles didn't know whether they talked like this all the time or just for him, but he didn't care. He just sat and listened, a bit more attentively than he would in class.

"You know," said Jim, "that new chick Joan's got a nice ass. You wouldn't think so when you first look at her, but she does."

Charles flushed—he didn't know whether from anger, jealousy, or shock—and tried to think of something to say.

Luiz said, "Yeah, I seen it, but I don't know. I think we gonna have to wait for this cat here to tell us. Won't be long, will it, cat? Chick like that wouldn't look twice at dumb shits like you and me, Jim. Queens and threes."

"You're right about that. Fuck. Pair of tens."

The sky to the east turned from black to purple, and a pink fringe formed over an outline of distant hills. Jim and Luiz put down the cards and patter and the three of them watched quietly as features in the landscape emerged from the night. A few minutes before the sun broke the horizon Joe walked into the circle of firelight looking haggard and smelling strongly of beer and rum.

"Shit, man," said Jim, "don't get any closer to the fire or you'll fucking explode." Joe said nothing but picked his blanket up from behind Jim and crawled under the truck to sleep.

"Ain't any of us gonna be good for shit today," laughed Luiz.

Lieutenant Fleming stepped out of his tent to take a leak. Charles coughed; he'd gone through two packs. "You guys want some coffee?" he asked his buddies.

The second day went better than the first, despite the heat and despite the beating they all took the day before. They paced themselves more sanely, ate more carefully, and took more breaks. After half an hour some of the boys began to sing and within ten minutes the whole column, counselors included, joined in "Roll Me Over." It wore thin after the fourth repetition, so they entered a period of relative quiet that ended when Jim began the "Yo Ho Song." Charles hadn't heard the "Yo Ho Song" before, but he picked it up after the first run-through. It had the tune of "When Johnny Comes Marching Home" and the first verse went:

> *I laid my hand upon her toe, yo ho, yo ho;*
> *I laid my hand upon her toe, yo ho, yo ho;*
> *I laid my hand upon her toe,*
> *she said "Yankee, you're mighty slow—*
> *get in, get out, quit fucking about"*
> *yo ho, yo ho, yo ho . . .*

From toe they advanced to shin, to knee, to thigh, and thence to twat, which led in turn to the final verse, which they sang slowly and solemnly right up to the third to last line:

> *And now she's in a pinewood box, yo ho, yo ho,*
> *And now she's in a pinewood box, yo ho, yo ho,*
> *And now she's in a pinewood box,*

at which the song drove quickly and ruthlessly to its conclusion:

> *for sucking too many Yankee cocks!*
> *Get in, get out, quit fucking about,*
> *yo ho, yo ho, yo ho!*

But after the third time Fitzroy had had enough so he taught them the words to "The Battle of New Orleans" and for the next fifteen minutes the baking plains of Luzon resounded with the voices of boys boasting about chasing the British down the Mississippi to the Gulf of Mexico. When that wore down, Dawes ground out a cigarette, spat, and bellowed out a few cadence calls, usually alone for the first line, but joined by the corpsman and the few other marines in the column for the response, as in:

> *Why you soldier looking down?*
> *Ain't no pussy on the ground . . .*

or,

> *I don't know what I been told,*
> *Eskimo pussy mighty cold . . .*

But again Fitzroy tired quickly of the vulgarity and visibly winced as 150 Boy Scouts echoed it through the countryside of an inoffensive ally. "Hey Carl," he said, "you boys know the words to the Marine Corps Hymn?"

"Ah heck," said the younger Wong, "that's boring. You might as well sing 'The Star Spangled Banner.'"

"Oh no," said Fitzroy. "Why don't you try it? Only instead of the regular tune, try it to the tune of 'My Darling Clementine.' Marines just love that."

So to rag Dawes and the other grunts, Post 360 did just that and soon the rest of the column picked it up, the counselors from Clark joining in with particular gusto. When Dawes finally broke down and told them to cut the shit, they did, but then Fitzroy whispered to some of his charges and soon the hymn rolled out again, only this time to the tune of "Gilligan's Island."

Sipko yelled out the truck at Dawes. "Looks like everybody wants to make fun of your song, grunt!"

Dawes lit up and said, "Well, they'd do the same for you, fly-boy, if anyone bothered to remember the fucking words."

They came to their first barrio of the day, a small collection of nipa huts in the middle of dried rice paddies. One wire strayed from the power line along the highway, dangling from pole to pole to light a few incandescent bulbs in the concrete church and a cooler and a jukebox in the one tiny, wood-framed sari-sari store. The scouts took their break there, and the store owner, suddenly confronted with nearly two hundred customers clamoring for sodas, met the challenge as best he could, manning the register, ordering his family into action, and accosting the uncomprehending crowd with a hundred Tagalog expressions of alarm and delight.

Others cashed in, too. A farmer set up a stand next to the store, producing from somewhere an old sheet-metal icebox filled with shaved ice and small bottles of locally produced pop. Charles ordered a root beer that came heavy with syrup and low on carbonation; he sucked a full Dixie Cup right down, though the Filipino serving it looked like he'd come straight from the fields and popped the bottles and threw in shaved ice with hands smeared with carabao dung and mud. The root beer made a cold sweet river through the rough dusty ditch that Charles's throat had become on the morning march, and that seemed well worth a few centavos and the risk of dysentery.

From the sari-sari store came the sound of a jukebox playing "Ob-La-Di, Ob-La-Da" from the Beatles' *White Album*, one of two songs the scouts heard in every barrio they passed through, along with "Yummy, Yummy, Yummy" by the 1910 Fruitgum Company. "Yummy," with its unique combination of catchiness and monotony, rapidly became unbearable. In contrast, the Beatles' song about Desmond and his barrow in the marketplace made a great deal of sense, both barrows and marketplaces constituting highly accessible concepts in the barrios. But neither song played too many times because thrice on the previous day and now for the first of probably four or five times on this one, Tom Sanders slipped a twenty-five-centavo piece into the jukebox for "I Will," also from the *White Album*. Two hours out of Subic he had already begun to get moony about Marsha, and it seemed to get worse by the hour. Sure enough, as soon as Charles heard the opening bars he looked around the corner of the store to see Tom stretched out in the dust on the shady side, nursing a San Miguel and crooning his intention to love someone forever and forever with all his heart. Then, as Tom noticed Charles, he held up another Philippine quarter and said, "Be a friend, would you, and play it again." By the end of the day the Explorers would divide evenly between those who wanted to murder Tom and those who simply wanted to nail him to a cross in the marketplace. But whoever had counterfeited the forty-five in Taipei for the Philippine market must have loved Tom because he played that song so many times he ruined every copy in Pampanga, Zambales, and Bataan provinces and fresh orders must have gone out each time the column moved on. The boys heard the song so many times that eventually it grew on them, and they worked it into the march repertoire, along with the cadence songs, "Roll Me Over," "The Battle of New Orleans," and "Yo Ho, Yo Ho, Yo Ho."

They marched out of the little barrio of the farmer/soda jerk and continued over the plains, the land gradually beginning to roll more as the line of trees crept closer to the road. Charles learned to gauge paces and tell when the column went at 120 or 90 and so whether to pick up or slow down the rear. At breaks he sometimes switched back to the front, where he found the pressure of setting the pace balanced by the feeling of leading everyone else into undiscovered lands. He learned miles the first day: what one looks like marked with a straight line of asphalt shimmering between dry fields. Now he learned kilometers from roadside historical markers commemorating the Death March. He learned how long a klick took at different rates and got to where he could see it stretched out before him on the road, six-tenths as long as the mile learned the day before. He found that time and the countryside pass on foot just like they do from a car, only in superslow motion, so he could see infinitely more than the usual quick procession of snapshots under glass. But he also felt more—more weariness, more pain—until somewhere around the outer limits of his strength he entered a state in which he seemed to float above it and could see the whole world turning, ever so slowly, under his feet, and feel his feet swinging on their own like heavy-booted pendulums, working the world around like the biggest treadmill imaginable.

They met no flagelantes or penitentes in those particular klicks, but at the end of the march day, at perhaps fifteen hundred hours, as they came into the barrio where they planned to bivouac for the night and entered the main square, they passed a cinder-block meetinghouse or town hall with a pair of large speakers flanking its double doorway. As the head of the column neared, a rich, piercing wail poured out; it seemed to Charles like a poorly recorded cross between a coyote and a Wagnerian soprano. The marchers stuttered to a stop and stared back at the unearthly assault. "Passionaras," said Luiz. "Move on!" said Lieutenant Fleming.

A hundred yards beyond the square they found their camp-site by a gray crumbling masonry church with a cornerstone marked "1804." Extending at right angles from each end of the church came an equally long, barrackslike wing; a four-foot-high stone wall finished the job of enclosing a large flagstone court-yard, half the stones of which had disintegrated or sunk into the dirt. One of the wings had also collapsed, forming a wall of rub-ble behind the remaining half of its facade. Nuns and uniformed schoolgirls watched the scouts from the high windows in the other wing. "Easy now," said Jim, talking to his pants.

With the support vehicles parked immediately outside the gate, the scouts unloaded and pitched their tents in the courtyard, packing them in tightly but finding room for all, just as they found room for the tent pegs in the cracks between or within the stones. A single water tap jutted from a three-foot-high pipe to the right of the door in the middle of the church and dangled a length of hose that Charles and 360 turned into an ad hoc showerhead. They stripped to their underpants and soaped up, ignoring a small crowd of Filipino onlookers and the shrill exclamations of the nuns as they shooed their charges back from the windows. Charles watched and felt a two-day layer of dust and grit turn to sludge and roll off him then hosed his hair till he could see and feel the water run clear. After he washed he changed more or less privately between two tents and, in clean shorts and T-shirt, accompanied Jim and Luiz into the barrio.

The first sari-sari store they reached had "I Will" coming out of it, so they passed it by. Two doors down on the narrow street they found another place throbbing with the bass of Creedence Clearwater Revival's "Born on the Bayou" so they checked it out. Inside the door they found a clean café with a dozen tables on a linoleum floor, a handsome wood-and-glass counter, and two valiant, if overmatched, ceiling fans. Carl Wong and Ed Sanders had staked out a corner table where they sprawled like two vets on leave, Carl in a loud Hawaiian shirt and Ed in an equally flamboyant dashiki, both of them sucking down San Miguel from long-necked bottles and staring fiercely at the Boy Scouts sipping Cokes at the next table.

Charles followed Luiz to the counter and tentatively ordered a beer. Maybe, he thought, it would taste different from the sour liquid his father had let him sample a few times. It didn't, but he decided not to let that bother him; by the time he finished it he felt very comfortable and quite happy that he had these particular friends and had discovered this particular place. At that moment Fitzroy walked through the door.

"Shit," said Jim, quickly setting his beer on the floor next to him. Carl and Ed hurriedly drained theirs. Fitzroy, standing like a scarecrow, looked around, his thumbs hooked in the front belt loops of his swabbie bell-bottoms, then walked to the counter and asked for a Dr Pepper. The proprietor didn't seem to know what he meant so Fitzroy settled for a 7Up and brought it over to the Explorers' table. "Mind if I join you, boys?" Without waiting for an answer he pulled up another chair and sat down. Ed and Carl stared at him, fighting the queasiness they felt from chugging their beers. Luiz looked him in the eyes, then glanced at his San Miguel and asked, "You don't mind, do you?"

"Nah."

"Okay," said Jim, picking his bottle up from the floor.

"Damn," said Carl. Ed got up and went to the bar for another.

"Yup," said Fitzroy, "help yourself, boys. Enjoy life. You wanna do something behind Mommy and Daddy's back, go right ahead."

"You sure?" asked Carl.

"Hell yes. Three, four years from now they gonna be more worried about you comin' home in a box than any old San Miguel. Get all you can and then some."

This is all right, thought Charles. When Ed returned he got up to get another beer for himself and even splurged on a pack of cigarettes—Marlboros made locally. "Under franchise," Luiz explained when Charles got back to his seat.

"Like San Miguel," said Jim. "That's really Lone Star. No shit."

"Franchise," repeated Fitzroy. "This whole damn country's a franchise. Look at all these poor people hereabouts. Look close. They all got a little tattoo behind the right ear, says 'Made in USA.' This is no shit." Then he looked disapprovingly at Charles. "You know, my daddy caught me with one of those there Marlboros when I was about your age. Took me out behind the woodshed and like to beat me half to death."

"Didn't want you smoking, eh?"

"Nah. He said—and I remember this distinctly—'Son, I don't mind you smoking, but if I ever catch you sucking on a Kotex again I think I'll kill you.' 'Cause that's all them filters is." He turned to Luiz and bummed a Camel.

They chatted a few more minutes until the door opened again and George walked in. He looked strangely natty in a short-sleeved white oxford carefully tucked around his girth into fresh bermuda shorts from which stout brown legs led down to dress socks pulled halfway up his calves, and ended in shiny black cordovans. When he saw his brother, he cried, "Carl! Are you crazy drinking beer like that? What if Mom or Dad heard about it? What if one of the counselors finds you?"

"One of the counselors?" replied Carl, gesturing toward Fitzroy with his bottle. "Guess I'd have to buy him one."

The others laughed and Fitzroy drawled, "Ain't you heard, George? Drinkin' age in the PI is around twelve."

"Oh," said George, "I guess it's all right then."

That night on the dawn watch, Charles left Jim and Luiz at the fire and patrolled the low wall and the wing of rubble. Occasionally he would stop and stare at a shadow until it changed from a ghostly bandit into a shrub or stray cat. He felt like a Roman Legionnaire on Hadrian's Wall with a lifetime to spend walking back and forth waiting for the barbarians. Before the watch he'd had a dream in which Commander Barker worked as a pipe fitter in the big Philippine Navy base on the Potomac and his mother smoked those long black cigarettes that everyone said had carabao shit in them to make them burn steady, only the ones she smoked came from Fairfax and thus didn't have the same cachet as the ones from Cebu. It unnerved him to the extent that he found walking the perimeter looking for phantoms calming.

The next day the road led them up into the hills of southern Zambales and then into Bataan. It rose like a gentle, slow-motion roller coaster, rising and dipping and turning until by midday they found themselves out of the hot, dusty plains and among hot, sporadically forested hills. They kept a steady pace and laughed and joked between songs. Feeling better about themselves and the march, they made fewer denigrating remarks about the Filipinos, their pigs and nipa huts, the proudly signed municipal latrines and rudimentary schoolhouses, or the smell of alien food. A few scouts even began to smile at the people in the barrios and to hand C-ration gum to the kids without treating them like beggars.

At the top of another gentle rise the road brought them to a kind of plateau, a plain where the asphalt bordered by a single thin row of trees on each side ran straight through rice fields about a klick and a half to the next barrio. All the way up the slope the scouts had sung cadence songs, mostly ones they'd just made up, and 360 felt pumped up enough to keep walking to Manila Bay. But when they got to the level stretch Fleming called a halt. Charles stood at the front with Jim, Luiz, Joe, Carl, and Ed; he looked back and saw the whole column fall apart and disperse under the trees as Finch walked along the shoulder to the rear to talk to Fitzroy, Tom, MacReady, and George. Charles didn't want to sit and throw away the momentum he felt. He looked at the other Explorers in front; they didn't look like they wanted to stop, either. They saw the supply truck drive up slowly with Sipko looking in the rearview mirror waiting for the pickups to get started and catch up. Jim ran up, jumped on the running board, and asked a few questions. Then he jumped back into the road and walked back as the pickups closed and the three vehicles took off down the highway.

"Man, this is bullshit," said Jim, pulling a four-pack of Salems from his shirt pocket. "Sipko says we're bivouacking just the other side of that barrio. If we hadn't stopped we'd be halfway to our next beer by now."

"Then what the hell are we waiting for?" asked Joe.

"Ah, they say some of the little tenderfeet are tired."

"Well, hell," said Carl, "why don't we just take off then?"

"Ah, I don't know. I don't wanna piss off Sipko and Dawes again unless I get more out of it than blisters and an early beer. Fuckers looked ready to lock and load on us last night after they found out how many of the smokes we got."

"Yeah," said Luiz. "Plus, I don't wanna piss off Finch."

"Oh, fuck *me*," said Joe. "What's anybody gonna do to us? Send us home?"

Jim looked back to the rest of the column, thinking. Then he turned to the other Explorers and, shrugging, said, "Okay. Fuck. Why not? But look, let's get a good head start. I'll nod, then we fall in and quickstep like hell, no singing. They're all jacking off

back there—we can get maybe a hundred meters off before anyone notices."

They all agreed and, on Jim's signal, took off. Charles thought
about forty seconds had gone by at 120 before they heard one of
the counselors shout, "Hey! Get your asses back here!" Carl sang
out an improvised cadence in reply:

> *Post Three Six-tee has got the gas*
> *you tenderfeet can kiss my ass . . .*

and the other four sounded off with him. Glancing back they
could see the column forming up behind them, the counselors
pulling boys to their feet and pushing them together, trying to
get the elongated herd in motion. Joe took the lead and the others half jogged to stay even. They clomped down the road in their
heavy boots at 150 or more, pushing themselves a great deal
harder than they'd planned, having an unspoken agreement that,
now that they found themselves pursued, they would not only
beat the other scouts, but beat them so badly that by the time the
rest caught up with them, they'd find 360 in the shade, sucking
down their second San Miguels.

Another minute passed of hot breathless racing when Charles
heard Jim gasp, "Who the fuck's that?" and looked back to see
a diminutive figure break from the column and begin to close the
gap at the run.

"Finch," said Luiz, "who the fuck you think?"

They didn't slow, even for him, but kept it up. Ed tripped at one
point but Carl and Luiz caught him on either side and held him
up long enough for him to get his feet moving again. Jim pulled
out his canteen, took a big swig without missing a step, then,
coughing, poured the rest out on his head and down his back.

Finch caught up with them, red faced and panting. Carl looked
over and said, "Don't be pissed at the others; it was my idea." Finch
shook his head, whispered, "My responsibility," and stumbled.

"Ah shit," said Joe. "Come on—give a hand, Luiz." They
pulled him up and pushed him forward and all seven kept up a
steady 130.

Charles felt his heart pounding and grew too tired to wipe the sweat from his burning eyes. In retrospect it seemed pretty silly to kill himself just to make a point—he had no idea what point—with the Boy Scouts and counselors, but he also knew that he wouldn't quit until he did die or someone else stopped first. The edges of his field of vision blurred and a black field began bobbing up from his feet, threatening to swamp up over the horizon; his head started to turn involuntarily. At that moment he heard a vehicle race up behind them, close, and erupt with high-pitched, twanging laughter. A jeepney appeared, packed with grinning Filipino men who waved at the exhausted boys, shouted, "Hey Joe!" and threw something back at them as they raced on. Luiz ran up to the object and picked it up—a clear plastic bag filled with what looked like glistening pieces of leather.

"Hey! Fried bananas!" He turned and waved toward where the jeepney had vanished in a cloud of khaki dust. "Thanks, man!"

"Joe food?" Ed wondered aloud. The others gathered around Luiz looking equally skeptical, but Luiz tore into the bag and pressed the greasy, sticky slices into their hands. Charles chomped his down, filling his mouth with a flavor at once sugary and salty, and a texture creamy and crisp. The boys licked their fingers and laughed at each other.

"Damn," said Jim, "that's the first time I ever got a handout from a Joe."

"Hey guys," said Carl, "the others are closing. Let's book."

Some fifteen minutes later Fleming stumbled into the main square of the barrio at the head of the thin leading strand of a long, disordered column and came upon all seven Explorers sitting and lying among the roots of a large shade tree, bottles in hand and cigarettes lit.

"Who the hell authorized you to leave the column?" Fleming demanded.

"I did, sir," said Finch.

"Bullshit," said Joe, "it was my idea."

"Hell, I'm the one who thought of it," said Carl.

"You lie like one big rug, cat," said Luiz. "It was my idea."

"No way," said Charles, "don't you remember . . ."

"Screw all of you," said Jim, "I was the one . . ."

"You boys think you're pretty funny, don't you?" said the lieutenant. "Well, your behavior has been noted, I tell you, and don't think it hasn't been."

"What in hell does that mean?" asked Ed as Fleming walked away.

Dawes stepped up and spat at his feet. "It means," he grinned, "that he don't have any fucking idea what to do with you but he don't want to stand here all afternoon like an asshole trying to figure it out."

"Oh," said Jim. "Thanks."

Tom, George, MacReady, and Fitzroy joined them a few minutes later.

"That was really thoughtless," said MacReady. "Don't you know how hard it is to wake Fitz up?"

George looked at Carl. "I certainly hope Father doesn't hear about this."

"Oh blow me," said Carl.

Tom stepped up to Ed but before he could say anything his younger brother flipped him a twenty-five-centavo piece and said, "Don't even be startin' with me, man. Just take your money to that sari-sari store over there and play your lame-ass white boy song for your lame-ass white cow girlfriend."

Tom sighed, picked up the coin, and left for the sari-sari store.

After they'd finished their beers and sodas the Explorers wandered through the barrio to the bivouac site in a grove on a small hill overlooking rice fields. Jim pulled a fatigue jacket from his pack, stuffed the pockets with Pall Malls and two complete rations of Ham and Lima Beans, and invited Charles and Finch to join him. "Luiz wants to go back to the barrio with Joe and see what's happenin', but I want to check things out a little farther down the road." Finch and Charles agreed to go. They took a dirt lane between the caked and stubbly paddies that led to a distant line of thin trees through which they could see the late-afternoon sun shining on a small arm of Manila Bay. After a couple of hundred meters they came across an old farmer sitting beside a hand pump in front of his hut. With a little bit of Tagalog and the rations, Jim got the three of them another bath. With the addition of a few packs of Pall Malls, the old farmer's wife came out, took their T-shirts, and washed them in a tin basin with a bar of Ivory Soap. Charles squatted beside her and listened as she chattered away in Tagalog. He couldn't understand a word, but she reminded him of Grandma Barker on the farm in Texas and he imagined her talking about the weather, or recipes, deaths, and births. When she finished washing the shirts she hung them on a section of old barbed-wire fence. Then, before going back inside, she pinched the boys' cheeks and arms by way of saying good-bye.

"Yup," said Jim, "take thirty or forty years off her and I could be in real trouble with this farmer here."

"Right," said Finch. "Another three days out here and the thirty or forty years wouldn't mean a thing to you."

The shirts dried quickly in the sun and they soon said good-bye to the farmer with handshakes and more packs of Pall Malls. They walked farther down the road, took a rickety wooden bridge over a creek, and came upon a clump of stilted huts on the shore of an inlet. Here the road just touched the water before heading back to the interior for the final run down to the point of the Bataan peninsula, just across the water from Corregidor.

Low on the horizon the sun turned the ripples orange and flashed them with white. A few dozen Filipinos worked at various jobs—the women mending nets, the men hammering and hacking at a big outrigger, a banca boat. The banca sat out of the water, held upright by a scaffolding of thick bamboo poles while men moved over and within it. Charles couldn't tell whether the work consisted of construction or repair; it occurred to him that any one of the Filipinos would know, and would think it odd that he didn't. The three scouts waved and smiled at the workers, who generally waved and smiled back. Jim tried to talk with a few but didn't get too far.

"Tagalog seems to be a second language here," he said. "Besides, most of mine doesn't really further polite conversation."

The workers tried a little English, but their accents and vocabulary held them back. One old man walked up to Jim and pulled on his green fatigue jacket. The old man only stood about five feet tall, wizened as a gnome, but the three boys would most vividly remember his mouth, a crude jagged slit that could not quite close to cover his rotted stubs of teeth. He seemed to want something; not the coat, but something, and murmured unintelligibly. "U.S.A., he say," explained one of the men.

"We're just Explorer Scouts, man," said Jim. "No army. No marines. Boy Scouts."

"We're on a hike," Finch tried. "The Death March, you know? The Bataan Death March." He pronounced it slow, as if they'd never heard the word *Bataan*.

The old man nodded and seemed to smile, as much as he could. The worker translating said, "He Death March. He Death March. Japanese, Japanese . . . they," he shrugged in frustration then, brightening, pulled on his lip and pantomimed the act of slicing it off with a knife.

"Oh my God," said Charles.

Jim stared.

Finch blinked several times. Then he took the old man's hand and shook it. "Thank you," he said.

The old man nodded slowly and held on. Not knowing what else to say or do, Finch, smiling and bowing, said, "Jim, give him the rest of the smokes and let's get out of here."

"I hear ya, man."

Later the whole post sat together in the trees watching the sun set and sipping smuggled San Miguel from their canteens. Charles lit one of his Pampanga Marlboros and blew the smoke at the gathering mosquitoes. The next day they would finish the march and would find themselves acting in a little ceremony on the shore of Manila Bay with American and Filipino dignitaries and reporters from the *Manila Times* and *Stars and Stripes* witnessing the distribution of merit badges and the usual speeches about Phil-Am relations. The scouts would play their roles as good dependents and then return to the base for showers, air-conditioning, hair cuts, and leisure activities at the appropriate U.S. Navy recreational facilities.

"As hot, filthy, tired, bug-bit, horny, and generally fucked up as I feel," said Jim, "I'm actually not looking forward to this ending."

"I sure as shit don't want to stand around with a buncha little Toy Scouts in some goddamn parade," said Joe.

"Why don't we like moon the reviewing stand?" suggested Carl.

"You don't have to get crazy," said Finch. "Fitz and I can stay and represent the post. Anyone else who wants can leave early."

"Does that mean we wouldn't get our merit badges?" asked Tom.

"You *know* what you can do with that, don't you?" replied Ed.

The next day, after they packed up the tents, Jim, Luiz, and Joe got an early ride back on the supply truck. Tom Sanders and George Wong stayed with Fitz and Finch, while Charles, Ed, Carl, and MacReady climbed into the back of a Navy pickup the corpsman would drive back to Subic. Dawes, still half drunk after a night in the barrio, climbed in the front to ride shotgun.

They pulled out in a cloud of dust and took the road back at as high a speed as the corpsman and the beat-up truck could manage. Dawes found it a bit too much, stuck his head out the window, and puked, sending a noxious spray past the boys in back. But things picked up when the corpsman stuck a cassette in a little Japanese portable and turned the volume all the way up so they could all hear a tinny, buzzing version of Cream playing "I'm So Glad" as they bounded up and down the wooded hills of Bataan.

The four Explorer Scouts stood up in back, leaned on the cab, and watched the road they'd come to know step by step race back in their faces like a storm blowing in from the South China Sea. And Charles looked down on the hills and the trees and the barrios all winding down below him in a rapid collage of tan, alabaster, emerald, and chocolate and tried not to think about the end of the ride or what his father might say about his skipping the final ceremony and the merit badge. Instead he thought about what he had seen and where he had gone while the landscape played back like a movie and the rock group broke out of a long instrumental with a sentiment that felt as welcome as seemingly odd.

"I *am* glad," Charles said, laughing to himself, his voice lost in the slipstream of the cab.

→ X ←

PO PRAHLER

The search for a new counselor to replace Fitzroy ended when George and Carl Wong's father found a candidate who appeared to have the right mix of responsibility and boyish enthusiasm. Mr. Wong discovered Petty Officer Second Class Henry Prahler in the course of his duties in the base finance office, while auditing accounts for Non-Appropriated Fund Activities, which included the Special Services Riding Stable. Prahler operated the stables with the assistance of about two dozen Filipinos. In the three months since assuming this responsibility, Prahler had goaded his workers into opening two new trails, increased the availability of horses (and thus revenues) more than 30 percent, and—perhaps most impressively— convinced the shady, half-off-the-books retired CPOs in his putative chain of command to invest several hundred dollars in facility upgrades and new equipment. When Mr. Wong mentioned Explorer Post 360 to Prahler, the young man fairly glowed, reminding the portly middle-aged accountant of no one more than himself when first put in charge of a section of accounts maintenance clerks many long years before.

The boys welcomed Prahler, too. In the weeks following the Death March they had made only a few hikes to the VC village, none of them overnighters, and a sense of boring routine had sunk in. That turned around when Prahler came to the monthly meeting at FICPACFAPFAPL. They might have cheered him no matter what he said, but in fact he made it easy. He promised hikes and campouts every other weekend if they wanted them. He listed the titles of a ship's company of friends in low places who could provide new backpacks and jungle boots, cocoonlike jungle hammocks, and camouflage fatigues. The boys sat up at the mention of camos: marines en route to Vietnam had just begun to wear them and, in contrast to the more workmanlike greens, the new uniforms made even pale, teenage dropouts look dashing.

Prahler also promised a different kind of campout from now on. No longer would the post loaf at the VC village grab-assing with exploding cans of peanut butter; henceforth they would trailblaze in the hills around the riding stables and sawmill. They would visit the Jungle Environmental Survival Training center and later apply their JEST skills out in the bush. Before they knew it, he said, they would run circles around Negritos. He might even get them a few days off from school so they could stay up to a week in the jungle like marine recon or SEALs. In a few months, he suggested, he could perhaps even get the Explorers basic weapons training and the boys could assist with perimeter patrols.

"Hard-core," murmured Carl Wong, while Ed Sanders nodded appreciatively and pumped his fist as if at a Black Power rally.

Finch sat stunned behind the desk at the front of the room, staring at Prahler, bedazzled—it seemed to Charles—by all the things he might learn before he got to Annapolis. Charles looked around the room and saw that nearly everyone appeared solidly on board with Prahler's program. Jim, Luiz, and Joe all nodded and grinned right through to the end of the petty officer's speech, while Tom Sanders and George Wong seemed to fade only when the idea of weapons training came up. Billy, too, looked enthused. Only Ford—the newest, least congruous member—squinted skeptically.

"Has it perhaps occurred to you," he asked Charles as they left the building after the meeting, "that our new counselor is psychotic?"

A week later Ford raised the question again as he and Charles sat in the back of a baby-blue Special Services jeep racing down the main avenue of the naval station at forty miles an hour while Billy rode a terrified shotgun and their counselor alternated demonic laughter with curses at the pickups, buses, and occasional dependent's sedan that dared to get in his way.

"This is crazy!" shouted Ford as a sudden swerve threw him half out of the stripped-down jeep. He and Charles held on tenuously to the sides, buttocks perched on the outer edges of the rear to make room for the pile of gear stowed safely between them.

"Stop being such a goddamn pussy!" shouted Billy from the front.

"Yeah," added Prahler, "I ain't lost no one yet!"

"You've never been a Scout leader before, have you?" demanded Ford.

"There is that," Prahler admitted.

Charles smiled, unwilling to show his terror, but also happy with the loot they had picked up. It all came from an unlikely Quonset hut near SRF where a third-class buddy of Prahler apparently owed him for unspecified, though highly winkable, services rendered. Instead of the road, Charles focused on the size-small camos and floppy broad-brimmed recon hat he picked out for himself.

Prahler accelerated to forty-five on the road to the stables and sawmill—two lanes of packed dirt held in place by twice-yearly applications of used motor oil in lieu of the asphalt the base could never seem to afford, and so beaten and cratered by the weather and lumber trucks that it seemed mined rather than maintained. The jeep bounced and skidded past the ruined facade of the old Spanish magazine, accompanied by Prahler's hectic narration over the plaintive squeal of a transmission that, in its senescence, remembered only second and reverse.

Just nineteen, Prahler had already seen a world far greater, as well as more twisted and dangerous, than had any of the boys of 360. As he told it, he had trained as a Navy SEAL for secret missions in the Mekong Delta, but then hurt his back and landed in Subic. SEAL training alone involved more than Charles would ever quite imagine surviving. To join that force of elite professional killers, one had to swim and run phenomenal distances, learn to use a full range of U.S. and communist small arms, fight several instructors at once bare-handed, eat lizards raw in the midst of thunderous rainstorms, and masturbate in a given number of strokes with a small dab of Vaseline and the coarse cardboard tube from the inside of a roll of toilet paper. After a while Charles lost track of where the training ended and the hazing began, or whether it all came out of the same secret special operations manual concocted in a dark and knowing corridor in the labyrinthine subbasements of the Pentagon.

Before SEAL training, Prahler said he had cruised the Mekong on Swift boats, manning a .50-caliber machine gun, unleashing its heavy, half-inch slugs in torrents that literally swept away houses, boats, pigs, goats, and, on occasion, suspected VC.

Prahler told all his stories with extravagant gestures and flashes of his bright blue eyes, seeming to dance in the driver's seat while the jeep steered itself with a series of hysterical reflexes of self-preservation. Lean and tan, a high forehead under a silver-blond crew cut, a snub nose and a little jutting chin that moved like a bullet tumbling after first hitting bone, he could, at a distance, easily pass for the All-American Boy.

"You scared?" he yelled back at Ford. Getting no answer, he tossed the pale scout a ragged paperback. "Read that!" Ford almost fell off the jeep reaching for the book, but he did as told. "Out loud, dammit!" Prahler demanded.

Charles looked at the cover. *Fanny Hill.* Prahler grinned and Charles and Billy chuckled as Ford read, in a quavering and reedy voice that strained to reach above the quavering and reedy engine, a baroque description of undergoing violation from an enormous, blue-veined, vermilion-tipped penis. He managed to cover half a paragraph before he gagged and said, "I really don't feel good about doing this." Billy and Charles laughed. Prahler ignored him and asked Billy, "You ever use orgy butter when you jerk off?"

Now Billy gagged. "Gross, man! No way!"

"Come on now," Prahler insisted, "admit it! How long does it take you, huh? Hey, if you can't do it in fifty beats, you ain't a man!"

"Christ, you're sick!" shouted Billy, his voice cracking.

"Come on, Billy," said Ford, "don't be such a pussy."

That weekend Explorer Post 360 held its first overnight camp-out since the end of Fitzroy's watch. The boys marched down the road from the stables to the sawmill, up a firebreak to the stream, then up the stream to the waterfall they'd discovered several months before. It took two hours to slog through the bush and shin-high water before the group reached the point at which the waterfall poured five meters into an icy pool some ten meters in diameter. The scouts lugged their equipage up the steep trail on the right bank then crossed back over the stream above the falls to set up on a rocky stretch where a steep escarpment faced downstream, a cliff faced the pool, and a thick tangle of under-story growth closed off the rest of their small perimeter. They set up two tarps in the event of a shower or anything else that might drop from overhead, and laid two more tarps under those for ground cover. Most of the boys then circled back down to the pool, stripped off their uniforms, and went skinny-dipping. Prahler loudly joined in, starting a splash fight by cannonballing from the rocks at the top of the waterfall.

After half an hour, Charles, Carl, and Luiz tired of water games and got out. They dressed without drying off, hoping the icy water would keep them cool and less attractive to bugs for a while. Luiz still wore the old-fashioned green fatigues and when Carl Wong teased him claimed that they actually provided better camouflage than the new ones. The three tried an experiment with Charles as a judge: covering their faces with their sleeves, Carl and Luiz slowly backed into the jungle until Charles couldn't see them anymore and told them to stop. Carl had to back up perhaps five meters farther than Luiz before disappearing. The patterns in the new camouflage fatigues actually made them stand out compared to the plain grayish green of the old ones. Anyone could see that. One would only choose the camouflage,

Charles realized, for the same reason the boys did, the same reason he preferred HO-scale Waffen SS toy soldiers to little plastic GIs: because they looked neat.

After the experiment Charles returned to the tarps and busied himself working a John Wayne around the top of a can of C-ration cookies. Ford, looking sweaty and uncomfortable, leaned against his knapsack and peered into a slim volume of Mo-tzu. Finch stepped in from the thick jungle side, saw the book, and asked about it.

"I find that philosophy reads better in the wilderness," Ford explained.

"You're not scared, or worried, are you?" asked Finch. "It's okay if you are; it's your first time out."

"No, I'm not scared. But I expect to be in the near future. Probably as soon as the sun goes down."

Finch smiled. "Well, we'll be there for you." He turned to Charles and said, "I found a trail that looks like it leads farther upstream. Maybe we could use it in the future instead of getting our feet wet."

Charles paused to swallow a cookie. "Yeah? Want to check it out?"

"That was the idea. Ford?"

"Oh no. Thank you, but I'll just stay here and wait for head-hunters."

"Have a cookie first," said Charles. He handed him the can and, after strapping on his web belt with its bolo and pair of canteens, followed Finch into the bush. They stepped carefully for a few dozen meters, parting branches and tendrils using the flats of their bolos or sleeves rolled down over their forearms. The slight break in the jungle canopy caused by the stream let in enough light to sprout a dense tangle: it would have taken hours to hack a way through, but far less time to ease through in a kind of slow-motion swim. In a few minutes they found the trail Finch had discovered, a track half a meter wide beaten into the leaf floor and winding among the tree trunks. It led them gradually uphill and ultimately to a short, sharp rise. At the top of this they found a few boulders and a gap in the canopy through which they could glimpse a sliver of the bay in the distance. They knew they still remained well within the borders of the naval station, at least on a map, but it didn't feel like it. It felt like nothing but jungle. A few meters to either side, Charles felt, they might find another Angkor Wat, untouched by man for centuries.

"Where did that trail come from, you think?"

"Dunno. Boars. Smugglers. Negritos." Finch fumbled in one of his jacket pockets and came up with a round, foil-wrapped C-ration candy bar. He broke it in two and gave half to Charles.

"How'd Joan enjoy the movie the other night?" he asked.

Charles looked at Finch. He forgot what he'd seen with Joan, but he remembered the walk back to her quarters in the muggy night, the acrid smell of the insecticidal fog a Navy truck laid down just as they left the theater, the trembling that briefly overtook him when he wondered if he should reach for her hand. Back at her place, her parents safely away in Hong Kong or Taipei, she put on a Janis Joplin album and talked about the kids stateside marching against the war. Charles thought Joplin screamed too much and that hippies didn't add up to much more than spoiled runaways fooling themselves into thinking that everything would work out fine if America simply walked away from the war. As if you could do that without walking into something just as bad, he thought, like a life of squalor and welfare, or as an accountant or something. But Charles kept quiet and after an hour left for home despite his mental image of Jim and Luiz telling him to go for it. He might have gone for it, and she might have let him get it, but probably not.

"Oh," he told Finch, "I think I'm in love."

"Right. You just want me to *think* you're joking."

"Could be. You never have that problem, do you?"

Finch grinned. "Too often. But I'm waiting for Miss Right."

"Oh yeah? What'll she be like?"

"Well, first off, I think she's gonna have to be short."

They laughed, then Finch added, "Seriously, though, not like I'd want this to get around, but I've yet to do the deed. I mean, I'm pushing sixteen and all, but I can't see doing a Filipino prostitute, or hooking up with some Navy man's daughter and getting into all that crap about getting hitched right out of high school and stuff. I mean, I want it to be right—right person, right time. You know?"

Charles looked at the distant bay and cringed with an unfamiliar discomfort. None of the boys he knew admitted to virginity, even the obvious cases like Billy and Ford. It upset the natural order. Dry mouthed, he said, "Actually, I've never done it either."

He looked over and saw Finch staring at him, lips pressed tight as if trying to keep his half smile from splitting his face.

"Well, gee, Charles," Finch managed to say, "that's pretty astonishing."

"Oh, fuck you."

"Wouldn't you rather save it for Miss Right?"

"I thought she was yours . . ."

"Hey, if it's her ass or mine . . ."

They could see the sky begin to blacken in the patch above the bay and so hurried back through the darkening forest to gain the tarps just as the sky cut loose. Rain fell heavily for about fifteen minutes, collapsing one tarp, soaking the treetops, and misting the air. After the storm passed the leaves above continued to drip, drip, drip into the sudden twilight and dense night that followed, and anyone who moved outside the single tarp became soaked the moment he brushed against the rain-laden leaves around the campsite. It took nearly an hour to get the second tarp back up and scrounge enough wood to feed a smoky, smoldering fire next to their sagging shelter. Chilly and soggy, the boys crowded around the struggling flames and tried to heat a few cans of dinner. No one felt like saying much, except Jim, who asked Luiz, "Okay, so why aren't we in town tonight?" To which Joe replied, "Just shut the fuck up."

Prahler stood in the dripping gloom on the jungle side of the campfire, his smirking face underlit sardonically by the coals and the brief flares of match strikes as boys tried to light damp cigarettes. He had heard about the war games at the VC village. Now curls of smoke and swaying sword leaves cast weird shadows on his camos as he told his charges that any pussy could play at jungle warfare in a dry forest lit by stars and moonlight but guys with real balls trained in all weather.

"What are you talking about?" Finch asked.

Prahler made a hatchet head of his right hand and hacked in the direction of upstream.

"We go back up there, one, two hundred meters. Red team, blue team. Blue holds the creek line, red attacks. How many flashlights we got?"

"What?" asked Ford.

"Five," said Joe. "Shit, it's gotta be better than just fucking standing here."

"I don't know," said Tom, "we didn't even get that far up in daylight."

"Oh, you just scared again," Ed told him. "Fuck, I'm game."

"It's fine," said Prahler. "Easy country. I checked it out myself. Who's ready?"

Charles looked at Finch, who seemed about to say something, but as the majority of boys began to choose sides, the post president first went over the rules with Prahler and then moved among the others to make sure they knew where they had to go and where they had to stay away from. Charles tried to find Billy only to see him disappear into the night with Joe. He turned to Ford instead and said, "Okay, just stick with me. Nobody dies."

Ford nodded, a little too quickly thought Charles.

The two teams split up and took their positions, stumbling in the pitch darkness over the unfamiliar ground, keening their ears for the sound of the waterfall and the stream, straining their eyes for obstacles and the sudden shock of flashlight beams poling hazily into the mist. Despite their initial enthusiasm most of the boys simply walked into the woods and sat down, afraid to move until the all-clear brought them back to the marginal safety and comfort of the fire. Prahler rampaged through the bush, intermittently screaming at the blue team, alternately urging them on or cursing them. Half an hour passed before Charles saw him, briefly illuminated by a killing flashlight—whose, no one knew or would admit. Charles pulled Ford to his feet only briefly abashed at having hid. In the scary and confusing dark, no one really knew if anyone had fought.

The post did not sleep much that night. They listened to Prahler tell endless and increasingly incredible war stories as the campfire slowly burned out. In the morning they marched out feeling wet, bug-bit, and beaten, not saying much but still listening to their scout leader's plans for new trails and campsites.

The next week at school Finch confided in Charles. "I don't know," he said. "That was kinda crazy, playing around the falls like that. It's a miracle we didn't lose anybody."

"Yeah," said Charles. "Kinda cool, though."

Finch looked away and nodded. Charles could tell he didn't find it cool, but something—neither fear nor intimidation—kept Finch from criticizing Prahler. Charles wondered briefly before he put his finger on it. Finch must have seen himself as a kind of executive officer to Prahler's commanding officer. Growing up in the Navy, Charles knew that an XO would probably have to find his CO foaming at the mouth and sodomizing midshipmen before he'd admit that perhaps someone on the outside ought to look into things.

In the few weeks after Prahler's debut in the battle above the falls, Post 360 went on several more all-nighters—a term especially apt now that no one knew when their scoutmaster might roust them in an emergency "drill" to ward off imagined attacks from nameless enemies. And in addition to fake firefights at two hundred hours, they held forced marches in daylight, two- or three-mile jaunts at double time through the bush, Prahler pacing them all the way, calling on from the front or appearing suddenly in the rear to boot stragglers back into the column.

"You think *this* is tough, boys?" he would yell with an expression that they could interpret as half joking or half insane, as they wished. "Just wait till Uncle Sam packs your ass off to Vietnam!"

No one complained and no one fell out. The ones Charles thought would drop first—Billy, Ford, and the elder Wong and Sanders—actually seemed the most determined. Like himself, he guessed. You get used to getting picked last for teams in gym class, he thought, picked on by bullies who can smell your fear no matter how much deodorant you roll on; you get tired of it. You get to a point where you'd rather die than give somebody one more thing to give you shit for; and if you got any chance they might drop first, well you would gladly die for that. And guys like Joe, Jim, and Luiz must have sensed that, because they seemed all the less willing to let the tenderfeet see them weaken.

After half a dozen outings with Prahler, Charles could feel himself toughen. He got no tan in the jungle, but his muscles hardened and the sight of a spider or centipede or scorpion, even the touch of one dropping on his arm, no longer frightened him as it once did. He spoke less, and when he did he sounded more like one of his friends than one of his teachers. He hadn't played a war game in quite a while, and dust began to collect on the last group of tin soldiers he had begun to paint. One night at dinner his mother asked him about that. When he brushed the question aside he thought he saw his father smile.

As the end of the spring semester neared, Las Casas asked his English class to write a five-hundred-word essay about an experience they'd had overseas. Charles thought about it and decided to write about the road up SOQ Hill, how long it seemed in the dark after he left the Teen Club, and how spooky it looked with the jungle creeping in on each side and the trees forming an archway over it, and how the shadows from the few streetlights waved around so one couldn't tell the cracks in the sidewalk from snakes. In the end he didn't write an essay so much as a kind of hysterical Edgar Allan Poe narrative in which the writer—Charles—went insane before reaching the top of the hill. It struck Charles as either a work of genius or frighteningly bad. Las Casas hailed it and made him read it in front of the class, which Charles did. Then a girl read the one other essay Las Casas liked, about her family's pet iguana during their tour in the Canal Zone. When Las Casas asked the class which they preferred the iguana came out a clear winner. Las Casas looked disappointed. Charles would have felt disappointed, but at least he seemed to have Las Casas' support, for all that mattered. But what, he wondered, did any of it matter? If the other students had enjoyed his essay, would that have reduced his real-world fear? Only making that walk over and over—and worse walks deep in the jungle with Prahler and the post—had done anything about the fear. Writing about it made no difference at all.

Charles saw Joan two or three times a week. She still hadn't met any boys in her own grade, or any she particularly liked, so he had a clear field, and while he would have given nearly anything for the accolades of Jim and Luiz upon the momentous occasion of scoring, "nearly" did not include the small sense of accomplishment he felt holding up his end of the conversation with a sophomore and knowing that she didn't mind people seeing them together. Or the conversations themselves, which wandered from school readings like *Romeo and Juliet* and *For Whom the Bell Tolls* to music and art, and even the Philippines. Sometimes they talked about the war, too, but never much. Joan wanted it over, like most girls said they did, but Charles couldn't quite imagine his future in the Navy if Vietnam ended before he graduated from college.

Luiz of all people came closest to reconciling Charles to his relationship with Joan, though perhaps not intentionally, and certainly not directly. "Cat," Luiz told Charles, "you really something. Like, I fuck girls all the time, but man, I can't never talk with them."

On a Sunday in May Charles saw Joan again, quite by accident, as he dropped by the Teen Club after another Saturday night in the jungle practicing war with Prahler and the boys of 360. He walked her home at twilight; as they reached the intersection at the base of SOQ Hill, the sky suddenly dimmed and turned a dull orange. They stopped. She turned to him and reached up to gently touch his forehead where the night before a thorny vine had ripped a narrow gash. She looked pretty in the half light, he thought. Her pale face seemed to glow and her long narrow nose cast a shadow that linked with the wave of her dark pageboy. It gave her eyes now fixed on him the look of an inquiring half-moon. *Luna*, he thought. Yet before either of them could say anything they became abruptly aware of a series of graceful creatures slowly swimming across the sea above them as it switched from orange to deep blue. Many at first, they soon became more, covering the air above Joan and Charles in a thickening cloud of large, purposeful creatures with the heads of intelligent dogs and the wings of strangely benign devils.

"Fruit bats," said Charles before she could ask. "Migrating."

"Oh my."

They both stared up. As the sky darkened to indigo the bats grew even more numerous, crowding it from horizon to horizon. Joan shook her head.

"It's like an omen. It should mean something."

She really did look pretty, Charles thought.

"It means the rains are coming," he guessed, "and they're following the fruit."

"They must have done this for millions of years!" she exclaimed.

"I don't know," Charles said. "I was home this time last year."

SOMEBODY ELSE'S WAR

This time of year, just before the rains, the giant fruit bats held regular twilight processions over the jungle and, despite a few early showers, the grass on the hills a mile beyond the Barkers' dining room window stood tawny and crisp. While sitting at the table one evening watching the bats, Charles listened to his parents talk about The Movie.

These days everyone on the U.S. Naval Station, Subic Bay, Republic of the Philippines, talked about The Movie. In Vietnam the war persisted like a geological era: on Hamburger Hill, red and green tracers crossed like luminous fountains; in one night the VC and NVA launched more than two hundred attacks on military and civilian targets around the country; Nixon came up with an eight-point peace proposal; and America made plans to draft nineteen-year-olds. But it all read just like the news everyone had heard for the last five or six years—no fresher than reruns of *The Dick Van Dyke Show*. In contrast, the report that Michael Caine and Cliff Robertson would come to Subic to make a movie about the British army fighting the Japanese in World War II had everyone's attention. It went well beyond the Navy's customary entertainment of swing combos, balladeers, and artists from various Filipino and other Southeast Asian folk ensembles. Charles remembered with some fondness, as well as embarrassment, watching a performance of the second corps of the Philippine national dance troupe, the Bamiyan Dancers, whose tightly wrapped, richly bosomed and buttocked female dancers shaking and spinning to a mounting climax of native percussion pinned him in his seat at the main naval station theater with an erection so fiercely insistent that it drained the blood from all his limbs and left him paralyzed and drooling. Still, it couldn't compare to Hollywood.

The maid set a plate of rice in the center of the table next to a platter of pork chops and a bowl of string beans. Mrs. Barker looked thoughtfully at her nails, her wavy helmet of Clairol Blonde making a not-displeasing, glossy continuation of the dry hillsides across the valley. She pursed her lips—full, but not overly so, lips that she didn't need to paint wider or narrower as did the mothers of some of Charles's friends—and said, "Of course we'll have to have a reception for them at the club just as soon as they get here, but I don't know. We can't look too eager. They'll think we're just a bunch of hicks."

Commander Barker looked at her from the other end of the dining table, chewed slowly on his chop, and swallowed. He had just started to gray, Charles noticed, but he still looked healthier than he did stateside. He'd gotten a tan, bronzing his balding forehead, and he'd lost weight. Twelve-hour days in the Tropics overseeing the construction of an extension to the naval hospital apparently agreed with him far more than eight-hour days at BUMED back in D.C. There he'd spent his tour constructing answers to mothers who wrote on various pretexts to request medical discharges for their sons, like the marine who'd lost his left testicle to his training company's bulldog mascot. "The loss of a single testicle is not considered an insurmountable impediment to continued service in the enlisted ranks of the United States Marine Corps," Commander Barker wrote in a memo that he read back to Charles the evening of its composition, laughing ruefully between swigs at his little blue plastic bottle of Maalox.

"Isn't the admiral's wife handling that?" he asked.

"And a wives' committee, which I'm on," she replied. "But it's not easy, honey. Lord knows what these people are used to, or what they expect to find out here. I just don't know."

She shook her head as she reached for the soy sauce. Charles passed it, having already liberally spritzed not only his rice, but his pork and string beans as well, a habit he'd picked up in Japan at the age of six. He almost felt sorry for his mother, except that he knew she would figure it all out in time, right down to exactly what dress to wear, not only at the reception, but to the PX the first time she heard a rumor that some of the movie people planned to shop there. She had spent nearly as many years as a Navy wife as her husband had in uniform, and in her own field had no less energy, insight, and skill.

"Well," said Commander Barker, "I know you'll figure something out, sweetheart. You always do. And those folks, wherever the hell they're from, are going to find out that there's more to the Navy than ships and planes. It's gentlemen and their ladies, too. No airs, but classy enough for them." He nodded and winked at Charles and for a moment the boy wished he had the next seven years behind him already and could go to that party with his father, both of them in their dress whites with their ceremonial swords. They'd show Hollywood.

A few days later Charles discovered that he might not have to wait to meet the movie people. Word had come that the film crew would need extras for group shots of a company of British infantry. With no carrier or battalion landing team in port at the time, the movie crew could only find that many Caucasian males by relying on base personnel and dependents old enough to pass for enlistees. All the boys of 360 thought they'd have a chance, except Luiz and the Wong and Sanders brothers, who took their skin color with varying degrees of equanimity.

"Motherfucking whitey," Ed spat disdainfully from his usual booth in the Teen Club snack bar.

"It's not racism," remonstrated his brother Tom; "it's supposed to be a *Scottish* regiment—they didn't *have* any Negroes in Scotland in World War II."

"Oh right," Ed replied, "like I'm supposed to take *this* bit of honky-assed repression because it's a historically accurate reproduction of *that* bit of honky-assed repression!"

"'Honky-assed,'" noted Ford, sitting beside Ed. "Interesting phraseology. Is that an authentic bit of Afro-American invective, or did you just make it up?"

"Oh bite me, white boy. Whatchoo gonna play in the movie— part of the elite midget Highlander company?"

Luiz and Carl Wong laughed while Tom and George Wong shook their heads in the neighboring booth.

"Actually," said Ford, "I'm too short to even bother to try out. I don't particularly mind; in fact part of me welcomes the chance to express my solidarity with my dusky-hued brethren . . ."

"Say what?" said Ed.

". . . but the rest of me is, to use the vernacular, pissed off."

Charles turned from his seat at the bar and a half-empty Coke. "Don't tell me you wanted to be in pictures, too."

"No, not that. It's just that I doubt that I'll stay this short when I reach draft age. I mean, I don't mind missing the movie war if I can skip the real one, too."

"What you scared of, little cat?" asked Luiz. "It's just a war."

They all laughed, except Ford, who replied, "Yeah, just a war. A war that's gone on since before I was born and doesn't look like it's ever gonna end. It just hangs out there, man, like some kind of macabre graduation present. It creeps me out."

"Hey, you know what?" George said to Charles. "Since we can't get to be extras, maybe the rest of you guys should stay out, too. You know, like Ford—show some solidarity."

"Oh fuck that," Ed said. "This fight is ours, brothers."

"'Brothers'?" asked Tom. "Does that include me?"

Ed glanced over at his older brother and grimaced. "Shi-it."

Saturday morning the rest of the post showed up in front of the PX by seven hundred and waited for the battleship-gray liberty bus to take them to the film site out past the naval air station at Cubi. When the moving van-sized vehicle arrived, they piled into the steel, unupholstered interior with a few score hungover sailors and marines, grabbed a bar or handle, and hung on.

"Why aren't there any seat cushions?" Charles asked.

"Think," said Jim, pushing his granny glasses up over puffy eyes. "Just think what's involved in getting a ship's company back from a night on the town in Olongapo. You want something you can just hose out and send back to the main gate for more, right?"

Between the whine of the diesel engine, the jostling of the enlisted men, and the sporadic reverberation of steel walls, the ride felt like a long one. By the time they arrived at the set a strange blend of enthusiasm and panic had set in and passengers began to leap from the bus before it came to a stop, seemingly afraid that the film wouldn't need everyone who'd come. But only Billy and a couple of other smaller dependents less honest with themselves than Ford got sent back. For the most part even boys like Finch and Charles, who really did look no more than their own ages, got taken to fill out the big crowd scene.

After spilling out of the bus, the applicants faced a series of shacks along the side of the dusty parking lot. Entering at one end they picked up their British uniforms piece by piece, ending in a crude dressing area where they could change from their civvies, dungarees, and fatigues. A technical adviser showed them how to lace up their boots Brit-style. Charles had not realized that the British had their own way of doing this, but a helpful marine explained that in fact any number of boot-lacing styles existed, including ones for paratroopers, rangers, and SEALs. And so for months after those in the know could look at the jungle boots of Explorer Post 360 and tell which pairs' owners had acted in the film.

Once the extras suited up they walked over to the set. This consisted of six stilted bungalows with thatched roofs and two European-type buildings representing a church and a store. The crew built the latter pair of plywood sheets sprayed with concrete and aged with paint and dirt; they looked quite real, even only a few feet away. The set buildings formed a rough U with the open end dotted by two mortar pits set a few meters back from a line of three sandbagged emplacements holding—Charles noted happily—authentic Vickers water-cooled .303-caliber heavy machine guns. The firing line faced a dry grassy field that ended several hundred meters away in a stretch of jungle. Brown hills bordered the field on either side. Behind the set sparse trees led perhaps fifty meters back to the beach where a few booths manned by hopeful Filipino vendors offered beer, soda, and cigarettes.

Soon after gathering on the set the extras found that their roles would require little more than standing in the hot dust within the U and staring off at the jungle as if it held something of compelling interest. Most of them didn't think this too demanding, especially at $12.50 a day and the possibility of a recognizable appearance, however brief, on a real movie screen. Still, before the first day ended boredom began to gain the upper hand over their hopes for stardom, and two hours into the second morning they began to think of ways to keep themselves engaged.

For several of the sailors and marines, as well as Jim and Joe, this meant sneaking away from the production staff and lolling under the trees or inside the buildings of the set with San Miguels they bought on the beach. Others tried to make themselves distinctive in the wide-angle crowd scenes. For example, Charles, MacReady, and Finch joined up with two sailors from the public affairs office and did a kind of dance where, in a line of five, two of them would step forward while the other three stepped back, then vice versa, hoping to create enough of a wave to notice when they saw the film later, but not enough to get the scene cut. Other enlisted men broke into the arms trailer and slowly waved Enfields over their heads until some of the film crew noticed and made them stop.

The film called for extras several weekends in a row, and much the same group kept returning. As time passed they grew even less content to stand in the sun with no better shelter than khaki shorts and strange drab berets with pom-poms. By noon of the third Sunday nearly half the extras had found San Miguels and shade, and it took a major effort of the crew to round up a quorum for the afternoon's camera work.

Charles decided that despite the difference in pay and exposure he would, as if he'd ever have the choice, rather work as an extra than as a star. Extras, he decided, could sneak off or at least stand in the shade of someone taller, and when the man came around with Vaseline to smear on to represent sweat, an extra could wipe it off on the ground and make do with his own perspiration while the star had to stand out there with a pasty covering of dirt and petroleum jelly, run a hundred-yard dash and dive down as if shot, then repeat that fifty or sixty times until some short dork with sunglasses and a floppy hat said, "Okay, that's a wrap." *Fuck that*, thought Charles. As the lunch break ended he and MacReady got their own San Miguels and played hooky by the beach for an hour. They teamed up with an overweight sailor from Supply who kept saying, "Man, this is the life. Easiest goddamn money you'll ever make."

The sailor remained good natured and continued to laugh when a short skinny marine with a map of Vietnam tattooed just below the rolled-up right sleeve of his British OD shirt walked up, waved a half-empty Schlitz, and complained about the whole idea of the film.

"Goddamn," he said. "Why the goddamn hell are we making a film about some pussy goddamn limeys in my daddy's war? Huh? Tell me, man. Here my bros are over in 'Nam getting their nuts shot off and these fucking limey faggots are making movies about a buncha fuckers in short pants. Fuck *me*, man."

"Bend over," chortled the sailor. "Didn't you get off watching *The Green Berets?*"

"Shit," said the marine, "that fat old fuck Wayne's a goddamn joke. You know they made that flick in *Georgia?* Whoever saw a fucking pine tree in Viet-goddamn-nam? Shit. That was just another World War II movie in disguise, man. Just like *Sands of Iwo Jima* and all that shit. Just like this crap right here—somebody else's army, somebody else's war."

By the next weekend the set had become even drier because that much more time had passed without the rains that now held back with as much threat as promise, making the sky heavy and the sun seem extra mean. Early Saturday morning the extras had a little excitement when the director marched them out into the field in front of the firing line and they got to stand someplace different, but things had become so dry that the brittle grass could not keep the dust down any better than the dust held itself down, and the extras sweated and choked for an hour while a helicopter flew back and forth and the director yelled at them not to look up. Matters became more exciting when a cameraman six meters up in a shaky tower dropped a lit cigar and burned a black patch ten meters in diameter before the twenty-year-old fire engine parked in back of the set could get started up and out there to do its job.

That ought to have made the right impression on everyone, but everyone didn't stay sober long enough to hold it. A little after thirteen hundred, when the production assistants had managed to assemble just over half the extras for another take of the stand-ing-in-the-ville-looking-at-the-faraway-jungle scene, three drunk sailors staggered out of the thatched bungalow next to the store just ahead of a sudden extrusion of thick gray smoke.

"Fire!" yelled one as they fell over each other in front of the church. A wave of laughter rolled off the crowd of extras. But then the bungalow erupted in closely bunched streamers of scarlet and orange and one of the crew repeated the cry, "Fire!"

"No shit," said MacReady, lifting his cap so that the sun glinted off his red curls in a weird echo of the blaze. "C'mon Charles. Let's go to the beach and get a beer before a line forms."

Charles looked around. Groups of marines and sailors walked or jogged in three or four directions around the fire; they blocked most of his view, but he could see flames beginning to sprout from the roof next to the bungalow where the fire started, while a wall of smoke began to curl off the church. Behind him the crew tried to bring the old fire engine in from the fields but got it hung up on an overhead power line just in front of the Vickers machine guns. It looked like the whole set would go in minutes and nothing anyone did would make much difference.

As Charles passed around the not-yet-burning side of the church a haze of smoke descended to meet the dust rising from everyone trying to walk or run away and, in less than a minute from the start of the fire, he had lost track of MacReady among all the other uniforms and could no longer see more than a few meters in any direction. He thought he might follow the crowd but the crowd dispersed like an expanding galaxy of slow-moving, confused pairs and trios of unarmed, choking men in unfamiliar clothing, some heading to the beach, some to the parking lot, and some to wherever they thought the smoke wouldn't follow. He slowed when he got to the gravel road behind the set and then stopped, wondering where to go. To his right the haze quickly grew dense as fog, his eyes watered, and an acrid stink rasped at his nose and throat.

Out of the smoke a big man, probably a marine, six-three or -four, more than two hundred, stumbled blindly, arms outstretched as if working on a Halloween party parody of Frankenstein. Charles stepped up to help him, thinking perhaps to give him some support on one side and show him the way to the parking lot, but as soon as he touched him the marine collapsed in his arms and knocked him down. Charles fell hard on his butt and then got thrown back and buried under the deadweight of the man he tried to rescue. Taking a deep breath of the nasty smoke he looked at the shadows passing around him and cried, "Help!"

Immediately three men in khaki grabbed the victim by his arms and legs and dragged him off in the direction of the parking lot. Another man, blond, filthy, maybe in his thirties, probably an officer, come out of the smoke in his Brit fatigues and helped Charles up. "You okay, sailor?" he asked.

"Yeah, sure," replied Charles.

"Okay, be careful," said the man as he disappeared.

Charles followed the rescuers a short distance when the smoke suddenly cleared to reveal a water trailer with three Filipinos standing by it smoking and smiling while Finch bent down and opened the taps wide into four gallon-sized cans. Joe, passing, said, "Give it up, man! It's over!" then stopped and moved to help him to his feet. Finch waved him off. Turning back to the spigots, Finch saw Charles and, as if he had just woken up, said, "You better follow Joe, Barker. If you see MacReady take him, too." *Right,* thought Charles. Like he could leave Finch there to contemplate something useless and heroic by himself. He ran over and grabbed one of the cans as water spilled over its top and shouted, "Where to?" because by now the air had filled not only with smoke but also the sound of hundreds of young men shouting over the gusty noise of flames eating buildings and acres of high, dry grass and scrub. Finch shouted back, "Follow me!" and Charles did, each of them with one heavy and altogether insignificant can of water, heading to where the smoke seemed thickest and flames four meters high spread their perimeter beyond the set, marching toward the supply trailers on the edge of the parking lot. Five meters from the flames the fire felt so hot and the smoke grew so choking that the two scouts could do nothing more than dump their cans at their feet, and even Finch could see that their efforts had no more use than trying to douse a chimney fire with an eyedropper you had to refill next door.

"C'mon!" Charles urged, "let's get out of here!" Finch nodded, doubled over with a vicious hacking cough, then grabbed Charles's arm and the two of them jogged down the road toward the parking lot. A few sailors and marines passed them, three or four others seemed to keep pace with them, but almost everyone else had already escaped to the lot or the beach, or perhaps hadn't escaped at all. Through the haze the two boys could see a large group milling or collapsed in front of the uniform and equipment shacks, but as they passed by a trailer parked between the gravel road and the flames an excited crew member in flared jeans and a photographer's vest emerged and shouted, "Hey! Give us a hand here! We got a ton of black powder and if it goes everyone goes!"

"C'mon," said Finch, straightening up and turning to the trailer.

"Ah, fuck," said Charles. "Okay. Sure."

They ran up to the trailer with smoke blowing past and the wall of flames cracking and shushing and swaying gracefully and impersonally toward them perhaps another trailer length away. Inside the trailer six extras busied themselves hoisting forty-pound crates, which they then began passing out in a chain of bodies. Finch and Charles took their places just inside the door, catching the rough wood boxes, Finch passing his to Charles and Charles passing his to the crewman, who passed his to someone else who'd just answered his call, and so to another and another into the rear of a truck that had just backed up as the first box reached the end of the chain. In a minute and a half they emptied the trailer and ran after the truck to the safety of the lot. In another two minutes the tall flames stopped at the gravel road, surrounded the trailer, and blackened and bent it like a beer can in a beach party bonfire.

It all ended shortly after that. Everywhere the fire hit the road it burned itself out and behind it, in the set where it had begun, the old fire engine, with the wind at its back and a crew of a dozen extras and technicians, stopped it from spreading into the fields. In the end only half the set burned and only five men needed to go to the hospital for burns or smoke inhalation.

After counting his cuts and bruises, Charles got up from the dust in the parking lot and walked back through the haze to the set with the other Explorers. Movie people had already raised a team of Filipino workmen to disassemble the charred framework of the church and two bungalows. Michael Caine, looking like he did at the end of *Zulu* but in a more modern uniform, stood by the mortar pits surveying the damage. Like the hero of a hard-won battle, thought Charles, but then an obsequious stagehand with buck teeth brought the star a paper cup of tea, tag hanging out at the side, and somehow broke the spell.

"Goddamn, that was cool!" said MacReady. "Fucking fire almost killed us all!"

Charles, Finch, and Joe all laughed, but Joe added, "You fuckers are crazy, you know that? That powder could have gone off."

"It didn't," said Finch, "but if it did, we wouldn't have been the only ones killed."

Joe shook his head. A little later they broke early for the day and the producer put five extra dollars in their pay for helping to put out the fire.

"Easiest goddamn money you'll make in your life," laughed the fat sailor as they boarded the liberty bus back to the PX.

Charles hung on to a vertical bar in the creaking interior and decided that he had done a brave thing. All the other extras talked about how high and fierce the fire had grown, and how quickly it had moved. Beyond that he knew how bravely he and Finch had acted by the number of sailors and marines who claimed that they, too, had helped move the powder. They might have, but only from behind, where the two Explorer Scouts couldn't see them. Still, he didn't feel brave. It seemed so much a part of everything else that he could hardly remember doing it at all.

And yet that night at the Teen Club he told Joan. He didn't exaggerate, he thought, but also made no attempt to diminish the height and heat of the fire, the size of the marine he tried to help, or the volatility of black powder. With some satisfaction he saw her eyes widen and her face take on an expression of shock.

"I can't believe you did that," she said.

"Well, someone had to."

"Charles, no one had to. You should have just gotten out of there."

"What?"

"Do you think that silly movie was worth anyone's life?"

"Well, no, but . . ."

"Then why, Charles?"

He thought for a moment. It seemed so obvious, and yet so unexplainable. "It's what guys do, Joan. Someone asks for your help, you give it."

"Charles, that's why boys kill themselves trying to get touchdowns. That's why they go to wars that make no sense. You know better than that."

He looked at her, and then away. "No. I guess I don't." She brushed her bangs aside with a thin pale hand and seemed ready to say something else, but he said, "Look, I gotta be getting home. It's been a long day."

He got up before she could say anything more and walked off, getting all the way up SOQ Hill before something in the air made his eyes water.

✢ XII ✦

THE WRECK OF THE *EVANS*

At ten hundred a small group of Explorers stood in their
camos in the riding rink, a large circular shed of sheet
metal over sand, and listened to the clanging rain. At
eight hundred, as he dropped Charles off, Commander Barker
had said it looked like rain and at nine hundred, as if on command, the sky proved him right. Through the two exits and the
top half of the rink below the roof, where the bleachers ended
and it opened to the elements, the scouts could see the jungle
blurred behind a pouring fabric. Mist and a gelatinous humidity crept inside and dampened their fatigues and spirits. For
today's survival hike Prahler had made only one concession to
the weather: to wait until after his birthday party when the rains
might have let up some. But the scouts knew that the march
would still mean plunging into dripping bush for a soggy march
to nowhere and none of them felt happy about it. Finch confided
to Charles that perhaps they shouldn't have bothered.

Lately Finch confided in Charles a lot. Prahler's marches had
begun to take a toll on the post. Joe spent more and more time
running with his Ace fraternity brothers at the Teen Club or out

in town. Jim more openly questioned why he should miss an evening with Lee Ann just to sleep in the mud with boys who, as he put it, could only get dates with each other. Tom and George now only appeared at monthly meetings to vainly plead for tours of carriers or sight-seeing trips and no longer hiked in the jungle. Ed and Carl still wanted to prove themselves tougher than their older brothers, but with their older brothers not going out at all anymore, they felt free to cut back on their own adventures. And even before Prahler, Not-Ready MacReady had never had a reputation for steady attendance. As a result, this day's expedition of Explorer Post 360 consisted only of Finch, Luiz, Charles, Billy, and Ford, and Billy and Ford only came because neither wanted to give the other an excuse to call him a pussy.

Prahler ignored the desertions and focused on his twentieth birthday party. The three dependent girls who worked at the stables—mousey thirteen-year-olds, observed Charles, who wouldn't have noticed the Explorers unless they had suddenly grown manes and hooves—brought Prahler a small cake from the commissary and a portable forty-five player from the PX. They spun the "Birthday" single from the *White Album* and sang to themselves as they laid out little paper plates and plastic forks on a card table in the middle of the rink. While they did this, Sparks—Prahler's short-haired little black-and-white mutt—divided his time between chasing his tail and sniffing at the boys' jungle boots.

None of the Filipino workers who cared for the horses and kept up the fences and trails bothered with them. Nominally they lived off base, but in fact they spent most evenings in a Quonset hut bunkhouse and only visited their families a few times a month. They kept their clothes and personal gear in the hut and had fit wooden cages with chickens above the stalls in the stables where snakes and civet cats couldn't get at them. A few of the older workers knew everything one needed to know about running the operation, so things had always worked well no matter who Special Services sent to manage the place.

Much of that had changed when Prahler arrived. He had ideas about running the stables just like he had ideas about running the post and he didn't much worry about the natives in either case. At the stables he enforced hours of work and a dress code and docked the pay of several workers who'd displeased him in some fashion. The Filipinos took it because they knew Prahler had increased revenues and gotten in good with his superiors and that, in any case, a petty officer second class had considerably more rank than any of them could ever attain as Filipinos. Besides, a lot of managers had started out hard before realizing that no one really cared, and that they would get just as far in the Navy by letting the old hands run the place. The workers must have thought that, sooner or later, Prahler too would figure it out, so they said nothing when he came up with new or long-forgotten rules to enforce, or when Sparks chased their chickens when they let them out to exercise during the day. They knew no one had authorized them to keep chickens anyway.

Luiz broke away from the party to chat with some of the workers, but Prahler sang the chorus for perhaps the tenth time, dancing with one of the girls while the other two, dancing in place, cut the cake.

Charles looked on, almost with admiration. "You're like a medieval lord here," he said. "You got your horses . . ."

"Yeah," grinned Prahler, "and my serving wenches . . ." pinching his dance partner, who smirked modestly.

"And your knights," said Finch.

"And dogs and stuff," said Billy.

"All to keep a lid on the peasants, right men?" Prahler laughed, looking at the Filipinos' Quonset.

Masked by the music, Ford muttered, "And let's not leave out My Lord's pigheaded arrogance whilst we're at it . . ."

Finch gave him a reassuring pat on the shoulder.

By ten forty-five they'd finished their cake and soda and the rain had tapered off to drizzle. One small ray broke through the clouds over the bay as the little file pulled on their packs and marched off to the sawmill and the wet woods beyond. Sparks barked, the girls waved and giggled, and a few Filipinos stopped their chores long enough to wonder why half a dozen children had chosen this particular form of penance. Half an hour into the jungle and the rain returned, spending much of its force in the canopy but surviving as thousands of little rivulets pouring down on the scouts. By the time they reached the campsite above the falls and rigged their ponchos into a kind of tarp, they had become too wet to really care, and the mist flowing under their makeshift roof kept them as damp as if they'd stayed outside. For a time the rain poured hard again and between it and the shade of the jungle and the dripping ponchos they could hardly tell when twilight came and passed, but huddled together in the dark and wondered what to say.

This sucks, thought Charles. *We've seen nothing, we've done nothing, we just walked over ground we walked over before, only got soaked and bored and miserable doing it.* He looked at Finch but Finch had turned to look after Billy and Ford, who trembled and looked pale. Luiz sat with his eyes closed and a half smile, seeming to have dreamed himself to a place with b-girls, Tanduay and Coke, and a Filipino band that could do a reasonable imitation of Sam and Dave. Prahler squatted in the glare of a flashlight and pared his nails with the tip of a Kabar.

Charles closed his eyes for a moment and listened as Finch tried to talk Billy and Ford into sharing a can of pound cake with him. A little later he felt him move closer and heard him whisper to Prahler like a loyal XO whose captain had just steered a little closer to the iceberg.

"Maybe this wasn't such a good idea. Maybe we should head out."

"Bullshit," said Prahler out loud. "This is a breeze. What the hell you little jerk-offs whining about? A little rain? Shit, man, hundreds of dudes die every week in 'Nam—thousands, if you want to get technical and count slopes—and you're complaining? Shit."

That night Ford kept them all up with his coughing and sneezing so they left in the morning as early as they could see. Luiz led the way and helped Billy while Finch and Charles practically carried Ford. Prahler picked up the rear, riding them all they way back. Charles looked at Finch but Finch just shook his head and bit his tongue.

A week later no one hiked and Charles went down to the main naval station to kill time. He hung out by the bleachers of the big ballpark and listened to a Navy band, some in whites, some in dungarees, as they marched up and down the diamond rehearsing "El Capitan." Finch walked up, from out of nowhere it seemed, and stood beside him for minute just listening.

"You know," said Charles as the sailors finished the piece and began to disperse, "they say that was the march Dewey had played on the *Olympia* right before they went off to sink the Spanish fleet."

"See this?" Finch asked, handing Charles a copy of *Stars and Stripes.*

Charles stared at the headlines. Five sailors with trombones and trumpets stood around in a rough circle by home plate and began a casual rendition of "Mercy, Mercy, Mercy." The headline said the destroyer *Evans* had gone down in the South China Sea. Part of it, anyway. Farther in the article Charles read that the *Evans* had cruised with a SEATO task force, running night anti-sub maneuvers with an Australian carrier. Somebody zigged when they should have zagged and the carrier caught the tin can amidships and cut her in two. When the destroyer's crew shut all the bulkheads the aft stayed afloat, but seventy-six sailors rode the fore straight to the bottom.

Charles looked up from the page at nothing. He had seen the ocean, not just on the flight from Travis or diving from a small boat off Grande Island, but as it had appeared to him at the age of four when his family had spent two and a half weeks on a dingy gray transport from Frisco to Yokohama: a world of gray forevers, a light smooth gray stretching endlessly above and a dark rippled gray spreading far beyond the horizon and covering a depth he could only begin to imagine. He saw the bow of the destroyer descending into that, momentarily visible like part of a model under dark, wavy glass, then nothing, and he began to shake.

"Take it easy," said Finch. "You know any of them?"

"No. I don't think so." He wondered how long it took the sailors trapped in their watertight compartments to realize that they would never leave.

That evening at the Teen Club Luiz told Charles about another tragedy of sorts. Prahler had chewed out one of the old hands at the stables and as the Filipino left the office he happened upon Sparks in the act of finally catching one of the chickens. The chicken screamed and flapped like crazy, said Luiz, which evidently pushed the Filipino over the line between angry and amok, because while Sparks dallied, intrigued by this suddenly more interesting dimension to the game of chase, the Filipino had time to get his bolo from the Quonset hut and come after him. Sparks could run quick, but not as quick as an angrily thrown bolo. The blade caught the little dog in the middle of his right rear leg and cut the lower half clean off. Prahler and the girls became hysterical and the old Filipino hid while Luiz and another of the workers got Sparks tied off and drove him to the base vet's. He'd recover fine, Luiz said, but he probably wouldn't catch any more chickens on just three legs.

For the next several days Charles heard about little other than Sparks and the *Evans.* The war faded, as did the approach of the last week of the school year and the prospect of summer jobs on base, while everyone he knew talked about the dog and the trapped sailors. The conversations differed according to whom he had them with. His English teacher, Mr. Las Casas, and his friend Joan, for example, would contrast the dog and the chickens, or the sailors and the thousands of others who died each week in the war, and from that they would try to draw some conclusion of universal significance. But Charles found himself more drawn to the talk of his fellow scouts and questions of more immediate importance: what should they do about the Joe bastards who'd mess with a little dog, in the one case, and in the other, which way would *you* rather get it?

"Blow me away in a hurry," said Charles, "but don't let me drown in the sea."

"Some Navy man," said Ford, and Billy, Luiz, and Finch laughed.

At Ford's suggestion they'd bought a case of sodas to celebrate the end of classes and carried it up to the new park overlooking the playing fields at George Dewey High School. No one ever came to the park except for the Filipino workers who maintained it. Most Americans found it too wild while the scouts found it too tame, so the boys had it pretty much to themselves. They'd toted the case up a steep series of log steps to a cleared trail along a ridgeline. A few hundred meters in they found a scenic clearing atop a cliff where a wide gap in the canopy gave them a panoramic view of Subic Bay. Here they set down the case while Ford brought out a church key and served them their first rounds.

"I don't know," said Billy. "I don't give a shit how I buy it as long as I get to kill a few slopes first."

"I wanna die in bed," said Ford.

"Yeah? Whose?" laughed Luiz. "I figure I go to Vietnam, it don't matter how I die. I gonna fuck so many whores, in sixteen years the whole country look just like me."

"You better watch out," said Billy. "I hear the VC got whores with razors in their cunts—split you right down the middle. I'm gonna take a year's worth of *Playboys* and get all my real pussy in Sasebo."

"We believe the first part of that," said Charles.

After a few minutes the mosquitoes began to get to them. Billy asked Ford for his comb and then scratched his ass with it. Ford grabbed it back and made as if to spray him with soda, which under the circumstances might have deadly consequences. But Luiz, smelling smoke, led them all into the jungle to where half a dozen Filipino workers had rigged a canvas sheet overhead and started a smoky leaf fire to keep the bugs away. The boys gave the workers some sodas and hung out in the smoke for a while.

Billy whispered to Charles. "You figure these Flips heard what I said about slopes earlier?"

"Maybe. I'm sure they understand the difference, though. Hell, maybe they already plan to kill us."

"Huh?"

"I mean, we just *thought* they were workers. Maybe they're smugglers. Or Huks."

"Shit. And me without a sixteen." He looked up and smiled at the workmen, several of whom smiled and nodded back.

"That," said Charles, "must be the same shit-eating grin the raj and the natives flashed at each other every time they met."

"Long as they don't attack," said Ford.

"Hey, look here!" Luiz shouted from their old position by the cliff. When the other three rejoined him their eyes followed his gesture to the far reaches of the bay. There they could see the task force bringing in the aft third of the *Evans*. It lay in the water lashed to the side of an American carrier like an injured papoose. Four destroyers escorted the carrier, neatly spaced around it in the corners of an imaginary box.

"I read about this," said Charles. "They were ready yesterday but they had to give the VIPs time to get down from Manila."

Finch said, "Yeah, well, who's in a hurry?"

They watched as the ships came in like little daggers then sailed in a broad sweep around Grande Island and began to grow to the size of tiny plastic models.

"Look at that," said Billy. "Seventy-six short. I bet those fuckers are so deep they'll never rot. If anyone ever finds 'em they'll be just as they were when they went down, playing acey-deucey in the foc'sle or jacking off in their racks."

"Just stow it a little while," said Finch, and Billy shut up while the models grew to real warships and finally merged with the mass of battleship-gray cranes, floating dry docks, masts, superstructures, and hulls down at the main naval station docks. Then the boys turned away and left, abandoning most of their sodas for the Filipinos to find.

Finch lagged behind with Charles.

"I'm a little concerned about the men," said Finch.

"The who?"

"The boys. Our buddies. Prahler's not going to get any saner after what's happened to Sparks. Things are already starting to unravel. Jim's always off whoring around, Joe I hear is into some really serious shit in town, and it's all going down on my watch."

Charles stopped and looked at him. "Hey, none of this is your fault."

"I'm talking responsibility, not fault. It's my watch."

Charles looked at the others getting farther ahead of them, nodded, and began walking again, Finch following closely. After a few moments, Charles said, "Maybe you could talk to him."

"Prahler?"

"Or your dad, maybe."

"Right."

That Sunday the Navy held a memorial service in the big airy naval station chapel, and it seemed that most of the base had come to pay their respects. The pews filled with officers and men in whites, civilian and dependent males in coat and tie or barong tagalog, and girls and women in dresses with veils and gloves. The sailors who played "Mercy, Mercy, Mercy" now played the Navy Hymn and everyone sang, "Oh hear us when we cry to Thee for those in peril on the sea" and, in the crushing silence afterward, a lone trumpeter played Taps.

As the Barkers left the chapel Luiz came up and told Charles that Sparks had made it through as predicted and had returned to the stables earlier that morning. "You wanna see him, cat?" Commander and Mrs. Barker smiled and agreed, so Charles rode out there with Luiz to see Sparks and a small crowd of well-wishers. Sure enough, despite a massive bandage, Sparks seemed as lively as before his injury and danced around Prahler's office chasing a red rubber ball one of the stable girls tossed for him.

But Sparks's high spirits didn't rub off on Prahler. Weeks before he'd had a sign made and hung outside his office as a joke. HEIN-RICH PRAHLER, it said, HOFMEISTER, SS RIDING STABLES, the SS standing for "Special Services." Now it didn't seem so funny. "Those fucking Flips will pay," Prahler said, angry but not out of control, which only made it scarier. "They're history," he said, "first fucking chance I get." Nobody knew what he meant, but they knew he meant it.

That night Charles dreamed that he'd just left Prahler's office, stepping past the box with the towels where Sparks had his bed into a long metal corridor belowdecks on a tin can. He entered a cabin off to the side and as soon as the bulkhead clanged shut behind him he realized he'd somehow gotten on board the *Evans*. The ship had already reached the bottom of the sea and filled with salt water. Somehow he could still breathe, but not easily. Strands of kelp drifted by his face and brightly colored angel and lion fish darted in and out around the sleeping and storage racks.

The sailors there looked beyond boredom. They moved around okay but their eyes had sunk and their flesh had already turned gray. They'd waited a long time for help and had pretty much given up on that. Now dead, they had nothing else to do but wait for the rest of eternity, playing cards and acey-deucey. Charles began to panic when he realized that he might have to stay, but they gave him to understand that he could leave if he could beat them at cards. They'd play war, an easy game.

Charles took the cards they dealt him and played them one by one. The sailors watched, disinterested, their eyes as wide and ever-open as those of the circling fish, their hair wafting in the deep current like seaweed.

Charles turned over the last card in his hand. Deuce of clubs, just like all the others.

BAGUIO

Perhaps it came about because of Sparks. Perhaps when the Filipino stable hand cut off Sparks's right hind leg at the knee with a well-thrown bolo, Petty Officer Prahler suddenly became alert to the fact that he did not have many friends. Even his superiors at Special Services, supportive enough when he boosted revenues a further 10 percent, declined to intervene. They didn't have much choice, really: no Americans witnessed the actual attack, none of the Filipinos would make a formal statement against one of their coworkers, and the possibility of firing the whole staff and starting anew with the sailor on whose watch this had happened had little appeal. As a result, word came down to Prahler through his chain of command that he should forget it, and perhaps for a moment the chop chain thought he really would.

In any event, at the next monthly meeting of Explorer Post 360 Prahler introduced, for him, a radically different scouting concept. Just as he had reached the point at which most of the boys had begun to show up primarily from morbid curiosity, wondering if their next outing would involve something like a quick march on short rations around the wrong end of a firing range in the middle of the next typhoon, Prahler let slip the word *fun*.

"Thing is, men," he announced from the podium in the FICPACFAPFAPL conference room, "Post Three Sixty works hard and it plays hard. We've been working pretty hard out there in the bush lately, and now it's time for us to go somewhere and play hard."

"I hear that," said Jim.

"Hell, I know a little place in town that'd be happy to see the whole post—even give us a little discount for our cherries," said Joe, reaching over to knock on Billy's head.

"Actually, I was thinking Baguio," said Prahler.

The room broke into a wave of nods, soul shakes, "right ons," and "fucking A's." Even Finch seemed to approve, although Charles could tell from his expression that Prahler had not bothered to consult with the post president beforehand.

But no one could object. Everyone wanted to go to Baguio. The city up north in the mountains had a full range of tourist stops, if one needed the excuse of wood carvings, silver work, or gaudy textiles crafted by Igorot hill people. And it had an Air Force base-John Hay—with no greater strategic or tactical rationale than a hill station in British India. Above all, it had cool, dry days, green meadows, conifers, and nights cold enough to call for blankets and fireplaces. Americans might go to Baguio for souvenirs and snapshots, but those who hadn't spent their lives on tropical bases went because for a few days they could almost convince themselves that they had gone home.

A few Fridays after the meeting, after emptying no more than half their modest treasury, the post departed Subic in a Special Services van and sedan: twelve scouts, one counselor, and two Filipino drivers. They saluted the marines at the rear gate and sang and joked all the way down the switchback through the Zambales Mountains. They waved and made faces at the Filipinos in all the little barrios between Subic and San Fernando. They ran through half their film taking pictures for their parents and the folks back home of carabao and calesas, nipa huts, and sari-sari stores, of farmers and armed men of uncertain allegiance. When that paled they took pictures of each other grab-assing until Jim and Joe and Finch pointed out that only a real asshole would shoot all his film before they even reached the mountains.

At San Fernando the caravan turned left instead of right toward Manila and Charles saw a new kind of country. For the last few hours little had changed from the rest of lowland Luzon: rice paddies, farmhouses on stilts above livestock pens, scattered thickets, faraway hills. But now the hills came closer to the road and brought trees with them. Houses began to look more solid, with planks, even logs, replacing mats, scraps, and undaubed wattle. The farther the scouts got from Subic and Clark and Manila, the more the Philippines began to look like its own country and not simply a place where Americans made their servants hide their families. When the boys reached the mountains they saw emerald-green sugarloaves lush with grass, flowers, and civilized trees: a land where platoons of leprechauns would not have looked out of place. The scouts rolled down their windows and breathed in fresh sweet air.

Baguio itself at first looked like many other Philippine towns, but it lacked noticeable squalor or the flocks of vendors who swarmed to Americans like flying foxes to rotten fruit. In other words, it looked to Charles unlike any other Philippine town he had seen.

At the gate to John Hay an airman in pale blue service dress waved the post through onto suburban American streets free of people and exotic smells. After a few blocks they came to an old housing area refurbished for U.S. military tourists and laid claim to two small cottages. Prahler and the boys off-loaded and stowed their gear while the drivers went to their own quarters on the other side of the base. After an impromptu meeting to talk over the options, Prahler allowed the post to disperse and go where they wanted, agreeing to rendezvous at the O Club at eighteen hundred. Tom Sanders, George Wong, and MacReady left for the marketplace to take color photos of authentic Igorot tribesmen, which George thought they might later sell to *Boy's Life*. Billy, Ford, Ed Sanders, and Carl Wong also aimed for the marketplace, but seeking instead authentic Philippine switch-blades and butterfly knives. Prahler went with them to make sure they got a good deal. Charles decided to follow Finch, Jim, Joe, and Luiz on the theory that the old hands would have the best chance of finding something special. But they went to the marketplace, too.

Baguio's market occupied a square of several acres in the center of town. Surrounded by old wood buildings that might have seemed equally apt in Chihuahua, La Paz, or Madrid, it embraced a mazy warren of stalls, shacks, and back rooms pressed together along the sides of narrow alleys each clearly marked by a luminous and aromatic center stripe of urine. Charles stayed close as the group followed Luiz deep inside the shadows where murmurs alternated with laughter and accidental rays of sunlight glinted off polished wood and silver ornaments. They stopped first at a stall where the Igorot proprietor, dressed in a vividly patterned vest of bright primary colors, squatted next to a meter-high carving of a warrior, touching it up with a can of Kiwi. The Igorot stared at his work intently: Charles thought of a story in a recent *Manila Times* about how a few Igorots, for reasons obscure, raided a Tagalog barrio not far from Baguio and killed eight residents. With spears.

Joe found a bolo in the shop and, with Luiz's help, bargained for it. Charles briefly wondered what might happen if they somehow insulted the Igorot and he killed Luiz, leaving the rest of them lost among hostiles, but then a few dollars changed hands and Phil-Am relations remained secure.

After this, Charles and Finch went off on their own to search for silver jewelry. Finch would not leave until Joe, Jim, and Luiz solemnly swore that they wouldn't go out for dinner at an exotic local whorehouse rather than the John Hay O Club. With that done, Finch and Charles looked over a dozen displays of silver in the space of a block before deciding that they had enough of an idea of local prices to go ahead and buy. Each booth they visited presented a variety of choices in the same general style: pins and brooches and pendants of leaves and blossoms in intricate filigree. "The Igorots mine this stuff in the mountains," Finch explained, "and missionaries buy it on the cheap. They have a school for orphans where they teach them to do it up. Pretty isn't it? It only costs a little more than if you bought it by weight."

But nothing cost much. Jewelry, vests, ponchos, carvings, cutleryall went for one or two or at most five dollars, perhaps a bit more if one tried to pay in pesos. Finch bought two brooches: one for his mother and one for a girl he knew back stateside and sometimes mentioned. Charles broke down and bought two as well: one for his own mother and one for someone else, perhaps Joan.

Finch found their way out of the marketplace and they started on the long walk back to their cabin. "I wish I could be sure about all of the men," he said. "Joe and Jim might blow off dinner just to razz me."

"Don't worry about it," said Charles, though now that Finch brought it up he worried about it himself.

"You're right," said Finch. "The XO can't always know where all the men are when they go on liberty."

"Yeah, sometimes Boy Scouts have the same problem."

Finch gave Charles an I'll-pretend-I-didn't-hear-that look and in a little while they passed back through the gate onto the base, where abruptly they found considerably less to look at. Yet as they approached the golf course they noticed a crowd gathering. Out of curiosity they investigated. When they slipped into the outer circle of onlookers by the clubhouse they could see a smaller circle in the center focused on a single Filipino teeing off. The knot comprised three or four well-dressed American civilians, some officers, half a dozen American and Filipino photographers, and some solemn and blocky Filipino men with dark glasses and pistol holsters clearly visible under the ornate embroidery of their barong tagalogs. The Filipino in the middle of them all wore a white golf shirt, orange ball cap, and lime-green trousers. He took several swings before lifting his head to smile back at the flashbulbs and polite applause.

"Did you *see* that?" asked Finch, sounding upset. "You see that? His bodyguard there must have said, 'Practice swing, Mr. President,' three times. That's Marcos, Charles, and the son of a bitch cheats."

Charles looked at the president of the Republic of the Philippines and his bodyguards.

"Why do they let those Joes carry weapons on an American base?" he asked.

"Son of a bitch cheats," Finch repeated, shaking his head. "Come on, Charles, let's get the hell out of here. I can't believe we need the bastard that bad."

All the scouts made it to the O Club for dinner except Joe, whose absence Jim and Luiz explained with knowing smirks. Prahler acted as if the missing scout would simply walk out of the head in the next minute and Finch looked sufficiently angry that no one mentioned it aloud.

At some time in the morning Joe returned to his cabin. He mustered with the rest at seven-thirty dressed in the previous day's clothes and red-eyed as a demon, but otherwise present and ready for duty. During breakfast at the O Club Prahler laid out the plan for the day: a hike to, through, and back from some caves he read about in a brochure he had found the evening before. No one had dressed for caving, especially Joe, so they spent an extra half hour after breakfast back at the cabins, changing into jeans, sneakers, and sweatshirts. When they reassembled they laughed at one another—none of them had ever before seen the post head out for the wilds in anything but jungle fatigues and combat boots.

To Charles the whole excursion felt like a funny dream. The approach march to the cave mouth took them down a path that seemed wide as a highway after all the clogged and crowded jungle trails they'd pushed down, and they marveled at pine trees standing straight and free of vines, the ground around them clean and bare as in a city park back in the World. Charles got all the way to the cave mouth before he realized with a kind of wonder that he hadn't stopped once to brush a web from his face, brambles from his leg, or sweat from his eyes.

For several hours they crept through the cave, chasing their flashlight beams and hooting and screeching to try out different echoes and their effect on their fellow scouts. In places the way widened to encompass a few meters of sand on either side of a black, trickling stream; in others it narrowed to a slender path of slick rock high above unseen water that sounded deep and rushing. Twice they had to cross a subterranean stream—half of them needing help from the others—and the confused shouts of encouragement or cries for assistance, mingled with half a dozen crossed rays, a jumble of shadows, and the flutter and almost inaudible whine of disturbed bats, all combined to create a scene that danced a mite too close to panic in Charles's mind. When Jim helped him over the second slab of limestone slippery with bat dung and condensation, he held on a little tighter and a little longer than his dignity would ordinarily allow. And when they all finally came to a point where sunlight shone at the end of a short, narrow crevice, they squeezed out without any thought as to where it might take them. Anyplace in the sun looked fine.

Covered with mud and damp, they sprawled on a jumble of gray rocks set in a steep grassy hillside. A small river ran far below, and a virtually identical hillside faced them across the valley. No one knew the way back to the base or the city. Jim reached under his sweatshirt, pulled out a plastic sandwich bag with a pack of cigarettes and some matches, and waved it in front of him like bait.

"How much am I bid?" he grinned.

"Tell you what," said Joe, "give me two and you won't have to suck my dick tonight."

"Yeah, for sure," said Luiz, "me too."

"You pussies wanna take a smoke break, fine," said Prahler, "but I'm gonna find a way back from here."

"Yowsa massa," said Ed and some of the boys chuckled. Prahler looked ready to lay into him but Finch said, "I think we'll find what we're looking for just over this hill in back of us," and started to climb.

"I know that," said Prahler, following. Half an hour later the two returned and led the post over the ridge and through a pine wood to a meadow from which they could see part of the base. They hadn't come this way, but no one objected to any way that got them back. Jim said, "Hey Prahler, I thought you knew where we were going."

"I did," said Prahler. "I just thought we'd head back a different way."

"Yeah right," Jim muttered when Finch gave him a look. Then Charles saw Finch look at Prahler the way he had at Marcos, but no one said anything and they marched back in decent spirits, even singing the "Yo Ho Song" as they approached the base perimeter.

In the evening after dinner Prahler wanted to have a post meeting but Luiz, Jim, and Joe skipped out again so the petty officer gave the rest of the post a dirty look and walked out into the night. Finch appeared upset, too, but he gathered the rest of the scouts in one cabin. While he waited by the phone, perhaps for a call from Base Security, Tom and George broke out a chessboard and Carl dealt a hand of poker to Ed, Billy, Ford, and MacReady. Charles sat by Tom and George, nominally kibbitzing but keeping an eye on Finch and the phone. Within an hour Prahler returned with a shopping bag.

"Listen boys," he said before Finch could get out a word, "I know I've been a little rough on you and we haven't gone out that much to do cool things like today, so how's about us sitting down and having a little party? Tom, George—why don't you guys get some sodas from the fridge?" While saying this he opened the bag and produced three bottles: Hiram Walker, Ron Rico, and Cherry Heering.

"All right!" said Billy, with Ed and Carl nodding approval.

Ford squinted uncertainly, while Tom said, "You know, we could get in real trouble for this."

"Oh bullshit," said Prahler. "This is an Air Farce base for Christ's sake. You think there are enough airmen on the whole installation to fuck with Three Sixty?"

"Damn straight!" said Carl.

"That is the most ludicrous rhetorical question I have ever heard," observed Ford, pushing thoughtfully on his glasses.

"And what the fuck does that mean?" asked Ed.

"It means I just realized that I'm too young to be held responsible for an offense of this gravity, and I believe I'll have a drink."

"That's the spirit," said Prahler, opening the bourbon.

Charles looked at Finch, who shrugged and smiled. "Well," he said, "at least I'm not going to have to worry about where you guys are tonight." He gave a little salute and walked out the door. Prahler followed him with a glare, then dropped it and raised his glass. "Anchors aweigh, fuckheads!" he said, and they all repeated the toast.

Apart from a few tastes of beer his father had slipped him on holidays, and four or five San Miguels on the Death March, Charles had never drunk alcohol before. Tonight, surrounded by friends in a strange place where none of the regular rules seemed to hold, he thought he'd try. While Prahler, Ed, and Carl knocked back bourbons and kept up a steady supply of rum and Cokes to Tom, George, Billy, and MacReady, Charles and Ford worked on the Cherry Heering. It didn't taste bad—something like one of the better cough syrups, Charles thought. After the first one-half a water glass full, he felt warm, relaxed, and mature.

"Our parents would be so shocked," said George, one pudgy hand wrapped around a nearly empty glass, the other resting peacefully on his belly.

"All our parents can go get fucked," said Billy with biblical conviction. The other boys laughed as if he'd said something particularly witty. Charles and Ford smiled indulgently and poured themselves another.

"You know," choked Ed, barely able to keep down his laughter, "I bet the principal and teachers at ol' GDHS would be kind of disapproving, too."

Billy stood, swayed, and, gesturing from the pulpit, declaimed, "They can go get fucked, too. Especially Principal Schutt. That motherfucker can go and get fucked twice as far as I'm concerned."

Carl applauded; Ed gave a clenched-fist salute. Tom said, "Oh my. I'm drunk."

"No shit," Ed laughed. "I'm gonna tell Mom."

"Look at you little pussies," said Prahler, his eyes focused several meters beyond the opposite wall. "You're all fucking drunk. Ain't nobody here can hold his liquor."

"I'm working on it," said Ford. "You rather I puked?"

"Suit yourself, kid."

"You could get in a lot of trouble," George told Prahler. "With your CO I mean."

"Fuck my CO," said Prahler. "Fuck the admiral, fuck CINC-PAC, fuck the secretary of the motherfucking Navy. Fuck 'em all. There ain't no such thing as gravity, boys: the Navy sucks enough to hold us all down."

Everyone found that pretty funny, but MacReady looked up from a pile of dropped cards and cautioned, "Better not let Finch hear you say that."

"Why? What's he gonna do? Jump up and try to bite my balls? What made you guys elect a little squirt like that, anyway?"

"Why, he's the best little Explorer Scout in the Navy," said Carl.

"Well, the Navy sucks," said Prahler, "we've already decided that."

Everyone laughed except Ford and Charles. Ford looked away. Charles stared at the sailor, trying to think of something to say.

"What's *your* problem, Barker?" Prahler demanded with a grin. Charles kept staring, studying him. Only part of the petty officer joked; the other part, the part he wanted to hide, really didn't like Finch. Charles looked away.

"You don't like me criticizing your boyfriend, do you, Barker? You know, I've been noticing how you two like to hang out a lot together. Reminds me of these two shipmates of mine once . . ."

"I don't think you should kid like that about Finch," said Tom. "Or Charles. Besides, everybody knows they go out with girls."

"Hey, I'm just kidding." Prahler raised his hands in mock surrender. "You guys shouldn't be so sensitive about these things. Hell, I'm not. A little liquor and who knows what a guy'll do . . ." He reached out quickly and grabbed Billy. "He-ey, Killer, sailor love you long time tonight."

"Shit! Jesus Christ! Get the fuck away from me!" Billy jumped up and ran across the room. MacReady laughed a little and then shut up.

"But seriously, Charles," Prahler continued, "a girlfriend? I didn't know." Suddenly, thought Charles, he seemed okay.

Friendly, even. "That's real sweet," Prahler said. "What do you two kids do?"

"She's a junior," said Carl.

"Oh, a *junior?* That's real special," said Prahler. "Tell me a little bit about her, Charles. What do you guys do when you go out?" Billy oinked provocatively, which got a few laughs, but Prahler said, "Cut the shit, Killer, unless you want to come back and sit on my lap. Charles and I are trying to have a serious discussion here. This is a reverent subject. I want to hear what Charles has to say. We might all learn something. Come on, Charles, what do you two sweet kids do when you go out?"

The other scouts quieted down. They all seemed to want to hear what Charles had to say. Charles felt a little queasy, a little foggy in the brain, but otherwise okay. He felt like he could sit in that chair and talk a long time.

"Well," he began, "we like to take walks, maybe see a movie. We both read a lot, so we talk about that, too."

"Jesus, that's so nice," said Prahler, reaching for the bourbon. "But tell me something, Charles. Seriously, man to man . . ." he leaned over, tottering slightly, but with a grave, sincere expression.

"Yes?"

"Does she give good head?"

The room cracked up and roared. Charles might have, too, if Prahler had pulled it on someone else, but at the moment he felt only a sickening rage and a profound appreciation of the tragedy of human existence. He stood up, eyes hot, legs twisting, stomach roiling, and spat, "Asshole!" Then he staggered to the front door, opened it, stepped through, and began to vomit on the shrubs beside the walkway. A few seconds later George came to the door.

"You okay?"

"Leave that pussy alone!" shouted Prahler as he pulled George back inside and slammed the door. Charles gagged and sobbed and started walking. As he walked he cried, part out of rage and sorrow and part because, in his state, it felt strangely good.

He walked an hour or more in the clear starry night, a night so cold and beautiful it reminded him of fall in Virginia. This only made him feel sadder, but he'd already cried himself out. He came upon a formal garden by a turn-of-the-century villa, still within John Hay, and stepped inside to take a seat on a lacy iron bench by a row of roses pruned back to their thorny canes. It looked so beautiful, all of it, that he wished he could show Joan, but when he thought of Joan he thought of Prahler's question again and wondered what drove the sailor to make things ugly- not just what Charles had with Joan, whatever that came to, but the jungle, the beautiful jungle, and the fine Navy of white dress uniforms and clean beautiful ships. Charles started shivering and then he got the sniffles. No jacket, but at least he'd brought some tissues, so when they found him dead of exposure at least he wouldn't have drenched himself in snot, too. He started laughing and crying at once.

"Here you are."

Charles looked up and saw Finch. "Hey, what's happening?"

"'What's happening?' You okay?"

"Yeah, I'm fine."

"Right." Finch sat next to him. "You're freezing to death, Joe's somewhere in town looking for a drug overdose, Jim and Luiz are catching clap in their cabin, and everyone else is heaving their guts, except Prahler, who's breaking empties in the sink like some kind of madman. Other than that, I guess you could say everyone's fine."

Charles shivered and shook his head. "What do you mean about Joe?"

"Forget it. What's with you?"

Charles blew his nose and said, "Prahler's an asshole."

"Tell me something I don't know."

"Man, he really pisses me off. Why are people like that?"

"Like what? What'd he do?"

"Ah, just yanking my chain, I guess. You should have heard what he said about you, though."

"I probably have. I tried to talk to him the other day."

"Yeah? What about talking to your old man?"

"My dad? I can handle this." Charles looked at Finch and Finch began to laugh. "Despite appearances at the moment. Come on, let's get you back." He took off his windbreaker and draped it over Charles's shoulders. Charles felt cold enough to leave it there.

When they returned to the cabin they shared with Joe, Jim, and Luiz, they found Joe still missing but, oddly enough, replaced by Tom. Luiz met them at the door with a sleepy satisfied smile and a Tanduay and Coke. When they stepped in, Jim greeted them with a cheerful, "Tough luck, shipmates, the whores just left."

"You're joking," said Charles, but the beds looked authentically disordered and Luiz said, "Oh no, cat," and gave him a wink that Charles thought you could perhaps only give after you had Done It.

Luiz insisted on making Charles and Finch some Tanduays and Coke. "I feel so good, cat," he said. "You know, sometimes I think, hey, life is okay." Jim laughed and lit a cigarette. Tom walked over looking deeply sorrowful. Charles wondered if he had gotten to the cabin before the prostitutes left.

"Tell me what to do, Charles," begged Tom. "What would you do? I feel so bad. I love Marsha so much. I promised her I'd wait for her . . ."

"Did you? . . ."

"Yes, Charles, I know. I came over and I saw them, and I thought, no way, man, not me, but then I thought, well, maybe I should, you know, practice . . ."

Jim and Luiz both laughed, Finch shook his head and grinned, and Tom continued with ". . . and she was such a sweet girl . . ."

"That's *whore*," corrected Jim. "She was such a sweet whore."

"And now I've lost my virginity!" Tom cried. "What am I going to say to Marsha?"

"Why are you telling me this?" Charles asked.

"Because *they* just laugh at me!" Tom wailed, pointing to Luiz and Jim, who doubled over onto one of the beds.

"I don't know if it last long enough to really count," said Luiz.

"Don't worry," said Jim, "even if it did there's plenty of doctors in Olongapo be happy to give you your cherry back."

"Oh, Marsha," Tom moaned. Finch took him away and tucked him in the farthest bed. Then he came back and let Luiz pour him another drink.

"Where's Prahler?" asked Jim.

"Other cabin," said Finch.

"That there is one dangerous squid," Jim remarked, stubbing out his smoke.

"He's not so tough," said Finch.

"That's what Jim mean," said Luiz. "He not tough at all. That's why he all the time fuck with the nice kids, never me or Joe or you. That's why he so fucking dangerous—all the time he want to prove something."

He handed Finch his drink. Finch paused for a moment, then raised his glass and said, "To the post!"

"Fucking A!" chorused Charles and Luiz.

Jim smiled grimly and said, "Yeah, the post. I just hope I live long enough to make it to Viet-fucking-nam."

⇥ XIV ⇤

THE DIVING BARGE

The Explorer Scouts returned from Baguio to summer jobs on the naval station at Subic Bay. Most of them chose outdoor work, like Luiz at the stables, Joe and Jim at the golf course, or Finch at the beach—stable hands, grounds crew, and lifeguards. Charles obtained a position as a salesclerk at the base hobby shop.

He did not face many demands. Every few days a new item came in that he had to record for inventory and place on the shelves; occasionally a customer appeared with a sudden need for a specific amount of balsa wood. On the whole the amount of business didn't seem to justify half the Filipino staff of four, much less Charles. But Charles never said this to the Filipinos, and they encouraged him to spend most of his time making models, ostensibly for display.

One week the USS *Enterprise*—the Navy's first nuclear aircraft carrier—took its turn at the huge carrier dock at NAS Cubi, and a rush of sailors came to the store seeking models of their ship, either to send home or to pass the time with asea between bombing sorties. Unfortunately the hobby shop had only three models of the *Enterprise* in stock and those had sat around for so long that the staff had marked them down several times, so they went quickly, and at a loss. The shop had others on order and, two weeks after the flattop returned to its duties off Yankee Station, they arrived, sixty of them, giant models three and a half feet long when fully assembled, motorized, highly detailed, bearing a complement of eighty tiny planes, all for twelve dollars each and of interest to no one perhaps except a crewman. Very shortly after these monsters arrived, the boss—Mr. Villanueva—began to mark them down, too. The store needed the space for a back order on the battleship *New Jersey*.

Mr. Villanueva and Charles got along fine. Villanueva—a middle-aged man of subdued yet firm dignity—appeared pleased when Charles called him "sir" just as he would an American adult, and Charles tried to match the Filipino workers in their outward attitude of deference to their supervisor. For his part Charles appreciated the Filipinos' constant, quiet courtesy and their general casualness about his hours of work. Once Charles and Mr. Villanueva both surmised that they both knew that the shop had nowhere near enough work to go around, Villanueva let Charles wander off and spend time downstairs in the ceramics shop with Traci and Cissy, the two queens of the Kittens sorority at the Teen Club.

Traci and Cissy spent most of their time making and painting ceramics for themselves because, as with the hobby shop, they very rarely had more customers than the Filipino staff could handle. But business did rise sharply when the *Enterprise* arrived: once all the sailors who couldn't find models of their ship upstairs discovered teenage American girls working downstairs in the ceramics shop, whole ship's divisions betrayed a sudden interest in pottery. The entire time the carrier sat in port Charles couldn't get anywhere near the girls. He could tell by the smell as he walked down the steps—a heavy blanket of aftershave over a whiff of PX perfume—that he'd find five or six sailors in freshly laundered whites interrogating the carefully coiffed and painted, yet studiously diffident, pair on the finer points of setting times and kiln temperatures. On those days Charles skipped out a little farther, crossing the parking lot to the snack shop across the way where Joan worked.

Yet Joan hadn't much time for him, either, although not because of sailors. Just as summer began the Navy had started a system of rationing to cut down on black market sales of PX and commissary items off base. Every dependent received a ration coupon and an individual ID number nine digits long that salesclerks would have to record for every purchase, even of items as small as a can of soda or pretzels. So Joan spent most of her days writing these numbers down. One day Charles bought a can of Coke and slipped into line to surprise her. When he stepped up for her to check him through, she recited his number perfectly without so much as glancing at his card. He felt quite special about this until the next person in line came up and she did the same thing, with an expression he now saw as somewhat glazed. Later that week, walking home from the movies, they ran into Finch.

"Hey man," said Charles.

"Hello kids," said Finch.

Joan smiled wanly and said, "Good evening, three-one-six-nine-five-four-three-two-seven."

After the *Enterprise* life slowed down again and Traci and Cissy didn't object to having Charles around to chat with. He tried initially to bring up subjects other than the Kittens, but not with much success. So for most of their conversations Charles simply listened as the girls discussed, in hushed and confidential tones, which of their sisters slept around, wore falsies, or had become secretly engaged, the whole time molding and painting little cat figurines for their families and friends.

It fascinated Charles. He had never seen far into the world of popular kids, and few exceeded Traci and Cissy in popularity. They helped put on dances and pep rallies and seemed to hold permanent and unchallengeable positions as cheerleaders. They went on dinner dates to the O Club and sometimes their mothers took them on shopping trips to Hong Kong or Bangkok. They considered Clark low class and the American School just too conceited. They found the Philippines beautiful, especially the beaches, but its people incomprehensibly slow and the jungle unhygienic. But they liked Joe and found him cute, if a little wild, and they could see why Charles would join the Explorer Scouts—it seemed a kind of fraternity to them—yet try as he might he could not get them to understand why any sane person would want to camp out in the jungle. They shuddered at the mention of snakes and Cissy thought fruit bats just too gross. Still, they found it okay for him: sometimes boys just did strange and childish things.

Charles watched them paint their statuettes and offered to help. They let him try a few and liked the results so he confessed that he used to paint toy soldiers. They found that funny but also okay. It seemed more like art than playing, they agreed.

In the weeks after Baguio, Petty Officer Prahler thought about playing a lot. Despite a few rough moments in the city in the mountains, he'd managed to begin and then continue the process of shoring up his popularity with Post 360. Survival hikes grew fewer, though not necessarily less intense, and he mixed in other activities. Once he canceled a hike and took the boys instead to the Jungle Environmental Survival Training school where they got to see the JEST Negritos explain the use of a few medicinal herbs and how the boys might save themselves if caught by pythons ("Poke him in the eye!" the little men said). They even got to see the Negritos feed rats to penned-up, five-foot-long monitor lizards.

The scouts wondered what sort of outing might follow this display, but at their next meeting Prahler surprised them again. He wanted to go on a picnic, he said, but not just any picnic. He had arranged with two buddies of his—a chief and another second class—to borrow the base diving barge for an afternoon. They'd park it over the reef by Grande Island, eat, drink, and dive. They could even, Prahler said, bring dates.

"Are you sure this is okay?" Ford asked.

"Hey, the master diver's a bro. Nice bottle of Scotch and everything's cool. As long as we don't sink anyone else we're fine."

Finch frowned at the potential misappropriation of Navy property, Ford looked uncertain, but all the other scouts seemed reassured. Immediately the talk changed to who would pick up the hamburgers and hot dogs, and how many and when. Luiz and Joe questioned Prahler about exactly where he meant to take the barge and made their own suggestions about the best places to look for shells. Prahler listened attentively and once, as he caught Charles's eye, winked as if to assure him that any bad blood from Baguio lay behind them now.

And so it seemed a week later when the hulking barge with its tennis-court-sized deck that rose a mere half meter above the waterline parked out over the reef by Grande Island. After an hour of diving and talking with scouts and guests under the canvas canopy, Charles leaned back on a cooler and looked up. Small clouds scattered over the sky, the aftermath of a mild front moving through the night before. The clouds cut back the sun and deepened the colors of both the land and the sea; they moved slowly among themselves in several layers of wisps and swirls of light blue-gray and white against an ultramarine backdrop. Charles watched them for a minute or so, tracing the circling flight of one gull against the dappled ceiling. Seawater soaked his trunks and T-shirt and made a puddle where he sat on the metal deck. His hair smelled of the ocean and made him vaguely uncomfortable with the thought of all the things that had lived and died in it.

He looked to his right a few meters away where Joan knelt in a dry, modest one-piece and laughed at four cowries crawling over the deck to the edge, slogging greasily toward whatever freedom means to a mollusk. Beside her laughed Prahler's friend, the second class, who'd caught them. He stood with his hands on his hips, tanned and muscled in faded tiger-striped camo shorts and aviator sunglasses. When Joan looked at him and giggled she showed a trace of girlishness—teasing girlishness—that she never allowed herself around Charles.

It stung him like an electric current. That look. You might hope to win it, to earn it, he thought, but the sailor had picked it up effortlessly within an hour of meeting her.

Charles watched them and began to smolder with shame and resentment—at his youth and inexperience, as if he could help it, as if thinking of it didn't make it worse. He tried to laugh along with Joan and the sailor but after a few minutes they seemed not to notice him and he stared moodily at the distant beach.

When Charles looked back he heard the sailor's voice, too low to make out the words, and saw him pointing toward a tattoo on his right bicep, faded under his tan, an improbable heraldic design of sea creatures, foliage, and motto designating a particular squadron or flotilla. It looked vaguely like the crest on a Prussian infantry standard and at any other time Charles might have wanted to hear about it himself. But he saw Joan lean forward and touch it lightly, running her finger slowly around the center design as if tracing a road map for a trip that may have made her nervous, but which she nonetheless wanted to take.

Charles felt his guts contract. All the shared stories, all the movies—none of it meant a thing against four slugs and a couple of sea stories.

All he needed. All it took to remind him that even after a year of doing things with other kids he didn't feel too much a part of their groups. Not the Aces and the Kittens whose lives revolved around the school and Teen Club, not the kids who drank in dark corners and ran secret missions of vice off base. Too bad the jungle lined the hills behind the beach; the jungle had seemed like his for a while, a place where perhaps he fit in and had a role where other boys depended on him. Now Prahler owned it, and to Prahler and this sailor moving in on Joan, Charles had no more rank than a child in elementary school.

To the whole Navy, top down, Charles had no rank. *Well, screw the Navy,* he thought. Screw the admiral, screw Prahler. Screw the Teen Club, the school, the PX, and the movie theaters. Screw the O Clubs where the officers and their wives sat around like they had royal blood while some Joe from Pampanga whose cousin whipped himself bloody every Easter sang "Because of You" thinking of a statuette of a half-naked pregnant girl holding a sailor cap. Screw the concrete duplexes decorated with inexpensive teak furniture from Taipei and resonating with American records on Japanese hi-fis and voices bitching about Joe maids stealing pocket change at the same moment those coins dropped into jukeboxes at the Teen Club. Screw the BOQ with junior officers in transit and high school English teachers pontificating to horny fourteen- or fifteen-year-olds about Great Works of Literature. Screw the Spanish Gate reeking with history and the urine of drunken sailors just come over the bridge from Olongapo. Screw the Olongapo River poisoned with Navy puke and sperm and blood and diesel fuel and avgas poured in from the brothels and bars and backwashed from the bay. Screw the go-cart track and the miniature golf course.

He stared at the beach damning everything to the deepest darkest shadows of the encroaching jungle. *Bring on the trees and the vines and the grassy clearings where the wild boar root,* he thought. Bring on the vipers and the cobras and the pythons glimmering softly in the dangerous night. Bring on liana and mahogany and mangrove and unnamed things with spikes and thorns. Bring on the spiders and the scorpions. Cover the white suits with dead leaves and dark segmented evils. Let flying foxes hang sleepily from the aerials and radar masts of abandoned warships tilting weakly in the silted-up harbor, streaks of rust striping their sides like the trails of bloody tears on the Flips' big tacky carved crucifixes. May parrots roost in empty hangars and civets stalk the echoing corridors of empty office buildings. In his mind Charles could imagine monitor lizards creeping dinosaurlike into an abandoned Teen Club and flicking out their forked tongues to taste the rotting bones scattered over the dance floor. Ha. He wished.

"Hey Charles! Come here!" Prahler, his shoulders bobbing out of the bay ten meters away, waved a camera encased in clear plastic. "I got an octopus down here—I'll get it, you take the picture! Come on!"

Charles glanced over at Joan; she still seemed stuck on the shells and the sailor. He stood up, fixed on his mask, and dived in.

Prahler swam about four meters down in a landscape of green, blue, violet, and red arabesques. He flipped over a small crusty rock with a paint chipper and Charles saw a quick puff of sand and dark serpentine legs scooting away in graceful frenzy. They surfaced.

"Did you get it?" Prahler asked.

"No, it was too quick."

"Shit, let's try again." Prahler gulped and dived back down. Charles stayed on the surface and breathed steadily through his snorkel. Prahler swept the rocks on either side of himself, surfacing every twenty seconds just long enough to get another breath. Charles held the camera and waited, following Prahler out about 150 meters from the barge, trying to keep calm but finding himself drawn into the chase. After a few more minutes Prahler stayed down nearly a minute, half of which he spent moving wildly over a coral outgrowth, his legs flailing like the wings of a gutshot bird. When he came up he gasped, "I got it. Don't you miss motherfucker."

Charles nodded and this time followed Prahler as he dived. At about three meters they reached bottom. The water pinched Charles's ears and sinuses and the colors made him wonder if they'd left the planet. He got ready, floating just above the surface of the reef, his flippers brushing a glassy fan. Prahler slipped his diving knife under the edge of an old giant clamshell and flipped it over. In the second before the octopus got out of range Charles snapped a picture. He thought he might have gotten another as it shot away.

They surfaced. "I got it!" Charles yelled, hoping Joan might hear. "I think I got it twice!"

"Great fucking job, Barker! Give me a kiss!" Charles splashed away from Prahler, laughing. They swam back to the barge like triumphant hunters with a pair of bull elephant tusks. Luiz and Carl helped them out of the water and when Prahler told them about the octopus—now rapidly growing to a size unknown in the scientific literature—Luiz grinned and Carl shook Charles's hand, saying, "That's really cool, man."

For a moment everything seemed the way it should. Charles caught a flash of himself in the starched whites of an Annapolis graduate holding the gloved hand of Joan, herself demure and adoring in a southern belle, taffeta kind of way.

But first the sailor. Before Charles could focus on the other picture he had to get rid of the one he saw now: her giggling with Prahler's friend and playing with his hand. Neither of them saw Charles, or even noticed that their four mollusks had jumped ship.

Prahler grabbed Charles's hand and held it up like he'd won a championship. "We did it!" he announced. "National-fucking-Geographic watch out! We are talking some serious mother-fucking nature photographers here!"

The chief and some of the scouts looked over and chuckled while a few of the dates blushed at Prahler's language. But Joan and the sailor still didn't notice.

Charles went aft under the canopy and got some fried chicken and a Coke from a cooler. He sat with his feet off the stern dangling in the sea like shark bait, ate, and brooded. Occasionally someone passed by and spoke to him before diving off into the water, but Charles just nodded, not really hearing. Huk frogmen might have just strapped on a demo charge for all he knew or cared. If the world held any justice Joan herself would come back to apologize for having ignored him (he would of course say he hadn't noticed) and to chastise him for not rescuing her sooner from that boring sailor (he would of course have complimented him on his mollusks). But the minutes passed and she didn't come by.

Billy did, and asked, "Hey, who's that squid with Joan?"

"Her brother. Didn't you know?"

"No shit? Oh."

When half an hour later Joan finally did come to Charles, she asked, "Charles, are you all right?" the way she might have asked a little brother if he'd had too much cake and punch.

"I see you finally tore yourself away."

She gave him a surprised look and asked, "Are you *jealous?*"

No bitch, he thought, *I could give a rat's ass.*

"Maybe," he said, looking at her shoulder and neck. She'd have to watch she didn't get burned.

She smiled, and the corners of her mouth rose like the blade of a guillotine. "But Charles," she said, "we've always been such good friends."

As she mouthed the last word he could feel his lower lip go numb. In the distance he saw Luiz coming up for air and then he felt salt water pooling in his eyes. He hadn't much time.

He dived into the ocean.

THE BATTLE OF THE SS
RIDING STABLES

A fter the field trip to the resort base in Baguio and the picnic over a coral reef on the naval station diving barge, the scouts of Post 360 expected their counselor to take them back to survival hikes in the jungle. Even those who really believed that the post could return to the old days of sampling ice cream in the galleys of nuclear attack submarines or spotting barracudas from the decks of aircraft carriers woke up when Prahler appeared at the next monthly meeting wearing his camouflage fatigue jacket and the hopped expression of a marine coming off a long night watch of suspicious noises and fanciful shapes.

"Okay, ladies," he said, pacing behind the podium at the head of the conference room in FICPACFAPFAPL, "we've had some serious R and R lately, some real good times. Like I said—we work hard, we play hard. But lately it's been nothing but play hard, am I right?"

The twelve boys murmured, some in approval and some neutrally, waiting for the tide to flow one way or the other. Finch stared at Prahler from his seat at the desk beside the podium. As post president he'd taken on the responsibility of rounding up the scouts during the group drinking spree at John Hay and had broken up an incipient fight between Prahler and one of his buddies on the picnic over the reef by Grande Island. On the whole he hadn't had a lot of time in which to play hard.

"Am I right?" Prahler repeated, his blue eyes darting over them like the weapon of an alerted sentry. He stepped to the front row where Tom Sanders and George Wong sat like dutiful students. He leaned down and smiled. "I mean, some of us *have* been a little light in our attendance at post events in recent months, haven't we?"

George smiled tentatively, looking a bit like one of the eight gods of good fortune caught with a can of spray paint near a rival high school. "Well . . ." he said, "I suppose I could do better."

"I'm looking forward to it," Prahler said. Turning to Tom, he asked, "What about you? Any truth to the rumor you only joined the Scouts to get a ticket punched on the way to higher aspirations, like the first NAACP chapter at Annapolis?"

"Certainly not, sir," said Tom with a hint of uncertainty. "I'm prepared to do whatever it takes to fulfill my commitment, sir." His younger brother Ed hooted derisively from the back of the room.

Prahler raised back up to look at the next row, the fluorescent light glinting off his silver-blond crew cut, winked at Jim, and continued. "Well, now that we've reestablished the commitment of our moral leaders, how about getting some from you whoring sons of bitches? Is there any chance you dudes can lay off the b-girls in Olongapo long enough to get in a little scouting?"

"Well," said Jim, brushing back his lush bangs, "it *is* getting a little sore . . ."

"Joe? You wanna show us the line between gettin' pussy and being one?"

"Shi-it."

And so it went. By the end of the meeting Prahler had gone eye to eye with each of the scouts and got them to agree: Saturday they'd march out from the stables, past the sawmill, and up into the jungle beyond the falls, carrying only a day's rations.

They'd make their own shelters for that night and march back out Sunday before noon.

"Nothing to it, men," said Prahler, "just a little trip to break us back in gentle."

Finch pointed out that Navy meteorologists forecast a typhoon in the next twelve hours, but had to admit, when Prahler challenged him, that they had also predicted only scattered showers by the weekend.

The storm did hit late Wednesday after the meeting, but few of the boys heard it as they slept in their families' concrete duplexes in the base housing areas. Air conditioners muffled the steady surf of rain and made the thunder sound as distant as the eruptions of firebases on the other side of the South China Sea. By Friday night the storm had worn itself down to waves of intense showers that the Filipino band in the Teen Club easily drowned out with their cover of Cream's "White Room." The drowning continued when the band broke at twenty-one hundred and Carl Wong grabbed the jukebox with a handful of coins and punched every Creedence Clearwater Revival tune on the chart. When he climbed back into a booth by the snack bar with Ed, Billy, and Ford, he swung and nodded his head in a kind of evangelical rapture, his half-closed eyes oblivious to the scowls of passing Psyche and Soul aficionados whose own chances at a few minutes of acid Frisco or mellow Motown he'd ruined with that evening's fourteenth playback of "Run Through the Jungle." His friends in the booth put up with it. Despite the incongruity of a lanky Sino-Hawaiian grooving to pseudo-Cajun C&W, they all felt a certain attraction to the black-toned bass and howling vocals crawling from the cheap speakers overhead. It seemed just right for boys who played at war at night in the jungle.

Charles walked in from the dance floor, saw them, and asked if he could sit down. Billy and Ford shifted over and he squeezed in.

"How you guys doing?" he asked.

"Man, I love Creedence," said Carl.

"And I hate that redneck shit," said Ed without conviction. Tonight he wore his jungle jacket over his dashiki. "What's happening Charles? Our man Finch still worried?"

"Don't you follow the weather?" asked Ford. "This rain is not going away for days."

"BFD," said Billy, his voice cracking on *D*. "Finch is a goddamn worrywart. I'm getting tired of him trying to mother us."

"That's not what you said when he was holding your head out of that toilet in Baguio, man," Ed replied. "You woulda drowned."

"Suck my dick," said Billy.

"Whip it out—I'll see if I can find it."

"You gentlemen are both very eloquent," said Ford, polishing his Clark Kent glasses with his well-used handkerchief, "but I think you may be digressing from the point of our little discourse."

"Why don't you speak English, you little dickhead," Billy replied.

"Okay, okay, listen up," said Charles. "Finch wants every one of us to bring a poncho tomorrow. A flashlight, too. It may be a survival hike but there's no need to get stupid."

Carl nodded, either because he agreed or because the jukebox had just switched to the opening chords of "Born on the Bayou."

"God, I love Creedence," he said.

"What the fuck," added Ed, "I'll be ready."

Billy brushed back his vestigial bangs as if his father hadn't made him go to the station barbershop the day before and said, "Man, I can't believe we're all sitting here for the big lowdown from the post pres and all he says is 'wear a poncho.' BFD, man."

"Let me clarify that for you," said Ford. "It's bring a poncho no matter what Prahler says because Finch is the one we listen to and Prahler's insane. There's a subtle yet nonetheless significant distinction there."

"Yeah, yeah—blow me, egghead."

Ed laughed. "'Egghead.' That's real original, Killer."

Joe walked up from a circle of his Ace fraternity brothers and their Kitten girlfriends in the corner booth. He wore his white denim Ace vest over an olive-drab T-shirt as if himself unsure whether his loyalties lay more with the Explorers or the Teen Club frat. As tall as Carl and as strongly built as Ed, when he leaned over the table from the open end of the booth he put a shadow over all five of the younger scouts.

"All the little wienies gonna wear their rubbers?" he asked.

"Sure, man," Ed replied. Pointing to Joe's vest, he asked, "You gonna wear that piece of shit?"

Joe grabbed his throat. "Hey, hold on!" said Carl as Ed gagged. Charles got up and pulled on Joe's arm. Joe let go of Ed but pushed back Charles as easily as he would brush away a dry leaf. He grinned.

"You little pussies think you're tough? You think wearing a jungle jacket to the Teen Club makes you any taller? Older? Stronger? Less of a dickhead?"

"You think a little random violence makes you less of a jerk?" asked Ford.

"Jesus, Ford," said Billy, sliding down in his seat.

"Oh, wow," said Joe. "You sound pretty tough hiding in that corner where I can't reach you."

"An astute observation," said Ford. "Sometimes your mental processes approach the hominid."

Joe shook his head, still grinning, but not reassuringly. "I'll see you girls tomorrow, in the bush," he said before returning to his friends.

Billy punched Ford in the shoulder. "You asshole! Why you gotta razz him like that?"

"Experience," said Ford. "Everywhere I go clowns like that try sooner or later to physically humiliate me. I might as well give them a reason."

"What's the matter, man," Ed asked Billy, "you only shit on your friends?"

The next morning at eight hundred the post assembled on the gravel parking lot in front of the stable buildings. A thick mist made it appear like a moment after dawn, but a growing mugginess and a bright patch of cloud low in the east confirmed the day. Twice on the drive over Commander Barker had asked Charles whether the scouts really wanted to make this hike and twice Charles said "sure" without enthusiasm but also without inviting further questions. An hour earlier the commander had entered his son's bedroom to find him in the midst of suiting up. Charles had already gotten into his boots and camouflage trousers, the latter so baggy on his skinny white frame that he thought he might have looked like some kind of grunt clown, but his father didn't notice that. Before Charles could get his OD T-shirt on, Commander Barker grabbed his hand and closed the bedroom door behind him.

"Good Lord, boy," he said, "have you seen your back?"

Charles made a weak attempt to free his hand but his father pulled him up and firmly pushed him over in front of the mirror atop the dresser.

"Look over your shoulder, boy."

"I've seen it," said Charles. He glanced over his shoulder anyway, glad his father hadn't seen his back two months earlier, but wishing he hadn't scratched himself so much. Still, as the administrative officer at the hospital, Commander Barker could probably guess what had happened, and when.

"Son, you better be glad your mother hasn't seen this. You must have had every bug in the Orient camping out on your back that last time. I don't believe I see a square inch that's clear skin."

A slight exaggeration, thought Charles, as he examined his back. Mottled with reddish, brownish, and purplish patches and bumps, interspersed with an occasional healing scab, it looked more like a miniature science fiction landscape than the back of a boy just turned fifteen. In places Charles could still see small pink mounds, a few millimeters in diameter, flanked by a pair of tiny indigo spots. Ant bites, he thought, wondering if he should have kept his shirt on during that last overnighter. But it had gotten full of mud in a mock battle and did better service rolled up as an extra pillow while his jacket served as ground cover.

"I'll do better this time, Dad. Look, I got my poncho and all."

The commander shook his head. "I'm telling you, son—I mean this—if you come back and that looks any worse, you are not going out again until it clears up, and if that takes another year and we're already on our way back stateside, that'll be just too bad."

"Yes, sir."

Now, at the stables, his father gave him another look and passed it over the line of scouts and counselors. His eyes met Prahler's and he seemed to size him up while the petty officer blinked in confusion. For a moment Charles didn't know whether he wanted his father to pull rank on the enlisted man and stop the hike, or to go ahead with it and a hundred others if necessary, until they got to the one where Prahler cracked and could never challenge them again.

Commander Barker nodded curtly at Prahler, as if acknowledging a salute, then got back in the Barkers' sedan and drove off. Shortly after, CPO Sanders and Lieutenant Commander Finch drove off in their own cars. With all the parents gone, Prahler turned to Charles. "What did Daddy say, Barker?"

"He said what he always says. He said, 'Be careful.'"

Prahler laughed and the other three counselors joined him. The scouts stared, never having seen the three before. Prahler introduced them. Ringo, a corpsman just back from Vietnam, stood as tall as Luiz but even slimmer, cadaverously so. With his dark, razor-cut hair, pale, blotchy jungle skin, and gray eyes fixed on a distant unknown point, he looked like he'd left half his baggage back in Da Nang. Chase, a hyperactive marine about Charles's height, compensated for Ringo's calm with furious chain-smoking. Charles noticed that once Chase lit a cigarette he never touched it again, but rolled it from side to side in his mouth, blowing smoke rings and French curls while keeping up a constant muttering patter to his buddies. His longish blond hair capped his ears and he wore a steady mirthful sneer under issue sunglasses. He moved in jerks like a windup toy. The third counselor, Moody, had served with Ringo. Prahler said Moody had caught a piece of shrapnel near his collarbone and had no feeling in his left arm. Moody confirmed it with a self-deprecating chuckle and rolled up his sleeve to show the boys a wide range of cuts and bruises, saying, "I don't know where the fuck I picked these up." He seemed all right; tall as Ringo but with warm brown curls as long as Chase's and a friendly expression. He moved easily but with a slight edge, as if he'd spent a lot of time expecting to step on the wrong thing.

"You cats are strange," said Luiz with a smile, and the counselors laughed again, a sardonic grin cracking even Ringo's face.

Strange seemed to cover the whole scene, Charles thought. Mist rose wispy from the ground, fog settled in all the hollows and indentations of the forest; the sky existed only as a low, soft ceiling of dirty white. A fine drizzle began that blurred everything—foliage, Quonset huts, faces, trees—and turned the uniformed group into a squad of brownish and greenish gray ghosts. It felt as if at any moment Rod Serling would walk up in jungle boots and tell them they had all just died.

Prahler paced in front of his buddies like a general with his staff, viewing the post with a kind of triumphant levity. All the boys had made it: Finch, Joe, Jim, Luiz, the Wongs, the Sanderses, Billy, Ford, MacReady, and Charles. Had Prahler simply ordered them to show he would have found himself with Finch and perhaps three others. But at the meeting he'd challenged them face to face and after the first few agreed the rest couldn't let them down. They remained ready this morning, even as they heard, far off, a boom of thunder.

The drizzle turned into a light rain. Prahler swept off his forage cap, leaned back, and opened his mouth. He shook his head like a boxer between rounds and laughing said, "Perfect! Let's move out!"

The scouts put on their packs and belts and shuffled into line as Sparks, yapping happily, hopped out from the Quonset that contained the office and the stables. After his run-in with the Filipino stable hand, he moved pretty well on three legs.

"Looks like he wants to come along," grinned Moody, while Prahler knelt in the mud and accepted his mutt's kisses. "Nice doggie," Prahler said as everyone stood and watched. "Good little Sparksie—Daddy not gonna let any nasty Joes get you ever again. Somebody lock this little guy in my office! Keep the goddamn Flips away from him!"

Luiz took Sparks away while the column moved off. A few Filipinos had stayed for the weekend riders whom the rain would keep away. Later they would leave, but for now they stopped their work for a moment to watch the scouts from the rink and stable doorways.

The scouts marched down the road, their boots kicking holes in the ground fog that the rain had washed from knee to ankle height. From the short bridge leading to the sawmill they could see that the stream had grown from its usual trickle to an irritated flow of respectable size. Beyond the bridge they passed between two large stacks of logs, leaving the sawmill behind on a rise to the left, then turned off onto a muddy firebreak that curved to their right into hilly jungle. The trees closed over them in the haze with drooping vines and ragged branches, looking vague and spooky. Twenty meters down the firebreak they could no longer tell the rain from the irregular dripping that could continue for hours after it ended. The scouts' boots sank over their ankles in the thick red mud and they made slow time. Under the persistent dripping of the canopy and the intermittent squelch of leather soles, the column kept up an unsteady patter of its own, three or four conversations alternately playing off or competing with each other before trailing off into disjointed whispers. In the rear Jim and Luiz sounded out the two marines, Moody and Chase.

"Tell me you wouldn't rather be in town," said Jim.

"Now what would you boys know about being in town?" asked Moody.

Jim and Luiz laughed and began to tell him what they knew about Olongapo, including which nightclubs, which bars, which stage acts, which bar girls, and which brothels.

"Shit, man," muttered Chase through a Marlboro cloud, "tell you what, Moody, let's get these boys on the team next time by God. Get some tour guides and pimps all in one, goddammit."

"I guess so," said Moody. "Hell, the wrong dude asked that question. Why don't you boys tell us why *you* aren't in town."

"Oh, I find Olongapo *so* depressing in the rain," said Jim.

"Yeah," added Luiz, "we like it lots more out here."

"That's the spirit!" called Prahler from the front.

"Yeah, shit," said Moody, "I just had to see what the jungle's like without some fucking gook in it taking shots at you."

"Hell, know what?" said Chase. "I still don't fucking like it. Remember that fucking academy second louey, whatever the fuck he was, kept sending guys up to take out that sniper kept droppin' us, till like that dude says, like, 'Pardon me, sir, but you can go fuck yourself,' and everybody backed him up? 'For the Crotch,' man, for the motherfucking Crotch."

"The Crotch?" Charles asked from behind Prahler.

"Translation, 'the Corps,' as in Marine," said Moody.

"Fucker finally got his, though, bunch lurps come in from three weeks in the shit and see a stack of cases of beer some chopper's just dumped off on the strip for the PX or something and they all start helping themselves. Man says, 'Hey, you men,' you know, all fucking John Wayne–like, 'put that back,' and they fucking shot him right there."

"Really?" asked Billy.

"Never happened," said Moody. "None of that shit happened."

"Seem like some of that shit happened, man," said Chase anxiously.

"Just cool down and shut the fuck up."

Halfway up a hill Prahler suggested they take five. Finch suggested instead that they continue to the top. Moody and Chase agreed while Ringo shrugged. Muttering, Prahler led them on and at the top they took a break, breathing hard and standing unsteadily in slimy, orange-brown goop. When the dripping got a little heavier Ford took off his pack and retrieved his poncho. Prahler saw it and for the first time realized they all had them.

"Who the fuck authorized you to bring ponchos?" he demanded.

"I did," said Finch, but as soon as he finished everyone else said the same.

"Don't pull that shit with me," said Prahler. "I know it was you, Finch, and I don't fucking care, because every one of you little pussies is gonna drop it right here. We can pick them up tomorrow on the way out."

"No," said Finch. His eyes met Prahler's and they locked for a long second while the rest of the group took an unconscious half step back. Prahler made a fist but Moody touched his arm and said, "Jesus, Hank, use your head. You wanna get some officer's son sick out here?"

Prahler looked away from Finch and at the others, a smile slowly irrupting under the shadow of his cap brim. "Sure, that's right. We don't want Daddy or Mommy's little boy to get the sniffles. Go ahead, Ford, wrap your ass up good and tight."

Some boys snickered. Charles exhaled. Now maybe things would work out, he thought: Finch got his ponchos and Prahler got to insult everyone. *Things should go just fine now.*

After the halt they continued another twenty minutes down the firebreak then cut left to the stream that would lead them up to the falls and the country beyond. But ten or fifteen meters from the bank their boots began to sink into soggy leaf litter and when they got to the stream itself they found it had deepened from several centimeters to about a half a meter, covering or isolating the stepping-stones they'd used in the past. They followed it anyway, knowing no other route through the jungle, and the conversations died one by one as they slogged upstream, the water filling their boots and soaking their camouflage fatigue pants to above the knees. Fifty meters up they found a newly fallen tree across their way, an obvious victim of the week's typhoon. It had dropped from the right but luckily hung itself up on some other trees so it presented them with a slanting trunk that they could slip under on one side at no greater cost than soaking their rears. Yet not much farther on they found a more troublesome blockade where a shorter, or more distant, tree had dropped with its canopy square across the stream, confronting the column with a thick mess of branches and vines. That took them half an hour to pass, as Luiz, Finch, and Ringo hacked a trail from the bank to the remains of the crown and around while everyone else stood in the stream and waited, the rain now steady enough, and the canopy above the stream open enough, that no one bothered with cigarettes. Their tightly woven fatigue jackets had shed water for the first ten minutes of the march, but they had long ago passed that point and now stood drenched and shivering despite the day's warmth.

In another hour they reached the waterfall and scrambled up the trail to the left of their old swimming hole. They stood in a confused and weary group at the top, uncertain whether to continue a while through the thick brush along the stream or plunge into the water itself, which here looked mean and roiling before the five-meter drop of the falls. George, standing on the very edge of the bank, fell in. At first the scouts laughed, but he couldn't get to his feet and, thrashing wildly, began to slide toward the frothing drop. Finch and Joe jumped in together to raise him up and push him to the reaching hands on the bank. Finch, despite his size, insisted on leaving last and would have ridden the stream off the falls if Ringo hadn't grabbed him. The three soaked scouts stood gasping on the bank but Prahler pushed on through the jungle, plowing ahead like Stanley or Livingston, confident that the bearers and gunboys would follow. They did, and Finch even recovered enough to pass up and down the column murmuring encouragement to the others. Charles caught Finch's eye; he wanted to ask how much farther but saw the fatigue in his friend's face and decided against it.

Above the falls they followed the stream for several more bends before it became shallow enough to wade again. Shortly after they came upon a clearing to the right where four large mahogany trees lay in a gap some forty meters in diameter at the foot of a steep ridge. Across the stream the jungle marched up steep hills and cliffs. Prahler led them out of the water into the clearing, where they discovered a wide path leading around the hill, thickly grassed over; it appeared that heavy equipment had once come in to drag away other trees. Finch took a few steps along it and said to Prahler: "This looks like it joins up with the firebreaks."

Other scouts stared at Prahler, who first seemed angry, then amused. "Stream's still shorter. If you want we can check it out later. But what the fuck, kid, look around! Isn't this gorgeous? We got a great view when the sun comes out and in the meantime we got all these hills to stop the wind." Finch nodded wanly and dropped his pack.

In the clearing they could tell the rain had stopped, but clouds still covered the sky thickly enough that the sun looked like a penlight behind used tissues. Under the threat of more rain they turned to the work of setting up camp. With bolos they chopped away fragments of mahogany to get down to dry wood. Joe and Luiz went into the hills in search of tinder from the center of thickets of bamboo. Carl and Jim followed, looking for green bamboo that they could use to rig shelters from their ponchos. Within an hour the scouts had fires in which to cook their lunch and simple cover to dry off under. Moody amused the scouts by retrieving their ration cans from the fire with his shrapnel-numbed hand, Ed Sanders and Carl Wong teased their older brothers with stories of rougher times they'd had, and Prahler walked from scout to scout telling them how proud they made him for marching through a rain that, to hear him tell it, had come on as hard and fierce as the typhoon two days before. Charles listened to him with disbelief but also gratitude. They'd had a bitch of a march that morning but at least Prahler seemed to appreciate it. Perhaps now he would relax.

Sitting on a stump by the shelter they'd rigged by joining their ponchos, Charles dug Turkey Loaf from an OD can while Finch spread regulation cheddar on a thick round cracker. The tree that the stump had once supported must have risen more than fifty meters. When Ford walked by they had plenty of room for him, too.

"How's it going," Finch asked as Ford gingerly perched on the stump.

"Miserably. Not only am I soaked, but I ruined my copy of Mo-tzu in the stream under that first tree."

"You still reading him?" Charles asked.

"Was. Rereading actually. He had the most interesting views on defensive warfare."

"The only defense is a good offense," said Finch.

"That's what you say, round-eye."

"Where's your buddy Killer?" Charles asked.

"Billy's no more my buddy than yours, you know. Luiz took him and Carl to look for snakes. I wish them success."

"You want something to eat?" Finch asked.

"No, Mother."

They sat quietly for a few minutes and watched Tom and George. The two older brothers had contrived to bring an extra poncho and now busied themselves raising a fairly elaborate shelter; neat and square, it used most of the poles Carl and Jim had cut as well as a full roll of twine Tom had tucked in his pack.

"Looks like they know what they're doing," said Ford.

"They'll be fine if it doesn't rain again," said Finch. "By the way, you'd be a lot more comfortable if you took off your poncho."

"Surely you jest. It's wet out here."

"It's wet in there, Ford. Condensation. There's no rain out here."

"Oh?" said Ford, holding out his palm. "Dear me, you're right."

Charles chuckled but no one heard because at that moment they heard and felt a boom of thunder. The vague glow of the sun went out and black clouds swept over their small window on the sky. Immediately a second boom sounded and heavy rain began to fall.

"Belay that last bit of advice," said Finch. "You two get inside."

"You, too," said Charles.

"In a sec. Got to check on things first."

The rain fell in sheets, the sky flashed, the ground shook, and the thunder roared like an incoming barrage. Gusts of wind ripped through the clearing, tearing down Tom and George's contraption of poncho, pole, and string in a few seconds. Charles saw them retrieve it and wrap themselves in the soaking mess just before the pour made him lose sight of all details. He and Ford struggled to hold on to their own shelter as the wind played the rain on them like a hose. In a few minutes Finch returned, pulling open a flap but not trying to enter.

"I'm going to need your help," he shouted at Charles, "just as soon as this crap lets up a little. Half the goddamn post is in the woods playing and I don't see the counselors. We're gonna have to get everyone together and get the hell out of here."

"Okay!" Charles shouted back, but Finch had already gone. Charles looked at Ford. Ford watched drops of condensation form streams and run like tears down the inside of their fragile shelter.

In twenty minutes the storm blew over and the sun came out, lower and feebler than before. With Ford tagging along like a timid puppy, Charles went out into the jungle and yelled and yelled. He figured some of the scouts had probably tried to run back to the camp when the storm hit and instead got turned around deeper in the jungle. After a few minutes of yelling he heard a rustling in the undergrowth that turned into Carl and Billy, Carl laughing with relief and Billy bearing the same addled stare as Ford. Charles led them back to the campsite, where they found the counselors waiting with Tom Sanders and George Wong. A little later Finch brought back Jim and MacReady, then Luiz brought in Ed. Joe came back on his own. By the time the whole bedraggled post gathered around the puddled black dregs of their campfires, their few watches read seventeen hundred— maybe an hour before twilight.

"I think we should think about leaving," said Finch. "Or maybe just getting some of the guys out. Some of them aren't up to this."

"Oh bullshit," said Prahler. "That was just a goddamn shower. 'Scattered showers' the weather said. That's what happens after a storm. Ain't nothing, little brother. Some day you'll have to do this under fire. Charlie don't wait for sunshine."

Charles stared at Prahler from under the wide, sodden brim of his recon hat. *Bullshit yourself,* he thought. But he knew Prahler wouldn't go back. Finch had blown it. If Finch had only said *he* needed to go back, or if he had said others had to go back and then sneered at them the way Prahler would, Prahler would have gone. But not this way. Not any way that involved Prahler having to take Finch's advice.

Charles waited for someone to back Finch up, to say they'd had it and had to go back. Maybe Tom and George. But Tom and George, bad as they looked, didn't look ready to take any more crap from their little brothers for copping out. Billy and Ford might, but they both looked a little too shell-shocked to pick up on their chance. What about himself? He looked around at all the other guys, including the counselors. Would they believe him if he said he couldn't take any more? Did he even want to give them that chance?

"Come on guys," said Finch. "Nobody has to stay if they don't want. I'll take you back myself."

No one said anything. Most of them seemed to take a sudden interest in mud puddles and each other's bootlaces. Prahler let out a laugh. Finch turned away. Moody walked up to Finch and put his hand on his shoulder. "You're all right, bro. Relax. We're all gonna be just fine. Wet, maybe, but okay."

"All right, all right, all right!" shouted Prahler. "Everybody listen up! I know it's wet, I know it looks dark, I know this could be like one real fucking drag, but hey—who are we? Post Three-fucking-Sixty, right? Let me hear you say that: Three-fucking-Sixty! Okay? Three-fucking-Sixty! Come on! Three-fucking-Sixty!"

He pounded through the mud around them barking them into line and shouting the mantra with an ecstatic ferocity they couldn't ignore. They tried, for the first shout or two, and then they started laughing, but self-consciously rather than derisively, and then they began to join in, first a few, Carl and Ed and Billy, then Joe and Jim, then all of them, even the counselors, even Charles and Ford and then Finch, all of them shouting, "Three-fucking-Sixty!" loud enough to echo through the rain-laden hillsides and beat back the clouds and the coming dark, shouting till each of them felt tall enough to stand over the rain and kick through the jungle as easily as through an unkempt lawn.

"Fucking A!" Prahler shouted. "So we're wet! What the fuck! BFD, right Killer? DILLIGAF, huh, little bro? Yeah, old Killer looks like a wienie, girls, but let me tell you something: right now he's man enough to fuck a monitor lizard sideways! Fucking A! And look at my man Ford here! Wait'll the Crotch gets hold of this tough little motherfucker! They'll have to tie cinder blocks to his boots so he can drive his goddamn APC all the way to fucking Hanoi! All right!" Everyone laughed and when the laughter died Prahler turned to Finch. "And just catch this stud here," he said. "We are in the presence of the future fucking CNO, are we not? Is this John Paul Jones come back to life or what? Fucking A Finch! Let's hear it for him, man: *Fucking A Finch!*"

They all cheered, except Finch. He looked at the post with the same weak smile as before. *His men*, thought Charles; *they're Prahler's men now.*

Quickly Prahler explained the next step: "Now men, there was a reason I didn't want you to weigh yourselves down with those ponchos. Tonight ain't nobody gonna have to sleep in the rain. What I planned, see, was that we'll march back and have a battle for the stables. We'll divide up into teams and have maybe three or four rounds—the best team can bunk down in the offices and the losers get the rink. Everybody sleeps warm and dry and to top it off I got the key to the soda machine right here."

Charles watched the other boys applaud. He caught Finch's eyes and saw disbelief but also resignation. He caught Prahler's, but Prahler looked away. It didn't make sense, Charles thought. Prahler had no reason not to tell them about this before. Next to him Ford muttered, "I'll be darned, but I think he's making this up as he goes along. Not that I care. Shoot me quick—I'll be happy to sleep in the rink."

Prahler went over the rules again for the benefit of his buddies and any one of the scouts who might have forgotten: you died if you got hit by a stick or a flashlight beam. The scouts and counselors took stock of their flashlights and found six that worked. Prahler decided that the defenders would get two and the attackers four. Moody would take the first team of defenders, Tom and George.

"Heavy odds, I know," said Prahler, "but you'll have two flashlights and it's clear ground all the way around the stables. If you set up smart we're dog meat."

"Sounds good to me," said Moody. He took off his cap and shook his head, his brown curls shedding water like a spaniel's.

"Okay, clear off while we get our shit together. We'll give you half an hour lead and then take off ourselves. We should get there just at twilight."

The three defenders gathered their gear and walked off into the jungle along the path Finch had pointed out, the one they all now believed led back to the firebreak and the stable road. The rest debated the plan of attack. Prahler wanted everyone to stay in a group until they got over the bridge between the sawmill and the stables. They could then deploy in a broad line and overwhelm the defenders in a single quick rush. It might have worked, but few liked the idea of risking everything on one banzai charge. Luiz wanted to cut off to the left of the main body and take the stables from the rear. He knew where they could find a drainage ditch and get close in without exposing themselves. Then Joe came up with the idea of cutting over downstream and attacking from the road back to the base.

"I don't know about that," said Prahler. "I don't like the idea of anyone wading that creek in the dark, especially below the bridge. That's a lot of water. Could get hairy in the dark."

"Ah hell," said Joe, "I could cross that stream with Billy and Ford. It's no problem."

"Prahler's right," said Finch. "Let it drop, Joe."

"Bullshit," said Joe. "It's a cinch. You guys aren't scared, are you?"

All eyes turned on Billy and Ford. "Hell no," said Billy in a thin voice. Ford had a set look that could fit either determination or fatalism.

"Nah," said Prahler. "I don't think so. Luiz can do his thing; he works out here, he knows what he's doing, but I don't think . . ."

"Oh, fuck that," said Joe. "You're always saying what pussies we are, and here you're just scared you'll get in trouble with somebody's daddy."

"Take it easy, kid," said Prahler. "I said we'll see. We'll see what the creek's like when we get to the bridge."

Joe nodded, apparently satisfied. Charles asked Luiz if he could go with him; he didn't want to go with a group led by either Prahler or Joe.

"Sure, cat," said Luiz. "We take Ringo, too. I see him in the jungle today, knows his shit. But nobody else, cat, unless Finch wanna come."

The attackers packed up their gear, lit a few cigarettes, and waited the rest of the agreed-on half hour before marching out along the trail to the firebreak. As they left the clearing they entered deep shadows that in a few minutes deepened further, whether from thickening clouds or twilight they couldn't tell. In another quarter hour a light rain began to drip through the canopy, which as they turned onto the firebreak began to soak through their already damp fatigues, but no one cared to stop to put on ponchos.

All the way down the firebreak Charles could hear Creedence playing "Born on the Bayou" in his mind, the rhythm playing perfectly against the wet thud of jungle boots on the slick ocher road. He couldn't shake the tune until they reached the sawmill where the blacktop stable road passed between the big stacks of lumber by the bridge. The rain eased to drizzle and the sun had not yet set, so they halted to wait for the dark. The column had made much better progress than anyone expected.

"Finch, let's go reconnoiter," said Prahler. Finch nodded. Luiz said he had to get going.

"I need to get these cats to the stream before dark," he said.

Prahler and Finch agreed. The two groups shook hands for luck, kidded each other about who would get to sleep in the offices, and filled their good-byes with "fucking A's" and "kick asses." Jim asked Luiz, "Hey, man, if you like die in battle, can I have all your rubbers?"

"Sure," said Luiz, "but most of them are kinda stretched out, you know?"

"Good. I won't have to work 'em so much myself then."

Finch shook Charles's hand. "Take care," he said. "Keep an eye on that crazy Guamanian and enjoy your trip. Remember, nobody dies."

"Luiz says you can come with us. Let Prahler handle the rest."

"Yeah, I'm afraid he would, Charles. That's why I've got to stay."

"Well, anchors aweigh then."

Finch smiled, looked strong again, and gave a casual salute before turning to the others. Charles turned around, too, saw the dark-haired Ringo stoically checking their flashlight and Luiz adjusting his pack; the three looked at each other and without a word set off back up the firebreak. The music in Charles's mind came back, this time as Carl Wong's theme: Creedence again, doing "Run Through the Jungle."

They walked along the firebreak for a couple of minutes to a heavy bass and insistent drums, then turned right down a wet slope toward the creek, hoping for a point about two hundred meters above the bridge. The underbrush grew thick here—mainly saplings and bamboo—and they found the ground slimy with mud and waterlogged leaves. Ringo followed Luiz, and Charles brought up the rear. Perhaps halfway down the slope Luiz squatted down and held up his hand. Ringo and Charles dropped silently; when Luiz moved his hand forward they closed on him.

He whispered: "I thought I heard somebody. If they smart they put one guy by the bridge and one guy in the field, you know? Surprise us while we think they're all in the stables. If they smart. But then I think, Tom, George, they not too smart; Moody, he don't give a shit."

"Yeah," said Charles. Ringo smiled thinly, which they took for agreement. As they moved forward again they found the slope leveling, and when they could hear the stream clearly the undergrowth abruptly changed to mangrove, a maze of roots snaking up three or four feet before joining into thin branches and leaves. They couldn't stand up and they couldn't go over it, so they squatted down and duckwalked through—easy prey, Charles thought, for spiders or snakes, though he could hope that Luiz or Ringo would pick them up first.

The strip of sinuous roots ended only when they got to the creek itself. Climbing out of the tangle, they stood knee-deep in an eddy and looked at what they'd gotten themselves into. Some ten meters wide, the coffee-and-cream water carried a steady traffic of swiftly moving branches and leaves. On the opposite bank they faced a muddy wall about two meters high. Above that they could see a broad field of waist-high grass and, several hundred meters away, the final traces of sunlight striping the corrugated metal roof of the riding rink.

"Looks hairy," said Ringo.

"You wanna go back?" asked Luiz.

"Fuck no. Let's do it."

Charles didn't like the look of things but he felt too tired to go back, and going back would mean the mangroves and the thick wet bush in the dark alone. He watched as Luiz entered the creek, slowly wading deeper and deeper until the water climbed halfway up his butt and jostled him roughly maybe two-thirds of the way across. Luiz recovered and made it the rest of the way, then held his hand up for them to wait while he scaled the bank and crawled forward a couple of meters to observe the stables. Turning back, he motioned Ringo forward. Ringo looked at Charles.

"You gonna be okay?"

"Yeah. Sure."

"Right. Just remember to face the bank and keep your side to the stream. The water catches you full in front or back you're fucked. Got that?"

"Yeah. Thanks."

Ringo slipped into the flow and stepped steadily across, slowing down where they'd seen Luiz stumble, then picking up again. A few twigs and leaves snagged in his web belt on the way, but he soon gained the opposite bank and joined Luiz on top. They both motioned to Charles.

Charles got a third of the way across when he felt the water surge up to his hips. He stopped for a moment, feeling the stream and gauging its force before continuing. A passing branch caught his belt and nudged him. He wanted to say *okay, okay, hold it—let's start again* but he knew it wouldn't help. The creek wouldn't hear, not over its own noise, and it wouldn't care. The creek only cared to get to the sea and would take anything with it that got in its way—trees, rocks, mountains, and even Explorer Scouts who only wanted to play a game. It wouldn't even think twice about it.

"Come on," whispered Ringo, "you can do it."

Embarrassed, Charles took a big step. Immediately the creek tore him off his feet. He thrashed forward, too alarmed to even cry for help, though he thought he could hear Luiz cry "shit!" as the stream pushed him along. He twisted toward the bank, half swimming and half floundering, and felt the cold water soaking his fatigues and pulling him down. He struggled to keep his head above water but it grabbed his recon hat and tugged at the strap holding it around his neck. As it carried him he worked his legs and tried to stay upright. Twenty meters downstream from Ringo and Luiz he suddenly felt mud underfoot and could see the bank looming just before him. He clawed furiously in the darkness, slapping at foam and froth and welcoming the resistance of every shred of debris, from twigs and leaves and rotted pulp, to at last the mud wall of the other side.

For a minute he simply held on, his fingers sunk in the bank and his legs still pinned in the stream. At length Ringo and Luiz crept up to meet him and, with some effort, he scrambled up high enough to reach for their outstretched hands. Ringo grabbed one flailing wrist, Luiz the other. As they dragged him up Luiz said, "Cat, what you taking so much time for?" Ringo grinned.

The three sat a few more minutes to let the night finish setting in. When they went forward again they did so on their bellies, first carefully pushing the grass down in front of them and then creeping over it, slithering forward a few inches at a time. It might take forever to reach the stables that way, but in a little while Luiz found the ditch and the three of them slipped into it.

"What's that smell?" asked Ringo.

"This drains the stables," explained Luiz. "Take us right there."

"Well, guess I been in deeper shit."

They quickly crawled up the ditch, completely hidden from the defenders. When they got close to the rink they crept out and hunkered down under the bleachers where Navy parents liked to watch their children practice one of the finer social graces. Not having thought any farther than this earlier, they decided that Ringo and Charles would go around the rink in opposite directions with sheathed knives for weapons: Ringo counterclockwise to the offices and stables proper, Charles clockwise to the reception area and the workers' Quonset. Luiz would take the flashlight, climb up on the roof, and see what he could do. They shook on it and split up.

Charles stepped cautiously around the ring, trying to keep in the shadows of the handful of outdoor lights and stopping every few seconds to listen. Tired, wet, and filthy, only the prospect of meeting an enemy, even a fake one, kept him alert. He didn't want to come all this way and fail. After about five minutes he made it to the front of the rink and held back just short of the glow cast by the lights of the office and the reception area. He saw no one, not the defenders, not Prahler's group, not Luiz or Ringo. He turned back, walked a dozen paces or so, then collapsed in the shadows beside the rink and decided to wait.

A slight breeze brought the sound of leaves in the jungle and an occasional creaking in the metal roof and sides of the rink. It chilled him through his soaked fatigues, but when he wrapped his arms around his torso it only brought cold gritty mud against his skin and did nothing to warm him. Once he thought he heard a muffled report, another time a hushed voice, but nothing followed either. He thought he must have fallen briefly asleep when he finally heard footsteps.

Charles tensed in the darkness, clenched his chattering teeth, and gripped his knife. His pulse revved when he saw a shadow approach and his hand shook until he deciphered the figure's features as Ringo's. He waited till the marine reached him before stepping out.

"Shit! Take it easy," said Ringo. "War's over."

"What? No way!"

"Yeah. Fuckers were asleep on their feet. Luiz caught all three of them stepping out the back of the stables for a look. Bam, bam, bam. Three up, three down."

Luiz walked up with the three dead defenders. "Hey cat, we won!"

"Great, all that crawling around and you get the scalps."

"No problem, man. We got their flashlights, too. One for each of us. Let's nail the others when they come in."

"Good idea," said Moody. "Maybe if you hard-asses kill everybody we can call this shit off for the night and get some sleep."

"I want a rematch," said Tom. "We weren't ready."

"Tell Saint Peter," said Ringo.

"Listen," said George, "why don't you let us help you get the others. That way we can all have fun."

"Fuck it," said Charles. "You're dead."

"That's right," said Moody, "and I for one plan on enjoying it. You studs go ahead and do your thing. Me and these two boys are gonna suck down some root beers and play pinochle."

"Pinochle?" said George. "That's okay. Come on, Tom—let's play cards."

In the parking lot in front of the reception area a flagpole rose from a circle of low shrubs. Charles took his position there, the office and stables in one Quonset to his right, the reception area— a small screened-in waiting room—directly behind him, the rink farther behind both the office and reception area, the Filipinos' Quonset fifteen meters to his left. Luiz hid in the dark somewhere in front of that. Even farther to the left, Ringo set up to cover the road from the base and a possible flank attack from Joe. They didn't bother to cover the rear.

From his position in the shrubs Charles became acquainted with all the night shadows in his immediate area. After half an hour in which he managed to stay awake only through cold and the expectation of attack, Charles saw one of the shadows by the stables move.

He held his fire. Quickly three or four shadows, large shadows, thudded from right to left in front of his position—horses. He almost leapt up to go after them but four or five smaller shadows appeared to his right front, leapfrogging across the ground toward him. As they neared Charles could make out edges— straps, packs, the brims of fatigue caps. When they closed to no more than five meters Charles sat up, flicked on the flashlight, shouted "Bam, bam, bam, bam, bam! You fuckers are dead!" then dropped quickly and rolled over as a beam played over his head. In his light he'd seen Chase, Carl, MacReady, and Jim. They now sat up. "Shit," said Carl.

The light searched the shrubs in front of Charles. He lay down, burrowing into the mud, recon hat and sleeves covering his head and hands with wet muddy camouflage. The light moved away. MacReady yelled, "No, man! He's still in there!"

"Where? Where *is* the fucker then?" yelled Prahler from the right.

Then, a little farther to the right, "Bam, bam! Your ass is mine, Prahler!"

"Luiz!" exclaimed Jim. "You slick motherfucker."

"You bet."

"Get down," said Charles. "Finch and Joe are still out there with Billy and Ford."

"Fuck that," said Prahler. "Everybody out! Game's over!"

"It's a trick," said Charles. "Get down!"

"Will you listen to me, you little asshole?" said Prahler, walking over to the flagpole. "Everybody come on out and gather around! Somebody let the fucking horses out!"

Prahler's group stood and came up to the flagpole. The office door opened and Moody came out with Tom and George.

"Who the fuck let the horses out?" Prahler demanded.

"Horses?" said George.

"'Horses?'" aped Prahler. "Four-legged things that run, you dumb son of a bitch. Who the fuck let them out?" His eyes widened and his jaw shook with anger. "I bet the goddamn Joes let them out before they left! Goddammit! Where's my dog?"

"Your dog's fine, man," said Moody. "He's in the office where he's supposed to be."

"No shit? All right, bring him out! Goddammit, let's round up those horses!" Prahler ran off down the road after the horses waving his flashlight. Luiz and Carl followed. Moody went back to the office for Sparks. Chase and MacReady, Tom and George and Ed—all spread out to look for the escaped horses. Charles clutched Jim's sleeve. "Where are the others?" he asked.

"Ah shit, I don't know. Out there somewhere. I thought the stream looked pretty bad when we got to the bridge but Joe had a real hair up his ass—just had to take off on his own, and Billy and Ford just fucking dragged after him, and Finch just had to run after them all to make sure everybody was okay. I said fuck that shit, man, I don't exactly feel like a swim right now. Say, that was a neat ambush Barker. Christ, you smell like shit, you know that?"

"Man, I was hoping to knock everybody off at one go."

"Well, you can forget that shit. I think the games are over for tonight, anyway. Let's see if we can find some horses."

He turned to go but Charles held on to his sleeve.

"The horses weren't out till you guys showed up."

"Yeah? No. Can't be. Come on, let's help the others."

They went out into the dark following the beam of Charles's captured flashlight. A couple of horses let them get within a few meters before bolting but neither Jim nor Charles felt like running after them. Finally, after perhaps half an hour they came upon a horse grazing calmly by the stream and, with only a little gentle cajoling, they succeeded in leading it back. When they returned they found all the scouts except for Joe's group, most of the horses, and all three of Prahler's buddies trying to talk him out of going after the last pair of mounts. They could get them in the morning, they said.

"Goddamn Joes!" Prahler yelled. "Goddamn fucking lazy-ass Joes! They cripple dogs, let goddamn horses out into the goddamn jungle, walk around like they fucking own the place, breed their goddamn *chickens* in the fucking *stables* . . ."

Charles had never seen anyone actually foam at the mouth, but Prahler looked close. In an odd way it seemed funny—most of the boys stood around and grinned, even stepping closer to see where Prahler's rage would lead. Except for Luiz's group they'd spent the last several hours in bad country and bad weather, psyching themselves up for a battle in which they'd gotten blown away in seconds. Maybe Prahler's rage would lead to something they could get into.

"I am so fucking tired of those filthy goddamn stinking grease-ball good-for-shit Flips! Where's my motherfucking dog? Goddammit! They wanna get rid of the Navy's goddamn horses? Well I am gonna goddamn get rid of every motherfucking unauthorized piece of Joe goddamn garbage on these premises! Sparks! Where are you, Sparks?! Oh, there you are, boy—come to Daddy, Sparks! Sparksie wanna treat? Oh Sparksie baby, Daddy gonna give you one nice treat, yesss. You like chickens,

Sparksie? You want chickens? *You want chickens Sparks?* I'll give you goddamn chickens! Come on, boys!"

He ran to the stables with the post following him half out of curiosity. Inside he flipped on the lights, unsheathed his bolo, and jumped up on the door of the first stall. The horse inside neighed and reared; Prahler swung back and hacked at the cage overhead. All down the row of stalls, suspended from the ceiling for safety from predators, the Filipinos' chickens filled crude cages of sticks and twine.

"Come on, men!" Prahler shouted. "Come on Sparks! We're *all* gonna eat chicken tonight!"

Carl leapt up beside him, Ed went to the next stall, then MacReady, Tom and George, Ringo, Chase, and Moody. The stables echoed with the neighing of frightened horses, thundered with hooves pounding on dividers, and shook with young men's shouts and the varied cracks and thuds of bolos knocking apart the flimsy cages. The chickens began to cackle and scream and the young men laughed with excitement, their bolos flashing in the light of naked incandescent bulbs, first white and then scarlet as they caught the workers' chickens in midleap. Feathers billowed as if in a pillow fight, tossed by jets of blood.

Falling from their shattered cages the chickens hopped and ran, some managing short flights before the boys in fatigues cut them down in the passage. Some, missing a wing or leg or sporting the bright stripes of deep slashes, screamed in the stalls, jumping against the sides until they collapsed, quiet and ebbing in a corner with straw and horseshit, or bounced out like comical feathered comets when a horse kicked them free. Others somehow made it to the concrete floor intact and ran out the open door to the parking lot followed by scouts and counselors with Kabar and bayonet and bolo.

Charles watched from the flagpole, dumbstruck. He hadn't moved. Everyone seemed to have joined in except Luiz, who stared sullenly from Prahler's office door. Charles ran up to him.

"This is nuts, man! We got to stop this shit!"

Luiz shook his head. "Too late, cat. Too late."

Charles ran out into the parking lot in the midst of shouting scouts and screaming chickens, the horses in the stables neighing and kicking in a crazy choir behind him. Sparks appeared at his feet, barking with excitement, running down the injured chickens and tossing them gleefully into the air or shaking them back and forth like toys. Everyone yelled and then Charles yelled too. He yelled at every scout who ran by with a bloody blade, yelling at them to *stop, goddammit, stop it now.* He ran into Tom, grabbed him and shook him, but Tom just stared past him, his freckles spattered with blood and his fists clenched on the handle of his bolo, and howled.

"Build a fire!" Prahler shouted. "Let's build a goddamn fire! Bring me those goddamn chickens!"

He stopped MacReady and George and pushed them toward the workers' Quonset. "Come on, let's get this fucking door open! They let our horses out, let's see if they left us any tinder!"

George and MacReady threw themselves at the door two or three times till it started to crack and splinter, then Prahler knocked the lock free with a high stomp of his booted foot. Behind him the post and Moody, Chase, and Ringo began to heap up the chickens, many dead, but many still pulsing and kicking. Chase and Ed followed George and MacReady into the Quonset and began bringing out the Filipinos' gear. Charles grabbed Prahler's arm and tried to sound authoritative. "That's enough!" he shouted. "All right, everyone, that's enough! Cut the shit!"

Prahler slapped him and he fell. Blood streaked Prahler's bolo and smeared his face. Both glowed red in the light of the freshly kindled fire.

"Ever hear of the law of the jungle, Barker?" Prahler asked in a strained, high pitch. "Well, just where the *fuck* do you think you are?"

Prahler laughed and other voices joined in. As the firelight grew with fresh additions of tools, mattresses, and clothes, Charles could see the blood that painted everyone's faces and splashed over their fatigues like an extra color in the camouflage pattern. Prahler turned from him and joined the others in looting the Quonset. They piled on cards, tables and chairs, Filipino porn and movie magazines, wood carvings, and a foot-long foam-rubber dildo.

Charles picked himself up and turned away, flinching from the shrieking laughter. He walked to the reception area and reached for the door. A few feet to his left Ed and Carl had a chicken on the ground, working at its gristly neck with a bayonet as it thrashed and screamed. In the half light the blood that spurted out looked black. When the head fell back Ed tossed the bird toward the pile of other chickens. It landed short, got up, and staggered a few meters, its head dangling from its neck like a loosened tie. Charles entered the reception area and lay down on one of the two metal-and-plastic sofas. The plywood walls rose only waist-high before becoming screens. They shut out none of the noise or firelight. Charles wanted to puke but he felt too tired.

It will stop when Finch gets back, he thought. *All this shit will stop. I'll help him and so will Luiz. And Jim. Billy and Ford will join us and then the others will, too.*

A figure appeared beside him. "Wanna smoke?" Jim asked.

"No. Jesus. Can't we stop this?"

"What's to stop? The chickens are gone and so's most of the Joes' shit. Man, you think it'd be a problem, but it's just Joes' shit, isn't it?" He sat down in one of the chairs and took a deep drag.

"Can't we do anything?"

"Let's wait for Finch."

Charles sighed and put his head back. A moment later the door burst open and Carl asked, "Anybody for some chicken?"

"Fuck off," said Jim. Charles didn't look up.

"What's wrong with you guys?"

"You're all fucking nuts, that's what," said Charles.

"Oh blow me, Barker. The fucking Joes tried to kill Sparks and let the horses go. They had this coming."

"Right. And this is what the judge sentenced them to. It all makes sense to me now."

"Hey, eat shit and die, Barker," said Carl.

"Yeah," said Jim. "We prefer shit." He blew a smoke ring and looked away.

Carl stared at them, a charred chicken leg in hand. "Ah, come on guys . . ."

"We'll talk about it another time," said Charles.

Carl frowned and shook his head. He tossed the chicken leg over his shoulder. Sparks barked and suddenly the boys outside got a little noisier. Carl looked around and said, "Shit! Here's Joe!"

"'Bout time," said Jim, getting up. "Come on, Charles, let's try and help the cavalry. Boots and saddles, bro."

"I'm with you." Charles struggled to get up. Now they could put things in order. He followed Jim to the fire, which twisted under a light rain that had just begun. In its wavering light he could see Joe with scouts and counselors gathering around him. A couple of meters away Billy and Ford held each other up, wet and as beat up as if freshly keelhauled. He couldn't see Finch.

"Where's Finch?" he asked when he got to Joe. Several of the scouts turned away. Billy started to cry. Ford stared.

"Where's Finch?" Charles asked again.

Prahler stepped up and seized Joe by the arms. "What the fuck you mean he's still out there? Jesus Christ, Barone!"

Joe looked up, his mouth hanging open in exhaustion. "Billy and Ford went under . . . he got 'em . . . he . . ."

"He *what*, you fucking pussy?"

"I don't think he made it. We had to get . . ."

"Bullshit!" Prahler yelled. "Goddammit let's go back and get him!"

"Ah, Jesus," sobbed Billy.

Prahler clenched the front of Billy's jungle jacket and pulled him up. "Shut the hell up! If you hadn't gone under . . ."

"Christ, Hank," said Moody, "take it easy. Let's get Security out here. These kids aren't in any condition to find anyone—look at them for God's sake!"

"Security?" Prahler asked. "Security? Look around yourself, asshole!"

"Listen, Hank . . ."

Charles jumped between them. "Nobody's that beat! He's right! Jim, Luiz, Carl—let's go out there and bring him back!"

"Christ, Charles," said Joe, sinking to his knees.

"He wouldn't have left any of *us* out there!" Charles cried. "Not any of us!"

Moody grabbed Charles's jacket and shook him. "How you gonna see?"

Charles patted himself for the flashlight but couldn't find it.

"That's right, you lost it. You and everyone else running around here. Me, too." He looked at Jim. "Hold on to his ass. We don't need two of them out there. I'll call Security." Then, to Charles, "Your buddy'll be all right."

"Don't you fucking move," said Prahler. "Nobody calls Security."

Luiz spoke up by the office door. "Too late, cat. I already did."

"Motherfuckers," Prahler said, then sat in the mud by the smoldering fire.

Charles shook loose from Jim and ran toward the creek. "Finch!" he called. "Finch!" Luiz and Jim tackled him, then pulled him up and clumsily tried to brush him off. He wanted to scream again or cry but he could see that they did too, so he stopped their hands and they walked back to the fire where Prahler muttered at the sputtering flames and Joe stared at his hands, and the other boys stood or sat and looked around dumbly at the charred gear and the fresh and burned bodies of dismembered chickens. Someone came up to Charles and held on to him. He heard Ford sobbing and he put his arm around his shoulder.

They stood there staring as the rain got heavy and as it finally broke and a few stars came out to show the edge of the jungle. Other lights came, too, down the road from the base as the first two pickups drove up to let out half a dozen Filipino security guards and one very tired duty officer in khakis. The officer walked up to the dead bonfire and saw the figures in muddy tousled camouflage and he asked, "What unit is this? Who's in charge?"

"Explorer Post Three Sixty," said Charles. "No one's in charge."

Prahler jumped up. "I'm in charge here, sir. Petty Officer Second Class Henry Prahler, sir, managing the Special Services

Riding Stables. We're on a scouting trip here, sir, and one of our boys is missing."

"He's dead," Joe blurted.

The officer looked around at the area lit by the two outdoor lights, the pickups' beams, and the stars. He switched on a flashlight and lit up more. Feathers, blood, chickens, a charred pile of someone's possessions.

"Ramirez!" he shouted, and then told the Filipino noncom to get help: marines, sailors, MAAs, people from JEST, choppers with lights. They had a boy lost in the woods and they needed to get him, pronto. Then he stepped over to Prahler and said, "Petty Officer, I'm going to get some vehicles out here and make sure these boys get home, but I'm going to need you to stick around for a while. I'm going to be real interested in hearing you tell me what's been going on out here tonight."

"Sir . . ." began Prahler.

Charles interrupted. "We're Finch's friends," he told the officer. "We can help find him. We know what we're doing, sir, we can get him."

"Just hang on, son. Help's on the way. We'll find your buddy. Everything'll be all right."

Charles heard him and he saw the lights of the other vehicles beginning to arrive from the naval station, the headlights and the flashing lights, and soon he could hear the helicopters, too. And already he could see the men, the sailors and marines, Americans, Filipinos, and Negritos, and at the head of each contingent an officer in khakis or whites or camouflage brusquely delivering the same assurance: we'll find your buddy; everything will be fine. *Everything will be all right*, they'd say. But Charles knew it wouldn't. Not that, not anything, not ever again.

↛ XVI ↚

CORREGIDOR

It took the Navy several days to find what it could of Finch. Parts of him ended up hundreds of meters downstream from where he went under, although the creek, in its clumsiness, had let him catch on rocks and branches along the way. When the clouds blew through and the waters suddenly dropped, creatures of the land found the various fragments and, in their own fashion, gave most of them a terrestrial burial. The monitor lizard, the wild boar, the civet cat, and countless small things, hard and segmented and as yet unnamed, each came and did their part. The Navy planned a funeral service anyway, although what it recovered did not amount to much. Or so Charles discovered when he lifted the base's weekly security report from his father's dresser to see what it had to say about his friend. Well hidden among the classified narratives about the theft of engine parts and pharmaceuticals, VD rates on an aircraft carrier recently departed for Yankee Station, and barroom brawls between sailors and marines, he found the paragraph on Finch. It felt wrong, although he could not say what he expected. Everything Finch had ever done or hoped for lay between tightly printed lines of stark, objective detail, and ended with the statement "The remaining pieces of tissue were sent to the Naval Hospital Morgue."

George Dewey High School capped its summer activities by opening the doors of the multipurpose room for a memorial assembly. There student notables made speeches about Finch by pulling together time-honored, virtuous abstractions about duty and service. At the chapel on the main naval station the padre made a similar speech seconded by the admiral and several senior officers, including the grieving father. The sailors who played "Mercy, Mercy, Mercy" on breaks behind the bleachers of the baseball field now played a dirge, after which the congregation sang the Navy Hymn. Commander Barker put his hand on Charles's shoulder and Mrs. Barker looked at her son with tears in her eyes, but Charles did not cry. He remembered Finch saluting in the twilight before turning away to protect the rest of the scouts from their mad counselor and their own bad ideas. It seemed neither fair nor possible that he would not return.

But then it also seemed unfair that none of the memorial activities included Explorer Post Three Sixty. It felt as though the whole base, unable to fix blame on any one person, resolved the problem by generally shunning the one group of boys. Even the post began to shy from itself. The day they returned from the battle at the riding stables Joe disappeared for several hours in Olongapo, an act he repeated several times that first week alone. The scouts and the Navy gave him certificates, ostensibly for trying to save Finch, but Joe got no more of an uplift from them than Finch did from his. Joe soon resigned from the post.

Prahler had to quit as counselor, not just for losing the one scout but for endangering the others in the course of looting and destroying the Filipino workers' possessions. Clearly he would have to go as manager of the stables, too, but the Navy took its time locating a new billet; it seemed to find it awkward to discipline the petty officer for the destruction of property that should not have existed in the first place. And the scouts, pressed by the silence of the Navy and the questioning stares of parents and friends, wore their jungle jackets less frequently, and had yet to discuss how they might find a new counselor or when they might go on another outing.

Still, they all showed up for the first monthly meeting after Finch's death. They looked surprised to find each other there, Charles thought; he wondered whether they came out of curiosity or some indefinable need to get back as a group. With the president dead and the vice president resigned, the post had good cause to meet, but even there they faced problems. Neither of the two most experienced members wanted the top job.

"I mean, shit," said Jim, blinking behind his granny glasses, "you know me. I prefer to do my trailblazing between a whorehouse and the main gate. I never made half the campouts anyway. If it'd been me in charge at Baguio instead of Finch we'd all be dead or hitched to Igorot tribeswomen by now. I mean like, fuck *me*, man."

"Yeah, not me for sure," said Luiz. "You gotta arrange shit and get supplies and permissions and things, deal with officers, you know. Not me. Besides, my old man's a civilian; he don't have enough pull to get us out of the shit we're in now. You should do it, Charles. Finch trusted you and you tried to stop Prahler and all that shit. What the fuck—you do the office shit and maybe I'll take care of us in the bush, huh?"

"Sounds perfect to me," said Jim.

"Wait a second," said George. "Maybe Tom or I would like to run."

"You really want to put that to a vote?" asked Ed.

Thus Charles became president and Luiz vice president, both by acclamation. Yet in the first few weeks of holding office Charles found his duties largely confined to recording resignations. First Tom Sanders and George Wong quit, explaining that they needed to focus on their studies in their last year of high school in order to assure themselves of slots at Annapolis or at least a good NROTC program. Then Ed and Carl had to quit after their older brothers told their parents about the night of the battle, the trip to Baguio, and just what Prahler had meant by a "survival hike." After that MacReady left, but only because his father's tour ran out. Charles wondered when everyone else would go.

"I think I'll stay," said Ford one evening, as he shot pool with Billy and Charles at the Teen Club. "My parents once approached me about quitting, but they relented when I threatened to kill myself. I like the feeling of empowerment that gave me."

"My dad knows I'll kill him," said Billy, viciously chalking his cue.

"Sure," said Charles.

"Okay, so he doesn't. But I would, swear to God." He put the chalk down and looked Charles in the eye, conviction for once overcoming bravado on his pudgy face. "What I did say was that my bro didn't drown so I could be chickenshit. I asked the old man if he thought the Nav would let his ass go just because some shipmate fell over the side. I asked him what he thought he was protecting me from when three years from now I could be one of those grunts getting shot at in 'Nam."

"And he bought that?" asked Ford.

"I think so. I'm not sure which one, though."

That Saturday Commander Barker rented a small cabin cruiser from the Navy marina at Cubi, intending to take his wife and son out for the change of scenery he thought they all needed. Around nine hundred, with a two-man Filipino crew, the three Americans, and a picnic lunch, the roomy boat rumbled out of the bay, turned left at the sea, and motored south along the Bataan peninsula. The coast remained in sight the entire trip; at first heavily forested, past the boundary of the base it became increasingly pale and bare, a low irregular ribbon of olive-dotted dun and khaki under an enormous bowl of blue. Off the starboard bow, toward the open sea, Yankee Station, and the war, Charles saw a distant, high formation of clouds but couldn't make out their destination. To port the coast flickered with breaking surf; he saw so much of it that he could imagine the features as they appeared on a map: promontories, inlets, a dot for a coastal barrio, a line for a road. Overhead, seabirds circled, investigating the boat's wake.

In a few hours the Barkers reached Corregidor, the island at the mouth of Manila Bay first fortified by the Spanish, and the site of the Americans' last stand against the Japanese in 1942. At a small wooden wharf a Filipino soldier in starched, lime-green fatigues greeted them cheerfully and helped the crew secure the boat. A group of urchins in tattered T-shirts and shorts offered themselves as guides: Mrs. Barker took a picture, then shooed them away with smiles and a handful of centavos. The children ran off a few hundred meters to play among several long, neat rows of machine guns, mortars, fieldpieces, and vehicles, some American and some Japanese, but all similarly rough as coral and rusted to the same shade of mercurochrome orange.

The Barkers walked for a couple of hours along trails leading from one sign to another, sometimes with a bright sun and a sea breeze, sometimes in the muggy shade of the jungle that now grew over the open places of the installation. Thinking of Subic, Charles could half imagine those spaces: parade grounds, ball fields, clipped lawns by the barracks and officers' housing, fields of fire cleared in front of the batteries. Out of a thicket there appeared a reinforced concrete pit holding two twelve-inch, ship-killing mortars, one now lying on its side like a fossilized elephant, the other teetering on the broken bed of the pit like a gunner's mate on liberty. Passages let into the sides of the pit where the crews had stored ammunition and sheltered them-selves, but vines hung over the entrances and small trees grew from the cracks that began with a Japanese dive-bomber and continued with nearly thirty years of hot and rainy seasons. Not far from the pit they came upon a coast artillery battery and Charles climbed up to the barrel of a fourteen-inch disappear-ing rifle, bomb-frozen in mid-rise. Mrs. Barker took his picture while the commander pointed to the corroded rangefinder and the sea and explained how the rifle might have sighted in on Japanese ships, had any steamed in front of it during the actual battle. After the battery they reached the Mile Long Barracks and MacArthur's Headquarters, both now hollowed by war, weather, and scavengers into unadorned concrete shells as over-grown with jungle as Subic's old Spanish magazine off the stable road. Charles abandoned his parents by the bright World War II memorial overlooking the sea and went back to MacArthur's

Headquarters, hoping perhaps for a souvenir. A narrow rough path led through the brush to a side entrance, but with the roof and upper floors gone the difference between outside and inside seemed nominal, a matter of the concrete foundation reducing the number and size of plants within the walls. Nonetheless, he entered and began to walk down a sparsely vegetated hall. Not so very long ago, Charles reflected, this had served as the center of American power in East Asia and the last refuge of its largest garrison. Pampered, underequipped, and wholly unready to fight, that garrison scarcely gave the Japanese a good workout before dying piteously on a forced march to prison camps. Still, Charles thought, they'd done what they could. In that way, it seemed to him, they set a more realistic standard of bravery than any hero he could imagine, including the general who had abandoned them with a fatuous phrase. Charles wanted to see a real memorial here—a bronze statue of a cavalryman eating his horse, or a cook trying to set the sights on a Springfield rifle. It didn't seem right to boil it all down to MacArthur and "I shall return." It then occurred to Charles that most soldiers never did return from the wars he enjoyed reading about and re-creating with games and toy soldiers.

He discovered a stairway leading to the nonexistent second floor and decided to go up and see if he could imagine what MacArthur might have seen before the war. It looked solid: the concrete slab steps lay largely intact, only here and there crumbling enough to uncover rusted reinforcing bars. He tried the first step, just to make sure, then took the second one, and only then found himself face to face with a snake.

A pit viper, he guessed from the shape of the head. Its bright green body stretched several feet along the stair and its tail dangled an unknown farther distance into the shadows beneath. Near its neck its skin turned pale and striped; as it gracefully reared it flicked a dark purple tongue at him. Charles almost laughed. There seemed something incongruous about a snake on a staircase, even this staircase. He wished he knew its name so he could tell people about it later if it decided not to kill him. For a moment he thought he should feel afraid; in the jungle he usually only heard snakes, he rarely saw them. But then he smiled.

"I'm too big to eat, aren't I? You're wondering if you should kill me anyway." Charles held out his hand. The snake hissed. Charles closed his eyes, then opened them and said, "So, we do this now or we do this later, right?" The snake dropped off the stair into the shadows and rustled the weeds as it slithered away.

Charles rejoined his parents and they returned to the boat, stopping along the way for a look at the bombproof tunnels that formed the very last line of defense for the Americans before their surrender. Signs in front of the hillside told them this and provided a map of the simple grid of laterals and cross passages in the Malinta Tunnel. Opening before them, it looked large enough to drive a train through, so the Barkers took their flashlight and went in. Very soon, after passing the gaping mouths of only two or three side cuts, Mrs. Barker said she had to go back. Charles looked at her and didn't see fear; something else bothered her, perhaps because as a young woman working in Washington she had seen General Wainwright, MacArthur's successor, unloaded in a wheelchair from a plane at National Airport after his release from a Japanese POW camp. Commander Barker and Charles continued, but not much farther. The flashlight made only hazy inroads in the darkness and a few times they heard sounds that robbers or wild animals might make. Back in the daylight they returned to the boat with Mrs. Barker and ate fried chicken and potato salad on the deck before casting off.

But what does it matter if no one comes here? Charles wondered. What did it matter if people forgot defeat; sometimes they forgot victories, too. Someday people might not remember MacArthur any better than they remembered Wainwright or some platoon officer in the imperial marines, and Subic itself might look like Corregidor now, and Corregidor like an Indian campfire under a shopping center in Fairfax. Finch had plenty of company.

Charles nearly fell asleep on the boat ride home but a few miles from the bay the water turned choppy and the clouds he'd seen earlier came on them like an enemy armada. The waves grew whitecaps and the boat began to dip and rise like a dolphin. Charles climbed atop the cabin and held on to the mast to watch the sky darken and the wind toy with the flag. He could hear one of his mother's records now, Mendelssohn's *Hebrides Overture,* and see that each time the bow of the boat crashed down a squadron of flying fish darted through the waves on either side. After a few minutes he came down and joined his parents in the cabin. He knew they worried about him.

JUST LIKE SENATOR KENNEDY

About a month after Explorer Post 360 came out of the jungle surrounding the Special Service's Riding Stables, savaged the Filipino workers' quarters, and killed and ate their chickens, Charles decided to go back and visit. Ho Chi Minh had died that Wednesday, so Saturday he felt like doing something more celebratory than painting toy soldiers or going to the library with Joan. Something different, in any event. When Luiz drove by and suggested they go to the stables Charles quickly agreed.

They parked in front of the workers' Quonset. Charles looked for signs of the previous month's bonfire but couldn't see any: the workers had done a thorough job of cleaning up after their assailants. A pair of Filipinos at the door invited Luiz in and Charles followed, a little guiltily. Inside, eight workers relaxed in their bunks or played cards on the floor, their table having fallen victim to the scouts' pillaging. The workers appeared to have salvaged perhaps half of their belongings; either Post 360 had missed the items or they hadn't gone on the fire long before the rain and the masters-at-arms extinguished it. From their

expressions and the scraps of English mixed in with their pre-
dominantly Tagalog conversation with Luiz, it appeared they
bore the young Explorers no grudge. Not that they had much
choice. They had enough on their hands hating Prahler; they
didn't need to take on a dozen dependents as well. They smiled
at Charles, said "hey, Joe!" and played for small stakes, laughing when Luiz made jokes whose meaning Charles could only
guess at.

Luiz quickly gambled away four pesos—worth a dollar the
year before but now only sixty-five or seventy cents—and asked
Charles if he wanted to play. Charles didn't have more than a
quarter on him and didn't like cards anyway, so he pointed at a
game board and suggested they play that instead. Luiz agreed
and asked one of the workers if they could borrow it. A squat
Filipino with a hand-rolled cigarette blazing in the corner of his
mouth briefly glanced up from a hand of cards and nodded. Luiz
set up the board. The game seemed a kind of checkers, played
with cowries and centavo pieces that one moved along straight
and diagonal lines burned into a piece of monkeypod wood.
Players didn't jump but tried to box the enemy's pieces between
two of their own. Luiz set stakes of ten centavos apiece and
quickly found himself out a peso he didn't have.

"Cat, you too good," he said. "I forgot you like those war
games."

Charles waived the wager and talked him into playing again.
A few of the workers sat around to kibbitz, mostly for Luiz's benefit since Charles knew no more than half a dozen Tagalog words,
none of which would help in a tactical situation. Still, after six
or eight moves Charles got the upper hand in this game, too, and
found himself in a pretty good mood.

It certainly felt strange to hang out with the Filipino workmen,
he thought. At first he felt like an explorer of the last century
among a new and unusual tribe, but he gradually became accustomed to the smell of their cooking and bodies—both a bit like
sweat and a bit like fish oil, he thought—their heavily greased-
back black hair, gold teeth, faded dress clothes worn for working, muddy complexions, and occasional hairy mole groomed

into an auxiliary mustache. An old worker reached over, brushed Charles's forehead, looked at his palm, and uttered a word that made the others laugh.

"What's going on?" Charles asked.

"He say you 'half baked,'" said Luiz, smirking around a Camel.

"What the hell does that mean?"

"Old Malay story, cat. When God make man from clay, first time He fuck up—burn him too much and shrivel him. That how you get Negritos. They figure the same for brothers, only they not shrunk-up like. Then He try again, only this time he don't do it enough. Man comes out half baked, all pale and weak. That's you, cat."

"Yeah, well what about you?"

Luiz moved lightly, capturing a piece. "I'm just like the Malay, cat. Baked just right. Ask any chick you see." He said something in Tagalog and all the Filipinos laughed.

At that moment Prahler kicked open the door, rebreaking the latch he broke on the night of the attack. The Filipinos sat up, tense with expectation if not fear. Luiz looked worried, but perhaps angry as well. Charles stood, still holding the cowrie he'd meant to move, afraid—not necessarily of Prahler, but of not knowing what to do.

"What's this?" Prahler demanded of Luiz and Charles. "What are you two up to? There's no loitering around here. If you don't want to ride horses, get the hell out."

"Go to hell," said Charles. Luiz stood up slowly behind him.

"What's that, Barker? You resisting a lawful command?"

"Command? What the hell do you mean?"

"I said get out. Do I have to call the master-at-arms?"

"Oh right. What are they gonna do? Lock up two dependents for visiting a recreational facility on base?"

Prahler frowned. Luiz grinned, as did a few of the Filipinos. But then Prahler smiled.

"No, not loitering," he said, "gambling." He pointed to the cards and the money lying on the floor between the bunks with their scorched and water-stained mattresses. "Thanks for raising the question, Barker. Now we'll see how your daddy feels about his son wagering with monkeys and how long these fucking Flips can keep their jobs after corrupting some American minors." He drill-book about-faced and strode out.

The Filipinos became visibly nervous. Luiz sighed. Incensed and alarmed, Charles followed Prahler outside.

"You ain't got shit on anybody," he said. "And you haven't got the balls to call."

Luiz quickly caught up with him. "Christ, cat," he said, "let it go. We're already in trouble."

"He's not going to call anybody. He's just trying to scare these guys."

"You'll see, Barker," said Prahler, walking to his office. A chief in khakis stood by the door to the reception area and watched. Thirtyish, stout, tanned over fading tattoos, under his aviator shades he wore an expression that wavered between curiosity and amusement.

"Take it easy," Luiz told Charles.

"Fuck that," said Charles. "That asshole's the biggest bull-shitter on base. He's gonna call the sucs like he's gonna have us double time the base perimeter and build pagodas out by the pis-tol range."

"You wait right there!" yelled Prahler as he slammed his office door behind him. Luiz remonstrated with Charles. The Filipinos came outside and whispered to each other.

"Man, we should split," said Luiz, pulling out his car keys.

"Bullshit!" said Charles, loud enough for Prahler to hear in his office. "I'll bet you ten pesos that cocksucker doesn't have the balls to call Security!" Then, more quietly, "We can leave, man, but what about these Joes?"

"Okay," said Luiz, "but use your damn head. If Prahler don't already call, calling him cocksucker probably make him do it."

Charles frowned. "Sorry, man. I couldn't stop myself; it felt too good."

Luiz shook his head. The minutes passed. The boys waited while the Filipinos milled about. Then Prahler stepped out of his office and folded his arms. The chief watched.

"I know who let the horses out that night, you bastard," Charles said to Prahler.

"Just keep talking. Just keep talking."

"You couldn't even take on the Joes when they were here, could you, you piece of shit coward."

"You don't know dick . . ."

"I know a pussy when I see one . . ."

"Cat . . ." Luiz pleaded.

A gray security truck turned into the gravel lot and pulled up beside the chief. A Filipino noncom in a gray uniform got out and looked around. Luiz sighed again, Charles bit his lip, Prahler smiled broadly, and the Filipino workers began to slowly move away.

"Are you in charge here?" the noncom asked the chief. The chief slowly shook his head and gestured toward Prahler. The noncom, about the age of the boys' fathers, turned to the petty officer and pulled out a pad of paper.

"What is the problem?"

"These men were gambling," Prahler said, indicating the retiring workers.

The noncom looked at the Filipinos and spoke a few words in Tagalog, apparently "you come here." They obeyed reluctantly. He asked them a question and they all shook their heads. Turning back to Prahler, he asked, "Do you have any witnesses?"

"What do you mean 'witnesses,' goddammit? *I* saw them."

"Yes, Petty Officer, I understand. But do you have any other witnesses?"

"Hell yes," said Prahler. "All of them. And these two kids, here. Right, boys?"

The noncom looked at Luiz and Charles. Luiz looked down. Charles stared at the noncom, and then at Prahler. *Never lie,* Commander Barker always said. More important, Finch, most of whose body still lay in the jungle, said the same. Charles could hear Finch now, telling him to go ahead and tell the truth. The Navy would find a way to take care of things.

"What gambling?" Charles asked, his voice rising in studied indignation. "What the hell is he talking about? I didn't see any gambling!"

"Goddammit!" said Prahler. "He's lying! They're all in it!"

The noncom held his pen poised but wrote nothing. He looked at the chief. "Did you see anything?" he asked hopefully.

"Nope," said the chief. "Heard some sea language, but didn't see a thing."

"Jesus!" said Prahler. "Aren't you going to do anything?"

"I can take a report. You want me to do that?"

"Well, hell. At least."

"Okay: please, then—may I have your name?"

"*My* name? What about *their* names?"

"You're the only one who saw anything. I can't use their names."

"Shit," said Prahler. "Forget it." He returned to his office. The noncom looked around, gave the workers a stare that quickly dispelled their smiles, then got back in his truck and drove off. As soon as the dust covered his rearview mirror, Luiz said, "Okay, cat. We go now, right?"

Charles nodded, but the Filipinos briefly blocked the way. They crowded up to Luiz and joked with him, clapped Charles on his back, and even shook his hand. The man who owned the board game laughed and mimicked Charles: "'Gambling? What gambling?'" The old man who had rubbed Charles's forehead said another word that made them all laugh. This time Charles assumed it meant "fully baked." Then the game owner stopped laughing, took Charles's hand, and said, "You are okay. Just like Senator Kennedy." Commander Barker hated and despised Senator Kennedy almost as much as he did Jane Fonda, but Charles assumed the Filipino had meant it as a compliment.

Prahler emerged from his office again and this time the workers made themselves scarce. "I'm glad to see you finally turned Joe," he told Charles.

"Yeah, I'm a Joe," said Charles. "Where the fuck do you think we are?"

"C'mon cat," said Luiz, "time to go."

"That's right," said Prahler, "get that little pussy out of here before I kick his ass."

Luiz sighed yet again, this time in exasperation, and in a gesture so quick and graceful it left Charles breathless, whipped off his belt and whirled it around his hand, leaving the heavy buckle and a few inches of leather strap dangling. He took a single step toward Prahler and calmly stared into the petty officer's eyes. Prahler gaped, seeming to expect Luiz to say something, but Luiz only looked at him. After a moment Prahler blinked, then turned around and walked back to his office without a word.

"Say," said the chief, "I don't think my cab's coming. Can I get a ride back to base with you guys?"

That night, still feeling excited about his rescue of the Filipino workers and his showdown with Prahler, Charles went to the Kalayaan theater with Joan. Trying to keep as cool as he could, he didn't tell her about his day until the film ended and they left the theater for a warm, starless night. She listened attentively— too attentively, he thought, her expression never changing from the serious, objective, almost adult gaze with which she might greet a teacher's instructions before a pop quiz. Charles wanted very much to see something different, to see a smile break the almost birdlike edge of her nose and chin, to see her close-set eyes broaden and her long pale hands brush back her dark bangs in amazement.

"You lied for those Filipinos?" she asked.

"They would've been in a lot of trouble."

"But they *were* gambling, Charles."

"Yeah, well. They'd have gotten a lot more than they deserved, you know that."

"I suppose you're right. So everything's okay?"

"Yeah. Everything's fine."

They walked in silence to the corner and turned left, away from the Barkers' quarters on SOQ Hill and towards hers. He wondered what she meant when she used the word *everything*. Did she mean just the stables, or how he felt about Finch, or something else? He would ask in a minute; at the moment he just felt glad she let him walk her home again. They hadn't spoken much lately.

"The Kittens have asked me to join," she said.

"What?" He couldn't hide his surprise. When he thought of the sorority at the Teen Club he thought of Cissy and Traci, the cheerleaders who painted little ceramic cats, gossiped about their friends, and—had one not dyed her hair blond and the other brunette—could easily pass for the same model Barbie. Cissy and Traci and *Joan?*

"The Kittens. You heard me. I thought it was very nice of them to offer."

"Gee, Joan, I don't know. Don't you have to get a lobotomy before you join?"

"That's terribly unfair and you know it. What have you got against them, anyway?"

"They're like a herd, Joan. You see them running around the Teen Club in their little groups and their little identical outfits gibbering away and looking down on all the other kids—what's the point?"

But he knew the point, and he knew his real objection. Every school had popular kids on one level and everyone else on several lower ones. If everyone became popular, caste would lose its point. He knew where he fit on the popularity scale back in the big junior high he'd gone to in Arlington and he'd done only marginally better at George Dewey High School. Outside of a circle of perhaps half a dozen Explorer Scouts still clinging to their disgraced post, and as many as a dozen Filipino stable hands in a half-wrecked Quonset hut in the middle of the jungle, he had as much popularity as a doorstop. But until now he at least also had a girl to watch movies and talk about books with. She wouldn't have much time for that now.

"The point, Charles, is that I want to meet more people. I'd like to see what this place has to offer before I leave. And you should, too. You should find a girl your own age and have fun—we just talk about movies and books we could see or read anywhere. Don't you want more?"

He did want more, but he would never let himself say what. She took his silence for argument and tried again.

"And what do you mean 'herd'? What about your Explorer Scouts? What about the night that boy died out at the stables? Who was in a herd then, Charles?"

He stopped and let her walk on a few feet. She turned and he could see her eyes starting to tear as her voice began to quake.

"I was at home *reading!*" she said.

"Sorry," said Charles.

"Oh, I'm sorry. I didn't mean anything about that boy . . ."

"His name was Finch. Walter Finch."

". . . but what do you want from me?"

He couldn't even look at her. He would have said something really stupid then.

"We're still friends, aren't we?"

He nodded, said good night, and walked back home up SOQ Hill.

→ XVIII ←

WE'RE NOT TRYING TO
SCARE YOU

Thirteen months after the Barkers arrived in the Philippines, the MacReadys went home, Commandant Chapman of the Marine Corps held a press conference about racism in the ranks, and a new academic year began at George Dewey High School. Another rainy season passed, succeeded by the dry, only moderately hot, and comparatively pleasant weather that accompanied Thanksgiving and Christmas. Charles asked his father several times to ask Base Security to give the scouts permission to camp in the jungle again, but each time Commander Barker brought back a negative. And Post 360 still had no counselor, so even on the outings still allowed them—tours of cruisers and destroyers, a run to and around Grande Island on a PBR ("Patrol Boat, River—at ninety knots she sprouts wings" the chief in charge said)—they had to have a parent along. Commander Barker offered to escort the boys on another march from the Kalayaan beacon to the Binictican golf course, but that, the scouts decided, would have missed the whole point of going into the jungle, a place where their parents could neither restrain nor help them.

Charles wondered if he should try to ask Joe to intervene with Security through his father, but he didn't see Joe much outside school, and even at GDHS Joe remained unapproachable. No one but Joe himself knew whether this resulted from his failure to save Finch from drowning the night 360 trashed the stables, or whether the self-annihilation he'd carried on in the bars of Olongapo well before that night fueled itself. Perhaps many more people than Joe would have to rotate home or forget the battle of the stables before the Explorers could ever get back to the jungle again. In the meantime they snuck out on a few occasions anyway, three or four of them smuggling fatigues and jungle boots to the house of a friend whose parents had gone for the day, suiting up, then spending a few hours revisiting the VC village and other sites of past adventures.

At school some of the teachers turned over, going on to other countries and classes in the DoD system, but Charles kept Las Casas for English. Charles appreciated Las Casas for the arguments he incited over the stories, poems, and plays he assigned to his class, but Charles also believed Las Casas sometimes thought he knew more about his students than he actually did, or could. Las Casas thought, for example, that Charles should write more—even outside of class—and that he should write or say something about Finch. As the class broke for lunch one day, Las Casas asked Charles to stay for a few minutes.

"You should talk about it, anyway," the teacher said. He took off his round, imitation tortoiseshell glasses and wiped the lenses on the tail of his barong tagalog as he spoke. "I mean, at least with your friends. You shouldn't suppress it—writing's a good way to let these things out. At least a journal, Charles." He looked up, his green eyes hopeful, and absently scratched his bald pate with the hand that held his glasses.

"No, I don't think so."

"What are you talking about, Charles? It's important not to bury something like that, not to let it burn holes in your heart or your head and scar you for life . . ."

"Do I look scarred, Mr. Las Casas? Am I acting scarred? Maybe I should be scarred. Hundreds of dudes die every week in 'Nam. In a few years maybe I could use some scar tissue."

"Charles, I'm just saying it would be normal. I know how I'd feel . . ."

"Well, maybe I'm not like you."

"Of course, if you'd just as soon I fucked off . . ."

"I didn't say that; just don't assume I'm in some great turmoil . . ."

"Okay, so you're not. It's just that I don't get a lot of sophomores doing book reports on *Faust*, and not Marlowe's but Goethe's . . ."

"So?"

"Parts one *and* two, for Christ's sake."

Luiz looked through the doorway and then stepped in carrying a book as casually as in better times he carried a bolo in the bush. Suddenly Charles realized that he read.

"Hey cat, cool book report. That Mephistopheles, man, I think I see him in town, you know? Where you get that, anyway?"

"Maybe you should start with *The Devil and Daniel Webster*," said Las Casas. "Stop by the BOQ sometime. I think I have it in an anthology."

"Sure, teach. Cool." Luiz left.

Las Casas frowned. "See what you've gotten me into?"

As November came, *Stars and Stripes* reported the beginning of the withdrawal of the Third Marines from Vietnam, but no one in Subic expected the war to get any smaller or shorter. Then, in midmonth, a back-page article appeared about a "Mobilization" against the war. To Charles it didn't seem like much, just a short article, but it said that more than a hundred thousand students had gone to Washington to protest. He thought at first that *Stars and Stripes* might have made a typo, but he quickly realized that they printed big numbers like total deployments or enemy casualties too often to make a mistake. The next day, about a week before Thanksgiving, another article appeared, this one dealing with an Army action at a hamlet called My Lai that resulted in the deaths of over a hundred villagers. Over the next few weeks it seemed to grow into a big scandal stateside, but the boys Charles knew all had a great deal of sympathy for the company of Army grunts. The boys decided that the grunts could not have gone far wrong in suspecting the village adults of sympathizing with the VC because they'd lost a lot of people around there, so it made sense to kill them all. And you couldn't leave the babies to fend for themselves.

On Thanksgiving Day, a few hours before the midday meal, Charles snacked on a cold olive-drab can of C-ration Turkey Loaf and thought of the guys in the field. His father disagreed with him about My Lai. "Those men were trained to handle prisoners," Commander Barker said. "You can't let discipline break down like that." Charles didn't argue; when he got to 'Nam his father would have no way of knowing what he did from day to day.

Charles still frequently saw Joan at school and at the Teen Club, but since Joan had joined the Kittens sorority they didn't get together as much. Near Christmas they went out a couple of evenings, not going to movies but sitting after dark on the terrace between the Kalayaan O Club and the pool, talking about the war, My Lai, and the marches. Since they arrived in the Philippines both had changed and the war had become less of an abstraction. Charles had worn the clothes and seen the soldiers of this war, and had gotten a year and a half closer to the time of deciding. Joan, too, had met some of the boys going over and coming back.

"What would you do if they called your number?" Joan asked one evening.

Charles looked down from the terrace to the water of the pool where the ripples flickered with moonlight and the shadows of insectivorous bats. He liked the idea of war in the eighteenth century—the uniforms and banners, the brutal honesty of muskets and swords, the importance of horses, the seemingly total lack of concern with the justice of causes. But this war—his war—had nastier, less sporting weapons, treacherous civilians, and a domestic population apparently obsessed with a level of moral certainty that war never had and never could attain. *People never went to war just for just causes*, thought Charles. They went to war because people had always gone to war.

"What do you mean?" he asked Joan.

"If they drafted you, would you go?"

"I don't think they can draft you if you're at Annapolis or in NROTC."

"So you would go?"

He shrugged. "I don't think I'd know how not to."

She said she understood. They stayed friends and spoke frequently, but on New Year's Eve at the Teen Club, when he finally nerved himself up for a kiss, she offered her cheek.

Charles began to wonder who he might meet besides Joan, and how far they might get if his father didn't sign on for another two years in Subic. As Valentine's closed in, he came home from school one day to hear his mother say that he had received a letter.

Mrs. Barker smiled as she handed her son the envelope. He smiled back, thinking that the way she stood there stylishly puffing on a Parliament over the lipstick-stained rim of her manhattan with a look just shy of a knowing wink, he might have just gotten something from a girl, perhaps even a Valentine's Day card. But the envelope didn't look right for a card and when he turned it over he saw that it came from no one he knew personally. The black, preprinted script said OFFICIAL BUSINESS— POSTAGE AND FEES PAID/NAVY DEPARTMENT, and the blue, rubber-stamped script in the upper left corner read, COMMANDER, U.S. NAVAL BASE, SUBIC BAY. He took it to his room to read.

"Dear Charles," read the typed part of the letter. Immediately after that came a mimeographed page that ended with a ballpoint scrawl that might have come from the admiral, but probably issued from one of his aides. Within the blue body of the letter he read, "You are recognized as one of the leaders of the youth of the U.S. Naval Base, Subic Bay, therefore you are invited to attend a Special Meeting of considerable significance. This meeting will be an informal one at the Teen Club at 1300 hours Sunday . . . will include about 30 young people of high school age and attendance will be by invitation only. Light refreshments will be served.

"We have great expectations that this get together will be a fruitful one, and it may have a profound impact on many people. You are urged to attend if at all possible. Please do not bring anyone with you who does not have a specific (written) invitation."

An invitation to attend "if at all possible" translated, as far as Charles knew, into a direct order from the highest authority this side of CINCPAC, and any refusal might affect his future, and his father's present, in the Navy. This caused him some discomfort, but he quickly found that outweighed by curiosity and a certain pleasure at forming part of the small group selected for this Special Meeting. When Sunday arrived, "informal" or not, Commander and Mrs. Barker made sure their son put on a formal barong and a pair of dress slacks before he left for the Teen Club. When Charles arrived there he found that most of the other parents had done the same.

An officer and a chief in tropical white longs greeted Charles at the door, checked his letter and dependent's ID, and politely directed him to the dance hall. There Charles found five rows of half a dozen folding metal chairs each, already largely filled by three GDHS class presidents, leading Aces and Kittens, and a few other children of senior officers. A large projection screen obscured the stage where the In Crowd had played the night before, and a folding table against the far wall held several cases of sodas and a few platters of PX cookies.

Two men nodded at Charles as he took a seat in the back row. One looked about forty and had a crew cut and a face of broad features seemingly slapped together out of putty. He reminded Charles of Joe Friday, right down to the kind of narrow, cheesy suit none of them had seen since leaving the States. He gave the impression of wanting to look nice for this meeting despite having run down a few small animals on the drive over. The other man looked in his late twenties: tall, tan, blond surfer cut just within regs, green paisley shirt open at the collar. He could have fit in with any group of sailors on leave. The two made small talk with the students at the front as they set up a slide projector and glanced through some notecards. The young, good cop called the old, bad cop George. George called his partner Vince. From what Charles overheard, they came from NISRA, the Naval Investigative Service Resident Agency at Subic. They smiled— or in George's case, grimaced—as the rest of the kids came in, but Charles didn't see a lot of smiles going back. At thirteen hundred only one seat remained empty, the one on Charles's left. The officer and the chief stepped in and the two NISRA men looked at each other.

"Let's go ahead," said George, even sounding like Friday. "There's always one that doesn't want to get the message."

"I don't know, partner," said Vince, winking at the audience. "What's another minute?"

George scowled and for a moment Charles thought he might really see something interesting, but just then Ford rushed in, sweaty and breathless, to a chorus of disapproving and derisive murmurs.

"What are you doing here?" Charles whispered.

"President of the George Dewey Chess Club," Ford explained. "Sole member, actually. 'Leader of Youth,' that's me."

With the room filled, the officer and chief left, closing the door behind them, and George and Vince formally introduced themselves as criminal investigators working for NISRA.

"What we're about to discuss may shock you," said George. "It *should* shock you, as it should shock all Americans. We wish we didn't have to, but as young adults you have a right to be informed."

"And these are things you really need to know," said Vince, his voice slow and soothing, his eyes gentle and frank.

"I won't beat around the bush," said George. "It has come to the attention of the commander, U.S. Naval Base, Subic Bay, that some dependents have been in the habit of visiting Olongapo in the evenings and on weekends."

A few giggles and snorts broke out. Vince smiled indulgently while George quelled them with a few well-aimed stares. Then Vince said, "Okay, okay, so some of you know about this. But what you probably don't know is that some of your friends have gotten in over their heads. Some of them," he said, in a tone that bordered on a sigh, "have even gotten involved with drugs."

No one laughed. Kids looked around at each other, some with surprise and some with fear. Charles didn't know what to feel. Hippies smoked pot; Negroes in cities shot up with heroin; he couldn't see Navy kids doing either.

"When this came to the attention of the commander, U.S. Naval Base," George continued, "it was both his duty and his concern for the young people of this installation that led him to call on NISRA. We conducted a series of investigations and we reported accordingly to the appropriate authorities. The results will soon become known to everyone. Before that, however, it has been determined that appropriate representatives of naval base youth be informed of the exact nature and extent of the problems associated with narcotics addiction."

With some solemnity Vince and George turned out the lights and switched on the projector. The first slide showed a close-up of a black man lying horizontally on blood-streaked asphalt. One eye hung loose from its socket over a protruding cheekbone. The other side of his face crumpled shapelessly against the pavement.

"LSD," said George. "I'm not going to tell you that each time someone uses LSD this is what happens to them, but in twelve hours of wild hallucinations, you don't know. On the street they call it 'acid.' That should tell you something. This fellow thought he could fly."

"That's true," added Vince quietly. "We're not trying to scare you."

More slides came, no less interesting. When the NISRA men talked about heroin they showed filthy spoons, bloody hypodermics, and anonymous arms covered with festering lesions. Same for morphine. When they got to psychedelics—mushrooms, mescaline, STP, DMT, peyote—they showed haggard and obviously diseased hippies panhandling in Haight Ashbury, and bedridden young patients staring plaintively in mental hospitals. Ford raised his hand.

"Isn't it true," he asked, "that some Indians are allowed to use peyote for religious purposes?"

George looked at him then turned back to the screen and a frozen slide of a bedraggled girl in handcuffs. Vince answered patiently.

"Yes, I've heard that. Once each year, under strict governmental supervision, registered medicine men are allowed to use peyote as part of an ancient tribal ritual. I wouldn't want to scare you, but it's not a pretty sight. Once those guys get going they don't know what they're doing—wrestling cacti, cutting themselves with knives . . . I really don't think you'd want to try it. They'd probably think you were crazy if you told them about somebody who did it for fun." Some of the students looked at Ford and laughed.

Ford raised his hand again. "Excuse me, sir, but what about marijuana? Do people on pot fly off of buildings and wrestle cactus, too?"

Charles squirmed. He heard some snickers, either for or against Ford; either way he didn't feel comfortable. George turned around like a raptor.

"Let me take this one, Vince. Kid, a lot of people will tell you that marijuana is harmless. Fact is, most of the time that's true. But it's like any other illegal narcotic. You don't know when you'll 'freak out' and have a bad reaction. Fact is, half the marijuana in the Philippines is nothing but scrapings off the barroom floor. Think about that. And I know of a case in Los Angeles where two young men not much older than yourself grew up together as the best of friends. Like brothers, they were—probably better. Did everything together. Both good students, too. At first. But then they started smoking marijuana together. Got 'high' they called it. Went on to college together. Even passed some courses. But they got to like that 'high' too much. One day one of them just stabbed the other. When he came off his trip he was in a jail cell. Had no idea what happened. That's the problem with marijuana, kid. Most of the time it probably only makes you stupid. You just don't know when it's going to do worse."

Ford stood up. "That's crazy," he said. "When did that happen? Wouldn't that have been in the papers or something?"

Everybody looked at him. Some laughed, others shushed. "Ford!" Charles pled in a stage whisper. "Come on!"

"Look you," said George, "I've spent years in the field of criminal investigation. I know what I'm talking about. Why don't you tell me who's giving you *your* information?"

Charles could see Ford shaking. He pulled on his friend's belt but Ford pushed his hand away. "You'd like a few names, wouldn't you, George? You know what I think? I think you guys are just a bunch of narcs saying whatever it is you think you have to say to get us to behave however it is you think we're supposed to behave."

Various moans and sighs of disapproval came from the student audience, though not everyone, Charles noticed, joined in. For a moment George and Vince just glared at Ford, perhaps trying to square this short, pale, dandruff-plagued, and heavy-glassed nerd with their idea of a drug abuser. As George eloquently clenched his jaw, Vince reasoned.

"Look, we really aren't trying to scare you. We're just telling you what we know based on the facts we have. You're a bright young fellow and it's right to question authority—you need to do that so you can get the facts and make the right decision. But let me tell you something. You're not the only young man on base to think the way you do, but you'd be well advised to hear us out before you try to find things out on your own. Because some of those things are bad. Some of those things are so bad you can never get right again. You have your choices, just like others have had theirs, but you have got to seriously reflect on them. The wrong choice will have consequences you can hardly imagine."

A girl in a Kitten sweater started to applaud and most of the others joined in. Ford sat down. Charles looked at him but Ford stared ahead, his eyes locked on Vince's. No one but Charles saw that Vince looked away first.

"Well, kids," Vince said smiling, "that's really about all we have for you today. We would like you to stick around, though, and maybe ask some questions if you have any. And of course, if you have any of your own thoughts or experiences you'd like to share with us we'd be happy to hear them."

The kids applauded, even Charles and Ford, then stood and walked over to the sodas and cookies. Several of the Kittens and Aces went up to Vince and asked a number of questions, including how to get a job in the Naval Investigative Service. Charles and Ford hung around the perimeter, not wanting to make themselves conspicuous by leaving early. Joe, on the other hand, who had come to the meeting as a leading Ace, made himself briefly obvious by asking Vince why he thought he could always tell a marijuana cigarette from a regular one.

"It's just different material. It never looks the same."

"Yeah, but what if you use one of those rolling machines?"

"Lucky that boy's dad works for Security," Ford muttered.

"Yeah, well, yours doesn't," said Charles. "You should be more careful, for Christ's sake."

"Yeah? Think about that, Charles. Think about what you just said. I'm almost certainly the cleanest kid you know. What in God's name am I supposed to be careful about?"

"I don't know, man. I don't want to know."

"That's the spirit, Charles. That's the spirit that made America the great democracy we defend today against the godless communists of Southeast Asia."

"Just shut the fuck up, okay?"

"Well, since you ask me as a friend."

The following day at school everyone learned the reason for the lecture. Rumors began on the buses in and by the third period had spread to every class. At lunch the whole student body clumped around the schoolyard in knots of whispered conversations. NISRA had targeted twenty-six dependents as either drug users or otherwise guilty of "conduct unbecoming." Copies of formal Security reports went to each of their fathers, each bearing a signature line for acknowledging receipt. As the acknowledgments came in, orders went out, sending the families home.

"BFD, man," said Billy at lunch. "Nobody's arrested; nobody goes to jail. You get caught with dope or some Joe hooker and what do they do? They send you home! Fuck, wish I'd thought of that one. I've been doing the wrong crimes."

"Don't be a fool," said Ford. "If you were arrested you could at least get a trial, and how many convictions do you think they'd get? Where do you think they got their evidence? Joe informers? Pimps and bar girls worried about their Navy business? A little bit of entrapment here and there? Now we have twenty-six kids, maybe some who are guilty of something and some who are not, and they're all equally screwed."

"You talk like you know something we don't," said Charles.

"I do. I talked to Jim Sunday night. He goes home in two weeks. So do the Sanderses: they got Ed. You know that Jim and Ed were counting on being officers someday almost as much as Finch. I never understood why, but they did. They can forget it now."

"Damn," said Charles.

"Hell," said Billy. "Jim must have seen it coming—he went off base often enough."

"Yeah, but he told me he never did any drugs," said Charles. "What'd they get him for, Ford?"

"Suspicion of something, I suppose. 'Conduct unbecoming,' whatever that means. God knows what sorts of rules there are that we've never heard of."

"He just *says* he never did no dope," said Billy.

"Come on, Killer," said Charles, "who you gonna believe?"

Billy looked down. "I wonder when they nail Luiz and Joe," he said.

"Who knows?" replied Ford. "With these charges, just about anyone could be next."

Within a week the Navy assigned new managers to the Teen Club in lieu of the old rotation of parent volunteers. First a third class named Brock, who had short blond hair and wide green eyes that looked through the kids as if trying to find the words behind whatever they actually said. Perhaps twenty, he gave the impression of never having held a post as dangerous as this one. To assist him the Navy assigned a short, pale, and plump yeoman named Lansing, who wore her chestnut hair to the middle of her ears like a sailor just returned from a long leave. The first time Charles saw her she wore green stretch pants with what looked like a uniform shirt with the ribbons and patches removed. Like Brock she tried to mix with the kids but seemed unsure of the appropriate combination of casualness and decorum. In the first weekend after the great bust, Ford must have asked each of them a dozen times if they knew some guys named George and Vince.

Charles bumped into Jim at the Teen Club a week after the lecture. After Lansing's second pass they walked up to the corner to talk by the park bench.

"Tough luck," said Charles, the right words slipping away like a coin in the water. "I'll be sorry to see you go."

"Not as much as my old man," said Jim. He took off his granny glasses like he wanted to throw them in the street. "Shit, the poor bastard doesn't know who to believe—me for saying I didn't do anything, or the Navy, for saying I must have. Anyway, so much for handing his gold stripes on to his son."

"Shit," said Charles.

"I mean, so what do I do now? I never really thought of anything else, man. I hate to admit it, but I don't know dick about anything but this. I mean, just what do civilians *do*, Charles? Just what the fuck *is* an accountant or an insurance executive?"

"Beats me."

"Me, too. I'll tell you what I do know, dude. I know the name of every rank from E-one to O-six. I can tell a squid's job from the color of his jersey stripes and those fucking cartoons on their sleeves. I know carriers are named for battles, battleships for states, cruisers for cities . . . fuck. I know the price of a blow job in every port in the western Pacific and how much you can save by paying in the local currency. You know where we're going next? Great Lakes, man, fucking *Chicago*! Jesus, you know what the weather's like there now?"

"Not to mention the price of blow jobs."

"Right. Not like I need one now. This ass-fucking should last me the rest of my life."

Jim left for his quarters. Charles returned to the Teen Club but found little going on. No one played pool or bothered with the jukebox. The kids who used to drink in back had retreated to the darkness of playgrounds or unlit lawns behind the club and theater. The only music came from the Armed Forces Philippine Network over the insipid PA. Kids chatted quietly while the new managers hovered like dully genial wardens. Charles left early to visit Las Casas.

Ten feet from his teacher's door Charles could hear the moronic *thumpathumpa* of Johnny Cash's band. Las Casas greeted him at the door with a beer in hand, pulled him in, and sat him down while he went to get a soda from the fridge. Over the singer's woofer voice he said, "I know—don't tell me. I would-n't go through my teens again for anything, Charles. Your parents will tell you how great these years are, but they've forgotten. Hell, I'd kill myself before I'd be your age again."

"Thanks a lot, Mr. Las Casas. I feel a lot better now."

"Hey, listen to this!" Las Casas turned around and grabbed the tone arm on his stereo and with a bit of a scratch cued up a song. As Cash sang about San Quentin and the inmates howled on the live soundtrack the teacher shook his head and clucked in grudging admiration. "Can you believe that? That guy is virtu-ally starting a riot! You and me, we'd be crucified if we tried some-thing like that. I bet he made a million dollars off this record."

"It's not bad," said Charles.

"Not bad? It's unscrupulously horrible! I love it!"

Charles listened to the rest of the album while Las Casas had a few more beers and tried to sympathize with him. Charles might have appreciated the sympathy if he knew quite how he felt himself. When the album ended he thanked Las Casas and left, thinking he'd go back to his family's quarters and try to get some sleep. At the corner he found Billy and Ed Sanders shar-ing the park bench while somewhere in the blackness behind them various dependents sucked down Tanduay and San Miguel between humorless laughs.

"Yo, Charles," said Billy. "Me and the brother here were just about to bust this fucking bench into kindling. Wanna help?"

"That won't solve anything," said Charles.

"Who the fuck wants to solve anything?" asked Billy.

"Say Charles," said Ed, "my asshole brother Tom say he heard one of the Kittens ask Joan if she was gonna ask you to the junior prom."

"Great. And what did Tom say Joan said back?"

"He said she just laughed, man. Tough break."

"Don't spare my feelings any."

"Don't worry. If she fucks all the Aces I'll be sure to let you know."

"You're a prince."

"Forget her, man," said Billy. "All those bitches think their shit don't stink. Fuck 'em all."

Charles looked at Ed. He wore a new dashiki over flared jeans and he had teased his hair out into a fairly respectable Afro. He looked ready to leave.

"Tell me something," Charles asked him. "Are you guilty?"

Ed blinked, then grinned. "Of doing dope or original sin or what?"

"You know what I mean."

Ed looked at the streetlight across the road and watched the bats run down moths for a few seconds. "I guess so," he said. "But *guilt's* some heavy word for it. You're a good boy, Charles, and you won't believe me, but whatever they told you about pot and the other shit is wrong."

"Yeah? You think so?"

"Yeah," Billy cut in, "who you gonna believe, Charles?"

As Charles began to think that over a gray van and a covered jeep came down the street on their left, opposite the rise of SOQ Hill. As the vehicles crested the last low hill in the junior officers' housing area they doused their lights, cut their engines, and coasted toward the boys on the corner. Behind them the three heard muffled exclamations and the rustle of kids fleeing through the playground with their booze.

Charles, Billy, and Ed sat together on the back of the bench, feet on the seat, as the vehicles pulled up and disgorged nine sailors in a mixture of whites, khakis, and dungarees. Some had flashlights, some wore helmets; all carried billy clubs. A chief aimed a flashlight at the boys' faces and then over the playground as the sailors fanned out in a line.

"Where are the others?" one of the sailors demanded.

"What the fuck you talkin' about, squid?" asked Ed.

The chief stepped up. "You boys hear anything about a rumble?"

Charles blinked. Billy laughed. A few of the sailors smiled, others shook their heads; they all seemed to relax. "I'd say we'd been had," said one.

"No shit," said Ed.

"Watch your lip," said the chief.

"What're you gonna do?" asked Billy. "Send him home? Too late, motherfucker."

"Okay, that's it," said the chief. "Get up off the bench and come here."

"Fuck you, suc," said Ed. Two sailors grabbed him off the bench while others approached Billy and Charles.

"Come on, boys," the chief said, "assume the position." They did, going over and standing with their hands on the side of the van while a sailor frisked them. The sailor pulled a butterfly knife off Ed, a switchblade off Billy, and a Boy Scout pocketknife off Charles.

"Dangerous customers." The chief gazed at them paternally and said, "Look you little shitbirds: I don't care who your daddies are or what kind of crap you think you can get away with. What I got right here could get all three of you into some serious shit. Are you reading me?"

The boys said nothing. A petty officer said, "Let's take 'em in, chief. Let's take 'em in or let 'em go. We got places to be."

The chief said, "Okay, turn around." He gave Charles back the scout knife and said, "If you young gentlemen see anything we ought to know about, call Security. Other than that, you didn't see us." Without waiting for a response he waved his team back into their vehicles. They started their engines, pulled away, and after a block turned their lights back on.

Billy stepped up on the bench and showed Ed and Charles how easily the seat planks bent under his heel.

"It's pointless," said Charles.

"Look, if they can get a war going when I'm eight and have it waiting for me at the end of high school, I can bust a fucking bench."

Ed laughed and jumped up with Billy, saying, "You can leave if you want to, Barker."

"Yeah. In a minute. Let me give you a hand first."

⇥ XIX ⇤

OPERATION SILVER HAMMER

Between NISRA drug busts and the normal rotation of families to other duty stations, Charles's circle of friends in Subic Bay tightened like a garrote. NISRA's hand held back from slapping down Luiz and Joe, but it remained present, and in the weeks following the great bust all the students of George Dewey High School lived under it like nervous flies.

Charles and Luiz went to say good-bye to Jim at his family's quarters the morning he shipped out. Luiz smiled but couldn't seem to find many words. Charles figured he and Jim had spent too many nights in the bars and brothels of Olongapo, wooing b-girls and singing with Filipino bands, or camping out in the jungle to the music of roosting fruit bats and prowling pythons, for Luiz to sum up what he felt in anything less than a long speech that neither he nor Jim would admit they wanted to hear. Besides, they didn't have time. The van from the Naval Air Station in Cubi would arrive within half an hour.

"I shouldn't say it," said Charles, "but I'll miss ya, ya cocksucking son of a bitch."

"Yeah, Jesus Christ for sure," added Luiz.

Jim smiled joylessly. His appearance had hardly changed since Charles first met him eighteen months earlier. He'd let his hair grow since the bust and it now came halfway over his ears, but he still had baby fat in his cheeks and braces that made his lips pout. He picked at a pimple on his chin and said, "Yeah, well, you two can split all my old rubbers. Your share should last you about twelve lifetimes, Barker. Wish I could say I'll miss y'all, but you know how it goes. Another tour, another buncha buddies for life. The only dude I'm really gonna miss is long gone already."

"Edgefield?" Charles asked.

"No, jerk-off. Finch. That was a goddamn shame, for sure, him dying like that. You'd a figured he'd a taken an enemy fleet with him."

"Ah, shit," said Luiz.

"A shame for all of us," Jim continued. "I mean, I really want to know what's gonna happen to this country, man, ten, twenty, thirty years from now when we get our asses into the war he was supposed to win for us."

"Maybe that was this one," said Charles.

"I don't know where it all went wrong. Like it matters now. Used to be, they said, ships would come into port and the crews would hang out—they all had their favorite bars and whores, like coming home to mother, the Joes said. Almost goddamn whole-some. Now there's some weird shit out there and no fucking esprit. I'm glad to be going. When the fucking Nav starts eating her own, ain't no reason to stay."

"It don't have to be that way," said Luiz.

Jim stood up and the three exchanged soul shakes. "Yeah, well," he said, "anchors aweigh fellow fuckups."

"Bye Jim."

"See ya around, cat."

"Don't count on it."

The Wongs left next, on normal rotation. By the spring of 1970, the height of Charles's second dry season in the Philippines, the ranks of his friends had shrunk with those of Explorer Post 360 from a dozen to just Luiz, Billy, and Ford. At school, sitting out on the grounds at lunch with Charles and Ford, Billy spoke for them all.

"This bites," he said. "Did you see the mug shots outside the principal's office?" A rhetorical question: since the bust everything had tightened up. Principal Schutt had taped up photos of boys in crew cuts in the window of his office under the legend BOYS' HAIR SHOULD LOOK LIKE THIS. But nearly all the boys' hair looked like that already; the pictures simply rubbed it in. Kids newly arrived from the States couldn't believe it. One boy told Charles that he had to shave off his mustache before the Navy would let him in the country. Charles couldn't believe the boy's old high school had let him grow one in the first place. America had changed since he left Arlington, and he began to realize how much.

"I heard somebody say," Billy continued, "that we're about the only place where they still do this shit. Like in Sasebo, man, and Yokohama, dudes can wear their hair any fucking way they want."

"I don't believe it," said Charles.

"I do," said Ford. "Things are really changing everywhere. Have you seen some of these new enlisted men? They're growing mustaches and sideburns and they're dressing like hippies when they go off base."

"See?" said Billy. "And the Nav still floats. All this shit about hair is just bullshit, man; it's just a way to keep us down. You look at the *Manila Times* and even the back pages of *Stars and Stripes* these days and you'll see there's marches and shit back home, and dudes blowing away their officers in 'Nam—these pricks here, they're just pissed that the country doesn't wanna let them have their war anymore. They're losin' it, man. They're losin' the folks back home, Charlie won't die, and their own damn grunts and squids are turnin' on them. Our own damn parents. It's like all they can control is their kids. It's like the only thing they still got hold of is our hair."

"And there isn't much of that," said Ford.

"I'm really sick of this shit," said Billy. "It wasn't so bad for a while, you know, when I could get out into the jungle and fuck around . . ."

"Yeah," said Ford.

". . . but now I really want to bomb this fucking place."

The three sat quietly a few moments, soaking in the frustration.

"Where would you start?" asked Charles.

"Right fucking here, man. The school."

Another moment of quiet passed as the three thought about that.

"The school?" said Charles. "Our teachers already catch as much shit as we do. Besides, they *expect* you not to like school."

"Well, they're fucking right about that," said Billy.

"What would *you* hit?" Ford asked Charles.

Charles paused before replying; he knew they had passed the point of joking. "The Teen Club," he said. "That wonderful place we're all supposed to love so much."

"Fucking A," said Billy. "That'd be like a buncha officers trashing the O Club."

"What exactly did you have in mind?" asked Ford.

"Nothing we haven't talked about before. Sodium chips, ammonium disulfate, and the light switch at the back of the club."

"Oh yes," said Billy, rubbing his hands together and squinching up his freckled cheeks.

Ford peered over the tops of his spectacles. "You're serious?"

"Can you still get the stuff?" Charles asked.

Charles and Billy studied Ford's face. Ford looked first at Charles, then at Billy. Then all three of them began to laugh.

Charles called his last official meeting of Explorer Post Three Sixty at twenty-one hundred hours Saturday night, April 11, 1970. He, Luiz, Billy, and Ford sat a block away from the Teen Club at a metal table on the terrace between the Kalayaan O Club and the swimming pool. Billy brought a Sanyo portable cassette player with him. He put it on the table and played a tape he'd recorded off bootleg forty-fives from Taipei via Olongapo. First some Cream, then some of the new Beatles songs from *Abbey Road*. As Ford set out the contents of a shopping bag the tape scratched out "Maxwell's Silver Hammer" with its cheerful chorus about the eponymous hero bang-banging upon his teacher's head till she was dead. Billy sang along off key while Ford showed them an amber jar of sodium chips packed in greasy wax and four small glass vials of ammonium disulfate. Luiz grinned, reached into the pocket of his jungle jacket, and brought out Edgefield's old packet of marker dye. Charles nodded toward the cassette player, then toward his friends, and said, "Okay, listen up. This is the Silver Hammer Operation. Let's synchronize our watches."

"I got twenty-one-oh-seven hours," Billy said gruffly.

"And what is that in English?" asked Ford.

Charles translated. "That's nine-oh-seven P.M."

"Not that I have a watch," added Ford.

"Look, it's simple enough," said Charles. "We're going down there in about ten minutes. Here are some paper cups from the PX. Just like the cups from the snack bar. You fill these at the watercooler in front, one at a time. Manage to leave one in each room where you can get to it easy. Don't be obvious, just look thirsty and then absentminded."

"You can do that, Ford," smiled Luiz.

"What?"

"About half an hour after we get started Billy's gonna hit the switch at the back of the club. We backtrack and dump a few chips in each cup. If you're right about that stuff it's gonna start popping and dancing fire."

"So?" said Ford.

"It's called a diversion. Get out as soon as you get all the cups. Luiz and Billy will each take one of the vials of the stinky stuff. Billy: hit the lights, count to ten, then hit the snack bar and leave. Luiz: hit the dance floor as soon as the lights go. I'll take two vials and get the lobby and the poolroom. After that we split."

"What happens if they catch us?" asked Luiz. He sounded more curious than concerned.

"I won't shit you," said Charles. "I have no idea."

"What would Finch say?" Ford mused.

"He's dead," said Charles. "We're not."

"Fucking A," said Billy, as his tape shifted from the Beatles to Creedence.

"Yeah, let's go, cats," said Luiz.

"Morituri te salutamis," said Ford.

The new managers, Petty Officer Brock and Yeoman Lansing, had their eyes on the four Explorer Scouts from the moment they walked in the door wearing their camouflage jungle jackets and grim secretive expressions to a fuzzy version of "Suzie Q." But they could hardly watch all four boys, and quickly lost them among the teens dancing, playing pool, racing from room to room in the gossipy rituals of high school romance, or drinking themselves senseless out past the parking lot. At approximately twenty-one forty Billy hit the switch.

The entire club went dark and, momentarily, silent. Then Kittens shrieked and Aces said "hey!" and less exalted classes of children yelled for their friends or muttered in confusion. The Filipino band relaxed as soon as their amps went out, brushed their hands through their shiny pompadours, and lit cigarettes, waiting to see what would happen next. They waited perhaps thirty seconds before little hissing volcanoes spat up from Dixie Cups in first one room and then the next, followed shortly by the crack of small glass tubes, almost unheard among the swelling hubbub. A strong stench evocative of rotten eggs fermenting in the bellies of beasts with especially unwholesome diets rose like ground fog from the floors of all four rooms. Kids began to scream, in indignation and surprise, and then to push for the doors.

Charles had gone in the front as soon as the power went out, stepping into a jumble of shadows caused by the streetlight outside. He threw his first vial on the floor in front of the managers' office then turned left and entered the poolroom, elbowing kids aside in the dark in order to get a clear shot at the linoleum floor and not splash himself. Once he tossed the second vial he tried to head out with the crowd in the general stampede. At the back door he felt a hand grab onto his fatigue jacket and pull him back. He heard Joe's voice.

"What's this?" Joe said loudly. Brock appeared from the crowd; in the dark his face looked as if someone had unexpectedly taken a shot at him. "You think you're gonna get away with this?" Joe demanded. Charles pulled free and got outside with the rest of the crowd. Billy and Ford joined him, beaming.

"Split up, beat it," Charles whispered. "If you see Luiz tell him to ditch the marker dye. He must have said something to Joe."

"Fuck," said Billy.

"That fascist," said Ford. "Let's go, Killer."

Charles retreated to the back of the parking lot and hung around a few more minutes, hoping to hear that no one really had any idea who perpetrated the attack, despite what Joe said. Failing that, he thought he might at least defend himself if accused. After all, he thought, he couldn't possibly have hit the switch, planted the chips, then crushed all the vials by himself, so if they only had one suspect, they really had no one.

While waiting, Charles listened to the reactions of the kids around him. Girls in sorority sweaters and boys in white denim Ace vests threw around the words *juvenile* and *immature* like angry confetti. Others laughed and a few even said, "Far fucking out."

He smiled, then saw Rich, a civilian kid from his math class, slipping through the crowd toward him. Rich had arrived in Subic a few months earlier, just after Christmas; he wore bell-bottoms, a dark shirt with a long pointed collar and puffy sleeves, and hair that fell over his ears but that he tried to camouflage in school by greasing it down and combing it back like a blond Filipino. He grabbed Charles's arm and said, "Good job, dude."

"Hey, I'm innocent," said Charles, lightly.

"For sure, man. But you're just as busted, right?"

"What do you mean?"

"I heard that Brock dude calling somebody as I passed the office on my way out. They like already knew, man. Somebody must have told somebody who told somebody, man. They were waitin' on your ass."

"Shit."

"But, hey, what can they do? Send you home? Big deal, right? See you around, man. Take it easy."

Charles stared at the club, trying to decide how he felt now. He didn't mind the suspension but couldn't shake his surprise at having received an indictment, trial, and conviction in absentia within ten minutes of the incident. That made him angry. Then he realized that this sort of thing might go on his record and prove as indelible and damaging as the unknown crime that sent Jim home and ended his future in the Navy. Now Charles thought of his father and became both sorry and afraid.

After an hour of first staring, then walking, then milling around anxiously, Charles returned to the Teen Club. It had aired out enough for people to enter and the power had long since come back on. He entered the lobby and then went through the managers' door without bothering to knock.

"I hear I've been accused," he said, trying to keep his voice from shaking.

Brock looked up at him from behind the desk. He had a cowlick in back of his blond razor cut and his green eyes quivered between anger and anxiety. The look made Charles smile.

"You heard right," said Brock. "And you're suspended from the Teen Club for thirty days. Starting now."

Lansing entered and stood beside Charles, her arms folded. She looked at the floor when Charles looked at her.

"What for?" Charles demanded.

"You know what for," said Brock.

"No, actually I don't."

"People saw you just now," said Lansing.

"Saw me what? Saw me hit the lights and bomb every room of the Teen Club inside of five seconds? You think you can prove that?"

"We don't have to prove anything to you," said Brock, standing up. "As soon as I heard I called the XO and he cleared the decision. That's all she wrote."

"Bullshit," said Charles. "This is still America, isn't it? You want to do something to somebody you still have to prove it, don't you?"

"It's not my decision," said Brock. "What's done is done. You can take it to the admiral or you can take it to the XO."

"Yeah? Well what's the XO's number?"

Lansing sighed in exasperation. "The executive officer is having dinner with his wife at the O Club. You really want to call him?"

Charles picked up the phone on Brock's desk and dialed the O Club. He told the steward whom he wanted to speak to and then waited, looking from Brock to Lansing as each of them looked away. How bad could it get, he wondered? The XO lived three houses down from the Barkers on SOQ Hill and had a son in Charles's grade at GDHS. An okay kid.

The XO picked up and gave his rank and name as if he'd just received a call from one of his men on watch. When Charles identified himself the XO just said, "That's right, the Barker boy. Well, you've just been suspended from the Teen Club for thirty days. Didn't they tell you that?"

"What for?" Charles shouted into the receiver.

The XO's voice sounded unused to the question and torn between ordering Charles spanked or shot. "For conduct unbecoming an American dependent," he said.

"What the hell is that?" Charles asked, incredulously. "Is that some law anyone's ever heard of? You got that written down somewhere or do you make this up as you go along?"

The XO hung up. Charles dialed the club again but this time the steward returned to say that the XO wouldn't speak to him. Charles slammed down the receiver and walked out on the verge of tears, only slightly cheered by the surprise in Brock's and Lansing's faces.

Charles stomped up SOQ Hill, enraged but also nearly hysterical with the prospect of having to face his father. But he couldn't go anywhere else. All his camping gear lay under the bed in his room.

A third of the way up the hill Charles saw something wrong from the corner of his right eye. He stopped, turned, and laughed. Below him, about two hundred meters away, the pool by the Kalayaan Officers' Club blazed bright orange under the outdoor lights. Luiz had ditched the marker dye. In a little while, the XO would see it on his way home.

Commander Barker greeted Charles at the door with an expression that Charles had never seen, but that he imagined might have faced several unlucky Chinese soldiers in Korea a number of years before. Charles stepped in and faced his father, almost unconsciously standing at attention.

"Son, you interrupted the base XO at dinner with his wife!"

"But Dad . . ."

His father's hand caught him across the right cheek and ear and sent him stumbling against the wall. Charles reached for his face and bit down on a sob, knowing his old man could hit a lot harder and might still do so.

Commander Barker looked Charles directly in the eye. "Did you do it?"

In the space of a second Charles could see everything that would happen to him and his father. The report from Security, the acknowledgment, the trip home and condemnation to life as a civilian, a life he knew nothing about. But what could he admit—that he had done everything himself? That he had help from his friends? That he had their names? His father wanted a truth Charles did not have.

"No sir."

"Let me see your jacket."

Charles stripped off his jungle jacket and handed it over. His father searched it, running his hands through the bellows pockets and sniffing inside to make sure. Finding nothing, he shook his head.

"You know, I had seriously thought about signing on for another tour. But I just don't think that's a good idea. Do you?"

"I don't know, sir."

"They can dust those vials for fingerprints, you know."

Who? Charles thought. Vince and George, the two NISRA men who lectured students on the lethal consequences of marijuana? "They can't prove a thing," he said.

His father shook his head again. "Son, I just don't know what's come over you these last few months. Why the hell would you do something like that?"

Charles didn't try to answer and his father didn't ask again. Commander Barker handed the jacket back to Charles and went upstairs. Charles followed and went to his room. The maid had left earlier. He didn't see his mother.

A few days later NISRA sent a letter to Commander Barker's office at the naval hospital. They attached a copy of the report of the incident at the Teen Club and asked him to sign at the bottom acknowledging receipt. Commander Barker sent it back without signing. They sent it again and he sent it back again. Charles overheard his father mention it to his mother. "Hell," Commander Barker said, "I told them that even a sailor picked up drunk in town gets some kind of hearing. Even a traitor gets a trial."

After the third try, NISRA just gave up.

THE LAST MARCH

A week after the Silver Hammer Operation, Charles invited
Billy and Ford over for another war game. Luiz found out and
came over, too, just to watch he said, but he ended up splitting
the Austrians with Ford, leaving Charles to debate which elements of the Prussian army he could trust Billy with. As they had
before, they fought on the dining room table in front of the wide
window and a view of the Zambales Mountains. With those and
the jungle as a backdrop, Charles had set the table with a mock
central European landscape of felt pasture, cardboard villages,
paper streams and roads, hills of stacked books, and forests of
stained lichen. On either end of the table the boys deployed their
tin regiments, squadrons, and batteries, moving them tape-
measured distances and resolving fire and melee with rolls of the
dice and quick references to the rules. While they played they
talked, about the progress of their forces, the outcomes of encoun-
ters, and the world beyond their battle. About an hour into the
engagement Charles revealed that his father had decided not to
sign on for another tour in Subic.

"Lucky mother," said Billy, scratching his navel through the same Jim Morrison T-shirt he'd worn when he first met Charles. "How short are you?"

"I forget. Two or three months." Charles measured the range from his most forward battery to an advanced squadron of Pandours and tried not to think about good-byes, or how his old neighborhood in Arlington might have changed in two years.

"If you'll excuse me," said Ford, hunched over the table and looking like a dwarf Clark Kent who would never find the right phone booth, "I think I'll run down your hussars with my cuirassiers before I mourn."

"Been to town lately?" Charles asked Luiz, hoping to distract him from the inch or two he'd just added to the move of a battalion of Feldjagers.

"Nah, cat. Too dangerous. Election coming up." He brushed back his long black bangs and added, winking, "Your guys move pretty quick."

They all knew what he meant about the election. The American armed forces had restricted nearly all personnel to their bases as Filipino politicians and their hired guns maneuvered for bloody advantage at the polls. Factions of Marcos's Nacionalistas and the rival Liberalista party daily picked each other off in twos and threes, and innocent bystanders by the half dozen. But the Nacionalistas held the incumbent's advantage. The *Manila Times*, for example, reported the forced closure and dismantling of Liberalista headquarters in Marcos's home province of Illocos Sur by unidentified men in Philippine army uniforms. Delivery of American aid accelerated along with news stories and photos of Ferdinand and Imelda delivering the goods to the barrios. The United States and Marcos went back a long way and everyone knew it. Each time an American officer or housewife asked their maid or houseboy how they planned to vote, the Filipino servants always said "Nacionalista" and the Americans always nodded approvingly.

"I remember what Finch told me about Marcos," Charles said. "In Baguio. We saw El Presidente at the John Hay golf course taking a lot of free shots. He got all pissed about Marcos cheating and bringing his armed bodyguards on the base. He said we didn't need him that bad."

Ford snorted. "That's true. But it only makes it worse."

"What?" asked Billy.

"That we're not going to do a thing to help these people get a fair election. That with everything we have we're still so scared we don't even want to give them a chance to change puppets."

"Hey, it's a free country," said Billy.

"I think you missed his point," said Charles.

But with the mention of Finch they stopped their game in midbattle and the topic quickly moved away from elections. They drank their sodas and told stories about their fallen post president—one more dead soldier to add to the empty cans, the tin figures lying on the tabletop, and the weekly lists broken down by service in the back pages of U.S. papers. Charles told Billy and Ford what Jim had said about Finch and our next war.

Ford said, "A country keeps the heroes it deserves."

"What the fuck is that supposed to mean?" asked Billy.

"I don't know," Ford replied. "Maybe it just sounds like it ought to make sense."

"You know," said Charles, "I'd like to do the beacon march just one more time before I ship out."

"I think we'd just get in more trouble," said Ford.

Billy snorted. "What are they going to do to us? Send us home?"

The following Saturday each of the boys crammed fatigues, boots, and canteens into backpacks, threw on a cosmetic layer of flippers and masks, and told his parents he planned to spend the day at the beach. Luiz picked up the other three and drove to the gap in the security fence by the firebreak leading to the beacon. He parked on the side of the road, explaining that anyone seeing his car there would probably just think he'd run out of gas or taken a girl into the woods. When they got to the Binictican golf course they could take their street clothes out of their backpacks and change, then split a Special Services cab back. The rest thought it sounded like a plan and changed inside the car as quickly as they could, slipping into their camouflage and lacing up their boots. In a few minutes they'd completed the change, left the car, and put fifty meters between them and the road.

The air hung hot and muggy. Charles trudged forward and up, regarding the trees closing in on the steep track and their thick, latticed walls of branches, leaves, and vines. They did not bother him as they once had. Instead he now felt as if he walked among, if not friends, then at least benign creatures whose world appealed far more to his sense of reason and justice than the one he left behind on the road out of Kalayaan.

After an hour struggling up weathered and overgrown fire-breaks they reached the top of the hill and the aircraft beacon. From there they could see the main naval station laid out below them in the distance, just like one of their tabletop villages, oddly immersed in jungle by the sea. They spent ten minutes resting, swigging water from their canteens, and looking at their toy world as it gleamed under an enormous sky only here and there spotted with small clouds that sailed slowly past like widely scattered caravels. Then one by one they got up and began to search for a way to get down. It took several more minutes, but Luiz and Charles agreed when they found a break in the canopy at or very near the spot where Edgefield began his descent the year before last. With a brief nod to the view from above, Luiz led them down into shadow with Charles in the rear, sandwiching the less experienced Billy and Ford between them. Charles tied an old rope they didn't plan to need again to a tree at the summit, which they all used to hang on to as they clambered down the steep rocky hillside from branch to trunk to giant buttress root.

Despite a few halts and stumbles they reached the bottom without injury. There they gathered themselves up, checked their compass bearings, and marched off on a route parallel to the old one. Most of the time they passed easily through the undergrowth that sparsely stubbled the shadows of the huge trees, and they only occasionally stopped at the sound of something rustling through the dead leaves at their feet or calling from the dark, distant, and weirdly intricate canopy. Where a

tree had fallen and the forest closed the wound with a lush outburst of scrub and sapling, the boys revived the old trick of
rolling down their sleeves, masking their faces with their forearms, and plunging ahead blind, gambling their safety at, as the
jungle had taught them, favorable odds. When they got through
and marched again in the clear they answered the calls of the
monkeys and birds they'd never seen with choruses of "Roll Me
Over" and the "Yo Ho Song." Sweat soaked their jackets,
squished between their booted toes, and ran down their faces
stinging their eyes like tears. In his mind Charles heard the
album he'd put on at the end of that last toy soldier battle
when they spoke of Finch: Wagner, *Siegfried's Funeral March*. The
low strings and muted horns slipped between the trees like
morning fog and reached through his camos and sweat to nest
in his guts.

After a few hours they came to the stream at the base of the
last long ridge that separated them from the golf course. There
on the rocks they took another break, removing their web belts,
pouring water from their canteens over their heads, and leaning
against the trees to rest. Charles worked a John Wayne around
the top of a can of C-rat cookies and Ford gave Billy one of his
round candy bars. Luiz reached into his breast pocket and
brought out a long black Philippine cigarette.

"You know," said Billy as he unwrapped his chocolate, "I bet
we could stay out here as long as we wanted to."

"Yeah?" said Ford.

"Shit, yeah. Remember all that crap we learned at JEST? Juice
of papaya for snakebites, water vines, rubber sap and fruit to trap
bats—hell yes."

"I'd never go back," said Luiz. "I'd be happy right here, you
know?"

"Well, why don't you two go ahead and stay then?" suggested
Ford.

Billy looked suddenly unsure. He moved his feet restlessly
away from the trickle of the stream. "That night," he explained
when Charles looked at him. "Goddamn that night was dark."

Ford pulled his cap brim down and stared at his knees.

"I don't know," said Luiz, ignoring them. "Maybe I go back after all. You know, Charles, Mr. Las Casas is crazy, but he thinks I got a future. Ain't that a laugh, cat?"

"Las Casas is crazy but he's not an asshole. Have you actually been reading the stuff he gives you?"

"Sure, cat. You think I couldn't?"

"It's not as if you've been broadcasting your erudition," remarked Ford.

"I'm gonna look that word up," said Luiz. "Someday nobody get anything over on me, man. Someday maybe I'll be an officer. Then I come back here and really kick some ass for them fucking with Jim."

"Sure," said Billy, "and when you make CNO you can sneak him into OCS. Shit."

"I always figured you could do anything," Charles told Luiz. "Find a trail, get laid, make a deal with an Igorot for a new bolo. I never thought you couldn't read. I just thought it was a question of what you wanted."

"Thanks for the vote, cat."

Billy looked up, searching for sky and blinking. "How long till dark you think?"

"It'll be okay," Ford said quietly.

"What the fuck you talking about? You think I'm scared?"

Ford gave Charles a sickly look. "I'm sorry. It's got to me, too."

Luiz toked slowly on his cigarette, gazing at Ford and Billy through unfolding blossoms of grayish smoke. Charles squinted at Ford as if a ray of sun had penetrated the canopy. "What really happened that night?" he asked.

"I don't know," said Billy. "I don't know."

"Really?" asked Luiz.

"Really. I was scared shitless and don't remember a thing till I got to the bank and then I thought everything would be okay. Swear to Christ I did."

Ford whispered, "I held on to a branch caught on a rock while Finch dragged him over. I could hardly breathe I was so tired."

Charles reached over to touch his shoulder but at the last moment pulled back. "It's okay," he said.

"No it's not," said Ford. "I wish to God I could at least have said no, but he came back for me. I remember his eyes. He was tired, too. That's all I remember till Joe was leading us through the woods back to the stables."

"Where was Joe when you were in the stream?" asked Luiz.

"Watching from the bank," Ford said. "Guess he was tired, too."

"And fucking Finch half his motherfucking size," spat Billy. "He never did like him. Finch beat him out for post president and knew he was getting into some heavy dope every time he went out in town. He couldn't stand Finch knowing that."

"You don't know any of that," said Charles.

"Yeah, but it's true," said Luiz, throwing his cigarette into the stream. "Goddamn, everybody know that."

"Are you guys saying Joe killed Finch?" said Charles. "Because if you are, let's turn the motherfucker in."

"Sure," said Ford. "You, the Mad Bomber of Subic, are going to accuse the son of Mr. Base Security of murder for not risking his own life to save a hero. I don't see a lot coming out of that."

"Can't do shit," said Billy. "Can't nobody do shit about anything."

Luiz lit another cigarette and got to his feet. "C'mon cat," he said to Charles, "let's get these two home before dark." They all got to their feet and got squared away, buckling up the web belts with their canteens and hoisting their packs onto their shoulders. Luiz said he thought he could find a better route to the golf course than the first time, so instead of going straight up the ridge and perhaps running into another precipice at the top, they followed the creek downstream a few hundred meters until it became too overgrown to follow any farther. They checked compass bearings again, then cut over a few small ridges and a side valley until they reached a gentle downward slope. They followed it down to a field of elephant grass that they knew would lead them to one of the greens. A few minutes after sixteen hundred they emerged from the high grass onto the eleventh hole to startle a quartet of ensigns and j.g.'s with their caddies.

"What the hell?" said one. "What the hell unit you with?"

The boys ignored him, walked across his line of fire to the road, and turned toward the clubhouse. Along the way any number of Americans and Filipinos stopped to stare at them but the scouts continued oblivious. Charles and Luiz had their minds on the jungle and the cab and Billy and Ford still looked lost in the rainy night of the battle at the riding stables.

Things had changed from their first beacon march. By the time they reached the clubhouse one of the employees had seen them coming and called Security. Six MAAs greeted them at the door and asked for their authorization for leaving the base.

"We don't need any authorization," said Luiz. "We came from Kalayaan. Look at a map. It's all on base. Everything off base already been cut down."

"Don't backtalk, son. Show me your ID."

After a brief consultation the MAAs decided to hold them there and call their fathers to come and get them.

"You got change for a dollar?" Charles asked the chief. "I'd like to get the guys a few Cokes."

"Sure," said the chief, reaching into his pocket. "But stay in sight."

"Can we change into our civvies?" asked Ford.

"No, you stay just the way you are."

Over the next hour the fathers drove up, but the MAAs had made a mistake if they expected to witness any angry lectures. Mr. Ford arrived first and reacted with bemusement.

Charles had never met Mr. Ford. He now saw a slight, youngish-looking adult with dark hair curling forgetfully beyond regulation length, a reddish batik shirt, and khaki pants. He stood taller than Charles would have expected—almost as tall as Luiz—but wore the same dark-framed glasses as his son. He looked at Ford and his fellow scouts, then at the MAAs, then back to the scouts. He stepped forward and carefully touched Ford's sleeve, rubbing the camouflage fabric thoughtfully between his fingers. "Well, I'll be damned," he said, shaking his head and smiling. "I'll be damned."

He looked at the MAAs. "Tell me again what the problem is? Why is my son in trouble?"

The chief said, "These kids aren't authorized to be in the jungle."

"It's not allowed?" Mr. Ford said. "Why?" Then immediately, "Oh, I'm sorry. That's not something you would know, is it?" He pulled on his son's sleeve again and said, "Well, I will be damned. Let's go home, son."

After the two left Charles asked, "What the hell was that all about?"

Billy grinned. "His parents knew he hung with us but they never knew he went out in the jungle. He always said he was spending the night at my place. I kept his fatigues and other shit with me. They never guessed."

"Never?" Charles asked.

"Well, hell—look at him," said Billy. "Would you?"

"What about the night at the stables?" asked Luiz.

"Same deal," said Billy. "I guess something might have slipped out if they'd ever talked to any of our folks, but Ford's old man's a civilian. I guess he's not comfortable consorting with officers."

"Well, I'll be damned," said Charles.

Luiz's father drove over from SRF in a gray panel truck. When he got out he looked angry. Charles hadn't seen him before, either, but would easily have picked him out. He looked like Luiz, tall and limber with dark hair, except he had no Oriental in him. All the Guamanian must have come from Luiz's mother. When Luiz's father got to the group he gave the chief a disgusted sneer and said, "Don't you birds have anything more important to do?"

Billy's father showed up at the same time as Commander Barker but didn't even look at the MAAs. He just shook his head wearily and said, "Come on, Killer. Let's try to get home before your mother finds out, okay?"

Commander Barker said nothing. On the drive home he mentioned that he'd received his official orders and that the family would soon return to the D.C. area, back to their house in Arlington. He would write the tenants in a few days and let them know to start looking.

Charles spent Sunday afternoon at the dining room table packing up his toy soldiers. They would accompany the rest of the Barkers' household goods by sea while the family itself would fly home to spend the next few weeks wondering which of their material possessions would not make it. Wagner played on the stereo again, setting off the view of the Zambales Mountains while the maid walked through a few times on inscrutable missions of her own.

Charles could not recall speaking to the maid. In fact, between school, the Teen Club, and his outings with the Explorer Scouts, he had scarcely seen her. He looked at her now and saw a tiny, thin, ancient woman with a tight bun of gray hair, strong features, and a complexion the color of darkly stained, well-oiled wood.

"You know," he said as she passed, "you have a beautiful country." He gestured toward the jungle beyond the backyard fence.

"Thank you," she said with a slightly anxious look, as if he had just asked her a trick question.

After she left Charles looked through the window again and realized with a start that he hadn't watched a single television program in nearly two years. He'd caught glimpses: *Ninoy*, the Filipino student comedy, and once for a few minutes he'd watched the moon landing—a fuzzy picture of Neil Armstrong hopping around like Alice's White Rabbit in a desert landscape. But for the most part he'd seen nothing that his friends back in Arlington had seen. Even in the newspapers. Back home they'd read the *Washington Post* or the *Evening Star*. Here he'd read the *Manila Times*, filled with comparatively bizarre stories of drought, miracles, and crazed jeepney drivers gone amok, or *Stars and Stripes*, a chronicle of endless military optimism, whose front page always profiled another successful operation in a war that seemed to have room for all the successful operations America could mount for the next thirty years.

A few days later he went out with Luiz, Ford, and Billy again. This time they really did go to the beach. Charles wanted one more good close look at the sea before he left, the kelp beds a hundred meters from shore, and a stretch of reef that made him think of Mars. Luiz drove; they had just reached the intersection of the road from Kalayaan and the road from the main base to

Cubi when they had to stop for a convoy. Scores of dark green trucks, their headlights on in the full glare of late morning, filled one lane of the road for what looked like a full kilometer.

The four boys watched the trucks roll past, each one filled with a squad or more of marines in full combat dress, the canvas tops of the trucks rolled up so one could see every grimly apathetic face. Once the entire convoy got on the road to Cubi an SP waved Luiz forward and the boys moved on, passing the trucks on the left. After getting beyond the first four or five Ford leaned out the window from the right rear seat and made the V peace sign with his upraised hand. If Security stopped them, Charles thought, perhaps they could argue that they only meant to copy Winston Churchill. But despite a scowl from a second lieutenant in the seventh truck and a disgusted frown from an old sergeant in the eighth, Ford met no objection from the marines. When Luiz flashed the sign with his left hand out the driver's window and Billy leaned out from shotgun with both his hands making the same gesture, the marines began to respond, first one and two, then fire teams of four, and finally whole squads and platoons. By the time they reached the middle of the column Charles too had his hands up and the whole convoy seemed to have responded. In silence the boys watched as a forest of peace signs sprouted alongside the quiet emotionless stares of men returning from war.

When Charles next saw the *Manila Times* the headline shouted yet another piece of news he knew and couldn't use: Marcos, reelected in a landslide.

→ XXI ←

GOING HOME

The Blaylocks bus, boxy and dirty and dented, carried Charles to the last stop on base as if tottering under his slight weight. Once out on the street corner a block from the main gate, he watched as the bus limped off in a cloud of petrochemical flatulence and, for a moment, felt sorry for it. He would soon leave, but the base itself—teeming with Filipino servants and workmen who strained the buses' riveted seams twice daily, and with American dependents tormenting its drivers with weekly pranks and an intense ritual egging every Halloween— would remain, and the bus would just have to deal with it.

Charles stayed on the corner a minute and looked around. On one side he could see, in sequence, the main gate, a muddy streak of Olongapo River, and, beginning immediately on the other side of the water, as if jostling for a spot from which to jump in, the dark ramshackle buildings of the town itself. On Charles's other side, clean concrete and metal buildings with neatly trimmed lawns led in disciplined steps toward well-ordered docks and piers where slim gray warships lay like thoroughbreds in expensive stalls. Charles took a deep breath of sea air mingled with fuel oil, paint, and a trace of the open sewers of the town—the smell of the U.S. Navy on the far fringes of empire.

He shook his head as if to clear it. *You always get nostalgic when you leave*, he told himself. But he felt more than simple nostalgia. The Quonset huts, signs with stenciled acronyms, uniforms and shoulderboards with familiar patterns of symbols and stripes, the resting warships and the white warplanes, all spoke to him of more than the armed forces described in newspapers, books, or civics classes. Together they said *navy base*, and together with every other navy base in the world they made up Charles's home, hundreds and thousands of places that would always feel like home, wherever he went, whatever he did, even as over in the ballpark a brass quintet of sailors still broke from marches with "Mercy, Mercy, Mercy" and other sailors on their way to town more and more wore love beads and peace signs, dashikis and Afros, and shook hands in funny ways that made their officers feel afraid.

He had found it easier than he thought to say good-bye. But, after all, hellos and good-byes formed a regular part of life in Subic. Maybe that in itself made the Navy feel more like a religion than a job: people, ships, and wars all came and went on the tide, but the Navy remained, like a flag that never wore out no matter how many hands raised and lowered it over the years. Charles could let go the halyard but other hands would take it up. The same with Post 360: Edgefield let go and Finch took it up, then Charles. Luiz, Billy, and Ford would take over from him and then pass it on to other hands, of kids they hadn't yet met.

Earlier Charles had gone to say good-bye to Las Casas without any idea of what he would actually say. As it turned out, he didn't feel he had to say anything. Las Casas made him promise to write and Charles agreed, knowing that his teacher meant novels and plays and poems, while he himself meant only a letter or two before forgetting the address.

Joan presented more of a quandary. Charles had liked her a lot; maybe he even loved her. He didn't want to say good-bye because as long as he put it off he could go on imagining that they had not in the last six months become more and more like distant acquaintances. Until he said good-bye he wouldn't have to accept that she would not make a last-minute declaration of love and rip his clothes off in a vibrant reenactment of several hundred masturbatory fantasies. Still, he couldn't just walk away, either. He hoped she'd agree to write. They'd always had good conversations; why not a correspondence? He wouldn't lose the address.

They got together the night before, his last night. He gave her the pin he'd bought in Baguio and his address back in Arlington. She agreed to write and when they said good-bye she even let him kiss her on the lips.

Now he walked through the base for the last time. He still had an hour or so to kill before he had to get home and finish preparing for the short hop from NAS Cubi to Clark AFB and the longer flight to Yakota. The Barkers planned to spend a weekend in Yokohama before they flew back to Travis to stay for a few days with friends on Treasure Island. They had friends in a lot of places: by the time they got home their tenants would have left and their household goods might even have arrived.

A little way past the miniature golf course Charles saw Mr. Villanueva, his boss from his summer job at the hobby shop. They spoke only briefly: Villanueva, Charles realized, must have seen thousands of dependents come and go and Charles didn't have much to say beyond thanking him for a number of small kindnesses. To Charles it felt like little enough. He wished he could say and do a lot more to make up to the Filipinos for freely referring to them as Joes and Flips, albeit never to their faces, and generally regarding their country as no more than a scrap of pagan wilderness hardly worth colonizing. He felt he owed them. Two nights before, the Filipino workers of the naval hospital had thrown a party for the Barkers in Olongapo. Much to his surprise, Charles enjoyed it.

For two years Charles had heard nothing about Olongapo outside of Base Security reports with terse paragraphs about fights, robberies, and venereal disease, or his friends' lurid stories of pimps, whores, drugs, booze, rock and roll, and strange stage acts involving cigarettes, bottles, and the occasional carabao. But two days earlier his parents told him to get ready for dinner there; they even made him dress up first.

Once beyond the main gate they got into a Joe—no, Philippine—cab, Commander Barker in service dress whites, Mrs. Barker in the blue silk Chinese dress from Hong Kong, and Charles in his best barong, black slacks, and cordovans. The taxi took them down narrow streets and alleys, some of asphalt, some of cobbles, and some deteriorated beyond useful identification. They passed by crowded wooden stalls and storefronts, ditches glowing with urine, two- and three-story structures of wood or cinder block—houses, churches, and schools. Seemingly in the middle of it all, at a corner from which they could see no sign of the base, not even a high mast, they alit from the cab and entered a small stucco, vaguely Hispanic, club with a tiled dining room and, in back, a courtyard with tables set up for the Employees' Association and their honored guests.

Charles stared and spoke haltingly as Commander and Mrs. Barker shook hands, kissed, and made small talk with the employees. One of the gentlemen explained to Charles that the workers had not had an employee association before, and would not now had the commander not allowed them.

"Your father is a good man," the Filipino said. "We'll miss him."

"Thank you," Charles replied.

"You must be happy to be going home. But maybe someday you come back, yes? When you are officer?" He laughed and lightly patted Charles's arm. Charles smiled back.

It felt warm in the courtyard but not unpleasant, and the food tasted good. They had an appetizer of lumpia—the real thing, with bits of fruit and shredded meat, not the hamburger-stuffed egg rolls served by Navy wives at cocktail parties. For the main course they had pork with vegetables and clear rice pancit noodles; for dessert they had hearts of palm. A three-piece band played after the meal and men in barongs danced graceful fox-trots with women in butterfly-shouldered gowns. After several numbers the band picked up the pace and the association president got up and jitterbugged with his wife. Then the band played slower songs again and people began to go to the mike and sing along. They started with Filipino popular songs that Charles did not recognize, then asked the Barkers to come up and sing something of their own. Mrs. Barker goaded her men into accompanying her for "Deep in the Heart of Texas"—fortunately for Charles and his father, the Filipinos joined in after the first few bars and spared them the embarrassment of actually having to carry a tune. When that song ended everyone applauded each other and two young Filipino couples took to the mike to sing "Dahil Sa Iyo" so beautifully that all the women cried and all the men held them with indulgent tenderness and a trace of tears in their own eyes. When the evening finally ended and the Barkers got back to their quarters on SOQ Hill, Charles knew he had just received a memory of Filipinos that would forever push the Security reports and the stories of Jim and Luiz into the background. And for that, he realized as he went to sleep that night, he felt grateful.

That memory of dinner in Olongapo carried him to the naval station library, a low small concrete box with a flat overhanging roof. He thought he'd go in, not of course to check anything out, but to see if anyone else had any of the books he'd enjoyed, like *Ordeal on Samar*, or that history of the Anglo-Indian invasion of Tibet in 1904. To his surprise he saw Prahler behind the checkout desk. It had taken a while, but the Navy seemed finally to have found someone else to manage the Special Services Riding Stables.

When Prahler saw Charles he laughed and stuck out his hand in greeting. Nothing in his manner or voice betrayed any resentment at his loss of power or at the bitter words they'd had in the past. He seemed just like the Prahler Charles had first met—part man, part boy, part imp: a tan, balding blonde, with wide blue eyes and the edgy manner of a fair number of young men who found themselves in the service at an age at which, at home, they would have needed a fake ID to buy a shot of booze.

"Hey Charles! What's happenin', bro?"

"I'm leaving."

"No shit? Shipping out, eh? How short are ya, buddy?"

"A couple hours."

"Jesus Christ, dude; any shorter than that and I wouldn't be able to see you. Come over here and have a seat on the edge of this dime."

They talked for a few minutes but didn't promise to write. Prahler did say that he'd buy Charles a beer the next time he saw him, but Charles shook his head.

"Nah, I still owe you for the booze in Baguio." Then, after a moment of studying the petty officer's face, he added, "You never were in 'Nam, were you?"

Prahler grinned but his eyes didn't join in. "Yeah, well, guess where they're sending me next?"

"Really."

"I shit you not. PBR in the Mekong."

"I don't know what to say."

"Say 'thank you, Jesus, it's him and not me' and don't pass up that beer. I get back alive, everybody I know gets a beer."

"Okay." Charles held out his hand and Prahler grabbed it in a soul shake, fist over fist.

"Take care, kid."

Half an hour later Charles stood in the carport of the Barkers' quarters off Finback Drive and said good-bye to Luiz, Billy, and Ford. Over the last week he'd turned over all the post's equipment to Luiz. Now he asked the three of them to do what they could to get the post back on its feet.

"If you don't want to be the last president," he told Luiz, "you're going to have to get some new blood in."

"Don't worry, cat; the situation's in good hands, you know?"

"Damn straight," said Billy.

"I think things will work out," said Ford.

"Yeah, I'm sure. Take it easy, guys."

He clapped Ford on the shoulder and gave Billy a soul shake. As he went to shake Luiz's hand, Ford said, "And if you run into Joe on the way back tell him 'fuck you' for me."

"What?"

"I realize the phrase is not in my customary lexicon, but I mean it from the heart."

"What are you talking about?"

"Didn't you hear?" said Billy. "They finally busted his ass. He's going home with a big turd on his record."

"What about his old man?"

"Him, too. And the horse he rode in on," Billy added. "Someone tipped off the IG about a hole in NISRA's dragnet; they must have used him as an example. When they finally nailed him doped up with a whore off base, Security couldn't do shit."

Ford looked up at Luiz and raised his eyebrows. "Very fortuitous, I'd say. One might wonder who could have given them such copious details."

Luiz flushed. "Nah, don't look at me, cats. Besides, I think he wanted it."

Billy said, "So who gives a fuck? Son of a bitch didn't deserve to be in Finch's Navy."

The four boys looked at each other. "Well," said Charles. "Maybe I don't either. Or maybe Finch's Navy's already gone. Anyway, I think when I get back I'm going to study up on civilianhood."

"Far out," said Billy.

"Write me," said Ford, "I'll give you lessons."

Luiz shook his head. "What you gonna do if they draft your ass, cat?"

A Navy van turned off Finback into the cul-de-sac and pulled up to the Barkers' drive.

Charles shrugged. "I don't know. I know what I can't do, though."

As the van pulled into the carport Commander and Mrs. Barker came out the front door. Luiz, Billy, and Ford smiled at each other conspiratorially, then stood at attention and saluted. Charles, surprised, looked at his father, waiting for him to salute them back, but Commander Barker only grinned and gave a little nod to Charles.

Charles about-faced and saw that his friends had saluted, not with the full hand of the Navy, but with the three fingers of the scouts. They meant it for him.

Eyes burning, he returned it sharply, then looked at his father and said, "Okay, Dad, let's get this show on the road."